As a child **Sarah Morgan** dreamed of being a writer and, although she took a few interesting detours on the way, she is now living that dream. With her writing career she has successfully combined business with pleasure and she firmly believes that reading romance is one of the most satisfying and fat-free escapist pleasures available. Her stories are unashamedly optimistic and she is always pleased when she receives letters from readers saying that her books have helped them through hard times.

Sarah lives near London with her husband and two children, who innocently provide an endless supply of authentic dialogue. When she isn't writing or reading Sarah enjoys music, movies and any activity that takes her outdoors.

Readers can find out more about Sarah and her books from her website: www.sarahmorgan.com. She can also be found on Facebook and Twitter.

Summer fling

Sarah Morgan

This edition published in Great Britain 2014
by Mills & Boon, an imprint of Harlequin (UK) Limited,
Eton House, 18-24 Paradise Road, Richmond, Surrey, TW9 1SR

SUMMER FLING © Sarah Morgan 2007

Originally published as *A Bride for Glenmore* and *Single Father, Wife Needed*

ISBN: 978 0 263 88960 4

024-0711

Harlequin (UK) policy is to use papers that are natural, renewable and recyclable products and made from wood grown in sustainable forests. The logging and manufacturing processes conform to the legal environmental regulations of the country of origin.

Printed and bound by
CPI Group (UK) Ltd, Croydon, CR0 4YY

KYLA

CHAPTER ONE

THE ferry docked in the early morning.

It was the start of summer, a fresh June day with plenty of cloud in an angry sky, and Ethan stood by the white rail with the other foot passengers, his eyes on the shore. The cool wind whipped playfully at his dark hair as if to remind him that this was remote Scotland and that meant that even summer weather was unpredictable.

Despite the early hour, the harbour was already busy and people were milling around the dock, buying fish straight from the boats and passing the time of day. From his vantage point high on the boat, Ethan could see a cluster of cottages, a café, a gift shop and an old-fashioned greengrocer with fruit and vegetables artfully arranged to draw the eye and the customer. From the harbour the road rose, snaking upwards and then curving out of sight along the coast.

Even without the benefit of local knowledge he knew where that road led. In fact, he felt as though he knew every contour of Glenmore island, even though he'd never been here before.

As if to remind himself of his reason for being

there, he slipped a hand into his pocket and fingered the letter. He'd done the same thing so many times before that the notepaper was crumpled and the writing barely legible in parts, but he didn't need to read it because he'd long since committed the contents to memory.

The description in the letter had been so detailed, the words so vivid that already the island felt familiar. In his mind he'd felt the cold chill of the wild, inhospitable mountains that clustered in the centre of the island and he'd walked the rocky shores that had sent so many ships to their doom. In his imagination, he'd sailed the deep loch and scrambled on the ruins of the ancient castle, the site of a bloody battle between Celts and Vikings centuries earlier. Glenmore had a turbulent past and a rich history thanks to the fierce determination of the locals to maintain their freedom.

Freedom.

Wasn't that what everyone wanted? It was certainly one of the reasons he was there. He needed to escape from the throttling grip of his past.

Suddenly Ethan wanted to sprint to the top of the highest point and breathe in the air and then he wanted to plunge into the icy waters of the Atlantic Ocean and swim with the porpoises that were reputed to inhabit this area. It felt good to escape from external pressures and the expectations of others and he had to remind himself that being there wasn't about escape, it was about discovery.

He'd come for answers.

And he intended to find those answers.

If he happened to enjoy being in this wild, remote corner of Scotland, then that was a bonus.

Ethan felt a sudden lift in his spirits and the feeling was as surprising as it was unexpected.

Well-meaning colleagues and friends had told him that he was mad to bury himself all the way up here on a Scottish Island. With qualifications like his, he should have been returning to Africa with all its medical challenges, or working at the renowned London teaching hospital where he'd trained. *They'd warned him that Island life would be dull.* Nothing but ingrowing toenails and varicose veins—old ladies moaning about the pressures of advancing age. He would be bored within a week.

A faint smile touched Ethan's classically handsome face. It remained to be seen whether they were right about the lack of job satisfaction, but at the moment it wasn't boredom he was feeling. It was exhilaration.

And a deep sadness for the loss of something precious and irreplaceable.

He breathed in deeply and felt the salty air sting his lungs. It was time to leave the ferry. Time to begin. He started to move away from the rail and then he paused, his eye caught by a tall, slender girl who was weaving her way through the groups of people hovering on the dock, awaiting the arrival of the ferry. She walked with bounce and energy, as if she had a million things to do and not enough time, returning greetings with a wave and a few words, hardly breaking stride as she made for the boat. Her hair was long and loose, her smile wide and friendly, and she carried a large sloppy bag over one shoulder. Anchoring it firmly, she leapt onto the ramp of the ferry with the grace of a gazelle.

Not a *girl,* he saw immediately, but a young woman, perhaps in her early twenties, and everything about her was vital and energetic.

The wind drew the conversation upwards.

'Hey, Kyla, you can't come on without a ticket.' The ferryman strolled towards her, a grin on his weathered face, and the girl reached up and planted a kiss on his cheek, her eyes twinkling.

'I've come for my deliveries, Jim. Logan ordered some equipment from the mainland and I've orders to collect it before breakfast, along with the post and the new doctor.'

Ethan frowned. *Kyla.* The letter had mentioned Kyla and finally he was putting a face to the name. And it was a lovely face. *So lovely that he found that he couldn't look away.*

The ferryman was hauling a sack onto the dock. His boots were dusted with sand and there were streaks of oil on his arms. 'The new doctor?'

'That's right. We ordered him from the mainland, too.' The woman stooped to help him with the sack. 'He'd better be good quality. If not, he's going right back. My poor brother needs help in the surgery almost as much as he needs a decent night's sleep.'

Jim snorted. 'Not likely to get it, with that bairn of his almost a year old.'

Ethan watched as Kyla's pretty smile faltered for a moment. 'He's doing all right. My aunt's been really busy at the café so one of the Foster girls has been helping him for the past few weeks. She's good with the baby. It's working out well.'

'Until she starts building up her hopes and hearing wedding bells, like everyone else who goes near that brother of yours.' Jim reached behind him and picked up a parcel and a bag of post. 'I suppose this is what you're after. You're up early for a girl who went to bed late. It was a good party last night. Don't you ever lie in?'

She dropped the post into the bag on her shoulder and lifted the parcel carefully, balancing it in her arms. 'Find me someone decent to lie in with, Jim, and I'll be happy to stay in bed. Until then I may as well work. Somebody has to keep everyone on this island healthy and strong.'

'Any time you want company in that lonely old cottage of yours, just say the word.'

Kyla opened her mouth to reply but the words didn't come and the beautiful smile faded as she stared at something.

It took a moment for Ethan to realise that he was that something. And another moment for him to realise that he was staring back and that he'd walked almost to her side without even noticing that he'd done so. He'd been drawn to her and the knowledge unsettled him. He was accustomed to being in control of his reactions, especially when it came to women.

Irritated with himself, he kept his tone cool. 'I heard you mention that you're meeting the new doctor. I'm Dr Walker. Ethan Walker.' He watched her face for signs of recognition, relieved when he saw none. *Why would there be?* It wasn't a name she'd know. And he had no intention of enlightening her. Not yet. He needed time to establish himself. Time to assess the situation without the complications that revealing his identity would inevitably arouse.

He watched as the wind picked up a strand of her blonde hair and blew it across her face.

'You're Dr Walker?' Her gaze was frank and appraising with no trace of either shyness or flirtation. She made no secret of the fact he was under scrutiny and he had the strangest feeling that if she hadn't liked what she'd seen she would have sent him back on the ferry to the mainland.

A strange heat spread through his body and he gave a faint smile.

His lifestyle wasn't compatible with long, meaningful relationships and he was careful to avoid them, but that didn't mean he wasn't capable of appreciating feminine appeal when it was standing in front of him.

At another time, in another place he might have done something about the powerful thud of attraction that flared between them, but he reminded himself that romance would only tangle the already complicated.

He tried to analyse the strength of his reaction— tried to provide a logical explanation for the primitive thud of lust that tore through his body.

It was true that she was striking, but he'd been with women more beautiful and more sophisticated—women to whom grooming was a full-time preoccupation. No one could describe Kyla's appearance as groomed. She was as wild as the island she inhabited, her hair falling loose over her shoulders in untamed waves and her face free of make-up. But her smile was wide and her eyes sparkled with an enthusiasm for life that was infectious. She looked like a woman who knew the meaning of the word happiness. An optimist. A woman who was going to grab life round the throat and enjoy every last second.

Aware that he was still staring, Ethan reminded himself firmly that his reasons for coming to the nethermost reaches of Scotland didn't include a need for female company.

'I'm Kyla MacNeil. Logan's sister.' She balanced the parcel on one arm and extended a hand. 'Welcome to Glenmore, Dr Walker. If you come with me, I'll take you straight up to the surgery and then I'll show you your new home and help get you settled in.'

'You're Logan's sister?' Ethan stared down into her blue eyes and searched for a resemblance. 'He talked about a little sister…'

'That's me. I'm twenty-five years old but that's six years less than him so I suppose that makes me his little sister. Are you going to shake this hand of mine, Dr Walker? Because if not, I'll put it away.'

Wondering why he was at a loss with a woman when he'd always considered himself experienced with her sex, Ethan shook her hand and nodded to Jim. 'Thanks for the lift. I'll be seeing you around.'

'If you're the new Island doctor, I hope you won't. The only time I plan to see you is in the pub or when I'm waving you goodbye as you leave this place.' Jim stepped back as the last of the cars clanked its way down the ramp and onto the quay. 'I intend to stay healthy.'

'Talking of which, how's that diet of yours going?' Kyla clutched the parcel to her chest and Jim pulled a face.

'Ever since she talked to you about what I should be eating, all Maisie seems to cook these days is fish and porridge. No bacon and eggs and I haven't seen a piece of cheese since the sun last shone, and that's a while ago. Life's just miserable. The only good thing is that Logan's stopped nagging me because he's very pleased with my cholesterol. It's come right down on that new drug.'

'That would be the statin he switched you to. Glad to hear it's working. Well, we need to go. I need to get to the surgery or Logan will be grumbling. Take care of yourself, Jim. The forecast for the end of the week is storms.'

Jim gave a grunt and watched as the last car clattered its way over the ramp and onto the island. 'Wouldn't be Glenmore if we didn't have storms.'

She turned to Ethan. 'Didn't you bring a car?'

'I've been working abroad until recently. I took the train but my car is being delivered later today. I gave them the address of the surgery.'

'In that case, you'll need a lift to the surgery. It's too far to walk.'

Ethan shifted his case into the other hand. 'Let me carry the box for you.'

'All right. I'm not one to reject a chivalrous gesture, even in the twenty-first century.' She relinquished the parcel and adjusted the bag on her shoulder. 'Don't drop it. It's a new defibrillator. One of those ones that talks to you, although, knowing my brother, if it starts to give him instructions he'll probably argue with it.'

Ethan took the parcel from her and followed her along the quay, watching the way everyone converged on her.

'Kyla.' An elderly woman crossed the street to speak

to her. 'I read that leaflet you gave me about strengthening your bones...'

'Glad to hear it, Mrs Porter.' She paused, her smile friendly. 'All OK?'

'Oh, yes. It advised you to walk more and lift weights. I'm a bit too old for the gym, so I filled some empty milk bottles with water and I've been using those.'

'Great idea. Well, if you have any questions you can find me in surgery and we can have a really good chat. And don't forget to speak to Evanna about doing her exercise class.'

She walked on a bit further before she was stopped by one of the fishermen who was untangling his net. 'Nurse MacNeil—I need to have those stitches of mine taken out.'

'How's the leg feeling?'

'Sore.'

She nodded. 'It was a nasty cut. You need to keep it up when you're resting. Pop in on Friday and I'll take the stitches out and take another look at it. If you need antibiotics, I can have a word with Logan.'

She walked on, somehow managing to acknowledge everyone's greeting in a friendly manner while avoiding lengthy conversation.

Ethan watched in silent admiration, trying to imagine something similar happening in London and failing. In London everyone kept their eyes forward and went about their own business. 'You know everyone.'

'This is an island, Dr Walker. Everyone knows everyone.' She scraped her unruly hair out of her eyes

and lifted an eyebrow in his direction. 'Is that going to
be a problem for you?'

'Why would it be?'

Her glance was assessing. 'You're a city boy and the
one thing that you can guarantee in a big, soulless city
is anonymity. And that suits some people. Not everyone
wants folks knowing their business.'

A city boy.

Ethan thought about the places he'd worked in, the
dust, the heat and the sheer weight of human suffering.
She had no idea. Oh, yes, he'd experienced anonymity.
The sort where you shouted and no one listened.

Kyla lengthened her stride, nodded to an elderly
woman who passed and then paused to stroke a baby
who was cooing in a pushchair. 'Can't believe he's two
months now, Alice. Make sure you remember to bring
him to clinic for his injections.' They moved on and
Ethan watched as she pulled a set of keys out of her
jacket pocket.

'Anonymity is one thing but time off is another. How
do you switch off and keep people at a distance?'

'On the whole people are pretty good about not
invading our privacy. If I'm wearing lipstick and heels
and have a drink in my hand, they know better than to
expect me to discuss their haemorrhoids.' She juggled
the keys in her hand. 'But it's definitely a close community and that can be a good thing or a bad thing, depending on the person you are or what you happen to
be doing at the time. If you're not careful you can find
yourself doing impromptu consultations on every street
corner. Not that I mind in some cases, but generally

speaking I want to feel I have a life outside work. We need to get a move on. The surgery is ten minutes' drive from here, in the village.'

He glanced around him. 'This isn't the village?'

'No, Dr Walker. This is the quay. People live dotted all over the place, which makes it a laugh a minute when you have an urgent house call, as you will soon discover.' She stopped by a tiny car in a deep shade of purple. 'Hop in. We'll go to the surgery and I'll introduce you to my brother and then I'll drop you at your cottage before I go back to my clinic.'

'This is your car?' He glanced at it in disbelief and she scowled at him across the top of the car, the expression in her blue eyes suddenly dangerous.

'If you're thinking of making a derogatory remark about the colour, then I advise against it. I happen to be very attached to my car. And so should you be, Dr Walker, because if it weren't for my car, you'd be walking up that hill with your luggage as we speak.'

Even on such a short acquaintance, he could see that she was a woman with a warm heart and a fiery temper. The combination was intriguing. For the first time in months he found himself fighting the desire to smile. 'Would you believe me if I told you that lurid purple is my favourite colour?'

'Very funny.' She glared at him for a moment and then grinned. 'All right, I'll be honest. I got it at a knock-down price from the mainland. Apparently no one else liked the colour.'

'You astonish me.'

'Sarcasm doesn't become you, Dr Walker. The boot's

open if you want to get rid of that suitcase.' She slid into the driver's seat and he somehow jammed his suitcase into the tiny boot and then climbed in next to her, wincing as he tried to fold his six foot three frame into the tiny vehicle.

'It may be an awful colour,' he muttered, easing the door shut, 'but at least it's roomy.'

'Are you being rude about my car?' She glanced towards him and burst out laughing. 'You look ridiculous.'

'It's the car that's ridiculous.'

'The car is fine, but you're too big for it.'

Ethan winced and tried to ease his legs into a more comfortable position. 'I'm aware of that fact.' He shifted down in the seat to give himself more head room and found his knees under his chin. 'Well, this is comfortable. Drive on. Wherever we're going, we'd better get there quickly or I'll need physiotherapy at the end of the journey and I don't suppose that's available on an island this remote.'

'Don't you believe it. Glenmore may be remote but we've a thriving population here. Physio is Evanna's division. Especially massage. She's great with crying babies and pretty good with moaning adults, too.' She started the engine, checked her rear-view mirror and started up the coast road at a frightening pace.

'Evanna?' Ethan wondered how a car so small could go so fast. 'I heard you mention her to the lady who spoke to you back on the quay. She's the other practice nurse?'

'That's right. We each have different responsibilities. Evanna is a midwife as well as a practice nurse and she's had some basic physio training. We all do a bit of everything if we can. It saves folks travelling all the way to the mainland.'

To one side of him the coast flashed past and he had a glimpse of rocky coves and sandy beaches. The island had a dramatic history, he recalled, with a good number of wrecks littering the seabed. He stared out to sea, his mind wandering. There were so many questions he wanted to ask but to do so would reveal too much so instead he turned back to look at her, studying her profile. From this angle he could see that her nose turned up slightly and that her eyelashes were long and thick. She had a sweet face, he decided. A happy face. There were no lines. No shadows. Nothing to suggest that life had sent her anything that she couldn't handle.

'You're staring at me, Dr Walker, and it's putting me off my driving.'

'Then I'll keep my eyes straight ahead.' He gave a faint smile. 'Given the proximity of this road to the edge of the cliff, I certainly wouldn't want to put you off.'

'I've lived here all my life. There's not a kink in this road that I don't know. And I'm a jack of all trades. I'm the dietician, the asthma specialist and the diabetes nurse. I'm trained in family planning but we're not exactly encouraging that at the moment because the population of the island is dwindling. If anyone comes to me for contraception, I send them away to have more sex and make a baby. We need babies on the Island or the next thing you know they'll be taking away a doctor and trying to close the school.'

Despite the dark clouds in his head, Ethan found himself laughing. 'Well, that's a novel approach to family planning. Are you serious? Is the school under threat of closure?'

'No, not yet.' She glanced towards him with a quick smile. 'Actually, this is a thriving, busy island and we're doing all right. But populations dwindle. It's a fact in rural areas like this. People find the life hard and they leave for the bright lights of the big cities. And they don't come back. They marry a mainlander like you and have their babies somewhere else.'

She changed gear and took a corner at an alarming speed.

'Do you always drive this fast?'

'I do everything fast. It means I can get through twice as much in the day, which is a definite advantage in a place like this. But that's enough about me. What brings you here? What are you running from, Dr Walker?'

He felt his body tense. 'Why would I be running from anything?'

'Because mainlanders don't generally choose to spend their summer up here in the wilds unless they're running from something,' she said cheerfully. 'Unless they're locals, people come here for space and to regroup. Was it work or something more personal? Love?'

His head started to throb. He'd expected questions. He just hadn't expected them this quickly. *And he hadn't prepared his answers.* 'Are you always this direct?'

'On an island, it's impossible to keep secrets.' She opened the window a crack and the breeze blew in and lifted her hair. 'They have a habit of following you. Better to get it all out in the open.'

Ethan stared at her profile and then turned his head

away to stare out of his own window. *If she knew his secret, she'd probably stop the car and push him off the cliff.* 'I'm not in the habit of talking about my sex life.'

'Right.' She shifted her grip on the steering-wheel. 'But I wasn't asking about your sex life, I was asking about your love life.'

It occurred to him that she would have got on well with his last girlfriend. *You don't have a heart, Ethan. You're not capable of intimacy.*

'I'm here because you advertised for a doctor. Logan told me he needed help.'

'He does need help. But that wouldn't be enough to attract a mainlander to a place like Glenmore. And Logan told me that you're a hotshot. First in everything. Top of your class.'

'Being a good doctor isn't about exam results.'

'Well, it's good to know we agree on something.' She shifted gear and slowed down to take a corner. 'Anyway, we're just pleased to have you here. It's been a tough few months. I don't know whether Logan mentioned it but he lost his wife almost a year ago.'

Ethan stiffened and the throb in his head intensified. 'Yes,' he said quietly, forcing his body to relax. 'He mentioned it.'

'It was a hideous time.' Kyla's voice was soft and her hands tight on the wheel. 'Awful.'

Ethan felt the sickness rise inside him. 'How did she die?'

'Having the baby.' Kyla shook her head slowly. 'It seems so wrong, doesn't it? In this day and age to die having a baby. You read about maternal mortality rates but you don't actually think it's going to happen to anyone you know. You think that if you monitor carefully, everything will be all right. But it wasn't all right. And I know Logan still blames himself even though he did absolutely everything that could have been done. She had an undiagnosed cardiac condition.'

Ethan took a deep breath. 'And how's he managing with the little girl? It must be difficult.'

'How did you know they had a girl?' She shot him a surprised look, her blue eyes narrowed. 'Did I mention it?'

'Logan mentioned it,' Ethan said, correcting his mistake swiftly. 'Kirsty. Eleven months.'

'That's right. She's a sweetie. She isn't walking yet but her crawling could earn her a speeding ticket and she's into everything. Gives us all grey hairs. And Logan manages. He's a great father and he has a lot of help from the islanders. One of my aunts runs the café on the quay along with one of my cousins, and they often take Kirsty for him during the day.'

'*One* of your aunts?'

'My grandmother was obviously preserving the future of the island. My mother was one of six.' She grinned at him. 'I have five aunts and eleven first cousins. Some of them have moved away, of course, but most of them still live on the island, which is handy for Logan. He hasn't cooked himself a meal for months, lucky creature. It's useful to have family around, isn't it?'

It was a concept so alien to Ethan that he found it impossible to answer. To avoid the inevitable questions, he took the conversation off on a different tangent. 'You don't like cooking?'

'Not one of my skills, but I do like eating.'

'And Logan has worked here since he finished his training?'

'No. He worked in London for a while, gaining the experience he needed to be able to work in a place like this. Out here it's the real thing, Dr Walker. No back-up. It takes skill and confidence to deal with that. Most islanders escape for a while just to see if the grass is greener on the other side and when they discover that it isn't...' She gave a slight shrug of her shoulders as she flicked the indicator and turned the car into a small car park '...they come back again. We're here. This is Glenmore Medical Centre.'

It was larger than Ethan had expected, a modern building with clean lines and glass, attached to a stunning house, painted white and with several balconies that faced towards the sea. 'Your brother lives here.'

'Yes. The surgery is attached to the house and, of course, people take all sorts of liberties, banging on his door when he's in the bath and that sort of thing.' She smiled and switched off the engine. 'But he loves it here.'

'From what I've heard, your brother is well qualified. He could have worked anywhere.'

'That's right. He could.' She reached into the back seat for her bag, her movements swift and decisive. 'And he chose to work here, where he grew up—where his talents really count for something. On Glenmore you're not one of hundreds of doctors, you're the only one. Sometimes you're the only person who can make a difference. You're truly needed.'

'And you love it.'

'Oh, yes.' She pulled the bag into her lap and then paused, a wistful smile on her face. 'As it happens, I've tried leaving. I've tried living in other places but they never feel right. When I'm here on Glenmore, somehow everything falls into place and I know I'm home.'

'It must be nice to feel that way about a place.'

'Everyone has somewhere that feels like home,' she said cheerfully as she opened the car door. 'Where is it for you? London?'

Ethan sat in silence, thinking about the question. 'That depends on your definition of home. Is it the place where you were born or the place where you grew up?'

She paused with her on the door as she considered the question. 'It's not necessarily either. Home is the place where you feel completely comfortable. You arrive there and suddenly you can't remember why you ever left because it's the only place you really want to be.'

Ethan studied her face for a moment. 'Then I don't think I have a home,' he said quietly, 'because I've never felt that way about anywhere.'

CHAPTER TWO

KYLA opened the boot and removed the box, trying not to stare as Ethan Walker uncurled his powerful body from the front seat of her car and stretched.

All the way in the car she'd been aware of him. Aware of the shadow of stubble darkening his jaw, of long, masculine leg brushing against hers and the long, searching looks he kept casting in her direction. She'd felt those looks—*felt him looking at her*—and something about the burning intensity of his gaze had disturbed her so badly that she'd driven fast to keep the journey as short as possible.

Her nerve endings had snapped tight and she'd been breathlessly conscious of every movement he'd made during the short journey.

She knew everyone who lived on the island. She was used to men who were safe and predictable. And she sensed that Ethan Walker was neither.

When her brother had given her the lowdown on the new island doctor, she'd conjured up a vision of a bespectacled, wiry academic who'd spent his life looking down a microscope and seeing patients from the other side of a large desk.

She hadn't expected to be knocked off her feet by the sight of him.

It wasn't just the handsome face and the athletic body that made it hard not to stare at him. It was the air of quiet confidence and the dark, almost brooding quality that surrounded him. She sensed that his emotions were buried deep inside him. Were those emotions responsible for the hard, cynical gleam in his eyes?

And what was he doing up here in the wilds of Scotland?

He'd evaded her question but she wasn't a fool. If Logan was right, then Ethan had been on the fast track. Hadn't he said that Ethan had been the youngest consultant they'd ever had in the hospital? A single-minded, ambitious over-achiever? Why would a man with that sort of career ahead of him suddenly leave it to work in a backwater?

It had to be something to do with his love life.

Hadn't he ignored the question when she'd asked it? Which was entirely typical of a man, she thought to herself, because since when did men ever talk about their feelings? They were all completely hopeless.

She slammed the boot shut, deciding that it would be interesting to get some answers. And interesting to spend some time with him.

The thought surprised her because it had been a long time since she'd found herself wanting to spend time with a man.

The problem with island life, she reflected as she

slipped the postbag onto her shoulder, was that she knew absolutely everyone. There were no surprises. She wasn't suddenly going to look at Nick Hillier, the island policeman, and feel a hot flush coming on. She wasn't going to go to bed dreaming of Alastair and his fishing boat. She knew everyone on the island as well as she knew her family.

But Ethan—Ethan was a surprise. A surprise that promised to make the long days of summer more interesting than usual.

Her mouth curved into a smile as she anticipated the days ahead.

It would be interesting, she decided, to find out more about him.

She pushed open the surgery door.

Her brother was sprawled in a chair at the reception desk, hitting keys on the computer. 'I've a full list here, Kyla. Did you book these in?'

'And good morning to you, too.' Her eyes scanned her brother's face, looking for signs of strain. Tiredness. Logan was the toughest person she knew but all the same she worried about him. He was doing all right, she decided. She was proud of him. 'Have you been here all night?'

'It certainly feels like it.' He pushed the chair away from the computer and stretched. His hair was dark and touched the edge of his collar, but his eyes were as blue as hers. 'I need every second of the day to see these patients. We have to stop booking them in.'

Kyla threw him an exasperated look. 'Well what do you expect me to do, you idiot? Tell them to go away and pick another day to be ill?'

'Nice to get some proper respect around here,' Logan drawled, but there was a twinkle in his eyes. 'I'm just pointing out that there's only one of me and at the moment I'm spread rather thinly.'

Kyla slammed the post down on the reception desk. 'Well, despite what you may think, I don't spend my time going round the Island drumming up business for your surgeries. Can I help it if people think you're the answer to their problems? Anyway, there isn't just one of you any more.' She turned with a wave of her hand. 'I brought you reinforcements from the ferry, Dr Ethan Walker. I expect you already know that because he's the only stranger that stepped off the ferry this morning so I dare say the jungle drums have been beating for the last half an hour. Treat him well and perhaps he'll help you with your surgery.'

'Ethan—pleased to meet you.' Logan straightened and the two men shook hands while Kyla tilted her head to one side and studied them both. They had a similar physique and yet they were entirely different. Both dark, both tall, both broad-shouldered, but the resemblance ended there. While her brother looked rough and rugged, as though he'd just strode off the hills, Ethan was smooth and slick. *City slick*, Kyla thought as she turned away and started stacking the post neatly for Janet, their receptionist, to open later. He was a man who looked...she searched for the right term...*expensive*.

And he probably wasn't going to last five minutes in a place like Glenmore.

The two men were deep in conversation when the phone rang. Reaching over the desk, Kyla lifted the receiver, her hair falling forward.

'Glenmore Medical Centre.' Her voice was bright and friendly and she ignored a look from Logan that warned her that trying to cram another patient onto his morning list would put her life at risk. 'Hello, Janet! How are you doing?' She straightened and pulled a face. 'Oh, no—that's awful! I'm so sorry to hear that. Don't move her. Logan will be right over.'

She replaced the receiver to find Logan gazing at her in disbelief. 'Remind me to fire you and replace you with a moody, scary battleaxe who frightens away patients. If you've booked me a house call two minutes before my morning surgery starts then I'm going to strangle you with my bare hands,' he growled. 'What do you think I am? Superhuman?'

'A good doctor.' Kyla scribbled the details on a scrap of paper and then walked across and gave him a swift kiss on the cheek. 'A good but exceptionally *moody* doctor. That was our Janet. She popped round to check on her mum this morning and found her collapsed on the floor.'

'Gladys?' Logan's frown changed to a look of concern and Kyla thrust a piece of paper into his hands.

'You see? You care really, you know you do. You just hide it well. This isn't going to wait, Logan. She needs to be seen right away.'

'I have surgery—I can't be in two places at once.'

'Well, I think the place you need to be is with Mrs Taylor. Janet thinks she's broken her leg. You go. I'll keep the patients happy. Evanna and I will see the ones that we can and the others will just have to wait.' Kyla waved a hand towards the door. 'Go forth and heal, oh great one. I can sing and dance and generally entertain them while you swan off like a knight in shining armour.'

'I'll start your surgery.' Ethan stepped forward, cool and unflustered, watching the exchange between them with puzzled curiosity. 'Why not?'

Logan ran a hand over the back of his neck. 'Because you've been travelling all night? Because you must need a shower and a rest? Because you don't know the patients or the island? How many more reasons do you need?'

Ethan gave a faint smile. 'I'm used to travelling and the shower and the rest can wait. As for not knowing the patients or the island...' he gave a dismissive shrug of his broad shoulders '...I don't see why that should that be a problem. Presumably Kyla's on hand if I need help. Keep your mobile on. If I have any questions, I'll call you.'

'All right, then. If you're sure.' Without further argument Logan reached for his bag. 'If she's fractured her hip, I'm going to need the air ambulance, Kyla. I'll call you.'

'You do that.' Kyla watched her brother stride through the door and then picked up a set of keys. 'All right, Dr Walker. Looks like you're on duty. I'll show you your room then I'll fetch you a cup of coffee. Hopefully that will see you through until we have time for something more—' She didn't finish her sentence because the surgery door crashed open and a large man staggered in. His face was pale and shone with sweat, his hand pressed against his chest.

'Doug!' Kyla was by his side in a flash, her arm sliding around him in an instinctive offer of support. 'What's happened? Are you ill?'

'Pain.' His face was contorted in agony and tiny drops of sweat clung to his forehead. 'Terrible pain in my chest. I was down in the basement, shifting crates of beer, when I started to feel funny. A bit sick, to be honest. Then it hit me all of a sudden. It's like an elephant on my chest.'

'Can we lay him down somewhere?'

'In the consulting room.'

Ethan took the man's arm and he and Kyla guided him down the corridor into the room. 'Let's get you up on the couch, Mr...?'

'McDonald,' Kyla said quickly, raising the back of the couch and helping the patient to lie down. 'Doug McDonald. Fifty-six years of age, been treated for hypertension for the past three years. He's taking beta blockers, an ace inhibitor and a statin.'

Ethan lifted a brow as he took Doug's pulse and reached for a stethoscope. 'You know every patient's history by heart?'

'Small community, Dr Walker. What do you need?'

'Start with oxygen?'

'There's a cylinder to your right with a mask already attached, and I expect you'll want to put a line in. I'll fetch you the tray.' Brisk and efficient, she reached into the cupboard, removed the tray and placed it on the trolley next to him. 'Just breathe normally through that mask, Doug. That's great. I'll squeeze while you find a vein, Dr Walker.' She put her hands around Doug's arm, watching while Ethan stroked the back of his hand, searching for a vein.

'Do we have the facility to start an IV?'

'Of course. I'll run a bag of fluid through for you.'

'You have good veins, Doug.' He cleaned the skin,

inserted the cannula with the ease of someone who had performed the same procedure successfully a million times before. Kyla gave a faint nod of approval and released her grip on Doug's arm.

'You're doing fine, Doug. Dr Walker will soon have you feeling better. I'll get the notes up on the screen for you,' she said to Ethan. 'That way you'll be able to see what Logan has been doing.' She moved over to the desk, flicked on the computer, crossed the room and grabbed the ECG machine from the corner. 'That computer will just take a minute to wake up.'

Doug gave a grunt of pain, his hand on the mask. 'I was always afraid that this might happen. It's why I tried to lose weight. I managed to stop smoking but I just ate more.' He grimaced and leaned back against the pillow as Ethan connected a bag of fluid. 'I've been trying, really I have. But it's so hard.'

'You've been doing brilliantly, Doug, you know that. Don't worry about it now,' Kyla said quickly, wrapping the blood-pressure cuff around his other arm. 'We just need to find out what's happening.' She checked his BP, showed Ethan the result and he gave her a nod.

'Can we do a 12-lead ECG?'

'Already on it.' Kyla quickly stuck the pads onto the patient and applied the chest leads and limb leads. 'Just hang in there, Douglas, you're going to be fine. Dr Walker is a real whiz kid from the mainland. People usually pay a fortune to see him, but you're getting him free so this is your lucky day.'

She was aware of the sardonic lift of Ethan's dark brows but chose to ignore him. This was her territory, she reminded herself. There was no way she was going to allow herself to be intimidated by a locum doctor, no matter how slick and handsome.

Doug closed his eyes and gave a wan smile. 'It doesn't feel like my lucky day, hen.'

Kyla felt her heart twist at the endearment. *She'd known Doug since she'd been a child.* 'Of course it's lucky because I'm on duty,' she said lightly, switching on the machine. 'If you had to be ill then you've done it in the right place. You're going to be OK, Doug.' She chatted away in a steady, reassuring voice and then looked up as the door opened and a dark-haired girl in a blue uniform hurried into the room.

'I just drove past Logan breaking the speed limit on the coast road and, judging from the look on his face, I thought you might need some help here.' Her eyes were gentle and concerned and her ponytail swung as she moved her head. 'Doug? What have you been doing to yourself?'

'This is Ethan Walker, the new GP. Ethan, this is Evanna, the other island nurse. Logan's gone to see Janet's mother who's had a fall and our Doug here is having nasty chest pains. Can you call the air ambulance?' Kyla glanced up at her friend and colleague and used her eyes to transmit the message that the request was urgent. 'Whatever happens, we're going to need to transfer Doug to the mainland. Doug, I need to call your wife and let her know what's happening. Is she home?'

Evanna slid out of the room without argument and Kyla felt a flicker of relief. She knew she could trust her friend to get the air ambulance to the island as quickly as possible.

'No.' Douglas turned his head, his face pale and sweaty and his voice urgent. 'You're not to worry Leslie. She's got enough on her mind at the moment with our Andrea going through a rebellious phase. She doesn't need this. I'm having a heart attack, I know I am. It'll be too much for her.'

'She loves you, Doug,' Kyla said firmly, starting the machine and watching the trace. She didn't like what she saw but she was careful not to let her worry show on her face. *But she was definitely calling his wife.* 'You're a partnership. A team. What do you think she'd say when she discovers that you've flown off on a mini-break to the mainland and left her here?'

ST elevation, she thought to herself, studying the pattern. She'd seen it often enough in her short time in A and E.

Doug gave a wan smile and shook his head. 'She's always on at me to leave the island for a break.'

'Well, there you are, then.' Kyla stood to one side so that Ethan could watch the trace. 'There's ST segment elevation in two leads. I expect you'll want to give him heparin and reteplase. I'll get it ready.'

Ethan looked at her and she saw approval and a flicker of surprise in his eyes. 'Do we have morphine and GTN spray?'

'Of course.' The question amused her. So he thought he was working in a backwater, did he? She unlocked the drug cupboard, found what she needed and prepared it, listening as he talked to Doug.

'I'm afraid the ECG shows that you're right about the heart attack, Doug. Probably caused by a blood clot in one of the vessels leading to your heart.' His tone was calm and steady. 'I'm going to give you a drug that will break it down.'

'One of those clot-busters I've been reading about?'

'That's right. We need to get the blood flowing back through that artery for you. Before I give it, I need to ask you a few questions.'

Doug winced, his face pale behind the mask. 'I ought to warn you that I hate quiz night at the pub. I never go. If you're about to start on capital cities, you can forget it. I left school at sixteen and went out on my father's boat.'

Ethan smiled. 'You don't suffer from any bleeding disorders? Haven't had surgery lately?' He asked a series of rapid questions and then took the drugs from Kyla. 'How long does the air ambulance usually take to arrive and where do they land? I'm not sure he's stable enough to travel.'

'The paramedics are skilled and you can go with him. They carry a defibrillator, along with all the other gear you're likely to need.'

Ethan administered the drug carefully. 'And they can fly here?'

'Oh, yes, providing the weather is all right, and today it should be fine.' Kyla took the empty syringe from him and disposed of it with swift efficiency. 'We need to call the hospital and fill out details for the transfer.'

'If I go with him, that will leave you with no doctor.'

Kyla smiled. 'Logan's still on the island and he won't be long, I'm sure. Don't make the mistake of thinking that you're indispensable, Dr Walker,' she said cheerfully, her eyes sliding to Doug's taut features. 'We nurses are extremely versatile.'

His gaze followed hers and he frowned and checked Doug's pulse. 'How's the pain now? Any improvement?'

Doug nodded. 'Better,' he rasped, just as Evanna came back into the room.

'Air ambulance will be here in fifteen minutes,' she said in her calm, gentle voice. 'I've explained to the patients in the waiting room that there will be a delay until Logan gets back.'

Kyla looked up. 'Did you call him?'

'Yes. Mrs Taylor has a nasty laceration of her leg and she's very shaken up but nothing's broken. He's going to bring her back here to be sutured and I've said that one of us will spend some time in the home with her, discussing how to avoid falls.'

Kyla frowned as she reached for the phone. 'She ought to join your exercise class, Evanna. Did she trip over something?'

'Not sure. Janet just found her at the bottom of the stairs. It was fortunate that she didn't break anything or we'd be keeping the ambulance busy today.' Evanna glanced at her watch. 'If you don't need me here, I'll get started. I'm going to filter Logan's patients and see as many as I can for him.'

She left the room and Kyla handed Ethan the phone. 'You'll want to speak to the head of the coronary care unit at the Infirmary. His name's Angus Marsh. He's a nice guy.' She walked over to Douglas. 'It's time we let your wife know what's going on. This is an Island, Doug. She'll see the air ambulance and pretty soon someone is going to tell her who the patient was. The first thing she'll do is worry and what will be going on in her head is going to be worse than the real thing. The second thing she'll do is kill me.'

As if to prove her point, the door flew open at that moment and Leslie hurried into the room.

'Who needs phones when there's the island grapevine?' Kyla breathed, stepping back from the couch and watching as Leslie lifted her hands to her cheeks.

'What have you been doing to yourself, Douglas Rory Fraser McDonald?'

Doug gave a feeble groan but there was no missing the affection in his eyes. 'What are you doing here, woman?'

'I was buying fish from Geoff on the quay and he told me he'd seen you looking really off colour and heading up this way.' Leslie stared at the ECG machine in horror and then turned to Kyla. 'Nurse MacNeil? What's going on?'

Kyla's gaze flickered to Ethan but he was on the phone, talking to the consultant at the hospital, arranging the transfer. 'Douglas has had some chest pain and it looks as though he might have had a heart attack,' she said gently. 'He's doing very well and there's certainly no need to panic. We're going to transfer him to the mainland just until they're happy with his condition. Just a precaution. The helicopter is going to be here in a minute.'

Leslie gave a soft gasp. 'You're going to the mainland? You've had a heart attack? And just when were you planning on telling me this, Doug? Next Christmas?'

'Stop fussing. Kyla was just about to ring you but

they've been working flat out since I arrived.' Doug kept his eyes closed and his voice was thready. 'Go back and check on our Andrea. I'll call you from the hospital.'

'Andrea is fine. She's thirteen now. She can get herself to school.' Leslie looked at Kyla, her face grey with shock and worry. 'Can I go with him?'

Kyla nodded. 'You should be able to but I'll have to check with the crew. Leslie, you look very pale. Sit down.' She quickly dragged a chair across the room and the other woman plopped onto it gratefully.

'I'll be fine in a minute,' she muttered, rubbing her hand across her forehead. 'It's just a bit of a shock, that's all.'

Ethan replaced the phone just as Evanna popped her head round the door again. 'The helicopter is here. The paramedics are bringing a stretcher in for you.'

'I've spoken to the hospital and they're expecting him.' Ethan checked Doug's observations again and then helped the paramedics move him onto the stretcher.

They loaded Doug into the helicopter, helped Leslie on board and then Ethan sprang up beside him in a lithe, athletic movement. 'How do I get back?'

Kyla grinned. 'If you're lucky, they bring you back. If you're unlucky, you swim. Don't worry, the water's quite warm at this time of the year. See you later, Dr Walker.'

She ducked out of range of the helicopter's blades and made her way back into the surgery. Walking into the crowded waiting room, she explained what had happened and quickly assessed who could see her instead of a doctor.

'Is Doug going to be all right?' Paula Stiles, who

worked in the gift shop, asked the question that was on everyone's mind.

Patient confidentiality was a total nightmare, Kyla reflected as she gave as little information as possible while still providing the necessary reassurance.

Then she opened the door of her own room and switched on the computer. Interesting start to the day, she mused as she tapped a few keys and brought up her list for the morning. Not even nine o'clock and already she felt as though she'd done a day's work.

And she didn't want to think about how Ethan must feel. He'd travelled for most of the night to catch the first ferry and now she'd had to send him back to the mainland, and she knew from experience that he'd be lucky to make it back before lunch.

She hoped the new doctor had stamina because he was going to need it.

CHAPTER THREE

HER first patient was the headmistress from the local primary school, who had been hoping to see Logan and be back in time for the start of the school day.

'I'm sorry you've had a wait, Mrs Carne,' Kyla said, her tone apologetic as she reached for a pen. 'If it's your asthma that's bothering you, I could discuss it with you and then we could talk to Logan later.'

'It is my asthma.' Ann Carne put her bag on the floor and sat on the chair. 'I've been having problems on the sports field. Can you imagine that? I'm dealing with six-year-olds and I'm getting out of breath.'

'Six-year-olds are extremely energetic,' Kyla said dryly. 'Don't underestimate the impact that can have on your breathing. I went to sports day last year and I was exhausted just watching. So what's happening? Are you using an inhaler before you exercise?'

'Sometimes.' Ann looked uncomfortable. 'I try to sneak off to the staffroom but it isn't always possible.'

'Why would you need to sneak?'

'I don't want the children knowing I have an inhaler.'

Kyla looked at her, trying to work out what the

problem was so that she could tackle it in a sensitive way. 'Are you worried about them or you?'

'Both?' Ann gave a rueful smile. 'I hate admitting I'm ill and I don't want the children worrying that I'm going to collapse in front of them.'

'Would they think that?' Kyla frowned and tapped her pen on the desk. 'There are a couple of asthmatics in your school, as you well know. The children are used to seeing inhalers and spacers.'

'But not in their teachers.'

Judging that the situation was more about Ann than the pupils, Kyla sat back in her chair. 'It's nearly a year since you were diagnosed, Ann. How do you feel about it all now?'

There was a long silence and then Ann breathed out heavily. 'I still can't believe it's me,' she said finally. 'I mean, I'm fifty-two years of age. It's ridiculous! How can I suddenly develop asthma out of nowhere?'

'Peoplc do. It isn't about age. There are many other factors involved.'

'Well, I can't get used to the idea.'

'Is that why you don't use the inhaler?' Kyla's voice was gentle. 'If you don't use the drugs then you can't be ill?'

'How did you come to be so wise?' Ann gave a faint smile. 'I remember you when you were six years old, Kyla MacNeil. You brought a frog into my class and hid it in your desk.'

'I remember. It was my brother's frog. He was pretty annoyed with me.'

'And he came thundering in to steal it back.' Ann

sighed. 'I still think of myself as young, you know. I don't feel any different. It's only when I look in the mirror that I realise how many years have passed. And when my body starts letting me down.'

'Your body is still ready to work perfectly well if you give it the little bit of help it needs.' Kyla reached into her drawer for a leaflet. 'Read this. A bundle arrived last week and I think it's good. It talks about living with a condition rather than being ruled by it. You wouldn't dream of not using a toothbrush and toothpaste, would you? All part of body maintenance. Well, your inhalers are the same. Body maintenance.'

Ann took the leaflet and gave a thoughtful smile. 'Body maintenance. That's a nice idea, Kyla.'

'For the next two weeks, promise me you'll use your inhaler as we agreed. Then come and see me and we'll discuss how things are. But don't hide it from the children. We try and teach the children that it can become a normal part of life. Something they can live with. If they see you hiding it then it won't do much for their own acceptance of asthma.'

'I hadn't thought of that but you're right, of course.' Ann stood up and gave her a grateful smile. 'You've come a long way since you made a mess of your geography books, Kyla MacNeil. Can I ask how Doug is or will you tell me to mind my own business?'

'I don't think I'm ever going to be able to tell my old headmistress to mind her own business.' Kyla laughed. 'But the truth is that it's too soon for us to say.' The entire island had obviously noted the arrival of the helicopter. 'Our new doctor went with him. Hopefully we'll have good news when he arrives back. I'll remind Ben to pin a bulletin to the door of the pub.'

'You do that.' Ann gave a brisk nod. 'We all care, you know.'

'I do know,' Kyla said with a soft smile. 'That's why I choose to live on Glenmore, Mrs Carne. Have a good day, now. And don't let any of those little monsters bring frogs into the classroom.'

Ethan arrived back towards the end of her surgery, about an hour after her brother had returned from seeing Janet's mother.

Kyla showed him into his consulting room and together the three of them swiftly cleared the remaining patients in the waiting room while Evanna played the role of receptionist.

'Any house calls?' Logan stifled a yawn as they finally collapsed at the reception desk.

'Just the one. Helen McNair. Had some bad news from the hospital and wondered if you'd call.' Evanna picked up the book. 'I managed to persuade the rest of them to come to surgery this afternoon to save you going out again. I thought you'd need some time to show Dr Walker around.'

'You talked someone out of a house call?' Logan's drawl was tinged with humour. 'Evanna, consider yourself promoted, my angel. From now on you're officially our receptionist and my favourite woman.'

Kyla noticed the betraying pink of Evanna's cheeks and glanced towards her brother with sudden interest, but he'd picked up the latest copy of a medical journal and was flicking through the pages, apparently oblivious to the effect that his endearment had had on her friend.

Shaking her head with frustration, Kyla resisted the temptation to hit him over the head with a blunt object. Didn't the entire Island population praise Logan for his amazing sensitivity? Didn't everyone think her brother knew everything about everything and everyone?

Well, there were some things that he was totally dense about, Kyla thought wearily as she tucked a set of notes back into the cabinet. It had been almost a year since Catherine had died. Long enough. Sooner or later she was going to have to interfere.

Looking at the wistful expression in Evanna's kind eyes, Kyla decided that it might just be sooner. 'I had a visit from Ann Carne this morning.' Dragging her mind back to the job in hand, she handed a set of results to her brother.

'Did you, now?' Logan leaned back in his chair, his long legs stretched out in front of him. 'And how was our favourite headmistress?'

'Still in denial. If she doesn't learn to use those inhalers, she's going to find herself in trouble.'

Logan nodded thoughtfully. 'And did you speak to her about it?'

Kyla lifted an eyebrow. 'What am I—stupid?'

'You want me to answer that?'

'Don't start, you two,' Evanna said hastily, sending an apologetic glance towards Ethan. 'You mustn't mind them. It's just brother-sister stuff. They're always the same. They bicker and needle. You get used to it after a time. They adore each other really.'

There was no answering smile on Ethan's face and Kyla frowned slightly as she noticed the grim set of his mouth and the tension in his broad shoulders. Oops, she thought to herself. Trouble there. There was a bleakness and a shadow in his eyes that made her wonder and want to ask questions. Did he object to humour in the work-place? Surely not.

She caught Logan's eye and he shot her a warning look. 'Mind your own business,' he murmured softly in Gaelic, and she smiled and replied in the same tongue.

'Perhaps I'm wondering whether to make him my business.'

Logan rolled his eyes and stood up, switching to English. 'Women. I'll never understand them.'

'Well, that's perfectly obvious,' Kyla muttered, her eyes sliding to Evanna. 'But don't give up trying. Believe me, you need the practice.'

'I'm practising on my daughter. Talking of which, if we've finished here I'm going to spend an hour with the girl in my life who should be just about waking up from her nap and ready to dress herself in her lunch. Ethan, I'd invite you to join us but you'd end up covered in puréed vegetables. Take some time to settle in. My sister will show you the cottage we've arranged for you. I hope it suits. It's only a short drive from here. If you need anything, you've only to ask.'

Kyla watched as some of the wariness left Ethan's handsome face. 'Do you want me to do the house call so you can spend more time with the baby?'

'No need.' Logan shook his head. 'I'll take her with me. Helen McNair has been asking to see her.'

Kyla gave a soft smile. 'That's a clever idea, Logan MacNeil. Give her something else to focus on.'

'She's had a hard time lately. It will be good to spend some time with her. And she makes the best chocolate cake on the island.' Logan strode across the reception area towards the door that separated the surgery from his house.

Kyla turned to Ethan with a smile. 'Are you ready for another trip in my car?'

'That was an exciting morning.' Ethan unravelled himself from the car and followed Kyla down a path that led towards a pair of cottages. The sea stretched ahead of them and he breathed in deeply, enjoying the cool, salty breeze and the freshness of the air. 'Is it always like that?'

'Sometimes.' She pushed open a gate and held it while he followed her through. 'It's often all or nothing. You were good.'

'Was it a test?'

'No. But if it had been, you would have passed.' She let the gate swing shut and tilted her head to one side as she studied him. 'Don't be angry with me. Working on this island isn't for everyone. We see everything here, and we're the first line of defence. Does that worry you?'

'No.' What worried him was the hot flare of lust he felt whenever he looked at her. Gritting his teeth, he concentrated on the view of the bay. 'It's spectacular. Who lives here usually?'

'Holiday let. The cottage is usually rented out for the whole of the summer season but Nick Hillier who owns it had a bad experience last year.' Kyla fumbled for the keys and opened the front door. 'A group from London had a bit of a wild party and left the place wrecked. So he decided that this summer he'd let it to the locum doctor. He's assuming that, with all those letters after your name, you'll know how to behave yourself.'

'I'll do my best.' Ethan strolled into the cottage behind her, trying to ignore her delicious scent and the incredible shine of her honey-blonde hair. 'Who's Nick Hillier?'

'Our policeman. I went to school with him. He used to tie my plaits together.'

For some reason that he couldn't identify, this piece of news simply racked up the tension inside him and Ethan drew in a breath and rolled his shoulders. He needed a swim. A run. Anything to drive the unwanted thoughts and images from his head.

He watched as she threw open doors and windows, letting in light and air. She was obviously an outdoor sort of person. 'Did you go to school with everyone on the island?'

'Not everyone, but most of the people of around my age who were born here. It's a small community. Mind you, that can be a disadvantage. I sometimes think Ann Carne still sees me as the little horror who led the strike against school dinners.' She turned and smiled and he felt a vicious kick of lust deep inside him.

Her pretty smile faded and was replaced by something entirely different as they stared at each other.

Back off, Ethan, he warned himself grimly. Not now. *And not this woman.*

That wasn't why he was there.

'You led a strike against school dinners?' He saw

from the slightly questioning look in her eyes that she'd picked up on the rough tone of his voice.

'I was a fussy eater. I protested loudly about every-thing they put in front of me and I expected everyone else to protest, too. I told all the other children to fold their arms and refuse to eat until they produced some-thing decent.'

He could imagine her doing it. Imagine her with those sapphire-blue eyes flashing and that chin lifted in defiance. 'And how old were you?'

'Five.' She smiled without a trace of apology. 'My mother said she'd never been so embarrassed. They called her down to the school. I was given such a talking-to.'

Ethan found himself smiling, too. 'And did you eat your dinner after that?'

'No. I used to scrape it into my napkin and then hide the evidence.'

'And they never found out?'

'Sadly, they did.' Kyla opened a door and walked ahead of him into a beautiful glass-fronted living room, her feet echoing on the pale wooden floor. 'But only because I was stupid enough to slide it into Miss Carne's handbag on one occasion. I think it was lasagne or something really sloppy. Vile. I'm surprised I wasn't expelled. After that, they watched me eat.'

'I don't blame them.' He glanced around him in surprise. 'This is nice.'

'You should have seen it two years ago. Complete wreck. It had been lived in by the same man for about ninety years. After he bought it, Nick spent every weekend doing it up. We all helped.' She walked over to the window and stared out across the sea. 'He was lucky to get it. There was a lot of competition because this is one of the best spots on the island.'

'So why didn't you try and buy it?'

'I didn't need to.' She turned to look at him, amusement in her eyes. 'I own the place next door. You might want to remember that before you run naked into the waves for your morning swim, Dr Walker. Or are you southerners too wimpy to take a plunge into the Atlantic?'

Was she challenging him? He held her gaze with his own. 'I swim well.'

Her eyes slid to his shoulders, as if she were assessing the truth of his quiet statement and suddenly the tension in the air snapped as tight as a bow and Ethan felt something dangerous stir inside him.

'So this place is mine for the duration of my stay?' His voice was hoarse and he cursed himself. *Could she feel it, too?* Was she aware of the sudden change in the atmosphere?

'It's yours for as long as you want it. When you leave it will be winter and no one but the locals brave this island come November.' She watched him for a moment and then walked over to the French doors, her movements as smooth and graceful as those of a dancer. But then she lifted a hand to touch a switch and he saw that her fingers were shaking. 'Flick this to the right and the doors open. The garden leads down to the beach. Just make sure you close the doors if there's a storm or you'll be sweeping the sand from your living room for weeks.'

'Storm?' Ethan fixed his gaze on the perfect blue sky. *He needed to stay away from her.* Far, far away.

'Jim, the ferryman, mentioned storms. It's pretty calm today. Hard to imagine the place in a storm.'

'You won't have to imagine it because you're going to see it soon enough.' Kyla gave a soft laugh. 'I hope you like your weather wild, Dr Walker, and I hope you're not afraid of storms. Because anything you've seen up until now will be nothing compared to this island in the grip of a seething temper.'

'I don't scare easily.' He turned, unable to be in the same room and not look at her. 'How about you, Kyla MacNeil? Do you scare easily? Do you take risks?' He was playing with fire. *Testing her.* He saw from the fierce glint in her blue eyes that she knew it.

'Life is there to be lived to the full. I was born on this island and it's part of who I am. Nothing about it frightens me. Not the storms. Not the isolation.' *And not you,* her eyes said, and he felt a flicker of envy.

What would it be like, Ethan wondered bleakly, to be so sure of everything? To live somewhere that felt like home?

The letter was still in his pocket and suddenly he wanted to read it again. *To try and understand.*

'I need to unpack and take a shower.' His tone was harsher than he'd intended and he saw the faint frown of confusion in her eyes. For a brief moment he wanted to take her arm and apologise, and the impulse surprised him as much as it would have surprised all of the people who knew him because he wasn't exactly known for gentleness.

You don't have a heart, Ethan.

And then he backed off, remembering that he wasn't in a position to explain anything.

He needed time.

There were things he needed to find out.

Kyla closed the front door behind her and jumped over the tiny hedge that separated the two cottages.

As she let herself into the cottage that she'd converted with the help of her brother and her friends, she considered the powerful chemistry between Ethan and herself. It was there. Pointless to deny it. And yet she sensed that the connection angered him.

He didn't want to feel it.

Kyla frowned as she flicked on the kettle. And what about her? What did she want?

She'd become so used to leading her own life she hadn't given any thought to the possibility that things might change.

He wasn't going to stay, she told herself firmly as she made herself a mug of tea and took it out onto the deck that overlooked the beach. Whatever they shared would be short-term because she would never leave the island.

'Nurse MacNeil! Kyla!'

She glanced up as she heard her name being called from the beach. Deciding that perhaps the prospect of leaving the island had possibilities after all, she gave a sigh and walked down to the end of her garden, still nursing the mug. At least in inner-city London she might get to drink her tea in peace. 'Fraser Price. What are you doing on the beach in the middle of a school day?'

Probably bunking off, the way she had as a child.

'Don't tell Miss Carne,' the boy begged, breathless

as he struggled in bare feet through the soft sand. 'She thinks I'm ill.'

'And you're not?' Reminding herself that she was a grown-up now and supposed to set standards, Kyla looked suitably stern. 'You should be at school. Education is important. Pretending to be ill isn't a good idea, Fraser.' She almost laughed as she listened to herself. *How many times had she sneaked off to play on the beach?*

'It was the only thing I could think of. And I needed to stay at home.'

'Why did you need to stay at home?'

'To look after Mum.' Suddenly he looked doubtful and unsure. 'She wasn't making sense this morning and I didn't want to leave her. I had a bad feeling.'

'What sort of bad feeling?' Kyla was alert now. 'Is it her diabetes? What do you mean, she wasn't making sense? Is something the matter with your mum?'

'I dunno. She just seemed…different.' He gave a shake of his head and then shrugged. 'She'd kill me if she knew I was here. I bunked off last week to take the boat out and she really did her nut. Don't say I was here. Couldn't you just call in on her? You know, like by accident?'

'Fraser, I don't call on anyone by accident.' Amusement gave way to concern as Kyla saw the look on his face. 'OK. OK.' She lifted a hand. 'Today I'll find a reason to call on your mum by accident.'

'Really?' He breathed an audible sigh of relief. 'That's great. Can the accident be right now?'

Banishing hopes of lunch, Kyla nodded. 'Just let me lock up here and get my car. I'll meet you back at your house. You can let me in. And, Fraser, about your mum…' She caught his arm. 'Can you describe how she looked? How was she different?'

'She was a funny colour. And her hands were shaking when she gave me breakfast. You won't tell on me?' He looked at her anxiously. 'I said I felt sick and needed a walk in the fresh air.'

Kyla thought of all the sins she'd committed at school. Didn't everyone need a little latitude? 'I won't tell. Off you go. I'll be there in five minutes.'

'What will you say?'

'I don't know, but I'll think of something,' Kyla said firmly, giving him a gentle push and turning back to her cottage. She noticed Ethan standing in his garden and had a sudden inspiration. 'Dr Walker!'

He turned and she gave an apologetic shrug. 'How badly did you want a shave and a shower? If you're not that tired, I need to enlist your help again. I think I might need a doctor.'

CHAPTER FOUR

'AISLA PRICE is a single mother.' Kyla snapped on her seat belt and pressed her foot to the accelerator. 'She moved to the island when Fraser was a baby because she thought it would be a good place to bring up a child. She has a small knitting business that she runs over the internet. Pretty successfully, I believe. She makes really pretty jumpers covered in bits of lace and beads and things like that. They live in a house right by the water.'

Ethan looked at her. 'And she has diabetes?'

'Yes. But her diabetes is very well controlled so it shouldn't be that.' Kyla frowned as she changed gear and flicked the indicator. 'But Fraser obviously thinks there's a problem so we'd better check it out. It might be nothing.'

'She hasn't asked you to call? You're making an impromptu visit?' Ethan tried to imagine something similar happening in London and failed. But in London a child wouldn't run across a beach to bang on the community nurse's door.

'That's right. An impromptu visit.' She stopped the car outside a row of whitewashed cottages and yanked on the handbrake. 'We're here.'

Ethan looked at her in disbelief. 'What on earth are you planning to say? You're going to bang on her door and say that her little boy thought she looked pale at breakfast?'

'No. That's why I'm taking you along.' She smiled and reached for her bag. 'You're the new doctor and I'm introducing you. She'll be your patient after all. You may as well meet each other.'

Wondering why he was on a wild-goose chase when he could be in the shower, Ethan slammed the car door and followed her towards the house.

The front door opened and it took less than a second for him to register the raw panic in Fraser's eyes.

'You have to come quickly! She's on the floor,' he said urgently, reaching out a hand and virtually dragging Kyla inside. 'And I can't get her to wake up properly. She's sort of moaning and trying to hit me.'

Ethan sprinted past him into the house, leaving Kyla to deal with the panicked child.

The woman was slumped on the floor of the kitchen, the remains of a cup of coffee spread over the quarry tiles. With a soft curse he dropped into a crouch and checked her pulse.

'Has she died?' The small voice came from behind him and Ethan turned.

'She's not dead. Fraser…' He kept his voice calm and steady so as not to frighten the child further. 'I need my bag from Kyla's car. Do you think you could fetch it for me? It's on the back seat.'

The little boy nodded and sprinted out of the room while Kyla dropped to her knees beside him. 'Aisla?'

The woman gave a groan and her eyes fluttered open and then closed again as she muttered something incoherent.

'Sugar,' Ethan instructed, glancing around him. 'Would you know where to find it?'

'Not a clue.' Kyla sprang to her feet and started opening cupboards. 'Come on, Aisla, where do you keep your sugar?' She rummaged through packets and bottles. 'Soy sauce, pasta, turmeric, honey. Harissa paste—what on earth is Harissa paste? Gosh, do people really use all this stuff? No wonder cooking confuses me.'

'Hurry up, Kyla,' Ethan growled, and she yanked open a few more cupboards.

'Lucozade. That will do.' She lifted it down just as Fraser ran back into the room with Ethan's bag. 'Can we get her to drink, do you think, or is she past that?'

'We should be able to manage it.' Ethan scooped the woman up and Kyla held the glass to her lips.

'Aisla.' Her voice was firm. 'You need to drink this.'

Aisla murmured something incoherent and tried to push them away, but Kyla held the glass and eventually she took a few sips.

'More,' Kyla urged. 'You're doing well, Aisla. Just a bit more.'

The woman drank properly and Kyla glanced towards Fraser, who was standing rigid, a look of horror on his face. 'She's going to be fine, sweetheart. Do you have any biscuits in the house?'

Fraser looked at her and some of the tension left his little body. 'Of course.' A flicker of a smile appeared.

'Chocolate ones. Really yummy. But I'm only allowed them on special occasions.'

'This is a special occasion,' Kyla assured him hastily. 'And a glass of milk, please.'

'Can you manage here for a second?' Ethan reached for his bag. 'I want to check her blood sugar.'

'She's coming round,' Kyla murmured. 'Why would she have gone hypo? Fraser, what did your mum do this morning? Anything different to usual?'

'She was late getting up.' Fraser was on a chair, reaching for a tin. 'I had to shake her. Why are you pricking her finger?'

'We're trying to find out the level of sugar in her blood.' Ethan read the result and nodded. 'Well that's your culprit. It's less than three. Perhaps she overdid the insulin. Fraser, has your mum done any exercise this morning?'

Handing the tin to Kyla, Fraser shook his head. 'No. But she went for a run on the beach last night. I know because I took my book down and sat while she ran up and down the beach. Is that why she's been acting funny?'

'I don't know, but I intend to find out. I'm going to take a blood sample and send it off,' Ethan told Kyla, reaching for a blood bottle. 'I want a more accurate blood glucose level.'

By the time he'd taken the sample and labelled the bottle, Kyla had fed Aisla several chocolate biscuits and she was rapidly recovering.

'I can't believe I let that happen,' she groaned, struggling to her feet with Ethan's help. 'It was such a sunny evening yesterday I just couldn't resist a trip to the beach. And then when I got there I thought I'd do some exercise.' I was going to eat as soon as I got in but Fraser's uncle rang and then I sort of lost track and just went to bed. I'm so sorry. How did you find me?'

Ethan opened his mouth to give the honest answer, but Kyla jumped in. 'We were passing,' she said quickly. 'I wanted to introduce you to Dr Walker.'

'Well, this isn't the way I would have chosen to meet you,' Aisla said with a weary smile, 'but thanks. I owe you both. If you hadn't called, goodness knows what would have happened.'

Ethan saw Kyla glance towards Fraser. Saw her smile of reassurance and praise.

Aisla followed that look. 'Fraser?' Her voice was gentle. 'Are you all right? Didn't you say something about feeling sick?'

'I'm feeling a lot better now,' he said firmly. 'Ever since I had that fresh air on the beach.'

'Fresh air can be a miracle-worker,' Kyla said blithely, and Fraser breathed an audible sigh of relief.

'I can't believe that this is an average working day. Do you ever get any time off for good behaviour?' Ethan slid into the car beside her and Kyla smiled.

'The nature of this island is that we're permanently on call. But it isn't usually this bad, honestly. And now you definitely deserve some time off. I'll drop you home on my way to the clinic. But have dinner with Logan and me tonight. It's the least we can do, having pushed you straight into the deep end.' She saw his expression change. Saw surprise flicker in the depths of his dark, dangerous eyes.

'You eat dinner with your brother?'

'Of course,' Kyla said comfortably. 'We're family.'

'But not all families eat together and socialise.'

'Well, we do. Usually several times a week. Is that so strange?' Kyla looked at him in confusion, wondering why that would seem odd to him. As far as she was concerned, it was so normal it wasn't even worth commenting on. 'I love seeing my niece and usually one of my aunts or cousins are there. It'll probably be a pretty noisy evening but it will be nice for you to meet some of the islanders. One of my aunts runs the café on the quay and another has a knitwear boutique in Glenmore village. Two of my other cousins are fisherman. They also man the lifeboat when it's necessary.'

'What about your parents?'

'They moved over to the mainland two months ago to be with my other aunt. My uncle died and she needs help on the farm, so my parents moved in and took over. But we still get together all the time.'

'You're a close family.'

'Are we?' She frowned and then gave a shrug. 'A pretty normal family, I would have said. We have our rows and disagreements and we're pretty noisy but, yes, we like each other's company and we're in and out of each other's lives. Why wouldn't we be? What about you? Are you a big family? Brothers? Sisters?' She saw the immediate change in him. His dark eyes were blank. Shuttered—as if something had slammed closed inside him.

'Just me.' His tone was cool and his eyes slid away from hers. 'My parents divorced when I was eight and my father's second marriage didn't last long either.'

'Oh.' Kyla tried to imagine not having her family round her and failed. Maybe that explained why he was reserved and slightly aloof. 'That must have been pretty tough on you.'

'On the contrary, it was a relief from the interminable rows. And it made me independent.' He frowned, as if he hadn't even considered the subject before. 'I had a very free and easy childhood because everyone was too busy fighting to be remotely interested in what I was doing. From my point of view, it was a good thing.'

A good thing? It didn't sound like a good thing to Kyla. 'But one of the joys of childhood is being fussed over. Knowing that someone cares. It's about loving and being loved.' Puzzled by his observation, she lifted her eyes to his and saw the faint gleam of mockery there.

'Perhaps it depends what sort of person you are. Don't feel sorry for me, Kyla,' he advised in a soft drawl. 'I've never been touchy-feely. I don't need hugs.'

'Everyone needs hugs.' *Even people like him.* He was tough and aloof. Independent.

'I prefer to handle my problems myself. In private.'

Kyla laughed. 'Actually, so would I sometimes. But it's virtually impossible if you live here. On Glenmore, people not only know everything about your problems, they all think they know the best way of solving them. And they let you know. Loudly and quite often in the pub when you're trying to have a quiet drink. Come for supper tonight. Really. It will be a gentle introduction to the realities of living on an island. Sort of sanitised nosiness.'

Her humorous observation drew a smile from him. 'I thought you didn't cook.'

'I don't. But luckily for you, Evanna does. Extremely well. And tonight it's seafood. You should come, it will be fun. If the weather holds, we'll eat in Logan's garden and no doubt my niece will create havoc.' She tried to keep her voice light. *Tried not to stare.* His hair was rumpled and his jaw was dark with stubble, but she'd never seen a more attractive man in her life.

'The baby will be there?'

Kyla dragged her eyes away from her surreptitious study of his mouth. 'Well, she's not really a baby any more. More of a toddler. Life has grown a great deal more complicated for everyone since she started crawling. But, yes, she'll be there.' She noticed the sudden tension in his shoulders. 'Is that a problem?'

'Why would it be a problem?'

'I don't know.' But she sensed something. 'You just seem…' There was something in his cool gaze that she found intimidating and she broke off and gave a small shrug. If he came from such a small, fractured family then he probably just wasn't used to children. 'Nothing. Anyway, you're welcome if you want to join us. I can give you a lift.' Her heart was pounding hard against her chest and she wondered what it was about him that had such a powerful effect on her.

'I think my relationship with your car has reached its conclusion,' he drawled with a sardonic lift of his eyebrow. 'My own car is arriving this afternoon. I'll give you a lift.'

'Does that mean you're coming?'

His hesitation was fractional, but it was there. 'Yes. If you're sure your brother won't mind.'

'The more, the merrier.' Her heart gave a little skip and she lectured herself fiercely. She shouldn't care whether he was coming or not. This was *not* a man to get involved with. There were too many shadows around his eyes. And the little he'd revealed about himself hinted at an extremely scarred childhood. And any man who didn't need hugs was never going to suit her. 'Can you pick me up at six? We eat early because Logan puts Kirsty down around seven o'clock and I like to have some time with her.'

He sat for a moment without moving. 'How does he manage?'

'With the baby? Very well. Logan's a brilliant father. Fun, loving and amazingly hands-on considering the job he does.' Kyla shrugged. 'He has to have help, of course, otherwise he wouldn't be able to work. My aunts work out a rota, and I help when I can. My cousins muck in and he's employed a few girls from the village, but that hasn't really worked out.'

'Why? Weren't they competent?'

'Perfectly competent. But they all had serious designs on my brother,' Kyla said in a dry voice. 'It would seem as though there's nothing more appealing to a single woman than a sexy doctor with a baby. Amy Foster is helping at the moment and we're all laying bets on how long it takes her to make a pass at Logan.'

'What about Evanna? She mentioned helping out.'

Kyla gave a soft smile. 'Evanna adores the baby.'

'And I suppose she's not likely to fall for your brother.'

Kyla laughed, wondering what it was about men that made them so unobservant. 'Evanna's been in love with my brother all her life. One day I'm hoping he'll wake up and notice. Otherwise I just might have to interfere and that won't be a pretty sight.' She pulled up outside the cottages and saw him staring out to sea, his handsome face an expressionless mask. 'You're very difficult to read, do you know that?'

He turned his head. 'Why would you want to read me?'

'It's easier to deal with people if you understand them.'

A faint smile played around his firm mouth. 'I have no particular desire to be understood,' he said softly, 'so you can relax.'

'Is it too isolated from civilisation for you here? Do you hate it?' For a long moment he didn't reply and she was starting to wonder whether he'd even heard her question when he turned his head away and stared at the sea once more.

'I don't hate it.'

What sort of an answer was that? He was a man who revealed nothing about his thoughts or feelings, she thought with mounting frustration as she switched off the engine. 'Thanks for helping me with Aisla. I'll see you at six, Dr Walker. Enjoy your shower.'

Ethan let himself into the cottage, changed into his running gear and let himself out of the back of the house. He needed a shower, a shave and a rest, but none of those options tempted him. He didn't want what he needed.

What he wanted was to run. Fast.

The conversation with Kyla had disturbed him and he didn't understand why.

All he knew what that he intended to drive out the thoughts from his head with hard exercise.

Despite the sunshine, a strong wind gusted, but Ethan didn't even notice, his expression grim and intent as he jogged to the end of the garden and down onto the beach.

As soon as his feet hit the sand he picked up speed, his long, powerful legs covering the ground in rhythmic, pounding strides as he pushing his body to its limits. His arms and legs pumped, his heart thumped and the sweat prickled between his shoulder blades, but still he ran, lengthening his stride until his pace would have been the envy of the wind. Still he pushed himself, giving himself no slack.

He ran until the sand ended and the cliff path rose upwards. He hit the slope with a fierce determination, maintaining his punishing speed through a mixture of willpower and physical fitness, his lungs and his muscles screaming a protest that he ignored.

He felt the rapid pumping of his heart as it responded to the demands of physical exertion, felt his body burn as his arms and legs pounded the earth. Felt his brain empty of everything except the need to focus on the physical task in hand.

Run, Ethan. Run.

And if he ran fast enough and hard enough, perhaps none of it would hurt any more.

Kyla stood at the bedroom window and watched.

Ethan ran like a professional athlete.

Or a man with the devil at his heels.

Even from this distance she could sense the grim

determination that drove his long stride. She could almost feel the power and force of his body as he took on the elements and pushed himself with almost super-human effort.

Kyla stared, unable to look away, captivated by the unexpected display of masculinity.

She'd only popped into the house to collect something for her afternoon clinic but then she'd happened to glance out of the window. She'd begun watching out of concern, sure that such physical exertion would cause an injury and then her gaze had turned almost greedy as she realised exactly what she was watching.

A male in his prime, at the peak of physical fitness.

This was no city boy out for a guilt-driven exercise session. This was a man who regularly pushed his body to the limit.

He ran with rhythm and surprising grace, drawing on all the strength and power of his body to meet the challenge he'd set himself.

She couldn't see his face and yet she knew that his expression would have been set and determined. Focussed. Bleak?

Sensing that his run was more than a desire to raise his pulse rate, Kyla turned away, giving him the privacy he so clearly craved, her curiosity well and truly piqued. Her own body suddenly stirred to an uncomfortable degree.

Who was he?

His cool indifference and aloof approach to life was completely alien to her.

Who was this man who held himself slightly apart from others? And why did he affect her so strongly?

She'd spent too long cooped up on an island with people she knew too well, that was why.

Ethan Walker was a stranger. And when you lived with people who were entirely familiar, strangers were always interesting.

It was no more than that.

She gave herself a mental shake and reminded herself that she had less than ten minutes to get back to the surgery or she'd have Logan on her back.

Logan's house was attached to the surgery and opened onto a huge garden crowded with mature apple trees.

Fresh from the shower after a busy clinic, Kyla pushed open the back gate and walked straight into the kitchen without knocking.

'Oh!' Evanna was standing in front of the range, stirring something in a pot. Her dark hair was caught up in a ponytail, her cheeks were pink from the heat and she was wearing a loose white dress that was summery and pretty. 'You're early. Can you pass me the coriander, please?'

'Coriander?' Kyla glanced along the work surface in confusion. 'Is that this green, weedy-looking stuff?' She picked it up, sniffed and handed it to Evanna. 'If we're early, you can blame Ethan's car. You should see it. All black and very growly. Very high testosterone rating.' She peered over Evanna's shoulder into the pot. 'Is that our dinner? It looks nice, but nothing like barbecued seafood. Did you lose the recipe?'

'It's chicken soup, and it's for Kirsty who hasn't woken up yet from her nap. Logan is hopeless with routine. He keeps waking her up for a cuddle.' Evanna swiftly chopped the coriander, sprinkled it on the soup and glanced at her friend, a curious look in her eyes. 'So I notice you're calling the new doctor Ethan now? Getting friendly, are you?'

Kyla grinned. 'No. Not yet. But I could probably be persuaded. You should have seen him running along the beach earlier. I thought my heart was going to stop. What a body! Not that you notice things like that.'

'I'm not blind, Kyla,' Evanna said mildly as she stirred the soup slowly. 'I do know a handsome man when I see one, and Ethan is certainly very good looking.'

'But?' Kyla leaned forward and dipped a spoon in the soup, tasting it cautiously. 'There's a definite "but" coming. This soup is good. Can I take some for lunch tomorrow?'

'There's more to a man than looks, Kyla.' Evanna gently slapped the back of her hand. 'Leave the soup alone. It's for Kirsty.'

'I'm the royal taster. And there's plenty more to Ethan than looks.'

Evanna frowned. 'That's what worries me. There are dark corners there. And mystery.'

'Dark corners? Mystery?' Kyla dropped the spoon in the sink, laughing to hide the effect that Evanna's words had had on her. 'You've been reading too many Celtic legends. Your imagination is in sprint mode. Spotted any fire-breathing dragons on your rounds?'

Evanna didn't smile. 'You can laugh, but I'm right. That man has secrets, Kyla.'

Kyla felt cold fingers of unease stroke her nerve endings. 'What sort of secrets?'

'If I knew that, they wouldn't be secrets, would they? But I don't think they're good ones.' Evanna stopped stirring and her pretty face was serious. 'There's something about him,' she said softly, glancing over her shoulder to check that they were on their own. 'Can't you feel it? A hardness. He's tough—a bit intimidating. I don't know...' She gave a shrug, obviously wishing she'd never said anything. 'Something's happened in his life, I'm sure of it. Something that he's living with every day of his life. He has issues.'

'Well, things have happened in our lives, too,' Kyla reminded her, trying to shake off the black, threatening cloud that hovered over her happiness, 'and we're living with them. We all have issues, Evanna.'

'That's true. Just be careful, that's all. I don't want to see you hurt by a man.'

'Wouldn't be the first time.'

Her friend looked at her and her expression softened. 'You haven't fallen for anyone since that rat, Mike Robinson, hoisted his sails and left for the mainland. It's time you found someone. I'm just not sure it should be Ethan. Is there something going on there or is it just wishful imagining on your part?'

'I'm not imagining the chemistry. I keep thinking we're going to burn the cottage down every time we look at each other.' Kyla chewed her lip thoughtfully. 'I just have a feeling he isn't very pleased about it. He's fighting it.'

'Probably because he knows he's only here for the summer,' Evanna said briskly. 'Thank goodness one of you is sensible.'

'Well, it isn't me,' Kyla said lightly. 'You know I always pick the unsuitable. And what about you? Talking of issues, you're wearing a white dress to feed my niece chicken soup. A strange choice from where I'm standing, knowing what I do about Kirsty's aim. You're going to have serious stain issues.'

Evanna's colour deepened. 'I happen to like this dress.'

'So you should. It suits you. It's nice to see you in something other than jeans.' Kyla opened the drawer, fished out a spoon and dipped it into the soup. 'My brother will probably like it, too. Which, I'm guessing, was the intention.'

Evanna gave a wry smile. 'Your brother wouldn't notice me if I stripped naked in front of him and danced a tango.'

Kyla tasted the soup again. 'I've come to the sad conclusion that my brother is obviously thick. One day I'm going to tease him about it. But not before I've eaten his seafood. My stomach always comes before sibling conflict.'

'You mustn't mention it.' Evanna gave a faint frown. 'And to call him thick is just ridiculous when you know just how clever he is. It's just that he can only think of Catherine. And that's normal, of course,' she added hastily, emptying the soup into a blender and securing the lid. 'She was his wife. He loved her.'

Kyla waited for the noise of the blender to cease before she spoke. 'Yes, I think he did. But that doesn't mean he can't love again.'

Evanna's eyes met hers. 'It isn't going to happen, Kyla. Please stop talking about it.'

Kyla leaned forward and gave her friend a hug.

'Give him time. Be patient.' She glanced up as Ethan strolled into the room and suddenly found herself unable to breathe.

'Logan has the barbecue going.' His voice was a smooth, cultured drawl. 'He wants to know what the pair of you are doing in here.'

'We're hugging. As friends should. Our Dr Walker isn't much of a hugger,' Kyla drawled, releasing Evanna and trying not to stare at Ethan. But it was hard to look away.

On the short car journey from their cottages, she hadn't had a chance to look at him, but she saw now that he'd showered and shaved and changed into a pair of black jeans and a casual shirt that clung to the muscles of his shoulders. Kyla felt her stomach flip and suddenly discovered that her fingers were shaking. She turned, dropped the spoon into the sink to hide her burning cheeks and gave herself a sharp talking-to. Evanna was right. She knew perfectly well that Ethan was complicated. But he was the only man who had ever made her want to sit down in case her legs gave way. It was pretty hard to ignore that degree of chemistry.

'We'll just get the prawns out of the fridge,' she mumbled, crossing the kitchen and tugging open the door. *Maybe cold air would help.* Plates of fresh seafood confronted her and she lifted them out and handed them to Ethan. 'Take these out. We'll follow with the salad.'

'You go out, Kyla.' Evanna poured some of the liquid soup into a bowl. 'I'll fetch Kirsty and join you in the garden.'

Logan and Ethan immediately started talking about

what had happened with Aisla, and Kyla stared at the pile of uncooked food with a distinct lack of enthusiasm.

'Logan, could you cook and then talk? If someone doesn't feed me soon, my blood sugar will do something dramatic,' she said in a conversational tone, and her brother lifted an eyebrow in mockery.

'Is there something wrong with your arms? What's stopping you putting food on the barbecue?'

'Possibly the memory of the stomachache I gave everyone last time I cooked.'

'Good point.' Logan grinned and she gave him a gentle push.

'Start cooking or none of us will be eating before midnight. Aisla is fine. And she's Ethan's patient now.'

'She's coming to see me at the surgery so that I can check her properly and we can talk. I'll cook.' Ethan stepped forward and picked up the plate. Soon he was placing food on the barbecue with swift efficiency and Kyla watched in admiration.

'You cook?'

He sent her an easy smile that had her heart racing. 'When I have time, I cook.'

Evanna was wrong, Kyla thought to herself, relaxing slightly. He didn't have demons. He was just naturally reserved. And here, in their garden, she could see him unwind.

Her theory lasted for as long as it took Kirsty to lift the baby out of her crib and bring her downstairs.

'You have to stop letting her sleep so late, Logan,' Evanna scolded gently as she cuddled the wriggling toddler against her body. 'She needs a routine.'

'So do I,' Logan said dryly, snapping the top off a bottle of beer. 'Would someone mind telling our patients? I need a regular bedtime and regular meals. I can't function like this. It gives me indigestion.'

'I'm serious, Logan,' Evanna said. 'She's really hard to settle in the evenings because she doesn't know whether she's supposed to be awake or asleep.'

Logan sighed and reached out his arms for his daughter. 'Routine is overrated,' he said roughly, as he buried his face in the little girl's blonde curls. 'If she goes to bed early then there are some nights when I don't see her, and I don't want that. I need cuddles.'

Kyla's heart shifted as she saw the two of them together and suddenly she found she had a lump in her throat. *He's a good father,* she thought to herself, and she knew from the soft expression in her friend's eyes that Evanna was thinking the same thing.

Then she looked at Ethan and something in his eyes caught her attention.

She saw shock, pain and desolation so huge that it almost hurt to watch.

And he was staring at the baby.

'I offered her some of my home-made soup,' Evanna was saying as she pulled faces at the little girl, drawing smiles of delight, 'but she wasn't interested.'

Had no one else noticed? Kyla wondered as she moved instinctively towards Ethan. Had no one else noticed the grim set of his mouth or the fact that his entire body was unnaturally still? It was as if he were afraid to move.

Did he hate babies? Had he lost a baby? What could

possibly have happened in his life to trigger that sort of reaction?

Her mind sifted through options and came up with nothing concrete.

Perhaps she was just being dramatic. He was single after all. It was perfectly possible that he just didn't like babies.

'She doesn't need soup, she needs attention. Give your daddy a cuddle,' Logan drawled in a soft voice, and the little girl gurgled with delight and lifted her hand to pull his hair.

'Ow—you have got to stop doing that, sweet pea, or Daddy is going to be bald and that is not a "good look", as your Aunty Kyla would say.' Logan wrapped his daughter's tiny fist in his hand and planted a noisy kiss on her cheek. 'Pull someone else's hair. Kyla has plenty.'

'Ethan?' Kyla moved over to Ethan's side and touched his arm. 'Are you all right?'

It was a moment before he even noticed she was there. 'Of course.' His voice was flat. 'Why wouldn't I be?'

'I don't know. You just seem—'

'Tired,' he supplied, his gaze cool as he turned to look at her. 'It's been a long day and it was a long night before that. I probably should have made my excuses and had an early night instead of accepting the invitation.'

Was that what was wrong? He was tired?

Kyla glanced towards her niece and then back at him, searching for clues. She wanted to ask a question but she had no idea which words would lead her to the right answer. Why would the sight of a strange baby affect him so badly? It didn't make sense. 'She's sweet, isn't she?'

There was a long silence and Ethan's knuckles were white as he gripped the bottle of beer. 'I don't know much about babies,' he said hoarsely, lifting the bottle to his lips and drinking deeply, 'but I'm sure she's very sweet.'

He was a loner, Kyla reminded herself. A man who clearly had no experience of family. It was perfectly natural that he wouldn't be comfortable with babies. But somehow none of her reasoning made her feel better and Evanna's words of warning rang in her head.

'I had a call from the Infirmary on the mainland,' Logan said, strolling across to them. 'Doug's doing well. They're going to keep him in for a few more days, review his drugs and then send him back.'

'We're going to have to add him to our cardiac rehab list,' Kyla said, her eyes still on Ethan. 'We need to try and get him to take some exercise. Evanna runs a class at the community centre once a week. When he's recovered, I'll talk to him about it.'

'It's Leslie who is going to need the support.' Logan winced as Kirsty grabbed another hunk of hair. 'She rang me from the hospital with loads of questions.'

'Don't they answer questions in hospital?'

Logan gave a laugh. 'She doesn't trust them. She wanted to hear it from me.'

Kyla rolled her eyes. 'What's it like to enjoy such godlike status?'

'Exhausting. Leslie is coming back over tomorrow to check on Andrea. She's staying with a schoolfriend but obviously she was pretty upset about the whole thing and worried about her dad. Those prawns are done, Ethan. There's a plate there and some of Evanna's lemon mayonnaise on the side. Help yourself.'

'Bit of a handful, our Andrea, by all accounts.' Kyla reached for a plate and held it while Ethan removed the prawns from the barbecue.

The tension in his body had lessened and Kyla watched as he shelled prawns and drank beer, chatting to Logan and occasionally tending the barbecue.

Had it been her imagination?

Maybe. Certainly he seemed fine now and he even handed Kirsty some bread to chew.

'I had Sonia Davies from the library in my antenatal clinic today,' Evanna said, speaking directly to Logan. 'She really wants a home birth.'

The smile faded from Logan's face. 'I won't do home births,' he said gruffly, 'you know that. Don't even bother asking me.'

Evanna bit her lip. 'It's her second baby and she's—'

'I won't do home births.'

'Logan, she isn't—'

'She can go to the community maternity unit on the mainland. It has all the advantages of home births, with none of the risks. This is an island, Evanna. I know you'll tell me that if something happens she can be transferred, but will it be fast enough? We do wonders here, but we have to be realistic. I can't provide neonatal intensive care and neither can I perform uterine surgery on a woman with an uncontrollable haemorrhage.' His tone harsh, Logan turned away and helped himself to another beer. Evanna glanced helplessly at Kyla, who gave a brief shake of her head to indicate that she should drop the subject.

They both knew what was behind Logan's intransigence. Catherine.

Feeling awful for him, Kyla strolled over to her brother and put a hand on his arm. 'Mum rang last night.' She kept her tone neutral. Steady. 'She's thinking of coming back over for Dad's birthday and spending a few days with her grandchild. They're missing her terribly. They loved the last set of photos you sent, especially the one of her sitting in the laundry basket.'

He was silent for a moment and then he breathed out heavily and she saw his shoulders relax. 'It would be good if they came. Kirsty loves to see them.'

'Mum's worried she's missing all the best bits.' Kyla gave his arm a gentle squeeze and then let go and helped herself to a baby tomato. 'I just hope she's here when Kirsty takes her first steps or we'll never hear the last of it.'

Logan's eyes settled on hers and she smiled gently, watching as some of the strain left his face. 'I'm all right,' he said roughly in Gaelic, and she gave a brief nod and replied in the same language.

'I know you're all right.'

And then she turned and caught Ethan looking at them, a curious expression on his handsome face.

He was a complex character, she thought as she strolled back over to Evanna. Deep. A real thinker. But that didn't mean anything was wrong.

She thought back to the way he'd looked when he'd first seen Kirsty.

It had just been her imagination working overtime, Kyla decided, her face brightening as one of her aunts arrived along with two of her cousins. She'd spent too long listening to Evanna's gloomy observations.

Ethan was a serious person, there was little doubt about that.

Some people were.

That didn't mean he had demons.

CHAPTER FIVE

THE next two weeks passed so quickly that it seemed to Kyla that they hardly had time to breathe between patients.

Doug McDonald came home from hospital, very subdued and worried about doing anything, and Kyla called in every day to check on his progress and reassure him. She knew that Ethan had called several times, too, and was pleased that he'd bothered.

Two weeks had been enough to prove to her that he was an excellent doctor. He'd settled into the routine and seemed to have no problem handling even the trickiest of cases. Remembering how some previous locums had panicked at being confronted by such complex cases with no local hospital support, Kyla was impressed.

But she still didn't feel she was any closer to knowing or understanding him.

He ran on the beach every morning as the sun rose, pounding hard across the sand and up onto the cliffs, pushing himself to the limit. Then he'd return to the cottage, shower and drive up to the village in time for morning surgery.

He was serious and committed but revealed absolutely nothing about himself to anyone.

Occasionally he joined her and Logan for supper and sometimes she saw him on his own in the garden, sitting on his own, staring out to sea.

Perhaps that was what came of living in a big anonymous city where you were one of millions, Kyla thought. You forgot how to relate to your fellow man.

She was clearing up after an immunisation clinic when Janet buzzed through and asked if she'd see an extra patient.

'It's Mary Hillier. She wants you to take a look at Shelley. Logan's gone out on a call and Ethan is back to back with patients so I don't like to bother him.'

Kyla thought of the six calls she had to make and the paperwork waiting for her attention. 'Of course, Janet. Send her in.'

She couldn't remember the last time Mary had come to the clinic for anything other than routine checks so the fact that she was asking for an appointment meant that she was must be really worried about something.

She tipped a syringe and needles into the sharps box and washed her hands just as Mary tapped on the door and walked in.

'Sorry to bother you, Nurse MacNeil,' she said in a formal voice, gently pushing Shelley into the room. 'I just wondered if you'd take a look at something for me.'

'Of course. What's the problem?'

'It's not me, it's Shelley. She's got these bruises all over her.'

'Bruises?' Kyla smiled at the girl. 'How are you,

Shelley? I saw you play in that netball match at the beginning of term. You were fantastic.'

Shelley blushed. 'You were watching?'

'I came down to give a talk to some of the children on healthy eating and I couldn't resist poking my nose in. So, where are these bruises? Can you show me?'

Shelley hesitated and then lifted her top. 'They're everywhere, really. And I've got these on my legs.' She slid her trouser legs up and Kyla bent down to take a closer look.

'How long have you had them?'

'They've just come up in the last few days,' Shelley muttered. 'At first I thought I'd just banged myself, but now they're everywhere so I don't think it's that. I didn't fall or anything.'

'Have you been ill, Shelley?' Kyla reached for a thermometer and checked the girl's temperature.

'No. Nothing.'

Mary looked anxiously at Kyla. 'Does she have a temperature?'

Kyla shook her head and forced a smile that she hoped was reassuring. 'No. Her temperature is fine. Why don't we ask the doctor to take a look at her? I'm just going to pop across to Dr Walker and see if he can fit her in.'

She left the room but Mary caught up with her in the corridor. 'Nurse MacNeil…'

Kyla turned and saw the worry in the other woman's face. She reached out and touched her on the arm, acknowledging the concern. 'I doubt it's what you're thinking, Mary,' she said softly, 'but we'll get it checked out immediately. Dr Walker is very, very good. If there's anything for us to be worrying about, he'll tell us soon enough. He trained at one of the top London hospitals, you know. You go back to Shelley or she'll pick up on your worry.'

Mary bit her lip but gave a nod and returned to the treatment room.

Kyla knocked on Ethan's door and walked in.

He was reading something on the computer screen and had a pen in his hand. 'Yes?'

'It's me. And you can put that frown away, Dr Walker, because I don't scare easily.' She kept her tone light and saw a glimmer of a smile in his eyes.

'I'm sure you don't. Can I do something for you?' He was wearing a dark, well-cut suit and he looked formal and more than a little remote.

'I hope so.' Trying not to be intimidated by the suit, Kyla came straight to the point. 'I've a patient I'm worried about. Eleven-year-old girl with bruising all over her body. My first reaction is to panic and think meningitis, but she looks well, apart from a bit tired, perhaps. Her temperature is normal and she's not been ill.'

'If meningitis even floats through your head, I'll see her straight away.' Ethan put the pen down on the desk and stood up. 'What's your second reaction?'

Relieved and impressed that he was taking her so seriously, Kyla came straight out with it. 'Leukaemia. I don't want to be dramatic but it has to cross your mind, doesn't it?'

'There are many possible diagnoses,' Ethan said calmly as he walked round the desk. 'Leukaemia is just one.'

'I know, but—' Kyla broke off and bit her lip. 'You should know that Shelley's mother, Mary, had a sister with leukaemia. She died about three years ago. Mary hasn't asked a direct question and obviously she doesn't want to frighten the child, but I can see from her eyes that she's frantic with worry.'

Ethan walked towards the door. 'Then the sooner I see her, the better. I'll have a better idea once I've examined her and obviously I'm going to need to do some blood tests. Bring her in.' His tone was crisp. Direct. 'I'll examine her here. And you'd better stay, if you have the time, given that you know the history.'

'I'll stay.' She wasn't going anywhere until she knew what was happening.

Ethan examined the child thoroughly, aware of the tension in Mary's body as she stood to the side of him, watching.

He questioned Shelley at length and then smiled at her. 'I'm going to need to take some blood from you, just to run a few routine tests. Is that all right?'

Shelley pulled a face. 'Will it hurt?'

'A bit,' Ethan said honestly, reaching behind him for the tray he'd prepared. 'But not much and not for long. Kyla?'

Kyla handed him a tourniquet and he tightened it round the girl's arm, stroking the skin as he searched for a good vein.

Kyla kept up a steady stream of chat. 'So did your netball team go over to the mainland and play the girls at St Jude's last week?'

A smile spread across Shelley's face. 'We thrashed them. Sixteen to one.'

'Brilliant.' Kyla turned to Ethan. 'The school is so small here that every single girl is in the netball team!'

'But we're still the best,' Shelley said quickly, and Ethan smiled, mentally blessing Kyla for her distraction skills.

'Sharp scratch coming up, Shelley,' he said smoothly, and slid the needle into the vein.

Shelley didn't stop talking. 'Mia Wilson was the best. She got it in the net about fourteen times.'

'Well, she's tall, of course, so that helps,' Kyla murmured, handing him a piece of cotton wool. 'And her mum is the sports teacher, which is another distinct advantage.'

Shelley laughed and Ethan withdrew the needle and pressed with the cotton wool.

'I'll do that while you sort out the sample,' Kyla murmured, her fingers sliding over his as she took over the pressure.

Her hands were so much smaller than his, her fingers slim and delicate and Ethan felt a sudden burst of heat erupt inside him.

Gritting his teeth and rejecting the feeling, he turned away and labelled the samples carefully. 'I'm going to send these off. As soon as I get a result, I'll be in touch.' Seeing the anxiety in Mary's eyes, he turned to Kyla. 'Can you take Shelley to your treatment room and find her a plaster, please? I don't seem to have one here.'

To her credit, Kyla immediately picked up on his intention. 'Useless doctors,' she said cheerfully, slipping her arm through Shelley's and leading her towards the door. 'They can do all sorts of fancy, complicated things but when it comes to something simple like a plaster, you can forget it. We girls will see you in Reception in a minute.'

Ethan waited until the door closed behind them and then turned to Mary. 'I understand that you're very worried about this.'

Mary was stiff, her fingers gripping her handbag. 'Do I have reason to be?'

'Obviously, until I have the results back, I can't be sure what it is, but I'm pretty confident that it isn't leukaemia.'

Mary's teeth clamped on her lips and he could see that she was battling with tears. 'If it is—'

'I don't think it is,' Ethan said firmly. 'There are other things that it can be, Mrs Hillier. I'm going to get these results back as fast as possible and then I'll call you. Is it useless to tell you not to worry?'

'Completely useless.' Mary gave a wan smile. 'But thank you for your thoughtfulness.'

'So you don't think it's leukaemia?' Kyla closed the door of his consulting room and stood with her back to it. 'Really?'

'Shelley looks well and there's no history of trauma. I've examined her thoroughly and her liver and spleen feel normal and there's no evidence of lymphadenopathy.'

'So what are the bruises?'

'Obviously until I see the results of the blood count I can't be sure, but I think she probably has ITP. Idiopathic thrombocytopenic purpura.'

Kyla frowned. 'I've heard of it but I don't know much about it and we've certainly never had a patient. What's the treatment?'

'Depending on the platelet count, it may just be a case of watchful waiting. In someone of Shelley's age the condition will probably be acute and it will resolve over a few months.'

'And if it doesn't?'

He gave a faint smile. 'What's happened to your cheerful, optimistic nature, Kyla?'

'I just like to know the options.' She looked away, struggling with her body's powerful response to his smile. He was indecently attractive. 'Mary is a friend of my mother's. She had Shelley late in life and she's very precious. I need to have all the facts at my disposal.'

'In a small number of children it can be chronic, and she might have to avoid contact sports...' he shrugged '...but so much depends on the blood tests. If her platelets are at a reasonable level then it becomes less of a problem. It's really too soon to try and predict the future for her.'

'So you're saying that she could just recover spontaneously?'

'That's right.' He studied her closely. 'You look as worried and upset as her mother. It doesn't do to get too involved with your patients, Nurse MacNeil.'

His comment stung and her shoulders stiffened defensively. 'Well, that's the theory certainly.' She lifted her chin. 'Try living on an island where you know everyone, Dr Walker. And, then try staying detached. It's a pretty tall order, I can tell you. And frankly, I don't think I'd like to be the sort of person who didn't care what happened to her patients.'

He frowned. 'Kyla—'

'And now, if you'll excuse me, I have things to do.'
She tugged open the door and left the room, taking
several deep breaths in an attempt to control her temper.
How dared he suggest that she was too involved with
her patients?

She cared about them.

What was wrong with that?

Thoroughly unsettled, she went back to her own consulting room and finished the clearing-up she'd started
before Janet had asked her to see Shelley.

Infuriating man, she thought as she pushed a box of
dressings back into the cupboard and slammed the door
shut. He may be amazing to look at but he was cold-
hearted and unemotional. Which made him completely
wrong for her.

Evanna was right.

It would be safer to steer clear of him.

Ethan vaulted over the fence that separated the two
cottages and walked up the garden.

The doors to the kitchen were open and he could see
Kyla standing in front of the stove, singing along to the
radio. Her blonde curls were pinned haphazardly to the
top of her head and her feet were bare. She wore a pair
of faded jeans that rode low on her hips, exposing a
tempting expanse of smooth, tanned abdomen. She was
lean, fit and incredibly sexy, and something dangerous
stirred inside him.

He gritted his teeth and reminded himself that he
couldn't afford the luxury of becoming involved with
this woman.

Life was about to become complicated enough without the extra dimension that a relationship would inevitably bring.

He was just working out the best way to begin what needed to be said when she glanced up and saw him. The singing stopped.

'I have a perfectly good front door with a working doorbell.'

'I heard you singing so I thought I'd come round the back.' He ignored her frosty tone and strolled into the kitchen. 'You can stop glaring at me because I've come to apologise.'

'You're saying that you were wrong?'

'No.' She had beautiful eyes, he decided. In fact, the whole package was beautiful. 'I still think it doesn't do to get too involved with patients, but I can see that it might be hard to do that on an island like this. And you're very caring, there's no doubt about that.' And it was impossible not to respond to her.

Suddenly he wanted to touch her. *Really touch her.* He wanted to taste and feel and immerse himself in the woman she was.

'Caring is what makes this community so special.'

'I'm sure that's true. But isn't it also true that caring too much sometimes makes it difficult to do your job?'

A shadow darkened her blue eyes and her slim shoulders sagged slightly. 'Perhaps. But it's hard to change your personality, Ethan. You just have to work with what you've got. This is me. This is who I am.' Her simple statement encompassed the differences between them and guilt gnawed at his insides.

She was open and honest. Transparent.

Whereas he…

Her quiet declaration reminded him that she knew nothing about the person he really was.

He clenched his hands into fists by his sides to stop himself from reaching out and hauling her against him. To make any sort of move would be inexcusable when he was hiding so much from her.

Cold and hard were adjectives that many women had applied to him but so far no one had thrown 'immoral' at him, and he didn't intend them to start now.

'I just think that you can do your job better if you can stay slightly detached. It makes it easier to think clearly.'

She gave a sigh and turned back to the pan on the hob. 'You sound like Logan. He always manages to get the balance right. I'm terrible. I take everything much more personally, but I can't help it.'

'And that's what makes you a nice person.' He realised that it was true. Even during the short time he'd been on the island he could see that she gave a great deal of herself to her job and to the community. 'What are you cooking?'

'Soup from a can. I can hardly bear the anticipation.' She stared at the gloopy liquid with a distinct lack of enthusiasm. 'I'd offer you some but frankly I wouldn't want to poison you. You're better off with whatever you have in your own fridge.'

'There's nothing in my fridge apart from milk and beer and neither of those is going to make a decent meal. Is there a good pub on the island?'

'The Stag's Head. Down on the quay. Given that

they know what you did for Doug, I doubt you'd even have to pay for your supper. You'll probably get a hero's welcome.'

'I don't mind paying but I need to eat something soon. I missed lunch.' He leaned forward and turned off the hob. 'Let's go.'

She stared at him and then at the saucepan on the hob. 'I'm eating soup.'

'Not any more. You're eating in the pub with me.'

Her eyes narrowed. 'What if I don't want to eat in the pub?'

'You'd rather eat congealed soup of indeterminate origin?' He watched her shudder and gave a smile. 'Come on. We both know that a stranger walking into that place is going to be given the third degree. If you're so committed to helping people in the community, the least you can do is give me some moral support.'

She looked at the soup and then back at him. 'It isn't that hard a choice.'

'Good.' He glanced down at her feet. 'Just put some shoes on or the locals will talk.'

And he hoped she'd change out of the jeans in order to allow his blood pressure to settle.

Kyla walked into the pub ahead of Ethan and felt every pair of eyes in the room fasten themselves on her.

Let them talk, she thought cheerfully, elbowing her way to the bar through the crowd of locals. It had been a long time since anyone had had reason to gossip about her. It would do them all good. 'Coming through,' she sang out as she wiggled and pushed her way to the front.

'This is a medical emergency. Starving hungry and gasping for a drink.'

The man behind the bar grinned and opened a fridge. 'So this is for medicinal purposes?'

'Of course, Ben. What else?' She settled herself on a stool at the bar and rested her arms on the bar.

Ben handed her a glass of white wine. 'We were all shocked to hear about Doug.'

'Logan spoke to the hospital today and he's doing all right. He'll be home before you know it.'

'All the same, I feel responsible.' Ben scratched his head awkwardly and Kyla looked at him quizzically.

'How can you possibly be responsible?'

'He was lugging my crates around,' Ben said roughly, and Kyla gave a soft smile.

'And from what I heard, you were the one to take him straight to the surgery, so you did him a good turn. Stop fretting.' Kyla glanced behind her and noticed that Ethan was hovering on the edge of the crowd. On impulse, she ordered for him and pushed her way back through to a vacant table, clutching the glasses. 'I ordered you a pint of the local brew. Hope that's OK. We'll sit here.'

'I feel like a zoo animal on display. Do they ever stop staring?'

'Only when someone more interesting walks in. Here. Try this.' Kyla handed him the drink. 'It will put hairs on your chest.'

His eyes met hers and she felt her heart skip a beat. *Now, why had she said a stupid thing like that when she was trying so hard not to think about his body?*

'Unless you want the whole island gossiping, I suggest you stop looking at me like that,' he suggested in a soft tone, and lifted the glass and drank.

'I am not looking at you. You're looking at me. And if I walk into the pub with a man, people are going to gossip. It's a fact of life.'

He put his drink back down on the table. 'Sorry. I'm not used to being the centre of attention.'

Wasn't he? Kyla was willing to lay bets that wherever he went women stared at him, but perhaps he just wasn't aware of that fact. 'Does it bother you?'

'No. Does it bother you?'

She smiled. 'I've lived here for most of my life. I'm used to it. But I know that it drove Catherine potty sometimes.'

He looked at her. 'What was she like?'

'Oh...' She wondered why he was interested. 'Lively, a bit on the wild side, flirtatious, quite amusing. She had a sharp tongue and she wasn't terribly patient.'

'How did she meet Logan?'

'She was travelling and arrived on the island one day. They met. Hit it off. Catherine became pregnant. They got married—and, yes, that was all in the wrong order so don't start my mother on that topic—and then...' Kyla broke off and sighed. 'And then it all went wrong.'

'And that's why Logan doesn't encourage women to have home births?'

'Can you blame him? Not that Catherine was booked to have a home birth, anyway, but, given what happened,

Logan wants every woman safely on the mainland the moment she starts to dilate.'

'And Evanna disagrees?'

'Evanna is a midwife. She wants to give every woman the birth experience they want. But she accepts the limitations of living somewhere like this. You can tell yourself that the helicopter can come and fly you out in an emergency, but what if the weather is bad, or there's been another accident somewhere and they can't get out to you?'

'I can understand Logan's reluctance.'

'He won't even consider it, and the women here respect that. To be honest, most of them want the reassurance of giving birth in a consultant-led unit so we don't get that many requests. I am completely starving. I need to order before I faint.' She turned and squinted over her shoulder towards the blackboard on the wall. 'The food here is amazing. See anything you fancy?'

'Why don't you choose for both of us? But I ought to warn you that I hate haggis.'

'That's because you're a soft Englishman.' She caught the eye of Jim, the ferryman, who was downing a pint with one of the local fishermen. He winked at her and she smiled broadly. 'Have the beef Wellington. It's amazing.'

'I feel as though I'm in a goldfish bowl,' Ethan said mildly. 'How does anyone ever have a relationship in a place like this? It's impossible to keep anything private.'

'The relationship bit is all right,' Kyla said easily, reaching for her wine. 'It's the private bit that presents more of a challenge. You just have to ignore it. And, anyway, we're not having a relationship. We're just colleagues, out for a civilised meal.'

His eyes held hers. 'That's right. So we are.'

It was impossible to look away. *Impossible not to feel the powerful spark of chemistry that drew them together.* She saw his mouth tighten and sensed his growing tension. 'We should order.'

'Yes.' He dragged his eyes away from hers and glanced over to the bar. 'I presume I have to fight my way through the crowd for that pleasure?'

'Actually, you don't.' Ben, the landlord, was standing next to them, a grin on his face as he looked at them. 'After what you did for Doug this morning, you're right at the front of our queue.'

'We'll both have the beef,' Kyla said quickly, 'and the treacle tart. Thanks, Ben.'

He scribbled on the pad in his hand. 'How's young Shelley?'

'Fine.'

'Mary's worrying herself sick.'

'I know that.' Kyla's voice was quiet. 'We're dealing with it as quickly as we can, Ben. As soon as we know anything, we'll be in touch with Mary.'

He nodded. 'Call me when you hear anything.' He walked off and Ethan stared after him in amazement.

'How did he know about Shelley? And how does he know so much about Doug? And how do you ever honour patient confidentiality in a place like this?'

'Doug works for him and Ben is Mary's cousin, but you're right that most people find out who's ill with what about five seconds after you've found out yourself. Anyway, Ben is on the crew of Glenmore lifeboat so he's an important part of this community.'

'The island has a lifeboat?'

'Yes. It has a berth by the quay. Haven't you seen it?'

'I haven't been down here since the day I arrived. Do they have a lot of callouts?'

'Unfortunately, yes. Especially in the summer. Usually walkers on the cliffs who drop down to pretty bays and then get stuck when the tide comes in. And if it's a medical emergency, they call on Logan. So, you see, we all work together and, yes, people are interested in one another, but we don't betray a confidence. There's a way of responding without giving anything away. But I can assure you that the moment you've spoken to Mary about the results, she'll be on the phone to at least five other people and they'll be on the phone to another five. But that's their business.'

Ethan shook his head. 'It's so different to London.'

'Of course. That's why we live here.' She tilted her head to one side, challenging him. 'You're missing all the positives. Like the fact that almost everyone on this island is part of an informal support network and that counts for a lot. When Fraser was in hospital with pneumonia when he was younger, everyone rallied round to help Aisla, even though she'd only just arrived on the island and knew no one.'

He sat back in his chair, his expression watchful. 'Go on.'

She shrugged. 'When Mrs Linton tripped down her stairs someone phoned us within the hour because they'd noticed that her bin hadn't been taken in. In London she probably would have been on the floor for a week before it occurred to anyone that something might be wrong.'

'Probably even longer than that,' Ethan said dryly, finishing his drink and sitting back as their food arrived. 'All right, you've convinced me. I can see that it has its advantages.'

'But it isn't somewhere that you could ever settle for good.' The words left her mouth before she could stop them and she froze, appalled at herself for being so indiscreet.

Why had she asked that question? What was the matter with her? It wasn't even as if she wanted him to be there for ever. She just wanted—she wanted—

A fling, she acknowledged finally, looking away from his searching gaze so that she didn't reveal any more. She wanted a wild, abandoned fling with an incredible-looking, intelligent man, and Ethan Walker fitted that description.

'What about you?' His voice was even as he handed her a knife and fork and reached for his own. 'You're obviously an extremely skilled nurse. Have you ever considered leaving here?'

'What's that supposed to mean? That the people on the island deserve less than mainlanders?'

'That wasn't what I meant.' His tone was wry. 'You're very touchy. Stop jumping down my throat. I just wondered whether you might be bored.'

'I trained on the mainland and that was enough for me. Here I have a great deal more autonomy than I would have on the mainland. I happen to think that anonymity is vastly overrated.' She poked the food on her plate for a moment and then looked up. 'I like people, Ethan. I like knowing what they're up to. I don't even mind the fact that they know everything that I'm doing before I even do it. I like the feeling of belonging. I like the knowledge that there is a whole community out there, pulling together, trying to improve each other's lives. In cities all you read about is stabbings and muggings, whereas here—' She broke off and gave an embarrassed shrug.

'I sense that we're back to caring again.'

'They probably care in the city, too, it's just that life is so fast and busy that no one has the opportunity to show it, and before you know it you don't even recognise your neighbours.'

'Is that really an excuse?' Ethan gave a short laugh. 'You're not exactly kicking your heels here and you manage to know everyone.'

'But we have a pretty static population except for the tourist season. Live in a city and people come and go. Here, everyone we see here is known to us. It's different. And I love the challenge of having to work with limited back-up. It makes you more resourceful.'

They'd both finished eating and Kyla suddenly realised that she'd been too absorbed in their conversation to even notice the food. 'Did you enjoy it?'

His surprised glance at his empty plate told her that he'd been similarly distracted.

'Very much. The treacle tart was delicious.'

'Shall I order some coffee?'

Ethan looked at her. 'Let's have coffee at home. That way we can drink it without everyone watching.'

She smiled. 'Good plan.'

What had possessed him to suggest coffee when what he really needed was to keep as far away from her as possible?

Frustrated with himself, Ethan walked briskly back towards the cottages and resolved to make the coffee quick and businesslike. If he kept the conversation fairly formal, that would help.

And he wouldn't look at her.

'Ethan? Are you OK?' Kyla's voice had a soft, breathy quality and he suddenly realised that not looking at her wasn't going to make any difference at all. He could have had his eyes shut in a dark room and she still would have had the same effect on him.

'I'm fine.' He could feel her looking at him and lengthened his stride. 'How is Doug doing anyway? Did Logan get any feedback from the hospital?'

'Oh. Better, I think. Seems a bit more relaxed. It's Leslie who's the problem. She's hanging over him every minute of the day, just waiting for him to collapse. I'm going round there tomorrow to see if I can help her get her head around the whole thing.'

This was fine, Ethan told himself as they reached the cottages. *This was good.* Talking about work kept everything on a safe level. He could handle this. Quick coffee. Small talk. And he wasn't going to touch her.

His resolve lasted as long as it took to follow her into her kitchen.

She was still wearing the jeans but she'd added a pair of sexy heels and a pretty cardigan in a shade of blue that matched her eyes.

'I'll put the kettle on,' she said cheerfully, reaching for mugs and coffee, 'and we can take it down to the beach if you like. It's lovely to sit on the sand in the dark and watch the stars.'

He felt a sudden rush of heat through his body. 'Here is fine,' he said hoarsely, running a hand over the back of his neck. He didn't need the darkness or stars. 'The kitchen is fine.' *There was nothing romantic about fluorescent light.*

'All right. If that's what you prefer.' She shot him a curious look and spooned fresh coffee into a cafetière. 'Do you realise that you've been here for two weeks and I still know hardly anything about you? We've been so busy we've hardly exchanged more than two words.'

And that was the way he'd wanted it. 'There's not much to know about me.'

'You mean there's not much you want to tell.' She poured water into the pot. 'Where did you work last?'

Hell? 'Abroad.'

She gave a soft laugh and turned to face him. 'You don't give anything away, do you, Ethan? Did anyone ever tell you that one-word answers don't make a conversation?'

'I'm not that great at conversation. You should have worked that out by now.' She had the bluest eyes he'd ever seen and her legs looked impossibly long. 'I ought to go…'

She hesitated and then walked towards him, narrowing the distance that he'd carefully placed between them. 'You haven't drunk your coffee.'

He wasn't even sure who touched who first.

He just knew that one moment he was standing there full of good intentions and then next she had her arms wrapped round his neck and his mouth was hard on hers.

His good intentions dissolved, as did his conscience and all the other better parts of his nature that had been holding him back.

His hands traced the soft curves that his eyes had already admired. His mouth devouring hers, he slid his hands over her hips, then over her bottom, anchoring her against him. The taste and the scent of her threatened to overwhelm him and he dragged his mouth away from hers and pressed his lips against her neck.

'Ethan…' She murmured his name and pressed closer and that movement alone was enough to snap the last of his self-control.

His mouth found hers again and his hands moved to the hem of her top, sliding underneath, finding the smooth, tanned skin that he'd admired earlier.

Her breasts pressed into his hands and he almost lost control as he felt her nipples peak under the brush of his fingers and heard her soft gasp of pleasure.

He lifted his head and their mouths met again in a fierce kiss, each demanding of the other, each hungry and possessive and increasingly desperate. His entire body was consumed by a ferocious heat and he felt her hands shaking as they struggled with the buttons on his shirt.

It was the touch of her fingers against his bare chest that brought him to his senses.

Another minute more and neither of them would have stopped.

'Kyla…' With difficulty he broke his mouth from hers and forced his hands to release her smooth, golden flesh '…we have to stop. This isn't a good idea.'

She gave a whimper of protest and leaned in towards him again, but he stepped backwards, breathing heavily.

'Kyla, no.'

She blinked, her eyes dazed and disorientated. 'Why—? What?' Her mouth was soft and bruised from his kiss and he gritted his teeth and reminded himself that she knew nothing about him.

She didn't know who he was or why he was there. But when she did… 'Trust me. This is a mistake.'

She took a step back and when she spoke, her voice was soft. 'Did it feel like a mistake, Ethan?'

Physically, no. But he had more sense than to take that route given the present set of circumstance. 'We need to forget this happened.'

'Why?' Her blue eyes studied his face, searching for answers to the questions bubbling up inside her. 'This wasn't just me, it was you, too.'

'I know that.'

'Then—'

'I can't explain, but it isn't you, it's me,' he growled, reaching for the door like a drowning man would have grasped anything that happened to float. 'And now I need to go home.'

'But—'

'Goodnight, Kyla. Thanks for dinner.'

He didn't wait to hear her reply, just strode out of her cottage and kept his eyes on his own front door.

Once there he switched on the kitchen light and pulled out the letter.

If nothing else, at least it would remind him of the reason he was there.

CHAPTER SIX

HE STRODE into her consulting room next morning with a piece of paper in his hand.

'I've had the blood results on Shelley.'

Kyla stared at him. That was it?

They'd shared a kiss that had probably shaken the foundations of the island and *that was all he had to say?*

Her heart thundering at a dangerous pace, she waited for him to make some reference to the previous evening, but he was remote and businesslike. Cold. *Unapproachable.* It was as if the kiss had never happened.

Clearly he hadn't suffered the same restless night that she had.

Kyla sighed inwardly, still unable to believe that he'd stopped so abruptly. The question was why? Evanna was obviously right. He had issues. It was just frustrating that he was unwilling to share them. Deciding that this wasn't the time or the place to try and fight him, she looked at him expectantly. 'And what do her results say?'

'It's definitely ITP. But her platelet levels are reasonable so hopefully it will resolve by itself in a few months. I've had a chat with the haematologist and his advice is to do nothing for the time being. We'll check her blood again regularly and see how she goes.'

'That's good news.' Kyla's relief was genuine. 'Mary will be delighted to hear all that.'

'I've called them and asked them to come to surgery this afternoon. Five o'clock. I thought you might like to be there.'

'I would. Thanks.' Was he ever going to mention the kiss they'd shared or was it just going to be consigned to the archives without further reference? Was that the usual end to an evening out for him? Did he kiss women like that all the time?

As if reading her thoughts, his eyes moved to hers and her heart started to beat faster. His mouth tightened and he cleared his throat. 'I need to get on.'

'Yes. Of course you do.' Her voice was a croak and he sucked in a breath and turned away from her, yanking open the door and leaving the room with a purposeful stride.

He was always walking away from her.

Kyla stared after him in mounting frustration. She wanted to run after him and ask the questions that were hovering on her lips.

What are you playing at?

Aren't you going to say anything about the kiss?

Are you going to ignore what's happening between the two of us?

Or maybe she'd imagined the whole thing and he just didn't find her attractive. 'Men,' she muttered to herself, cleaning the dressing trolley ready for her next patient. 'How can they accuse us women of being confusing?'

She tried to keep her mind focussed on the job all

day and then at five o'clock she joined Ethan in his consulting room.

'Mary and Shelley are just coming.' She looked at him, trying not to be intimidated by his cool, formal appearance. 'You're wearing a suit again.'

He gave a faint smile. 'I'm at work.'

'And does the suit help you keep the distance you need from people?' She asked the question without thinking and then immediately wished she'd kept her mouth shut when he looked at her steadily.

'This isn't the right time, Kyla.' His voice was soft and she felt the colour rush into her cheeks because she knew it wasn't the right time and she was furious with herself for even showing that she cared.

She wished she had the ability to be as indifferent as he obviously was.

Hurt and confused, she turned as she heard a tap on the door.

Mary Hillier walked in with Shelley, and Ethan immediately waved a hand at the two chairs he'd placed next to the desk. 'Sit down. I can see you're worried so let's get straight to the point.' He outlined the results of the blood tests, explaining in simple, precise language.

Mary was looking relieved. 'So tell me more about this ITP thing. What exactly does it mean?'

'It means that there aren't enough platelets in the blood. If you cast your mind back to biology, you'll remember that platelets are responsible for helping the blood to clot.'

'So if she doesn't have enough platelets, she could bleed?'

'That's right. That's why she has more bruising than usual.'

'And what's caused it?'

'It's an autoimmune disease. In other words, your body attacks itself—in this case it attacks the platelets. As to what causes it—most of the experts think that in children it's caused by a viral infection.'

'But there's no treatment? You're not going to do anything?'

'Treatment isn't always necessary, particularly in children. They tend to recover completely in a couple of months without any intervention.'

'But what if she has problems?'

Ethan reached for a pen and scribbled something on a pad. 'This is my number.' He handed the paper to Mary. 'If you can't get me in surgery, feel free to call me on that number if you have any worries. We will be checking Shelley's blood regularly to see if the platelet count is recovering.'

Kyla nodded her approval. He may be dressed in a suit and look unapproachable, but he was making himself accessible to worried patients and they didn't seem to find him intimidating.

Mary folded the paper and put it carefully in her handbag. 'And does she need to stop doing sport or anything? She loves her netball and they're playing loads of matches at school at the moment.'

'The way her platelet count is at the moment, it's fine for her to play.' Ethan scribbled something else on the pad. 'We'll monitor it and if it drops to a certain level then we may need to advise you to avoid contact sports, but at the moment it's fine just to carry on as normal.'

A relieved Mary left the room and Kyla managed a smile.

'You're very good at explaining.'

'Despite the suit?' There was humour in his eyes but she was too confused by her own feelings to respond.

'Thanks for spending so much time with them,' she said quickly, making for the door. She needed to escape. The effect he had on her was profoundly unsettling, but it was clear that he didn't feel the same way and the sooner she came to terms with that, the better for both of them. 'I need to get on.'

'Kyla, wait.'

She didn't turn but her grip tightened on the doorhandle. 'Not now, Ethan,' she said quietly, keeping her eyes forward. *Looking ahead.* 'As you said yourself, this isn't the right time.'

Ethan stared after her, feeling the frustration rise inside him.

Why now?

Why her and why now?

He lifted a hand to the knot of his tie and loosened it with a vicious jerk as he cursed softly.

He'd hurt her feelings. She thought he'd rejected her, and in a way he had, but only because he wasn't in a position to do anything else.

He turned and stared out of the window, watching the first threatening clouds appear in the sky.

He could tell her the truth, of course. He could tell her who he was and why he was there.

But he wasn't able to do that yet.

He wasn't ready.

There were still so many things that he didn't understand and he needed time to work out the answers to all the questions he had. Then, maybe then, he could do something about Kyla MacNeil.

Soon.

She felt such a fool.

Kyla slipped into the driver's seat of her car, stealing a glance at the low black sports car parked next to her. It was sleek, sophisticated and exclusive. Like its owner, she thought sadly as she started her own car and pulled out of the medical centre car park.

Ethan Walker would never fit into a place like this and he'd never be interested in a woman like her.

She frowned slightly as she analysed her own thoughts. *Pathetic,* she decided crossly, changing gear with rather more force than was necessary. She was being completely pathetic and selling herself short. It wasn't that she wasn't good enough for him, because she was. It was just that some relationships just weren't meant to happen, and this was obviously one of those. Yes, there was chemistry. *Amazing chemistry.* But their lives were different. They appreciated different things. They were just—different.

He drove a flashy sports car, he wore a suit to work— a suit that she guessed had probably cost more than two months of her salary.

And while there was no doubt that he was an excellent doctor and good with the patients, it was also true that he held himself apart. He was—she searched for the word—aloof? Sometimes when he joined them at Logan's for supper, she caught him watching them from the edges, almost as if he were studying them. But was that really so surprising?

She thought of the little he'd told her about his childhood. About his parents who had divorced. About how they hadn't been interested in him.

What must he make of her big, noisy, involved family? Was it surprising that he found them worth studying? He probably found them completely perplexing.

Kyla gave a sigh and decided to call in on Doug and Leslie. They needed the support and it would stop her dwelling on her own problems.

She was going to stop wanting Ethan, she decided as she pressed her foot to the accelerator and sped down the country road that led inland to the McDonalds' house.

She was going to stop watching from the window when he ran on the beach in the early mornings, she was going to stop finding excuses to go into his surgery to talk to him and she was going to stop dreaming about *that kiss.*

Everyone made mistakes, of course they did. But never let it be said that she didn't learn from hers.

Move on, Kyla.

She pulled up outside the McDonald house and walked to the front door without bothering to lock her car.

'Anyone home?' The front door was open and she pushed it open and stuck her head through. 'Hello?'

Leslie walked out of the kitchen. 'Come on in, Nurse

MacNeil,' she said briskly, wiping her hands on her apron. 'Your patient is just sitting in the garden but he's been for a walk this afternoon, just like they said. Just a short one. Up and down the garden. The kettle's hot if I can tempt you to a cup of tea.'

'Fantastic,' Kyla said, following her into the kitchen. 'Lunch feels like nothing more than a distant memory.'

Leslie gave a cluck of disapproval. 'You all work too hard in that surgery, but we're grateful for it. I certainly don't know where we'd all be without you.' She hesitated. 'Doug and I owe you so much—and that new doctor, too. The hospital was very impressed with the treatment Doug had with you. They said that you probably saved his life.'

'We did our job, Leslie,' Kyla said gently, 'and you don't owe us anything. It's just good that Ben brought Doug to us so quickly.'

Leslie nodded. 'Ben's a good man, no doubt about that. And now he's short-staffed at the pub, of course.'

'Ben will cope.' Kyla looked out of the window and saw Doug staring across the garden. 'How's he doing?'

'Well, he hasn't had any more pain but he's tired, of course. The hospital warned him that the drugs might make him tired. Said that Dr Walker could alter the dose if necessary.'

'Yes.' Kyla turned to her. 'I meant mentally. Doug's used to being very active. How is he coping with having to take it easy?'

'Well, he doesn't have much choice but I think he finds it frustrating.' Leslie stared at her husband for a moment and then gave a bright smile. 'Now, then. What was I doing? Tea. I'd offer you cake but when I came back from the hospital with Doug I went through the cupboards and threw out everything unhealthy. We've only fruit left to snack on.'

'I don't need cake, Leslie, thank you, and it's good to know that you're thinking about his diet.'

Leslie dropped teabags into a pot. 'Hard to think about anything else,' she muttered, and Kyla stepped closer and put a hand on her shoulder.

'Have you talked to anyone?'

'Me?' Leslie's hand shook and she sloshed boiling water over the side of the teapot. 'Why would I need to talk to anyone? I'm not the one who is sick.'

'This happened to you as well as him,' Kyla said quietly, taking the kettle from her and putting it safely back on the side. She reached for a cloth and mopped at the water. 'It's very stressful, seeing someone that you love suddenly taken ill. And you've had to stay strong for everyone. It must be incredibly hard.'

'I'm fine,' Leslie said briskly, her smile just a little too bright. 'You go on outside and check on Doug. I'll join you in a minute.'

'Actually, I wanted to talk to you first.'

'I'm not the ill one.' Leslie folded a teatowel with almost obsessive attention to detail and then her face crumpled and she curled her fingers around the soft cloth and gripped it hard. 'I keep waiting for him to die,' she confessed in a whisper. 'Every time he gets out of that chair I want to stop him from moving just in case it causes a strain on his heart. I want to yell at him, "Don't move," and here they are telling him to start gentle exercise. They want him to do this cardiac rehab…something.'

'Rehabilitation.'

'That's right. Rehabilitation.' She sniffed. 'But I don't want him to lift a teacup, let alone exercise!'

'Oh, Leslie.' Her voice loaded with sympathy, Kyla stepped forward and gave the other woman a hug. 'The rehabilitation programme is really important after a heart attack. I know it seems scary to you but it's really important to gradually increase the amount of activity. They've looked at his age and his lifestyle and worked out what's right for him. I spoke to the cardiac sister this morning and we discussed the programme that the unit want him to follow.'

'He's got a video and some leaflets. And he's going to have to lose some of that weight.'

Kyla nodded. 'Yes, he is. But it's not just about diet and exercise, Leslie. It's about giving emotional support to both of you. About helping you both rebuild your lives.'

'Is that possible?'

'Yes.' Kyla's voice was soft. 'We're here for you, Leslie. You know we are. Logan, Dr Walker, Evanna and I. We're here. You're not on your own.'

'But you can't guarantee it will be OK, can you? You can't guarantee he won't have another one.'

'No,' Kyla said honestly, 'there are never any guarantees for anyone in this life. But we're going to do our best. Many people go on to lead full and long lives after a heart attack.'

'I can't even bear to sleep at night in case he needs me.'

'That's natural, Leslie. It's still very early days. You

may not believe me now but that feeling will ease. You *will* grow more confident and both of you will eventually be back on your feet again. It won't go away but you'll be surprised how you manage to live with it. I've seen it happen before. I know at the moment this thing is dominating your lives, but as the weeks and months pass it will start to take more of a back seat.'

'Will it? I just keep picturing him lying on that couch with the oxygen mask on his face. I keep hearing all those machines beeping. I keep thinking of our little Andrea being left without a father—' Leslie broke off and covered her mouth with her hand, fighting back the tears.

'She still has her father,' Kyla said softly, 'and what you have to remember is that everyone is looking out for you. Both the doctors here and the hospital will be monitoring Doug and that's a good thing.'

'I hated those machines beeping in the hospital.' Leslie gave a humourless laugh. 'Now I'm missing them. At least when they were beeping I knew he was alive.'

'It's natural to feel a bit insecure when you're first discharged from hospital, but you're not on your own, Leslie. That's why we're here.'

'Leslie? Is that Kyla?' Doug's voice came from the garden and Leslie cleared her throat and turned on the tap to splash her face with cold water.

'Don't you go telling him I'm worried,' she said gruffly, drying her face with a towel and straightening her dress. 'I don't want him having any extra anxiety.'

'Do you think he doesn't know? Of course he knows you're worried!' Kyla shook her head and smiled. 'I'll go and chat to him while you take a moment for yourself. Maybe you can bring that tea out when you're ready.'

'I'll do that. And, Kyla...' Leslie's voice stopped her before she went through the back door.

'Yes?'

'Thank you, lass. You're a good girl.'

Kyla buried herself in work in an attempt not to think about Ethan.

She visited the McDonalds' most days on her way home and popped in on Aisla to check on her. She filled her clinics to the brim and saw everyone who wanted to be seen, usually on the same day. At night she fell into bed, exhausted. *And dreamed of Ethan.*

All his earlier reluctance to socialise with Logan and Kirsty seemed to have disappeared and he frequently joined Logan for supper, often in the garden and even turned up at Kirsty's first birthday party with an over-sized stuffed teddy, which the little girl loved.

In order to avoid him, Kyla took to visiting Kirsty during the day and spending the occasional evening with her aunt who ran the café on the quay.

'You've been visiting us more than usual,' her aunt observed gently as she placed a bowl full of steaming home-made soup in front of Kyla. 'Is something wrong?'

'Nothing at all.' Kyla sniffed the bowl 'Smells fantastic. Can you blame me for visiting? Given the choice of eating here or cooking for myself, there's no contest.'

'Kyla?' Her aunt sat down opposite her, ignoring the customers who had just streamed into the café from the ferry. 'I've known you all your life. There's something the matter, I can tell.'

'It's nothing.'

'And does this "nothing" happen to wear a suit and drive a flashy sports car?'

Kyla lifted her eyes from her soup. 'I don't know what you're talking about.'

'Don't you? This is an island, Kyla. It's hard for things to go on without anyone noticing.' Her aunt's voice was gentle as she stood up. 'You're entitled to your privacy, if that's what you want. But I'm reminding you that even though your mum's not around, you've still family here, Kyla Mary MacNeil. Family who love you. Don't you forget that.'

Kyla swallowed hard. 'He isn't interested, Aunty Meg.'

'Strikes me that he's a man with a great deal on his mind.'

Kyla gave a lopsided smile. 'You sound like Evanna. She thinks he has "issues".'

'Maybe he has. Maybe he just needs a bit of space to work a few things out and this is a good place for that.'

Kyla shook her head. 'I'm not pushing myself on him.'

'So is that why you're eating me out of house and home?' Meg pushed some more bread towards her. 'Because he's spending time with your brother and you're avoiding him?'

Kyla felt guilty. 'I love eating here and seeing you.'

Meg gave a snort. 'And do I need to be told that? Of course not. I'm not offended, lass, just worried about you.'

'You don't need to worry about me. I'm fine, really.' Kyla stood up to give her aunt a hug. 'Thanks.'

'Eat your supper.' Her aunt squeezed her gently and then released her. 'Before it gets cold.'

She loved her family. Kyla finished her soup, wondering if everyone else had noticed that she was suddenly spending all her time at the café instead of just strolling into Logan's garden in her usual fashion.

She thought about it all that night and the next day and when Evanna invited her to join them for a picnic on the beach that evening, she agreed.

She didn't want Logan making sarcastic comments, she thought as she slipped her feet into sandals, grabbed a cool-box and strolled down onto the sand.

Evanna was spreading a picnic out over a tartan rug while trying to control a thoroughly over-excited toddler. 'Don't eat sand,' she scolded gently, but there was a smile on her face as she scooped the little girl onto her lap and cuddled her. 'Go to your Aunty Kyla for a moment while I sort out the food.'

'I bought some things. It's just quiche and salad.' Kyla put the cool-bag down by Evanna and stooped to kiss her niece.

Logan strolled over to her, his body glistening with seawater. 'It's fresh.'

'In other words, it's freezing.' Evanna laughed, handing him a towel. 'Quick. Dry yourself off. We don't want you developing hypothermia. It's a bad advert for the practice.'

Logan cast a questioning glance in Kyla's direction. 'Well, if it isn't my long-lost sister. Where have you been all week?' He dried himself and pulled a shirt over his head. 'I've hardly seen you.'

'I called in to see Aunty Meg a few times,' Kyla said casually, eating a tomato and then pulling a face. 'Ugh. Sand. Remind me whose idea was it to have a family picnic on the beach when it's windy? It always sounds such a great idea, but then you start to eat and you realise that everything is crunchy because it's full of sand. I think I prefer the garden.' She looked up to say something to Logan and saw Ethan strolling towards them. The words stuck in her throat.

'Kyla.' Evanna's voice was gentle. 'You're dropping food on the rug.'

Flustered, Kyla glanced down and realised that her hands were shaking so much she'd dropped the tomatoes. 'Sorry.' *She'd had no idea he was joining them.* Her heart skipped and danced and she gave herself a severe telling-off.

She'd avoided him for most of the week. She'd made a concerted effort not to look out of the window in the mornings and watch him run, and she'd even managed to forget about the kiss for at least five minutes at a stretch.

She'd thought she was doing well.

Only now, feeling her heart hammering hard against her chest, she knew that she wasn't doing well at all.

He affected her just as much as he ever had.

'Sorry I'm a bit late.' He was wearing cut-off shorts and a soft, loose T-shirt that had obviously been washed a million times. His jaw was dark with stubble, his eyes were tired, and Kyla thought she'd never seen a sexier man in her life.

'Late? That's a real city-boy remark. I don't think

you can be late for a picnic on a beach.' Logan handed him a beer. 'Here. You can drink. I'm on call tonight.'

Ethan took the beer with a nod of thanks. 'I hope you have a better night than I did.'

Logan gave a wry smile and glanced at his daughter. 'I probably won't, actually, but for different reasons. I gather you were up several times.'

'For a small island, they certainly keep you busy,' Ethan drawled, lifting the beer to his lips, and Kyla found herself watching as he drank.

That mouth had been on hers. Those hands had—

Ethan caught her gaze and lowered the beer slowly, his eyes on hers. Neither of them spoke and the tension rose between them until Kyla was aware of nothing but him. She couldn't have looked away if she'd tried, and she sensed that he was experiencing the same inner struggle.

And then Kirsty crawled into her lap and reached for her hair.

'Ow.' The spell broken, Kyla gently prised open Kirsty's chubby fist and removed her hair. 'We need to teach you a new trick.'

To her surprise, Ethan put down his beer and leaned towards Kirsty. 'I'll take her.' He dropped down onto his haunches and smiled at the little girl.

'Fancy a paddle in the waves?'

Kirsty looked uncertain and when Ethan scooped her gently into his arms she went stiff and turned to look at Logan.

'She's a one-man woman,' Logan said smugly, reaching out a hand and smoothing his daughter's silky blonde curls to reassure her, but Ethan spoke softly to the child, pointed to a passing seagull, and Kirsty's face broke into an approving smile.

She forgot her reservations about the tall, dark stranger and with a gurgle of enthusiasm she grabbed a hunk of Ethan's hair in her fist.

'You're in favour, Ethan,' Evanna said cheerfully, reaching for the breadsticks. 'She only pulls the hair out of people she *really* loves.'

Ethan winced and extracted himself from that deadly grip, his dark eyes amused. 'Can I take her to the sea?'

'Of course. She loves it. Did you make any of your peanut chicken, Eva?' Logan leaned forward and studied the picnic, reaching into a bowl and helping himself to a slice of fresh mango. 'This looks delicious.'

'That's Caribbean fruit salad and it's for afterwards.' Evanna pulled the bowl of fruit away from him. 'Leave it alone. You always try and eat my picnics in the wrong order.'

Judging that this would be a good time to leave the two of them alone for a few minutes, Kyla scrambled to her feet and reluctantly followed Ethan towards the sea.

She didn't really want to approach him because then he'd think she hadn't listened to his 'hands-off' message. But she badly wanted to give Logan and Evanna some time on their own.

Frustrated that she suddenly felt so uncomfortable on her own territory, she walked a few paces and then stopped, her attention caught by the scene in front of her.

Ethan had removed Kirsty's shoes and socks and tucked them into the pockets of his shorts. He held her firmly round the waist, dangling her feet gently in the water, dipping her in and out of the breaking waves while she chortled with excitement and kicked her legs.

Kyla smiled at the delight on her niece's face and then found herself looking at Ethan. And couldn't look away. She'd seen him smile before, but not like this. That cool, remote look had gone. Instead, his eyes were gentle and he looked more relaxed than she'd ever seen him.

He lifted Kirsty quickly to avoid a slightly bigger wave, laughing and talking to her quietly, clearly enjoying her company.

He wasn't a man she associated with softness and Kyla watched, transfixed, as the two of them played together, each entertaining the other.

It was only when she tried to swallow that she realised she had a lump in her throat. There was something incredibly moving about watching this strong, reserved man transformed by his interaction with an innocent child.

And then he lifted Kirsty into his arms and she saw something else in his face.

A yearning. And an immense sadness.

Instinctively Kyla moved towards him and then she stopped herself. How could she offer comfort and support when he'd already rejected her? Any gesture like that on her part would be misconstrued. And, anyway, Ethan had already proved on so many occasions that he wasn't a man to open up and confide. What had he ever told her about himself? Hardly anything.

'Kyla!' Evanna's voice came from behind her. 'I've put some food on a plate for you and we're ready to eat.'

Kyla took one last, lingering look at Ethan's broad shoulders and turned away.

She had no idea what was wrong with him but she did know that he wasn't hers to comfort. *He didn't want what she was offering.*

And suddenly she wished she'd never joined them for the picnic.

Maybe, in time, she'd be able to treat Ethan like nothing more than a colleague and friend. Eventually she'd be able to laugh alongside him and enjoy a drink and a casual chat, but she hadn't reached that stage yet. She was painfully aware of him and it was only by a supreme effort of will that she managed not to just sit and stare at him.

Dropping onto her knees on the picnic rug, she reached for the plate. 'Thanks for this. I need to eat quickly and make a move.'

'What's the hurry?' Logan handed her some French bread. 'We've hardly seen you all week and it doesn't get dark for hours. What's the matter with you? You're behaving very oddly.'

'No, I'm not.'

'Well, usually you strip off and swim.'

Usually Ethan wasn't with them.

She just didn't know how to behave in his company any more. If she was chatty and friendly then he'd think that she was trying to flirt with him, and if she ignored him he'd think she was heartbroken. She couldn't win. All she knew was that she needed to put some space between them before she made a fool of herself.

'I have lots to do in the house. I haven't had a chance to tidy up this week.'

Logan frowned at her. 'But you hate tidying up, and—'

'Logan, shut up,' Evanna said gently, interrupting him and pushing a plate of chicken into his hands. 'Stop being so controlling. I'm sure Kyla knows whether she needs an evening at home or not. Why don't you just eat my chicken? Don't let Kirsty grab it—I've done something different for her.'

Kyla mentally blessed Evanna for her tact and then blushed slightly as she felt Logan's searching gaze on her face.

He knew.

She could tell by his face that he knew, and she gave a faint smile and a shrug.

Her brother was very astute about other people's problems, she mused, just not about his own.

When was he going to notice that Evanna was perfect for him?

Ethan returned to the picnic rug and handed Kirsty to Logan. 'She loves the water.'

'Of course. She's a local. She'll swim like a mermaid by the time she's four.' Logan grinned. 'Just like her Aunty Kyla.'

'I was three.'

'And you were always leaping off the rocks into the water. "Keep an eye on your sister Logan."' Logan gave a wry smile as he mimicked his mother's voice. 'You had no sense of danger.'

'You can't live your life looking over your shoulder.' Kyla finished the food on her plate, careful not to look at Ethan. She wanted to swim but not now. Not while he was there. She'd go back to her cottage, wait for them to finish the picnic and then come down later. 'I'm off.'

She jumped up and brushed the crumbs from her jeans. 'Thanks, Evanna, that was delicious. Logan, I'll see you tomorrow. Don't forget to phone Mum later. She keeps missing you when she calls and she wants to chat about the arrangements for Aunty Meg's birthday.'

Ethan was watching her. She could *feel* him watching her and she forced herself to cast a casual glance in his direction and smile.

'Bye, Ethan.' She felt as though her face was going to crack. 'See you tomorrow.'

Walk, Kyla, walk. And no looking back.

There are other men out there, she reminded herself as she made her way across the sand to the cottages. Nice men. Uncomplicated ones.

And one day she was going to meet one of them.

CHAPTER SEVEN

ETHAN hesitated by Kyla's back door, knowing that he shouldn't be there. But how could he stay away? She was avoiding her family and he was the cause of it.

She didn't want to bump into him.

Gritting his teeth, Ethan lifted a hand to knock on the door, but at that moment she wandered into the kitchen. And saw him.

She'd obviously just come out of the shower and was wearing a pair of tiny shorts and a skimpy top, and her hair fell in damp, curling waves over her shoulders. Her feet were bare and her legs long and lightly tanned.

Their eyes held for a long moment and he wondered fleetingly whether she might just ignore him.

But then she walked over and opened the door. 'Is something the matter? I was just going to bed.'

Bed? She looked like that to go to bed?

Ethan felt his blood pressure rise several notches and suddenly he wished he'd left this visit until the morning. Everything that needed to be said could have been said in the harsh light of day when she was wearing a navy uniform.

Not that her navy uniform did anything to disguise the tempting curve of her bottom.

'Ethan?' she prompted him with a frown. 'What's the matter?'

He pulled himself together. 'You're going to bed? It isn't even nine o'clock.'

'I'm tired.'

'Can I come in?'

Something changed in her eyes. Suddenly they were guarded. Wary. 'Why?'

'Because I need to apologise.' He came straight to the point, his voice rough. 'And because we need to talk about the other night.'

She didn't play games—*didn't pretend that she didn't know what he was talking about.* She wasn't that sort of woman. 'It was over a week ago, now. It doesn't matter.'

'I've tried pretending that it doesn't matter but it hasn't worked. And it hasn't worked for you either, has it? I haven't seen you at Logan's once this week.' And he knew she was protecting herself.

From him.

She inhaled sharply. 'I've been busy, Ethan.'

'Busy avoiding me.'

Her shoulders stiffened. 'And what if I have? I can read signals. You made your position clear and I'm not a woman who needs to be told anything more than once.'

'What if I told you that you misread the signals?'

'I'd say you were lying.' She tilted her head to one side. 'I know rejection when I see it.'

'No, you don't. That wasn't rejection.' Suddenly it was imperative that she understood that much at least. 'That wasn't rejection, Kyla.'

'Then my fluency in body language is less accomplished than I thought, because it certainly felt like rejection.'

He didn't associate her with coldness and yet her expression was anything but encouraging. He jabbed his fingers through his hair. 'It wasn't rejection. Far from it. But things are complicated.'

'And I certainly wouldn't want to make them more complicated—goodnight, Ethan.' She made a move to close the door but he stopped her easily and moved inside.

'I'll leave when you've heard me out. There's something I need to tell you. I probably should have told you earlier but I couldn't.'

She hesitated and then let go of the door but she didn't close it. 'All right. I'm listening. You're going to tell me that the kiss was a mistake.'

'It wasn't a mistake. I just didn't plan for it to happen.'

'And do you plan everything that happens in your life?'

'No. But there are things that I need to explain to you before we go any further with this.'

The chemistry was there again, pulsing between them, drawing them in. The wind was blowing outside and yet in her kitchen the air was thick, hot and pulsing with expectation. Suddenly his throat was so dry he could hardly speak and he guessed she was feeling the same way because she swallowed hard.

'You don't have to explain anything to me.'

'Yes.' The dryness made his voice hoarse. 'Yes, I do, Kyla. It's important.'

'Then tell me.'

He almost laughed. *Tell me.* She made it sound so easy and yet now the moment had come he had no idea what to say. He didn't know where to begin. He wasn't even sure where the beginning was.

'Are you married?' Her softly spoken question shocked him.

'Why would you think that?'

'Because I suppose it's the one thing that would stop this thing between us going any further.'

'I'm not married.'

'Then nothing else matters.' She sounded so certain. So confident about everything. And she made life sound simple. 'Ethan, you don't need to worry. Or feel guilty. This isn't right for you and—'

'It's right for me.' He growled the words against her mouth because his hands had reached out and hauled her against him even while his brain had been sending out warnings. He ignored the warnings and kissed her.

Later. He'd worry about everything else later.

Her arms slid round his neck and he felt her slender body press against the hardness of his. He was hot and aroused and more desperate for this woman than he'd been for any other in his life.

He forgot all the reasons why he shouldn't be doing this.

He forgot that she was probably going to hate him when she found out what he was doing there.

He just needed to answer his body's screaming need to possess her in every way.

His hands were on the rounded curve of her bottom when they heard hammering on the door.

Ethan didn't even lift his head but the hammering intensified and she pushed at his chest and he broke the kiss with a fluent curse.

'Yes.' Her flushed cheeks and faint smile told him that she agreed with his assessment of the timing. 'Not good. But I need to see who that is.'

Ethan ran a hand over the back of his neck and hoped that whoever it was could be despatched quickly. 'It's pretty late. Are you expecting anyone?'

'No. But around here people just call. Especially if they're in trouble.' She gave a frown, straightened her top and walked out of the kitchen towards her front door. 'Aisla?'

Ethan heard the surprise in her voice and wondered what on earth Aisla was doing calling so late in the evening with a storm brewing. Was it her diabetes again?

And then she spoke and he heard the raw terror in the woman's voice. 'It's Fraser. He's gone.'

'Gone where?'

'I don't know. He told me he was going to Hamish's for a sleepover but I needed to speak to Hamish's mother about a knitting order, so I rang and she told me that he wasn't with her. And Hamish had no idea where he was.'

Kyla frowned. 'Well, he's an imaginative boy. He's just playing.'

'But it will be dark soon.' Aisla covered her mouth with her hand and shook her head. 'I've told him over and over again that he can't just go off on his own, but he's so independent and he sneaks off when I'm not looking. I'm a terrible mother.'

'You're not a terrible mother,' Kyla said immediately, 'and try not to panic. He's probably gone to tea with someone else and forgotten to phone. Have you called Paul Weston? Henry Mason? They might know.'

'I've called them both and they haven't seen him.'

'Then I'll give Ann Carne a ring,' Kyla said immediately, reaching for the phone. 'She might have an idea what was in his head today.'

Ethan walked forward, ignoring the potential consequences of revealing his presence in Kyla's cottage. 'Where else does he normally play?'

Aisla looked distracted and her eyes were full of fear. 'I don't know—the beach? That's his favourite place. He's always sitting there, dreaming about Vikings and shipwrecks and making up stories in his head.'

Kyla came off the phone. 'Ann Carne said that he was in school until lunchtime and then said he had to go home because he had a doctor's appointment. He gave her a note.'

Aisla stared at her. 'I didn't give him a note. And Hamish didn't mention that he hadn't been at school this afternoon. Oh, God…'

'There's going to be a perfectly reasonable explanation.' Kyla slipped her feet into the trainers that she'd left lying by the door and reached for a coat from the peg. 'We just need to think logically and not panic. But I think, given the fact that it's going to be dark soon, we should phone Nick Hillier and tell him what's happening. He'll get the whole island searching, if necessary. In the meantime we'll take a look ourselves. I'll go down onto the beach and take a look around.'

Ethan stepped forward, reflecting on the fact that they all turned to Kyla in a crisis. 'I'll just go next door and grab a jacket and my car keys. Then I'll come with you. Two are better than one.'

'Go back to the house,' Kyla told Aisla. 'That way, if he turns up at home, you can let us know. I'll keep my mobile switched on. Call Nick and fill him in.'

Ethan grabbed what he needed from his cottage and then rejoined Kyla as she walked out of the back door and down onto the beach. Angry streaks were splashed across the darkening sky and the waves lifted and crashed against the rocks at the far end of the bay.

'The storm is closing in. Is it worth calling the coast-guard? If Fraser was walking on the cliff path, he could have been swept into the sea.' Ethan stared at the boiling, churning water, trying to not to think about the young boy being devoured by those waves.

'He hasn't been swept into the sea. Don't even think about it.' Kyla spoke briskly but her stride quick-ened. 'Fraser isn't stupid. And, anyway, we were down there earlier. If he'd been hanging around, we would have seen him.'

'Unless he went to a different beach.'

The both stopped and searched with their eyes and shouted, but their cries were snatched away by the rising wind.

'Why would he go to school for the morning and then leave? It doesn't make sense.' Kyla reached up to stop her hair blowing into her face, a frown in her eyes as she stared at the ocean. 'If you're going to play truant, why turn up at all? Why do half a day at school?'

'You think that's significant?'

'I don't know. It might be. I'm going to call Ann Carne again, but I'll do it from the house. It's too wild on this beach to hear properly. And, Ethan…' She put a hand on his arm and her blue eyes were worried. 'I think you might be right. Perhaps we'd better put in a call to the coastguard. Just put them on alert.'

He followed her to the house and made the call, and when he'd finished she was standing next to him, an urgent look on her face.

'I've spoken to Ann Carne.'

'And?'

'The last lesson of the morning was history. They were doing something on the Celts and Vikings.'

He looked at her blankly, failing to follow her train of thought. 'Why is that significant?'

'Because the bloodiest battle of this island's history was fought between the Celts and the Vikings.'

'And Fraser loves history. It's his favourite subject.' He looked at her, suddenly understanding. 'Where was this battle fought?'

'The castle.'

He gave a grim smile and reached for his keys. 'Let's go.'

Kyla huddled the coat around her and peered at the sky as Ethan pressed his foot to the accelerator. 'There's a wild storm coming. Let's hope we find him before it hits. We could walk from here but it's probably quicker to take the car.'

'He might not be anywhere near the castle. We might be completely wrong. Can we park near the ruins? How close can I get?'

'Pull in further up the road—that's right. This is good. We have to walk from here.' She undid her seat belt and was out of the car before he'd even switched off the engine. 'The kids do come and play up here sometimes. During the day there are guides, waiting to tell horror stories of the dungeons.'

'Just the sort of thing to appeal to a twelve-year-old with a vivid imagination.'

'Precisely.'

'But wouldn't there have been guides today? If he came up here this afternoon then surely someone would have seen him?'

She shook her head. 'It's only open from ten until two. My guess is he actually waited for them to leave so that he could explore.'

'I haven't even had a chance to look round the ruins yet.'

'They're brilliant. Remind me to bring you here under less stressful circumstances.' She broke into a run, thinking about Fraser. What would have been in his head? Where would he have gone?

She clambered over the crumbling stone wall that led into the main part of the castle. 'Fraser? Fraser!' The wind took her voice and carried it away and she looked at Ethan with frustration. 'Even if he is here, he's never going to hear us above the weather.'

'Then we just have to search.'

She looked at him helplessly. 'The place is a warren and it's getting dark.' She suddenly realised that she'd given no thought to the approach of night, and when Ethan pressed a torch into her hand she almost sobbed with relief. 'Thank goodness one of us was thinking.'

'You were thinking, Kyla,' he said roughly, switching on his own torch and sending a powerful beam over the surrounding landscape. 'It was your thinking that got us up here. Now we just need to search. If he's here then he should see the light.'

'Maybe. Maybe not. I've been thinking, Ethan.' Kyla looked round her, focussed her eyes on the dark, crumbling ruins of the castle. 'Fraser wouldn't want his Mum to worry. He wouldn't be hiding on purpose.'

'He played truant.'

'But for the afternoon.' Kyla bit her lip. 'I bet he was planning to home before the end of school so his mother wouldn't even know he was missing. Don't you remember that day on the beach when he came to get me? He didn't want his mum to know. He really cares about her. He thinks about her.'

'You're suggesting that he's injured.'

'Yes.' Kyla nodded slowly and forced herself to take a deep breath. 'Yes, that's what I think has happened. So he might not see the torchlight, Ethan.'

Ethan's mouth hardened and he gave a nod. 'So we need to look carefully.'

'For goodness' sake, be careful walking along the ramparts. There's a sheer drop on the far side. There is a fence but the wind is fierce.' And she desperately hoped that Fraser hadn't gone in that direction.

Zipping up her coat to give her protection against the rising wind, Kyla moved through the ruins methodically, making the most of her local knowledge to search.

But she saw nothing. Found nothing. And by the time she met up with Ethan again, she was finding it hard not to panic.

'Nothing. No sign of anyone. It was a stupid idea. He obviously isn't here.'

'Well, he's not home either because I just called Nick Hillier to check. I didn't want to worry Aisla, so I called him direct.' The wind howled angrily at them and Ethan caught her arm and drew her behind the comparative shelter of a wall. 'Earlier on, you said something about the guides telling stories about the dungeons.'

'Yes, but you can't go into the dungeons any more because they aren't safe. They've been closed off to the public for years and—' She broke off and shook her head in horror. 'No. No, he wouldn't have done that.'

Ethan closed his hands over the top of her arms and gave her a gentle shake. 'Where's the entrance? Where?'

'You go into the keep and there's a tunnel, but it's blocked off. At the end of the tunnel there's a door, but that's kept locked. There's no way he could—'

'And how do you know about the door, Kyla MacNeil?' He tightened his grip and then released her and started to run towards the keep.

'Because I did the same thing at his age,' Kyla whispered, as she followed him.

CHAPTER EIGHT

THE tunnel was dark and smelt dank and musty.

'At least we can hear ourselves think in here,' Ethan murmured, as he flashed the torch downwards to illuminate their feet. 'I'm beginning to see what you mean about Glenmore and storms.' His feet made a splashing noise and he shone the torch down. 'It's very wet.'

'The rain pours in here. The whole dungeon floods in the winter. Ouch.' She'd lost her footing and clutched at his arm, feeling his muscles bunch under her fingers as he took her weight and steadied her.

'Go slowly. It's treacherous underfoot.'

'Let's try shouting.' She stopped dead. 'Fraser? Fraser!'

Her voice bounced and echoed off the walls and then there was nothing except an eerie silence, punctuated by the sound of water trickling and dripping in the darkness around them.

'This could be a wild-goose chase,' Kyla said, as they picked and slithered their way further down into the tunnel. 'He could be sitting at home and—'

'Be quiet.' Ethan put a hand on her arm. 'I heard something.'

Kyla froze. And then she heard something, too.

'What was that?'

'I don't know. But it wasn't wind and it wasn't dripping water so it's worth investigating. How far is the gate that covers the entrance of the dungeons?'

'I can't remember. It's years since I came down here, but I don't think it can be far now.' Kyla flashed the torch and nodded. 'There. Can you see?'

'Yes. But the gate's shut. It hasn't been opened. Hold the torch while I check.'

Kyla shone both torches onto the gate and Ethan ran his fingers over the rusted bars. 'There's no way he could have got through here.'

'No, but he could have got through there.' Kyla shone the torch to the side and Ethan turned, his eyes on the crack in the wall.

'It's not wide enough.'

'Yes, it is,' Kyla said wearily, and he lifted an eyebrow.

'Are you seriously telling me that you once wriggled through that gap?'

'I was twelve at the time,' she muttered. 'I've eaten thousands of Evanna's dinners since then.'

And then they both heard the noise at the same time. And this time it was recognisable.

'Fraser?' Kyla yelled his name and moved closer to the gate. 'Fraser, is that you? Are you down there?'

'I'm stuck.' His voice was thin and reedy and Kyla felt her heart turn over.

'All right. Don't panic, Fraser. You're going to be fine. We're going to get you out.' She almost laughed as she listened to herself. How? That was the question that flew into her mind. How were they going to get him out? There was a storm brewing, Fraser was trapped underground in an unstable place and no one else knew where they were.

'We need to—we need to—' For once her ingenuity failed her and she looked helplessly at Ethan. 'I don't know what on earth we need. There's a drop, Ethan. He must have fallen in. I mean, there are no stairs or anything. Just a drop and then a small cramped room. It's a bit like being at the bottom of a well. How are we going to get him out of there?'

'A stage at a time.' Ethan was calm. 'First we find a way to get in. Then we find a way to get him out. But we're going to need help. I'm going to go back up to the top and call Nick. We need a team of people up here and some rope. And we need to call the people who run this place to see if there's an official way through this gate.' His quiet confidence gave her courage.

'Yes, of course you're right. Nick will arrange everything if you just call him. I'll stay here and see if I can work anything out.'

'I'll be back in a minute.'

'Kyla?' Fraser's voice came from far below her, weak and shaky. 'Are you still there?'

'I'm still here and I'm not going anywhere. You've chosen a good place to shelter, Fraser, on such a stormy night.'

'It's very dark down here.' She heard the quiver in his voice and her heart twisted with sympathy for him. He must be so scared. For a moment she contemplated dropping the torch down to him but then she realised that the fall would probably just break it and then they'd both be in the dark.

'How did you get down there, Fraser?' She slid a hand across the gate, shuddering when she encountered the softness of a spider's web. She didn't mind the storm or the dark but she hated spiders.

'I opened the gate. I only meant to look. And then I fell. I don't remember anything after that.'

He'd knocked himself out. 'Do you hurt anywhere, Fraser?'

'My head. I think it's bleeding but I dropped my torch when I fell and it broke. I've been lying here. I didn't think anyone would ever find me.'

Kyla closed her eyes for a moment, hardly able to bear thinking about just how frightened he must have felt. 'Well, we *have* found you, and we'll be getting you out in just a moment.' She glanced back up the tunnel and saw the reassuring flicker of Ethan's torch. He was on his way back. And then she suddenly realised what the child had said. 'You opened the gate? Fraser? Did you say that you opened the gate? How? It's locked.'

'But it opens on the other side. The hinges are rusted.'

'They're on their way.' Ethan stopped next to her and watched while she ran her hands over the gate. 'What are you doing?'

'He didn't go through the gap in the rock. He went through the gate. The gate opens, Ethan.' She tugged and pulled and the whole structure came towards her. 'Ugh. Spiders. I hate spiders.'

'Kyla?' Fraser's voice came from below them. 'I feel funny.'

'In what way funny?' With Ethan's help, Kyla opened the gate far enough for an adult to pass through. 'Talk to me, Fraser.'

There was a long silence and for a hideous moment she thought he'd lost consciousness. Then his voice came again, this time much weaker. 'Sort of swimmy-headed. And sick. Just not well. I wish I'd never come here now. I want Mum.' The childlike plea for protection went straight to Kyla's heart but before she could act, Ethan moved her bodily and handed her his torch.

'Hold on, Fraser.' His voice was deep and reassuring. 'I'm coming down to you.'

'You can't do that.' Kyla caught his arm but he shrugged her off.

'I have to. We don't know what his injuries are. He's afraid and on his own. Someone needs to be down there with him.'

'You can't just jump, Ethan. It's too far. You'll break something.'

'I'm not jumping.' He removed his coat. 'There are enough handholds in this place to climb down.'

'Are you kidding?' She eyed him with incredulity. 'The wall is completely smooth.'

'No, it isn't. Stay there for a moment and then hand me the torch when I say so. Fraser?' He raised his voice and wriggled his body through the gap in the gate. 'I'm coming down to you. Just hang on.'

There was no answer, only the hollow plop of water, and suddenly Kyla felt sick herself. She ought to stop Ethan doing something so rash but she knew now that

Fraser's life could be at stake. Why wasn't he answering? Was he unconscious?

Ethan gave a grunt as he anchored himself and held out a hand. 'Hand me the torch.'

'But you won't have any hands to hold on, and—'

'The torch, Kyla!'

'All right.' She bit back the impulse the tell him to be careful. They were all way past the point of being careful.

He took the torch in his mouth and started to descend with a smooth agility that astonished her.

And then she remembered the way he ran in the mornings. He may have been brought up in a city, but there was no doubting his physical fitness. Still, physical fitness was one thing. Climbing down a wall into a long abandoned dungeon was quite another.

Fifteen minutes, Kyla calculated, feeling the thump of her heart and the dampness of her palms. That was how long it would take Nick and a rescue team to reach them. Would that be fifteen minutes too long for Fraser?

They had no idea about the extent of his injuries.

All they knew now was that he wasn't responding to their questions.

She didn't dare flash the torch in case she distracted Ethan from his task. Instead she sat and forced herself to breathe steadily, braced to hear the sound of his powerful body crashing to the ground.

'I'm down, Kyla.' His voice echoed up to her from the bowels of the dungeon. 'Can you shine some extra light down here? It's pitch dark.'

She did as he'd asked, hugely relieved that he'd made it that far without injury to himself. And then she heard noise from above her and realised that the rescue party had arrived. 'They're here, Ethan. Have you found him? Is Fraser OK?' Suddenly she wished she'd been the one to go down the shaft. She felt so helpless, just sitting at the top. If she hadn't been holding the torch, she would have bitten her nails down to the quick.

'He has a nasty laceration to his forehead and some bruising, but I don't think anything is broken. He's OK. Conscious. Just a bit weak.'

And extremely frightened, Kyla was willing to bet. She could hear Ethan talking to the boy and then there was a crunch of footsteps behind her and she turned to see Logan standing there, along with Nick and two other members of the coastguard.

'We've brought ropes, and there's more equipment up top.' A light shone from the helmet on Nick's head. 'Give us an update.'

'Ethan is down there so it shouldn't be too hard to get him out,' Kyla said, moving onto her hands and knees so that she could get a better look over the edge. 'Ethan?'

'Drop a harness on a rope?' Logan turned to Ben. 'We can bring him up that way.'

Ben nodded agreement. 'That will certainly be the quickest way if the boy is up to it. Is he conscious?'

'Yes, I think so.' Kyla supplied the information they needed, and Ben frowned.

'How the hell did Ethan get down there?'

'He climbed down.' And Kyla was still wondering how a man who dressed in suits costing thousands of pounds could so skilfully negotiate a sheer and slippery face.

'Without a rope?'

Kyla heard the disapproval in Ben's voice and threw him an impatient glance. 'Fraser stopped talking. We were worried about him. If you were the one sitting here, would you have waited for a rope?'

'Probably not.' Ben gave a faint smile of apology. 'Good decision, then. Brave guy. That's another free pint I owe him. All right. Let's get on with this. The weather's getting worse and if he needs a lift to the mainland, it's going to have to be soon.'

Logan was shouting down to Ethan, trying to assess the medical situation and how best to extract Fraser. 'I still think the best way is to drop a harness. He's conscious and Ethan has dressed the wound on his head. He can use his feet to keep away from the side. We'll have him out in minutes that way.'

'Let's do it.'

After that everything happened quickly. They lowered the rope to Ethan and minutes later Kyla saw the top of Fraser's head appear over the lip of the dungeon. She breathed a sigh of relief and suddenly realised that her hands were shaking.

She'd been so afraid for him.

His face was streaked with dirt and blood and although he had a sheepish smile on his face, she sensed that he was struggling with tears.

Logan lifted him clear of the gate and sat him carefully down on the damp floor of the tunnel.

'You are such a brave boy.' Kyla took one look at him and wrapped her arms around him. 'If the Celts had had you on their side, those Vikings never would have stood a chance.' She could feel him quivering and cuddled him close.

His teeth were chattering. 'My mum's going to kill me.'

Ben nodded as he slipped some warm layers over the boy. 'Very probably. But then she'll be relieved you're OK. He's bleeding through that pad. Logan? Kyla?'

'I've got it.' Kyla gently lifted the pad on the boy's forehead and studied the wound under the torchlight. She could see that it was deep and the edges were jagged. 'I'll put a firm dressing on it for now just so that we can get you out of here, Fraser. Then one of the doctors is going to take a closer look at that.' It was obvious to her that he was going to need stitches and she glanced towards Logan, who gave a swift nod of understanding.

'I want you to answer a couple of questions for me, Fraser,' he said casually, shining a light into the boy's eyes to check the reaction of his pupils. 'What day is it today?'

Fraser answered correctly and Logan slipped the penlight back into his pocket.

'What's your mum's name?'

'Aisla. And she's definitely going to kill me.'

Logan grinned. 'I'll protect you. How's the headache?'

'Better than it was.'

'Do you feel sick?'

Fraser shook his head and at that moment Ethan joined them. 'He thinks he lost consciousness when he fell, but his GCS was fifteen when I checked it down there.'

Kyla looked at them. 'Will you transfer him to the mainland for a CT scan?'

'I wouldn't go down that route yet,' Ethan said easily, glancing towards Logan. 'It's true that he was knocked out, but he's not showing any clinical signs of a skull fracture. I'd suggest we just observe him and see how he goes.'

Logan nodded agreement. 'Let's get him to the surgery,' he said quietly, 'and then we can take a proper look at him under some decent lights. I'll stitch him up, check him out and then see what's needed. He can stay the night with me and then I can watch him.'

'Is Evanna with you?' Kyla was still holding Fraser and her brother nodded.

'Yes. She came over to stay with Kirsty when I got the call about Fraser. So she can keep an eye on him, too.' He put a hand on Fraser's shoulder and squeezed. 'You're going to have plenty of attention.'

'Will Nurse Duncan make one of her cakes? I've been down here since lunchtime and I'm *starving*.'

Logan looked amused. 'At this time of night? I doubt it. But I expect she'll whip you up something good to eat if you play your cards right.'

Kyla looked at Ethan. 'You never told me you could climb.'

'You never asked.'

Was it all about questions for him? 'You never reveal anything about yourself unless it's prised out of you?'

He wiped the mud from his cheek with the sleeve of his jacket. 'I'm not much of a talker, you know that.' He reached out a hand and touched Fraser's head. 'You did well. How are you feeling now?'

'OK.' Fraser looked at him and something passed between them. An understanding. 'Thanks.'

'You're welcome,' Ethan said, a glimmer of a smile touching his usually serious face.

Logan looked at Kyla and then back at Ethan. 'You two are filthy. Anyone would think you'd spent the evening scrabbling around in a dark tunnel. You're a bad advert for the surgery. I'm the one on call so go home and have a shower. I'll take over here but keep your phone switched on. If I need you, I'll call.'

The storm struck at dawn.

Hearing a consistent hammering, Ethan woke from a restless sleep, wondering whether the wind was rattling the windows. Then he realised that the hammering was coming from the back door.

Trouble with Fraser?

He'd rung Logan before going to bed and his colleague had assured him that Fraser was sleeping and seemed comfortable. He'd been sick once but that was to be expected after a head injury and Logan hadn't been unduly concerned. All his other signs were fine and they had been going to monitor him.

The hammering came again, louder this time, and Ethan forced himself out of bed.

Wondering what new crisis he was about to face, he tugged on a pair of jeans, jerked open the door and felt his entire body tense.

Kyla stood there, her face alight with excitement. 'Come with me. There's something I want to show you.'

Ethan pushed away the claws of sleep that were threatening to drag him down. 'Something's happened to Fraser? He was OK when I rang.'

'As far as I know, he's still OK. This isn't about Fraser. It's nothing to do with work.' She held out a hand. 'Come with me.'

'Now?'

She smiled. 'Now is the best time.'

'It's the middle of the night. There's a storm building. It's wild outside.'

'It hasn't even begun yet, and it's dawn. There's plenty of light.' There was a strange gleam in her eyes. 'Are you afraid, Ethan?'

Everything about her seemed vivid and full of life, and Ethan realised that the answer to her question should be yes. He was afraid.

But not of the storm. He was afraid of her. Of his feelings for her. Of where this wild, crazy chemistry was going to take them.

He still hadn't told her the truth about himself.

'There won't be anything to see in this weather. It's raining and the visibility is zero.'

'Now you're talking like an Englishman.' She thrust his coat into his hands and opened the front door. The wind tried to slam it shut again but Kyla leaned against it with her shoulders and zipped up her jacket. 'I hope you're feeling fit, Ethan.'

'Where are we going?' They were outside now and he had to shout to make himself heard above the screaming, howling wind. It slammed into them as they left the cottage, as if fiercely angry that anyone should dare to venture into its territory.

'Back up to the castle. Only this time we're walking.'

'Sorry?' He shot her an incredulous look, wondering what had happened to her. 'Kyla, we just came from there.'

'This is different. You said that you hadn't seen the ruins.'

'There's a storm and it's not even fully light yet.'

'It's the best time. Trust me.'

This time she ignored the car and crossed the road towards the grassy hill that led to the ruins, her hair blowing across her face.

The jagged outline of the castle was barely visible through the driving rain, and Ethan grimaced and wiped the water from his eyes as the spray of the sea mixed with the rain. He tasted salt, felt the air sting his cheeks and looked at Kyla in disbelief.

Being out in this weather was crazy, but she didn't seem to see anything odd in it.

The rain had turned her soft honey-coloured hair to sleek, dark gold and droplets of water clung to her lashes and her cheeks, but she didn't seem to care. In fact, he would have said that she relished being so close to the elements. He'd never seen her happier.

And her response intrigued him because he knew no other woman who would have been so comfortable in such filthy weather conditions.

She was half-wild, he thought to himself, watching as she scrambled over a gate and started up the grassy slope. The wind crashed across her path, trying to turn her, but she was graceful and sure-footed as she ran, and Ethan could do nothing but follow, exhilaration mingling with exasperation.

She scrambled over the outer walls of the castle that

were now no more than a few ruined rocks, and climbed across some uneven ground that led to the ancient, crumbling fort.

'We have to climb up.' She raised her voice to be heard above the wind and he followed her and then stopped, suddenly understanding why she'd brought him here.

Furious red streaks were splashed across the sky, as if an artist had just taken a brush and angrily thrown paint at a canvas. The grey, threatening outline of the ruins loomed from the rain and mist and beyond that stretched the sea, boiling and foaming with fury as the wind and the currents fought for supremacy.

'You can imagine it, can't you? The Vikings landing there?' She steadied herself, pointed down to the beach, and then lifted her hand to anchor her hair, which was blowing wildly. With a shift of her feet she balanced herself against the wind as she stared across the west of the island. 'They must have looked up and seen this castle and been afraid. They must have wondered whether to turn home and give up. When I stand up here in a storm I can feel the history of the place so strongly.'

He couldn't take his eyes off her profile. 'You're as bad as Fraser.'

'There's nothing wrong with being interested in your heritage.' She turned to face him and smiled. 'Was it worth the climb?'

He dragged his eyes away from her and stared at the ruins and then at the sea. He'd never seen a wilder, more atmospheric place. 'It was worth the climb.'

'This place is at its best when the weather is bad.'

He laughed and shook his head. 'You're crazy, do you know that?'

'Am I?' The wind gusted and she grabbed his arm for support. 'If we drop down to just below the ruined tower, it's sheltered. We can sit there and watch the sun come up.'

Ethan stared at the sky. 'I don't think there's going to be any sun,' he muttered, but he followed her across the patch of grass, over some stones and down again until they were sheltered by a large wall.

'Do you have any idea how old this place is? They reckon it's one of the earliest castles, although it's been built on over the centuries, of course.' She ran her hands over the grey, uneven bricks and looked through the tiny slit window. 'When I was a child I used to come up here with Logan and play warriors. He used to be the invading army and I used to be the one defending the castle.'

He could imagine her doing exactly that, with her hair streaming down her back, her chin lifted and her eyes blazing as she and Logan argued over who was in charge.

'Did you cover him in boiling oil?'

'No. Buckets of ice-cold water. My aim was brilliant. He used to complain like mad.' She stepped towards him and took the front of his jacket in her hands. 'You were brave last night with Fraser. You acted like an islander.'

Her face was so close that her cheek almost brushed against his. Ethan clenched his jaw and kept his eyes ahead because he knew that to look at her now would be too great a test of his self-control. And then she moved her head fractionally and he felt her touch her lips to his, and he just couldn't help himself. He was drawn to her in the same way that he'd been drawn to her on that very first day. He looked. And fell. Deep, deep into her stormy blue eyes that held both warning and invitation.

He issued his own warning. 'I'm not an islander.' There was so much that he still had to tell her and yet suddenly he couldn't remember any of it with the heat and awareness devouring them both like a greedy animal.

Her mouth was so close to his that he could feel her breath mingling with his. 'But you could be, Ethan. You could be.'

He was surrounded by her. The scent of her. The sound of her. The feel of her. His insides locked with lust. And in those tense, sexually charged few moments they both knew what was going to happen.

He was seeing it in her eyes and he knew that she was seeing it in his. And suddenly all the reasons that he shouldn't be doing this were eclipsed by all the reasons that he should.

He lifted his hand and cupped the back of her head, drawing her face towards his. 'It's got to be here,' he growled hoarsely, 'and now.' He was driven by an urgency that he didn't understand and she obviously felt it, too, because she pressed closer and lifted her face.

'Yes. Now.' She met the hot burn of his kiss and struggled with the zip of his coat just as he reached for her clothes. There was no gentle fumbling. No smiles or laughter. Each was deadly serious, intent on the other, eyes clinging and hands brushing in a feverish determination to discover flesh and be together. His mouth still on hers, he stripped her of her coat and then grabbed the hem of her strap top and slid it upwards.

She lifted her arms in acquiescence and he broke the kiss just long enough to jerk the top over her head. He looked, just for a moment—saw high, firm breasts and nipples darkening to a peak—and then looking just wasn't enough and he touched.

This time his hands were on bare, warm flesh and he held her against him, feeling the perfection of her slender body against his.

'Ethan…Ethan…' She murmured his name against his lips, pressing forward, boldly encouraging him. He felt her quiver under his hands—felt her skin sleek and soft as his fingers explored and discovered. She gasped against the relentless assault of his mouth and then he felt the scratch of her nails over the bare flesh of his chest and the nip of her teeth on his jaw. Only then did he realise that she'd ripped at his clothes with the same feverish desperation that he'd stripped her. His shirt hung open and her hands were on his chest.

And then she kissed and nipped and licked her way from his jaw to his neck and from his neck to his chest, touching, tasting and breathing in the scent of him until he was so aroused that his body ached with it.

And when he felt her fingers on the waistband of his jeans he sucked in a breath and clamped his hands over hers, his teeth gritted.

'Wait.' He held her away from him, struggling to find a control that had never eluded him before. 'You have to wait.'

'I can't wait. And neither can you.' She was on her toes, seeking his mouth with hers. 'Why wait?'

'Because I want you so badly.'

'That's the way I want you to want me, Ethan. What other way is there?' Her voice soft, she moved her face against his and he felt the soft brush of her lashes against his cheek before her mouth found his again. Her tongue teased his lower lip and then the corner of his mouth, accelerating the excitement between them to such a pitch that the very idea of control became laughable.

His mind and vision blurred, Ethan dispensed with the barrier of her shorts and panties and slid his hands down over her bottom. And this time when he felt her fingers at his zip, he didn't stop her but neither did he hesitate in his own quest to know all of her. He slid his fingers deep inside her and she was so wet and so hot that he cursed softly and buried his face in her neck.

'Now, Ethan.' She was almost sobbing as she freed him from his jeans and closed her hand around him. 'Please, now.'

And afterwards when he thought about this moment, he realised that he'd never really had a choice.

From that first moment on the ferry, this had been inevitable. Not here, perhaps, and not in this way. This frantic, greedy, desperate coupling that was almost primitive in its intensity. But it had always been there, waiting for both of them.

And when he pushed her back against the ancient stone wall and lifted her, he wondered how many other such acts of such sensual desperation this castle had seen over the centuries.

And then thinking became impossible because it was all about feeling and acting on the most basic of human instincts. She wrapped her legs around his waist and he moved his hand down and guided himself into her tight, silken heat, driven by a devouring, dangerous force beyond his control. His need was primitive and he deepened his possession, his hands supporting her as he held her still for his most intimate invasion. Dimly he registered her cry and tried to pause, wondering whether he'd hurt her, and then he felt the frantic movement of her hips, encouraging him, and gave himself up to his body's instinctive need to thrust into her.

The fire between them burned and licked as they moved and gasped and greedily devoured each other. And then the explosion came. Powerful and deadly, it took both of them with it and Ethan ground into her one last time, driven past control by the rhythmic contractions of her own body.

And then the storm left, as if satisfied that it had done its work.

Still breathing heavily, Ethan lowered her gently to the ground and tried to clear his head, still too stunned to form a coherent sentence. Would he ever be able to speak?

What was there to say? After sharing something so perfect, what was there to say?

She was shaking in his arms, her hair tangled and loose, her body deliciously naked.

And suddenly he wanted her again. And he knew that he'd want her again after that. And again.

He cupped her face in his hands, needing to communicate the way he felt but silenced by his natural reticence. 'Kyla—'

'Don't say anything,' she said shakily, her eyes shy as she looked at him. 'Don't say anything at all.'

And he knew that she understood and felt the same way.

There were no words that could possibly do justice to what they'd just shared.

He gently stroked her hair away from her face, noticing things that he'd never noticed before. Like the fact that her blue eyes were darker than he'd first thought and she had a few tiny freckles over her nose. He dragged his thumb slowly over her full mouth and she nipped at it, the look in her eyes reflecting his own thoughts.

He wanted her again.

But not here.

'The sun is coming up.' He spoke softly, even though there was no one around to hear them. 'The storm is over.'

'Let's watch. I'll show you where.' She stooped and retrieved her clothes, dressing quickly in a series of graceful movements that he watched with masculine hunger. Then she reached forward and started to fasten the buttons on his shirt. 'If I don't do this, I won't be able to leave you alone. I love your body—have I told you that?'

No. And he hadn't told her that he loved hers, although their frantic love-making should surely have left her in no doubt. But her observation that intimate conversations hadn't been part of their interaction to date was a sharp, uncomfortable reminder that this relationship was built on shaky, dangerous ground.

She took his hand and led him across a low stone wall and then sank to the grass and dragged him down next to her. 'This is the best view on the whole island. And this is the best weather in which to see it. Just watch.'

Ethan sat, silenced by the beauty of the scene unfolding in front of him. And as he sat there, watching the sun come up over an angry, boiling sea, he suddenly understood.

Kyla reached for his hand and curled her fingers around his. 'Do you think things happen for a reason, Ethan?'

'What do you mean?'

Perhaps she heard the wariness in his voice because she smiled. 'I mean that some things are just meant to happen. You came out of nowhere. Serendipity. You could have chosen to escape anywhere but you came here.'

Ethan felt coldness pour through his body.

It hadn't been serendipity.

And he hadn't come out of nowhere.

Her words were like a hammer blow to his conscience and the perfection of the moment was soured. 'Kyla—'

She covered his lips with her finger, preventing him from finishing his sentence. 'Not now. Now I just want you to kiss me again. And then we'll go home and do everything again in slow motion.'

CHAPTER NINE

UNFORTUNATELY, fate intervened in the form of a little girl with an asthma attack.

Logan was still tied up with Fraser, who was now being sick and complaining of persistent headache, so Ethan had no choice but to leave Kyla on her doorstep.

Once again he seemed distant, remote and Kyla felt a twist of yearning for the unconstrained, passionate side of him she'd discovered up in the ruins of the castle.

For a moment he'd lost control and finally revealed himself to her but now he had retreated back into his shell.

'I'll see the Roberts child, come back here and change and then go straight to the surgery. Logan thinks he may have to fly Fraser over to the mainland for a CT scan.'

They might have been no more than colleagues, discussing their plans for the day. Visit here. Clinic there.

Where had it gone? Kyla wondered as she stared wistfully into his handsome face—that incredible closeness and intimacy that had held them both in its grip. *Where had it gone?*

'On second thoughts, would you mind picking up a

suit for me?' He handed her his keys. 'I can take a shower at Logan's and change before surgery. It will be quicker than coming all the way back here.'

'Of course.' She took the keys and waited for him to say something that indicated he understood the way she was feeling. *Something that acknowledged the power of what they'd shared during the storm.* But he didn't even look at her.

His handsome face was grim and serious as if he had a thousand things on his mind and none of them related to her.

'That's fine.' She forced herself to speak normally and not show her disappointment. 'I'll bring the suit. Will I be able to find it?'

'In the wardrobe in my bedroom. Just choose one. And Kyla...' Finally he looked at her but there was a bleakness in his eyes that did nothing to alleviate the growing ache inside her. 'This evening, we have to talk.'

Talk? She watched him stride towards his car, the lump in her throat as big as the weight in her heart.

She loved him, she realised with a sinking feeling. Somehow, over the past weeks, she'd grown to love this complicated man. And up until five minutes ago she would have sworn that he had feelings for her, too.

Had she imagined what they'd shared in the castle?

No. She definitely hadn't. She was just being paranoid, she told herself as she turned and let herself into her own house. She'd shower and change and then collect his suit on her way to work.

She had nothing to worry about.

The fact that he was suddenly serious and detached

was just Ethan being Ethan. He was thinking about work. That was what he did.

As she stripped off her clothes she was suddenly deliciously aware of the unfamiliar ache in various parts of her body and a soft smile touched her mouth. He felt something for her, of course he did. How, otherwise, could he have made love to her in the way that he had? She just had to be patient and allow him the space he obviously needed.

He wasn't a man who opened up easily, she knew that.

She dried her hair, dressed in her uniform and picked up his keys.

Inside his cottage, she sprinted up the stairs, found the suit and carried it out of the house. It was only as she went to hang it in the rear of her car that she saw the letter that had dropped out of the pocket onto the road.

With a frown, she picked it up, intending to push it back into the suit pocket. And then a sentence caught her eye and she froze in shock. And started to read.

'So are you going to transfer Fraser to the mainland for a CT scan?' Ethan asked the question as Logan reached for the telephone.

'Yes. I'm pretty sure he's just displaying signs of concussion but I need to be sure. It's best to play it safe because I don't want any last-minute emergencies.' He broke off as the door crashed open and Kyla strode into the reception area. 'Oops. My sister obviously climbed out of bed on the wrong side.'

Ethan felt himself tense as she kicked the door shut behind her, dropped her bag by the reception desk and blew a strand of hair out of her eyes.

Then she looked at him.

And he saw that she knew.

There was contempt in her eyes as she stalked over to him and thrust the suit into his hands, her face unsmiling. 'Your suit, Dr Walker. Better put it on quickly. It's part of your disguise.'

Logan gave her an incredulous look. 'Are you hormonal?'

She whirled on her brother, anger sparking in her blue eyes. 'No. I am *not* hormonal.'

'Then what the hell is wrong with you?'

'You'd better direct that question to Dr Walker,' she suggested in an acid tone, and Ethan inhaled sharply.

'Kyla, why don't we go somewhere quiet and talk?'

'Don't you mean somewhere quiet so that we can carry on keeping our secrets? Or rather *your* secrets.' Her gaze was accusing. 'And what do you mean, *talk*? Since when did you ever talk, Ethan? You're more of a listener, aren't you? Especially when you're finding out about people.'

Wishing he hadn't taken so long to tell her the truth, Ethan watched her steadily. She was a woman of wild extremes. Whatever Kyla did, she did it with an abandoned passion. She made love as though she was enjoying her last moments on earth and she lost her temper with the same degree of intensity. With Kyla, there was no neutral. No grey areas.

So how on earth was he going to explain himself to her? Especially when he couldn't even explain things to himself.

'Surgery is about to start,' Logan pointed out in a

quiet tone, 'so whatever it is that's bugging the pair of you, you need to shelve it until later. There's enough gossip on this island without adding more.'

Kyla turned to him. 'Ethan is—'

'I don't want to hear it, Kyla.' Logan's voice was firm. 'Get set up for clinic. We'll talk later. And now I need to sort out Fraser.'

Kyla hesitated and it was obvious that she was struggling with her emotions. Then she blinked several times, swallowed hard and walked towards her room with her head down.

'Women,' Logan said wearily, watching her go. 'Don't you ever wish they came with an instruction manual?'

Kyla buried herself in her clinic but her mind wouldn't focus. She didn't know whether to cry or punch something and in the end she just did everything on automatic. She took blood pressures, she talked about asthma management, she syringed an ear, took a cervical smear and changed two dressings. Then she realised that she hadn't even noticed what the wounds underneath had looked like.

All she'd been thinking about was Ethan.

And the letter.

She gave up and went next door to Evanna.

'I'm sorry to ask you this.' Her voice was gruff. 'But have you got time to finish my clinic? I've only got three more to see but I'm not concentrating. I think I need some air before I put a dressing on someone who needs an ECG.'

Evanna put down the tourniquet she was holding. 'Of

course. What's the matter? Are you ill? Perhaps it was being stuck in that dark tunnel in the storm.'

'I'm not ill,' Kyla assured her dully, backing towards the door. 'I just feel a bit— I need to—'

'It's OK,' Evanna said in a soft voice, waving a hand at her. 'Just go. You don't need to explain.'

Kyla gave her a grateful smile and slid out of the room just as Ethan emerged from his.

They looked at each other and then she sucked in a breath and made for the car park.

'Kyla, wait.' His voice was a firm command but she ignored him and lengthened her stride. He'd had plenty of opportunity to talk to her and he hadn't bothered. And she certainly wasn't ready to talk to *him*. Maybe she wouldn't ever be ready. She felt completely betrayed.

She climbed into her car and sped away, determined to find herself somewhere peaceful to think.

Instinctively she headed for the ruined castle and then wished she hadn't because the place was now layered with memories of Ethan and it was impossible to think clearly with thoughts of earlier intruding.

There was no trace of the storm now and the sun shone in a perfectly blue sky, but still Kyla shivered as she sank down onto a rock and stared bleakly out to sea.

And then she heard a firm, masculine tread behind her and she rose to her feet, accusation in her eyes because she knew who it would be. And perhaps, secretly, she'd wanted him to follow her so that they could say what needed to be said, in privacy.

'Why did you follow me?'

'Because we need to talk and we don't need to do it

in public.' He stopped a little distance away from her and she turned away, ignoring the wisps of hair that blew across her face.

'You mean that you don't want anyone else to hear your secret.'

'I don't want them to hear it yet.' His voice was even. Steady. 'First, you and I need to talk.'

'Why?' She turned back to face him, so angry that she clenched her hands into fists. 'So that you can make excuses?'

'I'm not going to make excuses.'

How could he be so calm? 'You deceived us, Ethan.' Her voice broke and she hated herself for showing just how badly his betrayal had hurt her. 'You deceived us all. Not just me but Logan, Evanna—the whole island. We thought—we thought you were—'

'You thought I was Ethan Walker, and that's exactly who I am.'

She looked him full in the face, not giving him room for escape. 'But you're also Catherine's brother,' she said in a whisper. *'Catherine's brother.'*

He stepped towards her. 'Kyla—'

'You're not a stranger. It wasn't serendipity that brought you here. You came here for a reason. You came to find her child, didn't you? You came for your niece. *You came after Kirsty.'*

Tension stiffened his shoulders. 'I wanted to meet her, yes.'

'No, Ethan.' Kyla shook her head and hugged her arms around her waist. 'Wanting to meet her would have been you walking off that ferry and saying, "Hi, I'm

Kirsty's uncle." And you didn't do that. You stayed on the edges and watched. You ate our food and you drank our drink. You listened to our conversations and lived our lives with us, *and all the time you were just watching*.'

'There were things I needed to understand. I wanted to get to know you all.'

'And is that your excuse for making love to me? Did you need a few extra intimate details for your research?' She forced herself to say the words—forced herself to stare hurt in the face. 'I suppose that's the ultimate way of getting to know someone, isn't it? What are you going to do next? Move on to Evanna just to check that you know her, too?'

'Don't, Kyla—'

'Don't what? Don't face up to facts? I'm being honest, which is more than you've been up until now.'

His shoulders were tense. 'What happened between us had absolutely nothing to do with the fact that I'm Catherine's brother.'

'Yes, it did, because you wouldn't even have *been* here if you hadn't been Catherine's brother! We would never have met. You deliberately hid your identity from me. From all of us.'

'I tried to tell you.'

'But you didn't try hard enough, did you? What were you thinking?' The lump in her throat threatened to choke her and the anger burned inside her. 'Were you checking out whether Logan was a fit enough father? Because I can tell you now that he's worth six of you. Logan is honest and straightforward, and if you are thinking of doing *anything* that will hurt my brother or his child, I will personally see you off this island.' Breathless, she stopped, her chest rising and falling as she struggled for control.

A muscle worked in his lean cheek, an indication of his own rising tension. 'You want me to explain so let's start with that. You feel protective of Logan. You love him.'

'Of course I love him.' Her tone was both dismissive and impatient because she couldn't understand why he was wasting time stating the obvious. 'He's my brother. He's family.'

'You make it all sound so straightforward, but life isn't always like that, Kyla. It's complicated.'

'What's complicated about telling the truth? You should have just told us. That's what I would have done.'

Ethan swore softly and closed the distance between them. 'Maybe it is, but I'm not like you and my family is nothing like yours.'

Kyla tried to step backwards but he caught her shoulders and forced her to look at him.

'You want to talk about this? All right, let's talk about it.' His voice was raw with a depth of emotion that she hadn't heard from him before. 'Your family is a single unit. You're in and out of each other's lives, interfering and interacting. You're individuals but you're all small parts of a whole.'

She ignored the fact that his fingers were digging into her shoulders. 'So? That's what families are.'

'Not mine.' He released her then and his hands dropped to his sides, his tone hoarse. 'Not mine, Kyla.'

'I know your parents were divorced and remarried, but—'

'You don't know anything.' He stared out across the sea. 'Catherine and I didn't share the same brother-sister relationship that you have with Logan. You love Logan. Do you want to know how I felt about Catherine? For most of my life, I hated her. There.' He turned to look at her, a smile of self-derision on his handsome face. 'Now are you shocked?'

She didn't know what to say so she didn't say anything, and he turned away again with a humourless laugh.

'Oh, yes, you're shocked, because hating your family isn't something that really happens around here, is it, Kyla? Around here, on Glenmore, family is the most important thing. But the truth is that I hated Catherine. And she hated me, too. From the moment we met when I was eleven and she was eight, we hated each other. She hated me because my father married her mother and she liked it being just the two of them. It meant that she had to compete for attention. I hated her because she was the most selfish person I had ever met. She believed that the whole world had to revolve around her and it drove me mad. She took drugs, she stole, she did just about anything a person can do to gain attention. And I hated her.'

Reminding herself that he'd deceived her, Kyla tried to hold onto her anger but she felt it slipping out of her. 'You were a child.'

'Don't make excuses for me. Catherine and I spent the next ten years trying to make each other miserable, and usually succeeding. We argued, we fought, we each blamed the other for our terrible home life. She was half-wild, always running away from school and driving my father mad. Three times he had to collect her from the police station—did she ever tell you that? I thought she was incredibly selfish. She thought I was aloof, remote and judgmental. We couldn't wait to get out of each other's lives.'

'When did you last see her?'

'Ten years ago.'

'Ten years...' Kyla tried to imagine not seeing Logan for ten years. 'So—why did you follow her here? Why now if you didn't have that sort of relationship?'

For a long moment Ethan didn't answer. 'She wrote to me, a year ago, and I realise now that it was probably just a few days before she went into labour with Kirsty. It was the only letter I ever had from her and probably the only communication we had that wasn't tinged with bitterness. She wrote because she said that she'd discovered paradise. She told me that she'd settled in Scotland and suddenly felt different about life. She realised that family were important and she wanted to make contact. She told me that I was going to be an uncle.'

'Did you write back?'

'By the time I received her letter, she was already dead.'

'But—'

'I was working in the Sudan, Kyla. I was in Africa. I was battling heat and dust and disease like you cannot possibly imagine.' His voice was raw and she suddenly realised just how much of this man she didn't know. She'd assumed he'd worked in London. 'She sent the letter to my flat in London. For some reason it wasn't forwarded. I only received it two months ago when I finally came home.'

'So why not just turn up here and introduce yourself? Why pretend to be someone else?'

He frowned in response to her question. 'I didn't pretend.'

'But her surname was King. How can you be Walker?'

'Her mother refused to take my father's name. She was always King and I was Walker.'

'She never mentioned you,' Kyla told him. 'She always said that her family could have done with living on Glenmore for a while. I suppose she felt that having the baby was a time to make a fresh start.'

'That letter has tortured me. It left me with so many unanswered questions. The Catherine in that letter bore no resemblance to the Catherine of my childhood. She claimed it was this place that had changed her.' He breathed in and looked around him. 'She said that it was Glenmore. The sea, the ruins, the wildness. And most of all the people.'

'She arrived on the ferry one day with a backpack and never left. Glenmore has that effect on some people.' *But not on him.* The island hadn't changed him or caused him to open up to others. He was as reserved and self-contained as ever.

'Something in her letter affected me deeply. She described everything in such detail. Not just the scenery but the people. She talked about everyone as if she knew them. It was the first time I'd ever had the sense that she had been interested in anything other than herself. That letter showed me a completely different side of her.'

'She fitted in very quickly.' Kyla watched his face, trying to gauge his reaction, but as usual he gave nothing away. 'So what made you come here? Was it just Kirsty?'

'No. I felt as though I'd lost something. Which was ridiculous because up until that letter Catherine and I had never had anything that we could lose. We'd never shared anything. But she'd obviously discovered a different part of herself and new priorities. And maybe I had, too.' He gave a faint smile. 'A year working in Africa does tend to sort out your priorities. Her letter was intriguing. I suppose I wanted to see the place that had changed her so dramatically. I wanted to see Glenmore the way she would have seen it. And, of course, I wanted to meet my niece and the man who my sister fell in love with and married.'

'And you couldn't just have been honest with us?' Despite what he'd told her, she was still angry with him. *Angry that he hadn't told her the truth.* 'Couldn't you have told *me?*' Her implication was clear, and he didn't flinch from her gaze.

'I'm used to doing things by myself. I'm used to finding my own way. That's the person I am, Kyla.'

She refused to let him duck the issue. 'You deceived us.'

'Not intentionally and not in the way that you mean. I was always going to tell you. I'm just sorry you found out in the way you did.'

'The letter fell out of your pocket. I didn't intend to read it but then I saw Kirsty's name.' She took a deep breath. 'So what happens now? Are you going back to Africa?' Her question hovered in the air between them and for a long moment he didn't answer.

'Not Africa,' he said finally. 'I want very much to be part of Kirsty's life, so Africa isn't an option, but as to what else…' He shrugged and the fact that he still made no reference to what they'd shared—*made no attempt to touch her*—hurt more than she could have imagined possible.

'You have to tell Logan.'

'Of course.' His voice was quiet. 'I was always going to tell Logan when the time was right. I'm going now. Are you coming?'

She shook her head. She needed space. She didn't know what she thought any more. 'You go.'

'I'll see you later.'

She turned to look at him. 'This is an island, Dr Walker. Of course you'll see me later.'

CHAPTER TEN

'CAN you imagine that? Being given the chance to patch up your relationship with your sister and then realising that you're too late. How awful. Fancy having to live with that. And fancy Catherine never even mentioning that she had a brother. It was obviously such a thorny subject.' Evanna carefully turned the chicken on the barbecue. 'Poor Ethan. No wonder he always seemed so tense, poor thing.'

'Poor thing?' Kyla stared at her friend. 'Aren't you at all angry? Don't you think he should have told us?'

'I think it's lovely that Kirsty has more family to love her. We don't all live life by the same rules, Kyla,' Evanna said mildly, reaching down and scooping Kirsty into her arms. 'We don't all behave according to one rule book. We're all different people, looking for different things. None of us is perfect.'

Kyla scowled at her. 'Stop being so reasonable. He took advantage of our hospitality.'

'Over the centuries Glenmore was often a place of sanctuary for strangers,' Evanna reminded her softly. 'We've always taken a pride in our hospitality.'

'But if we'd known who he was—'

'Then the welcome would have been warmer still,' Evanna said firmly, hitching Kirsty onto her hip and letting her play with a wooden spoon. 'I think it's very exciting for Kirsty to have someone in her life who knew her mother as a child.'

'I can assure you that the memories aren't good ones.'

Evanna seemed unconcerned. 'People are all a mixture of good and bad. Perfection would be pretty hard to live with.'

'Kirsty will get attached to him and then he'll leave,' Kyla predicted, and Evanna looked at her.

'And does that matter?'

No.

Yes.

She didn't *want* it to matter.

Oh, she was being so stupid. 'No, of course not. Well, yes, it's just that—I—'

'This isn't about Kirsty, it's about you. You're in love with him and you don't want him to leave. Have you told him?'

Kyla stared at her friend, wanting to deny it. But her mouth wouldn't form the necessary lie. 'Don't be ridiculous. This is a man who doesn't exactly communicate his feelings, remember?'

'That's him. But you *do* communicate yours, usually pretty loudly…' Evanna gave a grin '…so you should be telling him, just so that there is no doubt.'

Kyla raised an eyebrow. 'The way you're telling my brother that you're in love with him?'

Evanna blushed gently. 'That's different. Logan

doesn't notice me and he certainly doesn't love me. Me telling him my feelings would just embarrass both of us. But Ethan definitely has powerful feelings for you. I suspect he loves you, too, but you might need to nudge him into telling you. I'm willing to bet that he has no idea how you feel about him. At the moment all he sees is your anger.'

Kyla thought about the frantic sex they'd shared in the ruins of the castle. It had been primitive, desperate and… 'If he'd loved me, wouldn't he have trusted me enough to tell me the truth?'

Evanna removed the chicken from the barbecue and put it on the plate. 'This is a man who isn't used to sharing and trusting so, no, probably not.'

'So perhaps he's wrong for me.'

Evanna smiled and handed her a plate. 'Perhaps. But isn't it worth finding out?'

'He isn't like us.'

'And isn't that a good thing? The planet would certainly be boring if we were all the same.' Evanna poured dressing on the salad. 'Eat. You're always cranky when you're hungry. Logan will be home soon. He's up at the surgery with Ethan.'

In the end, Kyla didn't wait for her brother to return home. She felt restless and confused and she needed to be by herself, so she drove back to her cottage.

And then she sat for ten minutes in her kitchen, looking out at the sea. And she still felt restless and confused so she slipped her feet out of her shoes and went for a walk on the beach.

It was only when she felt a hand on her shoulder that she realised that Ethan was standing behind her.

'I've come to apologise.' His voice was deep and she turned, feeling her heart leap into her throat at the sight of him. Would she ever be able to look at him and not react like this?

'For what?'

'For making love to you before I told you about Catherine. I certainly intended to tell you. But this thing between us is strong—' He broke off and she felt a twinge of disappointment.

He was talking about the sex, she reminded herself. 'I'm sorry I shouted at you this morning but I was angry with you.'

'I know. Justifiably so.' He didn't smile. 'And now, Kyla? Are you still angry?'

'I'm not sure. I keep going over our conversations and wondering how many of them were just about detective work for you.'

His hand dropped to his side. 'Is that what you think? That my relationship with you was just a means to finding out about Catherine?'

'You asked me about her in the pub that night.' She shook her head in disbelief. 'She was your sister and yet you were asking me about her and I answered without knowing who you were or why you were asking. And I can't help wondering if I said something that I shouldn't have said.'

'She was my stepsister and I wanted to find out who she was,' he said quietly. 'I didn't know her. The woman I knew would never have settled in a place like this. The

Catherine I knew was selfish and didn't think of anyone but herself. I wanted to hear you talk about her. And I wanted to hear you talk without knowing who I was because I didn't want my relationship with Catherine to influence your answer. I was trying to understand.'

'In that case, you should speak to Logan because obviously he knew her the best.'

'But different people see different things in a person.'

It was very much like something that Evanna would have said, and suddenly she wondered whether she'd been too hard on him. 'You want me to tell you more about Catherine?' She thought for a moment, trying to crystallise thoughts and images into something that would paint the picture he was looking for. 'She was— a bit wild, I suppose. She liked doing mad, crazy things. She flirted with every man she met. She was impossible to pin down and unreliable at social engagements. She wore pink shoes and high heels to the pub when it was pouring with rain and she never remembered to take a coat with her. But she was excited by life and enthusiastic about the island. She loved the beaches and Logan taught her to sail.'

'Was she pleased to be pregnant?'

'Oh, yes. She kept talking about family.' Kyla swallowed as she remembered. 'She kept saying that she was going to do it right this time, but when I asked her what she meant by that, she'd never tell me. I suppose I know now. Her death was a tragedy. It affected Logan very badly.'

'I can imagine.'

'She suddenly became ill but the weather on the

island was so bad we couldn't transfer her for a few
hours and the delay was critical. The hospital didn't
think that the outcome would have been any different
but Logan has always blamed himself.' She gave a sad
smile. 'He hates obstetrics now and he always refuses
to do home births.'

'You can hardly blame him for that.'

Kyla thought of her brother and her heart ached. 'I
don't blame him for anything. But I know he blames
himself. He carries it with him all the time.'

'Having seen your brother work, I know that he
would have done everything that could have been done,
and he did more for Catherine than anyone else had ever
done for her in her life. I wish I could have known the
Catherine that she became.' Ethan's voice was gruff
with emotion. 'When I read that letter I felt a tremen-
dous sense of loss. Not for what we had, but for what I
sensed we could have had. Those early years were too
traumatic for both of us and we were too young to be
able to adapt. You describe a Catherine who was happy
and yet I'd never known her that way. So I wanted to
come and see for myself. I suppose although it was too
late to change my relationship with her, it wasn't too late
to alter the picture in my head. I wanted to change my
memories. I wanted to understand her.'

'And have you done that?'

'I'm getting there.' He stared across the sea, his expression distant. 'I'm definitely getting there.'

'And you told Logan who you are?'

'Yes. He seemed pleased that Kirsty has more
family.' Ethan's mouth flickered into a self-deprecating

smile. 'Which just goes to show that they know me less well than you do. I'm not sure that I'm going to be the right sort of family for Kirsty.'

Kyla frowned. 'What do you mean, the right sort of family? Family is family. None of us is perfect but we all do the best we can and we're all there for each other.'

He turned to look at her. 'But that's the bit I'm not so good at, isn't it? Family, for me, has been no more than a word, but for you it's a way of life. Your family is reliable and sticks around no matter what. Your family shares. I'm no good at any of those things. I'm used to packing my bags and living where I want to live without thinking about another person's needs or happiness. I'm used to not needing anyone and to not being needed.'

Kyla looked at him, wondering what it must feel like to be so disconnected from the people around you. 'That sounds a lonely way to live your life, Dr Walker,' she whispered, and his eyes lingered on hers.

'It's the only way I know.'

'Feeling needed is good, and needing someone is good, too. For me, it's what life is all about.' She looked into his eyes and she willed him to kiss her the way he'd kissed her in the dawn light at the ruined castle. But he didn't move. He simply stood there, his eyes on her face, as if searching for something that he couldn't quite find.

And then he thrust his hands in his pockets and turned and headed across the beach and back to the cottage.

So this was how it felt, Kyla thought bleakly, blinking furiously to clear her vision. This was how it felt to be heartbroken.

Now she knew.

And the pain was worse than she could possibly have imagined.

'So that was it?' Evanna frowned at Kyla from across the best table in the café. It was right in the window and had a perfect view of the ferry and the quay. 'He didn't say anything about the two of you?'

'Nothing.' Kyla stabbed her triple chocolate ice cream with the tip of her spoon, wondering why she felt so totally flat and dejected. 'I really need to pull myself together. I'm being pathetic.'

'And what about you? Didn't you say anything to him?'

'What was I supposed to do? Beg?' Kyla frowned and lifted the spoon to her mouth, but the cold chocolate hit did nothing for her. 'I do have some pride, Evanna.'

'But he doesn't know how you feel.'

'I think it's his own feelings that are the problem,' Kyla said gloomily, putting the spoon down and staring out of the window as the ferry pulled away from the dock on the start of its crossing to the mainland. 'You said that the man had issues, and you're right. The man has issues.'

'And you're going to let that stop you?'

Kyla pushed the ice cream away from her. 'What do you suggest? That I hang a banner on the front of my cottage, declaring my intentions?'

Evanna grinned. 'In the old days you would have carved his name on your desk. 'K loves E. And Miss Carne would have put you in detention.'

'I feel as though I'm in permanent detention.'

Evanna reached across the table and squeezed her

hand. 'It's not like you to give up. What's he going to do now, do you know? Is he leaving?'

'He hasn't said.' Kyla gave a humourless laugh. 'That would be giving something away, wouldn't it? And Ethan never gives anything away. I dare say the first I'll know of it is when Jim tells me he's driven that flash car of his onto the ferry.'

'You need to speak to him.'

'I have my pride.'

Evanna sighed. 'Pride isn't going to keep you warm on a cold winter's night, Kyla MacNeil. You need to think about that next time you're lying in the bed on your own, staring up at the ceiling. Now, eat your ice cream. If there's one thing a girl needs at a time like this, it's chocolate. Lots of it.'

Kyla was in clinic the next morning when Aisla came in.

'I came to thank you. If you hadn't thought that Fraser might be in the dungeon, goodness knows what might have happened.'

Kyla smiled. 'I'm just glad we found him and that everything was all right. Logan said that the CT scan was fine.'

'They think he has concussion. Apparently he might suffer from headaches for a bit and I need to keep an eye on him, but they don't think there's any serious injury. And Dr Walker looked at his wound this morning and seemed to think that it was healing nicely. I still can't believe he climbed down into that filthy, dark dungeon for my Fraser.'

'He's a brave man. A good doctor.'

Aisla sighed. 'He'll be a loss to the island.'

Kyla felt her mouth dry. 'A loss?'

'Well, he was only ever a locum, wasn't he? He was reminding me of that this morning when I was trying to persuade him to stay, but I don't understand it really. The man fits in here. I mean, why leave?'

'I expect he's leaving because we can't offer him what he needs.' On impulse Kyla stood up and walked towards the door. 'I'm glad Fraser is on the mend, Aisla. Call us any time if you're worried.'

She saw Aisla out and then walked into Ethan's room. 'What exactly is it that you need?'

He was seated at his desk and he looked up, his dark eyes guarded. 'What do you mean?'

'I don't understand what it is that you need.' Restless and boiling up with emotions that she couldn't control, Kyla paced the floor of his consulting room. 'I mean, it's all here if you look for it. You love to run and you won't find better anywhere. Or do you prefer fumes and tarmac to sea breezes and sand? You like to swim and we have a whole ocean waiting for you, or do you prefer chlorine and public pools?'

'Kyla—'

'Or is it the medicine?' she continued breathlessly, turning around and pacing back again. 'Because I can tell you now that you won't find greater variety anywhere. This island is like a small world. We have births and deaths and in between we have all the things that are part of life. And we handle most of it ourselves because we can't refer someone to the hospital every time things get slightly complicated. You'll get more hands-on experience here than you ever would in a

London teaching hospital, and it's probably just as much of a challenge as Africa in its own way.'

He opened his mouth and she plunged on, afraid to let him speak in case he said something that she couldn't bear to hear.

'Or is it the people?' she said, finally standing still and daring to look at him. He was unnaturally still as he watched her, his eyes fixed on her face. 'It's true that everyone on this island is interested in everyone else, but that's because we're a community. We're not just a bunch of faceless individuals living isolated lives that never interconnect. We *care,* Ethan. We care in a way that you're never going to find in a city. We mind what happens to people. We care about each other and we care about you. I care about you. I love you, actually—' Suddenly awkward and embarrassed, she broke off, suddenly wishing she'd been born with some of his natural reticence because she knew that she'd given away far too much. She'd given away everything.

But then she decided that he'd probably guessed anyway, and remembered Evanna's words.

Pride isn't going to keep you warm on those long winter nights, Kyla.

He rose to his feet and walked round the desk towards her, and she felt the steady, rhythmic bump of her heart against her chest.

'You love me?' His voice was deep and she felt herself backing away.

'Yes, but that doesn't have to be a problem. You can stay on the island and not have a relationship with me. We could—'

'Can we start from the beginning? What makes you think I'm leaving?'

'Something Aisla just said, about your post only ever being temporary. I know that this island is different to everything you're used to. I know that you're used to living your life very much on your own. You say it's the only way you know, but that doesn't mean you can't learn a different way if you want to. Catherine did it.'

'Kyla—'

'You *feel* it, I know you do. The magic of this place. I've seen your face when you run on the sand in the morning. I've seen the tension melt away from you when you breathe in the sea air. I *know* you love it here. And you care about the patients. You cared enough to dangle off the end of a rope to save a little boy from a dark dungeon.'

He brought his mouth down on hers and kissed her hard.

Her head spun, her knees sagged and she gave a little murmur of shock as his hands slid into her hair and he held her firmly, exploring her mouth with feverish intent.

When he finally lifted his head she blinked and tried to focus. 'That isn't fair. You shouldn't do that when I'm trying to concentrate. W-why did you do that?'

'I was showing you that I care about the inhabitants of the island.'

She swallowed hard, her hands still clutching the jacket of his suit for support. 'I'm just one inhabitant.'

'But the most important one,' he said softly, the hint of a smile touching his mouth as he studied her face. 'I had no idea that you loved me. That changes a lot of things.'

'You didn't know?' She felt her cheeks colour. 'You think I strip naked in the ruins of the castle for every man?'

'I certainly hope not.' He stroked his fingers through her hair. 'But I thought the fact that I kept a secret from you damaged what we had.'

'I was angry with you and hurt that you didn't trust me.'

He drew in a breath and his eyes narrowed questioningly. 'And now? How do you feel now?'

'Now I just feel miserable that you're leaving.'

He released her then and walked over to the window, staring out across the fields that stretched from Logan's house towards the sea. 'When I first arrived here, I wasn't even sure why I'd come. It was too late for Catherine and me, but I suppose a part of me wanted to identify the last few pieces of the puzzle. I wanted to understand what it was that had changed her and now I do, because it's changed me, too. This place restores your faith in humanity. This place doesn't allow selfishness because it's all about sharing. The island only works because people share.'

'I think that's what Catherine discovered. She said that she suddenly felt as though she belonged somewhere.'

'Yes.' He turned to look at her and her heart pounded.

'I thought you were going to walk away from me,' she whispered, trapped by the look in his eyes. 'I thought you were going to walk away from what we have.'

'Never.'

'But—'

He walked towards her and put a hand over her lips, humour dancing in his eyes. 'I think when we're married I'm going to have to gag you for part of the day or I'll never get a chance to speak and then you'll accuse me of being hopeless at communicating.'

Her heart almost stopped and she wanted to ask him to repeat what he'd just said, but his fingers were still covering her mouth so she was only able to make a 'mmm' sound.

His fingers brushed her lips. 'You're right that I love Glenmore island. You're right that I love sea breezes and soft sand. You're right that I love to swim in the ocean, and it's certainly true that there's more than enough of a medical challenge here to keep me satisfied. And, of course, I love Kirsty and want to watch her grow up. But none of those are the reasons that I'll be staying here.' His gaze was gentle. 'I'll be staying here because of you. Because I love you, Kyla. I love everything about you. I love your warmth and generosity and the way you care for everyone. I love your slightly wicked streak and the way you love your family. And I want to be part of that family.'

He moved his hand from her mouth and looked at her expectantly, but now that he'd given her the opportunity to speak she discovered that the words were stuck behind the giant lump in her throat.

'Kyla?' His gentle prompt made her open her mouth and croak something incoherent.

'I didn't— You said…'

He lifted an eyebrow. 'I said?'

'A few sentences ago you mentioned…'

'I mentioned…?'

'Marriage.'

'Yes, I did.' He looked around his consulting room

and rolled his eyes. 'I'm thirty-two years old and when I finally propose to a woman we're surrounded by medical equipment.'

'I don't care about the surroundings,' she murmured, hardly daring to believe what was happening. 'I haven't even noticed them.'

'Good. So is the answer yes?'

'You came here to find Kirsty—'

'I came here because I was drawn by the letter that Catherine wrote. Because I wanted to see this place.' His ran a finger over her cheek. 'But I'm staying because of you.'

'You're staying on the island?'

'It's going to be hard to be married to you if I don't,' he drawled softly, 'because it's obvious to everyone that this is the place you were meant to be. And, anyway, we have a responsibility to the community to have lots of sex.'

She gave a gasp of shock and glanced towards the door, but it remind firmly closed. 'Ethan!'

'Stop looking scandalised. You were the one who told me that the population has a duty to have plenty of sex and produce lots of children.'

She started to laugh. 'Yes, but—'

'If you're worried about the school closing, we'd better get cracking. If we start now we can have a child in every class right the way through primary school.'

'Ann Carne would have an asthma attack if they were all little versions of me.'

'But their daddy would be delighted. I can't think of anything better than living my life surrounded by ten little versions of you.' He bent his head and kissed her. 'I love you. And I'm looking forward to populating the island with you. Just say the word and we'll start straight away.'

'Ten? I don't think we'll be having ten.' She wrapped her arms round his neck, unable to control the happiness that bubbled up inside her. 'I can't believe you mean this. We're so different. You don't say much. Oh, Ethan!'

'I'll try and say more,' Ethan murmured against her lips with a smile in his eyes, 'providing you're silent for long enough for me to speak. Is it a deal?'

She loved the feel of his arms around her. 'Do you think you'll be able to stand living here, surrounded by islanders who want to know what you ate for breakfast and a big noisy family who frequently turn up to eat that breakfast with you?'

The smile in his eyes faded. 'The answer to your question is yes. But you haven't answered *my* question yet. Will you marry me?'

'Yes.' Her voice was soft as she reached up and kissed him. 'Of course.'

EVANNA

CHAPTER ONE

A FRESH start.

Evanna Duncan drove her little car off the ferry, hearing the familiar clunk as the wheels left the ramp and hit the concrete of the quay. She waved at Jim, the ferryman, and then drove a little way down South Quay before pulling into a vacant parking space overlooking the harbour.

The city had been hot and sticky, the air trapped between the tall buildings with not a breath of wind to lighten the atmosphere, and she'd crawled through holiday traffic for hours to reach the ferry. She was hot, tired and desperate for the peaceful haven provided by her cottage on the cliffs. But first she had things to do. She was meeting a friend and she was already late.

Climbing out of her car, Evanna breathed a sigh of relief as she felt the wind lift her hair and cool her skin. At last.

Home.

Glenmore Island. Being a practice nurse on a remote Scottish island had its challenges, but she loved it and she could never imagine living anywhere else. She'd only been away for a month but it felt like longer.

'Good trip, Nurse Duncan?' A boy of about twelve strolled up to her, licking a towering ice cream in danger of imminent collapse. A baseball cap was pulled low over his eyes and he wore shorts, scuffed trainers and an ancient T-shirt that had been faded by endless washing. Two of his friends hovered in the background.

'Well, hello, Fraser. Are you enjoying the holidays?' Evanna slammed the car door shut. 'How's that head of yours doing?'

Fraser obligingly whipped off the hat and lifted his hair to show her. 'What do you think? Dr MacNeil says he thinks it's going to be the most *amazing* scar. Wicked.'

It was typical of Logan MacNeil to have turned a negative into a positive. Evanna ignored the way her heart jumped at the mere mention of his name. 'I'm sure he's right. Amazing.' Instinctively she reached out and took a closer look, noticing how well it was healing. *Logan had done a good job with the stitches.* 'And I hope you're staying away from the castle.'

'Sort of. But you'll never guess what's happened, it's *so* cool.' Fraser's voice was earnest as he filled her in on the local gossip. 'They've decided to open up the dungeons. Some archeologic—archolo—' He stumbled over the word and then gave up. 'Someone *really* important is coming to take a look and poke around. They think there might be stuff down there. Stuff from the Celts or the Vikings or something, you know? Like treasure. We're going to go up there and watch.' His eyes gleamed as he rammed the cap back on his head.

'That's great, Fraser.' Evanna slipped her keys into her bag. 'Just make sure you're careful. Those ruins can be dangerous and you've given all of us enough grey hairs this year. Your ice cream is dripping. You need to lick. Fast.'

Fraser grinned and caught the drip with his tongue. 'I'm careful.'

'I'm sure you are.' Evanna's tone was dry as she recalled the rescue effort that had been required to extricate him from the dungeon some weeks earlier. She flicked the brim of his hat with her finger. 'I'm meeting Nurse Walker. Have you seen her?'

'She's in the café by the window eating a *massive* triple chocolate fudge ice cream with extra chocolate flakes. She made me promise not to tell anyone because she says it's pretty hard to lecture people on eating a healthy diet when you're seen in public stuffing yourself with rubbish.' He frowned. 'Actually, she might not have actually said "stuffing yourself", but I think that's what she meant.'

'Disgraceful behaviour for a practice nurse.' Evanna's eyes sparkled with laughter. 'I'll go and tell her off, shall I?'

'Yeah. The ice cream looked good, though, and it's the only thing that really works in this heat. Bye, Nurse Duncan. See you around.'

'Bye, boys. Be careful, now.'

She was still smiling when she pushed open the door of the café and joined her friend at the large round table by the window. It had a view of the harbour and was a perfect place from which to observe the various comings and goings of Glenmore Island. 'You know, if you're going to eat that artery-clogging gloop you should at least do it behind a newspaper or at a table around the back. Eating it in the window is just asking for trouble. I've just heard all about it from Fraser.'

'You're late.' Kyla dropped the spoon and stood up to give her a quick hug. 'You saw Fraser? He's a cheeky monkey. With most of the summer holidays still ahead of us, I wouldn't be surprised if we're pulling him out of another hole soon. It's *so* good to have you back. We've missed you.'

'You've been too busy being newly married to miss me.' Evanna dropped her bag on the floor and pulled out a chair. 'I still haven't quite got over the speed with which you fell in love with our new doctor. You certainly didn't hang around.'

Kyla settled back at the table and dug her spoon into the ice cream. 'When something is right, it's right. And Ethan is perfect.' She waved the spoon. 'At least marrying him meant that he'd stay on the island permanently. Logan is pleased to have another doctor at the surgery.'

'Yes.' Evanna struggled to keep her tone casual. 'So, how is he? Logan is normally hideously busy at this time of year.'

Kyla considered the question. 'OK, I think. I don't know how he does it. It's only just over a year since his wife died but he's holding up really well. I just wish he'd talk about it more.'

Evanna thought of the conversations she'd had with him long into the night. *He'd talked about it with her.* 'I suppose everyone handles things in their own way.'

'Well, Logan always was tough and work keeps him going. That and having a thirteen-month-old daughter.' Kyla leaned back in her chair and called across the café. 'Aunt Meg, can we have another spoon here please? Evanna's tongue is hanging into my ice cream.'

'No, it isn't.' Evanna eyed the ice cream wistfully. 'I'm not like you. Fat never gives you a second glance. If I even *look* at ice cream, I put on a kilo.'

'That's rubbish and if eating ice cream gave me your fantastic curves then I'd eat it for every meal. You look great in that red top. A bit like a flamenco dancer.' She narrowed her eyes. 'Sort of sexy and sultry. All dark hair and dark eyes. But you need to wear your hair loose to complete the effect.'

'It's too hot.' Evanna ran a hand over the back of her neck. 'And the only reason I'm looking sultry is because we're in the middle of a heat wave. I'm boiling.'

'Was it hot in the city?'

'Unbelievable. I honestly don't know how people can live their lives in a place like that. It's all so—' Evanna frowned as she searched for the word '—closed in. There's no air. It's like being in a forest of buildings and everyone is busy, busy, busy. There's no room to breathe, whereas on Glenmore there's just so much space.' She shuddered at the memory and Kyla smiled.

'So you didn't enjoy yourself?'

'I enjoyed the work. It was fantastic to be back on the labour ward. You know I loved my midwifery and I don't exactly get the chance to practise much on Glenmore.'

'What are you complaining about? It's like a rabbit colony here.' Kyla waved the spoon. 'Both Sonia Davies and Marie Tanner are pregnant. And Lucy Finch's baby is only four days old, so you'll be visiting her for a while.'

'I know.' Evanna gave a soft smile. 'I actually delivered Lucy in the labour ward on the mainland. It was amazing and, of course, it's great that Sonia and Marie are pregnant. But it's hardly enough to make up an entire workload.'

'Well, Sandra King had a far-away look on her face this week and I know that she and Paul have been trying for ages, so I wouldn't be surprised if she's in the surgery soon. And we don't just want you for your midwifery skills. This island needs two practice nurses. I know midwifery is your first love, but don't even think about abandoning me!'

'I wouldn't leave you. I love it here and I love the variety.' Evanna glanced out of the window and caught sight of Janet, the practice receptionist, who was walking past, carrying two bags of shopping. She smiled and waved.

'But you love midwifery most of all. You're totally soppy about babies.' Kyla gave a wry smile. 'Go on. Has working on the labour ward made you broody?'

Evanna felt a grey cloud drift across her happiness. 'Of course not,' she lied, turning back to Kyla with a smile. 'How can I be broody when I don't even have a boyfriend? You know I believe in doing things in the right order.'

'You always were an old-fashioned girl.' Kyla watched her

for a moment and then looked up as her aunt approached. 'Aunt Meg, Evanna needs feeding.'

Meg was a plump woman with a generous smile and a mass of curling blonde hair. 'Good to have you home, Evanna.' She wiped her hands on her apron and reached for a pad. 'What can I get you? Same as Kyla?'

'Just a coffee, thanks. Americano. Decaff, no milk.'

'That's all? I've a chocolate cake that's enough to make a woman cry.'

Evanna ignored temptation. 'Just coffee.'

'And how's that going to give you energy through a long day?' Meg tutted her disapproval as she put the pad back in her pocket. 'You need flesh on your bones, lass.'

'I have flesh on my bones,' Evanna said dryly. 'I can't lecture people on losing weight if I'm overweight myself. At the moment I can still fit into my clothes and that's the way I want it to stay, especially given that it's the swimsuit season.'

'Could you stop being so perfect? You're ruining my enjoyment of this ice cream.' Kyla licked her spoon and looked regretfully at the empty dish as Meg removed it and walked back towards the kitchen. 'So—did you meet anyone gorgeous while you were away?'

Evanna hesitated. 'Sort of.'

'Really?' Kyla's eyes were suddenly interested. 'Tell me.'

'There's nothing to tell. He was a registrar in obstetrics and he was really…nice.'

'Nice? What sort of a word is *nice*? It doesn't tell me anything. Was he good-looking? Sexy? Intelligent?'

'All those things. We went out for a few drinks.'

'And?'

'There is no "and."'

'Did you sleep with him?'

'Kyla!' Evanna shot an embarrassed glance across the café

but everyone was engrossed in their own conversations. She answered the question in a low tone. 'No, I did not.'

'Shame.' Kyla was unrepentant. 'If you ask me, you could do with some unbridled passion in your life.'

'I didn't ask you, and my life is fine.' Evanna sat back and gave a smile of thanks as Meg put the coffee in front of her. 'We just had drinks. But it made me think. And I came to a decision.'

'What decision?'

Evanna blew on her coffee to cool it and waited for Meg to walk away before she spoke. 'I'm not doing this any more, Kyla.' Her voice was firm and steady. 'I'm not wasting any more of my life pining after a man who doesn't even notice me.'

Kyla's smile went out like a light bulb in a power cut. 'You're talking about my brother.'

'Of course. Who else? Who else has there ever been for me?' Evanna shook her head and gave a derisive laugh. 'Ever since we played kiss chase in the playground, it's been Logan. I've never even been able to *see* another man if he's in the same room as me. And when he's not in the same room as me, he's in my head. Even when I close my eyes I can still see him. I can see his smile, I can see that wicked gleam in his blue eyes. I can see the way he walks as if he owns the world. And it's a crazy waste of time, because he doesn't even know I exist.'

'He does know you exist.'

'I mean as a woman. When it comes to seeing his patients, making his dinner or caring for his child, he knows I exist,' Evanna said flatly. 'When it comes to anything more personal, I'm invisible.'

'He lost his wife, Evanna.'

'I know that. And I also know that it was over a year ago and, sooner or later, he's going to find someone else to share his life with. And no matter how much I dream that it might be, that someone is *never* going to be me. So I'm over him.' She said it for herself as much as Kyla. *To remind herself of all the promises she'd made to herself while she'd been away.* 'No more moping. No more pining. No more wishing for something that is never going to happen. I'm putting plan A into action. I'm moving on.'

'How can you move on? He's a GP and you're his practice nurse. We all work together.'

'Of course I have to see him at work. And of course I'll help him with Kirsty. He's had a horribly rough time and he's a single father now, so of course I'm going to help with his little girl. But I'm going to have my own life, too.' She felt the confidence rise inside her and suddenly felt strong and determined. Everything was going to be fine. After all, she hadn't seen Logan for a month and she'd survived, hadn't she? There had even been moments when she'd enjoyed herself. A few seconds when she'd managed to forget about him. And she was going to build on that. Seconds would become minutes. Minutes would become hours. 'I'm going to go out.'

Kyla raised an eyebrow. 'With?'

'I don't know.' Evanna sipped her coffee and gave a shrug. 'Anyone who asks me. Nick Hillier?'

'You fancy Nick?'

'No.' Nick was the island policeman and they'd been at school together. 'Not really. It's just that...'

'It's just that he isn't Logan. Wow. That's a really good way to begin a relationship.'

'I don't want to spend the rest of my life by myself,' Evanna said softly, resting her cup carefully back in the saucer. 'You asked me if I was broody and the answer is, yes, I'm broody. But not for a baby in isolation. I want so much more than that. I want to have a home and a family and a man who loves me, and I'm not going to find that while I'm blinded by your brother. I've been stupid about him, I can see that now. The way I feel about him has stopped me even noticing other men, but that's going to change. When I was away, I managed to talk some sense into myself. I went out with the people from the unit and had fun. It was good. And I realise now that it's up to me to build a proper life here and I'm going to do exactly that. No more waiting around and hoping. No more deluding myself. I'm really, really over him. Honestly.'

At that moment the door to the café opened and a man strolled in. He was taller than average, with lean features and a suggestion of stubble on a firm jaw that hinted at the stubborn. His hair was dark and slightly too long at the back, just touching the collar of the blue linen shirt that he wore tucked into a pair of light-coloured trousers. He had broad shoulders and blue eyes that were sharply observant, and all the females in the café turned to stare as he pushed the door shut with the flat of his hand and strolled towards the counter. 'Hi, Meg. Can I have a round of toast, please?' He spoke in a deep, sexy drawl and the coffee cup slipped out of Evanna's shaking fingers and clattered onto the table, spilling the contents.

Kyla uttered a sharp expletive and reached for a pile of napkins, dropping them on the table as she tried to staunch the flow of coffee. 'You're over him?' She kept her voice low so that no one else could hear. 'If you're over him, Evanna Duncan, why are you dropping things when he walks into a room? Plan A obviously isn't working so I hope to goodness you have a decent plan B worked out in that head of yours, because it might be time to make the shift. For goodness' sake—how much coffee was in that cup? It's like a lake here.' She mopped frantically but Evanna didn't even notice. She was too busy trying to control the frantic shaking of her limbs.

'I don't— I can't—'

'Evanna?' Kyla dropped more napkins on the soggy mess,

but her sharp whisper held a note of concern. 'You're as white as chalk—are you all right?'

No. She wasn't all right. Her pulse was thundering at a ridiculous rate and she knew that if she'd tried to stand, she would have sunk to the ground in a heap.

Oh, no, no, no! She'd thought she had her feelings well and truly under control. She'd thought—

Her thoughts froze altogether as Logan strolled over to them, a smile in his wicked blue eyes.

'So this is where both my nurses are hiding. Now that I'm here, we could have a practice meeting. It's long overdue.'

Evanna found it almost impossible not to stare. She'd always found it impossible not to stare at him. In primary school, when she'd been just five years old, she'd gazed at him from the corner of the playground—stared at the dark-haired, blue-eyed god who had come to collect Kyla from school. In secondary school she'd drunk in every detail with the dawning awareness that came with the onset of womanhood. And then he'd left the island to train as a doctor and had returned only for holidays and she'd stared at his photograph—*the one taken on the beach during the summer that he'd been a lifeguard.* His chest was bare and bronzed and he was laughing into the camera.

She still had the photo.

'Evanna.' His mouth moved into a smile and her gaze was drawn to his mouth. It was firm and sensual and, in her opinion, designed for kissing. Not that she'd know, she thought miserably as she tore her eyes away, because Dr Logan MacNeil had never kissed her and was never likely to. He'd kissed just about every girl on the island, but never her. He just didn't think of her that way. In fact, it was probably true to say that he didn't notice her at all. She was part of the island he'd grown up on, as much part of the scenery as the beaches and the mountains.

'Can I join you?' He spoke in that deep voice that always

turned her knees to liquid and made her think of sex and seduction.

'Of course. Hi, Logan.' She struggled to keep her voice casual and quickly moved her hands to her lap so that he couldn't see them shaking.

Her reaction was pathetic, she told herself. About as pathetic as hanging onto an ancient, dog-eared photograph.

Kyla scrunched up the saturated napkins and stood up to throw them in the bin, casting a long, meaningful look in Evanna's direction.

'Well, I'm certainly glad to see you home, Evanna.' Logan sat back as Meg placed the toast and coffee in front of him. 'I've missed you, desperately. Every moment that you were away seemed like an hour.'

Evanna's hands clenched in her lap and she felt an involuntary dart of pleasure at his words. *He'd missed her?* 'R-really? You missed me?'

'Yes, really. How can you doubt it?' He spread butter on his toast with those long, lean fingers that she knew were so skilled with patients. 'It's the summer. Glenmore Island is heaving with tourists and every surgery is packed. *Not* the best time for one of my precious nurses to go swanning off to the mainland for a month, even if it was part of her professional development.' He smiled the smile that had every woman on the island reeling. 'Of course I missed you. Did you think I wouldn't?'

Professional development.

He'd missed her at work. Evanna gritted her teeth and looked away from that charismatic smile. *It was always about work.* She was his practice nurse and nothing more.

She swallowed down the disappointment, reminding herself that she'd always known that. Hadn't she just spent an entire month dissecting their relationship in minute detail? Hadn't she been brutally honest with herself about the way he saw her? The answer was yes to both questions, so why did hearing him confirm her analysis hurt so much? If anything, she should take it as confirmation that she was doing the right thing. And no matter how hard it turned out to be—*and she knew it was going to be incredibly hard*—she was going to move on.

Kyla sat down again. 'Evanna had a good time on her refresher course.' Her tone was cool and pointed, and Logan glanced up from buttering his toast.

'Good.' He bit into the toast and lifted a hand in greeting to one of the locals who was strolling along the quay. 'It's busy out there today. Day-trippers as well as the usual tourists. The lifeguards are going to be busy on the beach. Let's hope it's a quiet one. There's a wind blowing so I wouldn't be surprised if the lifeboat sees some business today.'

Kyla's fingers drummed on the table. 'She met lots of people.' She emphasised each word carefully, as if English wasn't his first language.

Logan dragged his eyes from the window, obviously alerted by something in his sister's tone. 'Who did?'

'Evanna. On her course on the mainland, she *met lots of people.*'

Evanna blushed. 'Kyla…'

But Kyla was still looking at her brother, a dangerous light in blue eyes that were exactly like his. 'She's been away for a month, remember?'

'You're moody today. Of course I remember.' Logan buttered the second piece of toast. 'Why wouldn't I? We've all been covering her clinics because the agency nurse they sent was hopeless. As I said, it's good to have you back, Evanna.'

Kyla gritted her teeth. 'She went out a lot. Met a lovely registrar. Really nice guy. Good-looking. They got on brilliantly.'

'That's good to hear.' Logan finished his toast, licked his

fingers and rose to his feet, his eyes on the street. 'There's Doug McDonald. Excuse me. I've been trying to catch up with him all week. Since he had the heart attack he's afraid to push himself and I think he needs to do more. Perhaps he could go to your exercise class, Evanna? People always seem to like doing that. I suppose they have confidence because the instructor is a nurse. See you in surgery this afternoon. Janet's booked you a full clinic.' He patted her arm and walked towards the door, pausing by a table to exchange a few words with the couple that ran a small guesthouse near one of the island's best beaches.

'You see?' Evanna's voice was soft and she blinked several times to clear her vision. 'I'm just a piece of medical equipment. His practice nurse. He feels the same way about me as he does about the ECG machine. We're both useful tools that help his life run smoothly. If he could, he'd plug me into the electricity supply to make me function more efficiently.'

Kyla was simmering with frustration. 'I'm starting to think my brother is thick.'

'He isn't thick. He's very clever, you know that. He just isn't interested and that's fine.'

'It isn't fine. How can you say that it's fine?'

Because it had to be. What choice did she have? 'You can't make someone love you, Kyla,' Evanna muttered, reaching down to pick up her bag. Suddenly she just wanted to go home. Back to the peace and tranquillity of her little cottage. She needed to get her thoughts back together before she started work. *Needed to rediscover some of the strength and resolve she'd found during her time on the mainland.*

She dropped some money on the table for her coffee just as the door opened and Fraser stood there, his hat askew and his face scarlet. *'Dr MacNeil!'* He was breathless from running. 'I saw— You have to come—*now.*' He snatched in another tortured breath and Logan turned swiftly, concern in his eyes.

'Fraser? What did you see?' He strode over to the boy and put a hand on his shoulder. 'You must have run like the wind to be this out of breath. It's all right. Calm down. Now, what's happened?'

Fraser waved a hand towards the beach beyond the harbour. 'Drowning.' He sucked in a breath. 'Kid in a rubber dinghy thing. Fell in.'

Without wasting time on questions, Logan left the café at a run with Fraser at his heels.

Evanna and Kyla followed, dodging the throngs of tourists ambling along the quay before sprinting down the steps onto the sand.

'He's gone!' A young woman holding a tiny baby was running up and down the sand at the edge of the waves, frantically scanning the water. 'He was in the boat and now he's gone!'

'I saw him.' Fraser backed away from the mother and moved closer to Logan, instinctively seeking protection from the woman's mounting hysteria and the baby's howling. 'We were up on the cliffs. He leant out of the boat with this bucket thing and a wave caught the boat and he fell. Straight down.'

The woman's wails turned to screams and Logan took Fraser to one side, his tone urgent.

'Where, exactly?' He was ripping off his shirt as he spoke. 'And how long ago did he fall?'

Fraser shrugged. 'About two minutes? We started running down as soon as it happened. The wind's blowing off shore so I suppose it was probably there.' Fraser pointed. 'You want me to go in and look?'

'No. I want you to stay right here.' Logan thrust his clothes into Fraser's hands and handed him a mobile phone. 'Call the coastguard on that and then go to my car and get my bag. Here are the keys. Then stay here with Evanna and do everything she says. Everything.'

'OK.' Fraser nodded importantly and punched the number into the phone. 'I'll give them the details. Be careful, Dr MacNeil.'

Logan looked at Evanna, his ice-blue eyes sharp and alert. 'Beach duty.'

She nodded, reading his mind. He wanted her to coordinate efforts on the beach. He didn't want any of the tourists plunging into the waves on a rescue mission, because they were likely to get into trouble. *He didn't want little Fraser going in.* He wanted her to give support to the mother and then help the rescue services.

Logan lifted the buoyancy aid that he'd grabbed from the top of the beach and ran with a long-limbed, athletic stride towards the sea. At any other time she would have admired the strength and power of his body but the crisis was unfolding in front of her. The mother was screaming now, a thin, high-pitched panicky noise that cut through the air like a knife. A crowd had gathered in the way that humans always gathered when they scented disaster.

Kyla moved them back. 'Come on, now. Nothing to see.' Her tone was clipped. Efficient. 'Move right back, please. Go to the far end of the beach. Right back. That's right. We're going to need to land a helicopter here.'

Fraser was speaking to the coastguard on the phone and Evanna turned to the mother and slid an arm round her shoulders.

'You poor thing. You must be frantic with worry but try and calm down so that we can ask you some questions,' she said gently. 'How old is he?'

'Six.' The mother gave a gulp and jiggled the baby to try and soothe it. 'He's just six. Jason. He's so little.'

'And he was in some sort of boat?'

'I only turned my back for a minute. I was changing the baby.' She sucked air in and out of her lungs, her eyes wild. 'It was just a minute.'

And a minute was more than long enough when water was

involved, Evanna thought as she squinted towards the sea.
'What boat?' She couldn't see a boat. Only a small toy blow-
up boat of the sort that people used in swimming pools.

'There! That's it.' The mother pointed to the toy. 'We bought
it in the beach shop on the quay.'

'He was in that?' Evanna couldn't quite believe that anyone
would have considered such a flimsy toy sufficient protection
for a child in open water and her shock must have sounded in
her voice because the woman stiffened defensively.

'He was just playing near the shore. I thought he was fine.
It was just for a minute…' The woman was sobbing again,
clutching at Evanna who supported her and glanced towards
Fraser with a question in her eyes.

He slipped Logan's phone into the pocket of his jeans and
gave her a thumbs-up.

Evanna smiled her approval and watched as he sprinted
across the sand, arms and legs pumping as he went to fetch
Logan's bag. 'The lifeboat is on its way.'

The baby was red in the face from howling and Evanna glanced
towards Kyla. She gave a nod and strode up to the woman.

'Let me take the baby,' she offered briskly. 'One less thing
for you to worry about.'

'I don't want to let her out of my sight.'

'Kyla is a nurse at the local practice,' Evanna said quickly.
'We both are.'

'Oh—in that case, I know I'm just upsetting her.' Struggling
with her own sobs, the woman handed the baby over and Kyla
expertly tucked the squalling child against her shoulder and
walked away.

Evanna calmed the woman as best she could and watched
as Logan dived into the waves. He cut through the water with
a powerful front crawl, reached the little boat and then made a
guess as to where the boy might have fallen.

'Wow.' Fraser was standing beside her, Logan's bag at his feet, his eyes wide with hero-worship as he stared. 'Dr MacNeil must be diving down to look below the surface. He's a brilliant swimmer, isn't he, Nurse Duncan? He got a bronze Olympic medal, didn't he? And he saved that kid two summers ago and it was *all* over the papers. I'm going to be a lifeguard when I'm older, like he was. And a doctor. He's so cool.'

Evanna tried to look relaxed but the tension gripped her like a vice. 'He's a good swimmer, Fraser,' she agreed, as much to reassure herself as the little boy and the mother.

The woman was clutching Evanna's hand. 'We had a terrible night,' she whispered. 'The baby cries all the time and my husband and I are both exhausted so I said I'd bring them both down to the beach for an hour to give him a chance to catch up on some sleep. When Jason asked if he could take the boat in the sea, I didn't even think it would be dangerous. I imagined he'd just stay by the shore.'

'It shelves quite deeply here and the currents are strong,' Fraser said solemnly, and Evanna saw the woman's face pale. And then noticed something.

'There. Can you see the lifeboat?' She lifted a hand and pointed. 'They'll be able to help in the search.'

'But if he's at the bottom of the ocean…' The woman choked on the words.

Then Logan's head bobbed above the water for a few seconds before he disappeared again, this time further out to sea.

Three times his head appeared and then disappeared and on the fourth occasion he came up holding the body of the little boy.

'He's got him. Cool.' Fraser's voice was triumphant but Evanna saw what the mother immediately saw. *That the little boy was limp and lifeless.*

'Spread out your rug,' Evanna ordered. 'Dr MacNeil is going to need somewhere to put him. And get all the layers you can find.'

'It's August.' The woman looked at her blankly and Evanna saw the shock in her eyes.

'It doesn't make any difference that it's August. The sea is still freezing and we're going to need to warm him up. Fraser.' Evanna looked at the boy. 'You and your friends clear a spot for the helicopter to land. You know the drill. Everyone to secure everything that moves. Go. *Move.*'

But she spoke the last few words to the air because Fraser had already sprinted off to do what needed to be done.

Logan strode out of the water, carrying the boy level in his arms. 'I'm going to try tipping him upside down.' His expression was grim. 'He was stuck on the bottom. He must have caught his foot in seaweed. It took me several goes to free him.'

'No!' The mother was screaming with horror and another holidaymaker took her to one side and put her arms around her, giving the medical team space to work.

'Evanna?' Logan's voice was sharp as he laid the boy flat on the rug. 'Did you get my stuff from the car?'

'Fraser did. It's all here.' She flipped open the case. 'His name is Jason and he's six years old. Do you want to start CPR?'

'Not yet.' Logan felt for a carotid pulse. 'I'm hoping he's just bradycardic. Come on, Jason. Wake up, for us. Damn. He's in respiratory arrest.'

'Logan—'

'Respiratory arrest precedes cardiac arrest in drowning. He's got a pulse.' Logan started to examine the boy more thoroughly, his hands swift and skilled. 'Did Fraser manage to bring the oxygen?'

'It's here.'

There was a clacking sound overhead as the helicopter arrived but Logan was focused on Jason, leaving others to deal with the arrival of the helicopter. 'He's breathing but his core temperature is thirty-four degrees. We need to warm him up. What layers do we have?'

Evanna reached forward and covered the boy, noticing that his face was chalky white. 'Do you want to aspirate his stomach?'

Just then the boy screwed up his face and started to cough violently, and Logan gave Evanna a swift nod. 'We have lift-off. Jason? Speak to me. You're worrying your mother. Wake up.'

The boy's eyes fluttered open and he started to cough again.

Logan turned him into the recovery position. 'Good boy. You're all right. You've swallowed a bit of seawater but you'll soon be feeling better. Evanna, this oxygen mask doesn't fit properly. I need something smaller.'

The paramedic from the helicopter sprinted across to them with a case of equipment. 'How's he doing?'

Logan wiped a forearm across his forehead. 'Better than we could have hoped. He's breathing but he's very cold still and he seems to have aspirated water so he'll need to go to hospital for a check.'

The mother sank onto the sand beside Jason, tears pouring down her cheeks. 'He needs to go to hospital? Can't you just watch him here?'

'This is a small island,' Logan said gently, 'and while we are capable of dealing with dire emergencies if the need arises, we do try and anticipate and avoid them whenever possible. I'm sure Jason is going to make an uneventful recovery but, to be on the safe side, I'd rather he made that recovery in the hospital. I'm sure they'll only keep him in for a night.'

'They have rooms for parents,' Evanna said quickly as she found a smaller oxygen mask, 'so you can be with him the whole time.'

'I can go with him in the helicopter?'

The paramedic helped switch masks. 'Of course, but you can't bring the baby.'

'I can leave her with my husband. He'll be fine with her for a day, although the crying will probably drive him mad. We're in one of the beach houses just up there.'

'Go and give the baby to your husband and then you can come with us.' The paramedic squatted down beside Logan. 'Do you want to get a line in just to be on the safe side?'

'Yes, ideally, although he's so cold it's going to be pretty hard getting in a peripheral line.' Logan picked up one of the boy's arms and rubbed the skin. 'We might be lucky.'

With a last, frightened look towards Jason, the mother sprinted across the beach to Kyla who was still holding the baby. Kyla's husband Ethan, the other island GP, arrived and immediately took in the situation. 'You've had one trip to the mainland already today. I'll take this one, Logan.'

'I wouldn't mind, if that's all right with you.' Logan slid the needle into the vein and gave a nod of satisfaction. 'Good. Tape it firmly, Evanna. I don't want to have to try that again.'

Ethan went to supervise the helicopter landing and Kyla turned her attention to the mother.

'His colour is better.' Logan checked the child's pulse again.

'We're ready to transfer him.' Ethan arrived with a stretcher and they carefully lifted the boy, covered him with blankets and secured him. 'You'd better give me a handover.'

Leaving the paramedics to transfer the child into the helicopter, Logan pulled his colleague to one side, told him what had happened and detailed the first aid they'd given.

Watching the helicopter take off, Evanna suddenly realised that her legs were shaking. 'What a day. I think I've aged twenty years and I've only been back on the island for ten minutes!'

Logan sat down next to her. 'I only came down to the quay because I was trying to accidentally on purpose bump into Doug McDonald. I wanted to see how he was doing without looking too obvious.'

'If you hadn't been in the café, the child would have drowned. You were amazing.'

He brushed some sand from his legs and pulled his shirt back on. 'I was doing my job, Evanna. Stop making me sound like some sort of hero.'

'First aid for a drowning incident, that's your job, but going into that water to save a child?' Evanna's voice was soft. 'That's not your job, Logan.'

But he'd do it anyway because that was the sort of man he was.

Logan stood up and pulled on his trousers. 'Fraser was the one who saved the boy. If he hadn't had his eyes open and acted swiftly we would never have found Jason in time.' He lifted a hand and the boy came running over.

'Dr MacNeil. I did everything you said.'

Logan put a hand on his shoulder. 'You're a hero, Fraser.' His voice was gruff. 'You kept a clear head and you didn't panic.'

'You never panic.'

'I'm thirty-one years old. You're twelve.'

Fraser shrugged. 'Bet you didn't panic when you were twelve either. Will that boy be all right? Is he going to die, Dr MacNeil?'

'Thanks to you, I don't think he's going to die.' Logan ran a hand through the boy's hair. 'How's that scar of yours?'

Fraser grinned. 'Wicked. The girls all want to look at it.'

Logan winked and grinned at him, man to man. 'Then let them look. See you around, Fraser.'

'Yeah.' Fraser hooked his fingers in the waistband of his oversized surf shorts and scuffed a foot across the sand. 'The boys and I are going up to the ruins this afternoon. Just to look.'

'Well don't go falling into the dungeons.' Logan watched him go and gave a shake of his head. 'He's growing up.'

'Aisla will be so proud of him.' Evanna stood up, wiped her damp hands down her shorts and started gathering up their equipment. 'I ought to be going. I've got a surgery this afternoon and I haven't even been home yet. My luggage is still in my boot.'

He turned to look at her, his blue eyes searching. 'It's good to have you back. You're always good in a crisis.'

Evanna blushed slightly. And that was how he saw her, of course. Sensible, practical Evanna. Good-in-a-crisis Evanna. What would he say, she wondered, if she told him that she didn't want to be good in a crisis? She didn't want to be sensible, practical Evanna. For once in her life she wanted to be someone's hot fantasy.

She wanted to be *his* hot fantasy.

CHAPTER TWO

THE road clung to the coast, winding high above tiny bays that were accessible only by foot, bays that had once been fiercely defended against Viking invasion. Evanna drove carefully, alert for tourists too busy admiring the view to watch the road. To her right she could see the ruins of the castle where young Fraser had found himself trapped earlier in the summer. To her left was the sparkling ocean, waves crashing onto jagged rocks and, in the distance, the outline of the mainland.

There was nowhere like Glenmore, but today the excitement of being home was missing and she felt frustrated and cross with herself. *And disappointed.* She'd spent a month lecturing herself about the futility of being in love with Dr Logan MacNeil and she'd genuinely thought that finally she had her feelings under control, so the intensity of her reaction in the café was disheartening.

She'd wanted so badly to feel indifferent.

Her spirits lifted slightly as she parked outside her little white cottage with its blue shutters and views of the sea. Buying it had stretched her budget to snapping point but there was never a single moment when she regretted the extravagance. As a child she'd walked past the same cottage with her parents and had stared in wonder. To her it had always looked like the gingerbread house from the fairy tale. Roses clustered around the door and snaked under the windows. It was a friendly house and the fact that it was small had never bothered her. It was hers. And she'd made it her home.

She'd thrown cheerful rugs onto the polished wooden floors, hung filmy white curtains from the windows and filled tall vases with flowers from the garden and glass bowls with shells that she'd found on the beach. And if the second bedroom was so tiny there was barely room for a bed, did it really matter? All the people she knew lived on the island anyway, so she rarely had to find room for overnight guests. Her own bedroom was large enough, and that was what counted. Light streamed through the window and she'd placed the bed so that the first thing she saw when she opened her eyes was the sea. It was a perfect place to sleep, dream and wake up. A room built for lovers.

It was just a shame that she didn't have a lover.

Letting herself into her cottage, Evanna picked up a pile of post and walked into the sunny yellow kitchen that she'd painted herself over a gloomy February weekend earlier in the year. Usually the view from the window across the cliffs cheered her up but today she found it hard to smile.

Telling herself off for being pathetic, she sifted through her post, binning all the junk mail and putting the bills neatly to one side. Then she opened a white envelope and found a quote for redoing her bathroom.

Suddenly resolute, she picked up the phone. 'Craig? Evanna here. About your quote…'

Five minutes later she'd confirmed it all and written out a cheque for the down payment. It would be wonderfully indulgent to have a new bathroom and it was long overdue. The bathroom was the only room that hadn't been touched since she'd bought the cottage three years earlier. It would use the last of her savings but she decided that it was worth it.

Resolving to throw open all the doors and windows at the weekend to freshen the place, Evanna showered, changed and then climbed back into her little car and made her way to the surgery in time for her afternoon surgery.

'I gather you had a drama on the beach. You've a big list, Evanna.' Janet, the receptionist, handed her a computer printout and a pile of letters. 'Plenty of people have been holding on, waiting to see you. And Lucy wanted to know if you could call on your way home to check on the baby because the cord is looking a bit sticky and she's worried. You can tell it's her first. Every time the little one blinks, she rings Logan. He's incredibly patient with her.'

Logan was patient with everyone. 'I'll call, of course I will. I was going to anyway.'

'Who do I have first?

'Sandra King. She's sitting in the waiting room with a dopey look on her face so I think we all know the reason for her appointment.' Janet winked and Evanna thought back to Kyla's comment.

'Let's hope so. Is she first?'

'Yes.' Janet leaned forward and lowered her voice. 'I made it a double appointment, just to be on the safe side. I had one of my feelings. If I'm wrong, you can use the time to catch up on some of the paperwork that your replacement didn't touch.'

'Good thinking.' Evanna walked through to her room and sat down at her desk. It felt good to be back. She turned her head and glanced around the room. In the corner was a basket stuffed with toys that she'd selected herself and the walls were covered in posters that she'd chosen from the wide selection available to her. Everything was just as she'd left it. The heaviness that had settled inside her lifted and she switched on her computer and pressed the buzzer.

Sandra tapped on the door a few seconds later, her husband by her side. 'I'm pregnant, Nurse Duncan.' She was bursting to tell the news, her smile dominating her pretty face. 'I missed a period and I did the test yesterday and it was positive.'

Full marks to Kyla for observation, then. 'That's great, Sandra. Congratulations.'

'I couldn't sleep at all last night, just thinking about it. I want to have it here, on the Island, and I want you to deliver it,' Sandra blurted out, and Evanna gave a careful smile.

'Why would you want to have him, or her, at home?'

'Because I was born on Glenmore and I want the same for my children.'

'You were the third child,' Evanna said evenly, opening her drawer and pulling out the appropriate forms. 'First babies are better born in hospital, Sandra. I can quite understand your wish for the delivery to be as natural as possible, but we can achieve that in hospital.'

'But I'm young and healthy. Is it because it makes more work for you?'

'It isn't the work for me that's a problem. I love the home deliveries. But having a baby at home does come with risks,' Evanna said, her voice level. 'No obstetrician would ever advise a woman to have her first baby at home. And the other problem is that Glenmore is quite remote. No matter how carefully we monitor you, things can change very quickly in childbirth. Emergencies do happen and when they do, you want to be within easy reach of a specialist unit.'

'But there's the helicopter.'

The memories came rushing back. The evil weather. *Catherine critically ill.* 'If the weather is bad, it can't fly,' Evanna reminded her gruffly, and Sandra was silent for a moment.

'I'm sorry. I didn't think. You're thinking about what happened to Dr MacNeil's wife, aren't you? When Catherine became ill they wanted to fly her to the mainland but the helicopter couldn't get here. She died because of it.'

And Logan, griefstricken and racked by guilt, had made a heroic effort to save the baby.

His daughter. Little Kirsty, now a bouncy, healthy one-year-old.

Evanna felt sadness swamp her but kept her expression neutral. This wasn't the time to think about Logan. 'Catherine MacNeil was an extremely unusual case. It's unlikely that the outcome would have been different, even if she'd been in a consultant unit on the mainland.'

'But we all know that's why Dr MacNeil won't consider home births.' Sandra sighed and glanced at her husband. 'I hadn't really thought about it properly. Perhaps it would be more sensible to have it in hospital. What do you think?'

Her husband nodded, visibly relieved by her change of heart. 'Definitely. You know that was always my preference.'

'The community unit is lovely. I just spent a week there as part of my refresher course,' Evanna told them. 'I did three weeks on the labour ward in the hospital and a week at the unit. They've done up their delivery rooms to look like bedrooms so it's home away from home, really. I think you'll like it.'

'But I can have most of my care with you and Dr MacNeil?'

Evanna nodded. 'Absolutely.'

'Will I need to go to the hospital at all?'

'You'll need to go to there for an ultrasound scan between ten and thirteen weeks,' Evanna told her, reaching for a leaflet, 'and then again between eighteen and twenty weeks for another scan. Apart from that, providing there are no problems, we can do everything else here. Today I'll take some blood from you so that we can check your blood group and screen you for some conditions.'

She ran through all the tests that could be done and Sandra looked at her husband.

'We want all of it, don't we? I'm not taking any chances. You know how long we've waited for this to happen.'

'Can you step on the scales for me, Sandra?' Evanna stood up and reached for some blood bottles. 'I'll just weigh you and check your blood pressure and then I'll take the blood. You can make an appointment with Dr MacNeil to discuss the results and he can listen to your heart and lungs and that sort of thing.'

'I don't even dare look at how much I weigh. Mind you, I've been feeling so sick that I've stopped eating so that might help.' Sandra closed her eyes tightly and pulled a face. 'Is it awful?'

'No.' Evanna scribbled the number on a pad ready to input into the computer. 'Have you actually been sick?'

'Oh, yes.' Sandra stepped off the scales and slipped her shoes back on. 'The moment I wake up I just need to dash to the bathroom. It's awful.'

'Try eating a dry biscuit before you move in the morning.' Evanna checked her blood pressure and recorded the result. 'That's fine. Now, I'll just take that blood sample and you can do me a urine sample and then we'll leave you in peace for a while! Let me give you a pack of information that you can flick through when you have a moment.'

'Is it still all right for me to use the gym?'

'Absolutely.' Evanna took a pack out of her desk and handed it to Sandra. 'It's important to stay fit and active. You're not ill, you're pregnant.'

Sandra smiled. 'I know. And it feels fantastic. I don't even care about the sickness, I'm so excited.'

'It's normal to feel sick in the first few months of pregnancy but we'll keep an eye on the sickness. Let me know if it gets worse. Make an appointment to see Dr MacNeil and another to see me next week. That way, if you have any questions from what you've read, we'll have plenty of time to go over it. I'll send the forms through to the hospital and they'll contact you about the scan. They always try and give islanders a late morning or early afternoon appointment so you have time to get the first ferry out and the last ferry home.'

'Thanks, Nurse Duncan.' Sandra virtually floated out of the room and Evanna watched her go with a wistful smile.

What would it be like, she wondered, *to know that you had a new life growing inside you?*

Giving herself a mental shake, she stood up and walked into Logan's room. 'I've just seen Sandra. She's pregnant and she'll be making an appointment to see you for a check-up.'

Logan had his eyes fixed to the computer screen. 'Tell me you talked her out of having a home birth.'

'I talked her out of it. How did you know she was even thinking about it?'

'I heard a rumour in the pub.' His long fingers tapped several keys and the printer whirred. 'Why does everyone around here seem to be pregnant?'

'Because it's a natural consequence of relationships?' Evanna kept her voice steady. 'I've put all Sandra's observations onto the computer so it should be easy enough to just add in the results of your examination.'

'Thanks. Ethan just rang from the hospital. They've admitted Jason to keep an eye on him.'

'I can't believe she let a six-year-old go out into the Atlantic in a blow-up boat.' Evanna shuddered as she thought of what might have happened. 'Why do people leave their brains behind when they go on holiday?'

'I don't know.' Logan rubbed a hand over the back of his neck. 'That beach is clearly marked as unsafe for inflatable boats but perhaps she didn't see the sign.'

'The baby is obviously wearing them out.' Evanna thought

about what the woman had said. 'I might call later in the week and check on them. I hope Jason is going to be all right. I dread to think how long he was under the water for.'

'Hypothermia can actually give some protection against hypoxia. There have been cases of children recovering after being submerged in cold water for more than forty minutes.' Logan shrugged. 'Once the core temperature drops below thirty-two degrees Celsius, the brain needs less oxygen. Because children get cold very quickly, generally much faster than adults, they might reach that low core temperature before damage occurs from lack of oxygen.'

'But presumably you're worried or you wouldn't have called for the helicopter.'

'There can be late complications, obviously, which is why we transferred him to hospital, just to be on the safe side.' Logan stood up. 'But on the whole the prognosis is reasonable. He was submerged for less than ten minutes, he's young and his core temperature was thirty-four. On the downside, all the signs were that he did aspirate seawater, so they'll need to keep an eye on him until they're sure he's all right. They're going to miss a few days of their holiday.'

'In the circumstances, they're lucky that's all that they're missing.'

'Evanna, about Saturday…' Logan glanced towards her. 'Kyla and I are having a barbecue in your honour. Usual crowd. Six o'clock, my place. We're starting early so that Kirsty can join in. Is that all right with you?'

Evanna's heart lifted and then sank. She should say no. Hadn't she promised herself that she wasn't going to spend so much time with him? It was bad enough seeing him at work, without seeing him socially. But to refuse would look odd because they always socialised in a big group. She just had to adjust her own attitude. She had to try to look at him differently. 'I— That will be lovely.'

'What's the matter?' His eyes searched her face. 'You don't seem your usual cheerful self.'

What could she possibly say to that?

She could hardly confess that she was trying not to be herself because she badly needed to stop loving him! At the moment she would have happily become someone entirely different. Not that that would necessarily help, she thought gloomily, because half the women on the island were in love with Logan MacNeil. The other half was either too old or happily married.

He was perceptive, she acknowledged, about absolutely everything except her feelings for him. And perhaps that was just as well. She didn't really want him knowing how she felt. It would damage their friendship and make things too awkward.

'I'm fine, Logan.' She kept her tone light. 'Just a bit tired after the drive.'

He was still watching her. 'It's probably being in the city. It's far more exhausting than living here, on the island. Well, get some rest before Saturday. Meg, Kyla and a bunch of the cousins are going to be there and I know they'll be disappointed if you don't make it. And Kirsty has really missed you. You have a way with her that no one else has.'

What about you, Logan? she wanted to ask. *Did you miss me, too?* Instead, she smiled through stiff lips. 'In that case, I'll try and be there.' She left the room and bumped into Kyla, who grabbed her wrist and dragged her into the treatment room.

'You look as though you've just been to the dentist for root-canal treatment. What's wrong?'

Evanna told her and then gave a wan smile. 'What am I supposed to do? If I avoid him then I also avoid all the people I love, like Kirsty, you, Meg—your cousins—' She broke off and chewed her lip. 'That's the trouble. I promised myself that I was going to spend less time with him but if I do that then I don't have a social life.'

'It would be much simpler if he just realised that he loved you,' Kyla said gruffly, resting her hips on the couch. 'I've come up with plan B. Plan A, which was for you to forget about him, obviously isn't going to work. So plan B is to make him notice *you*. Once he notices you, he'll realise that he's been in love with you all his life.'

'He married Catherine. He was in love with Catherine.'

'Maybe. But life moves on and I also know that you're perfect for him.'

'Don't start that again.' Evanna started to turn away but Kyla grabbed her arm.

'Just hear me out.' Kyla's voice was urgent. 'I think one of the problems is that you grew up with Logan. You've been my best friend for ever and he's used to seeing you around. He sees you as my friend. His practice nurse. So we need to change all that.'

'And how are we going to do that?'

Kyla grinned. 'Operation makeover. Don't be offended. You're already stunning, it's just that we need to make your charms a little more obvious, so that my thick brother sits up and takes notice of something other than your skill with his patients.'

'What do you want me to do?' Despite her love for her friend, Evanna found it hard to keep the exasperation out of her voice. 'Strap a sign to my body?'

'Figuratively speaking.' Kyla tilted her head to one side. 'Fancy a shopping trip after work tomorrow? Alison has some really nice dresses in the boutique and she's open until eight in the summer. We could grab an early supper in the café afterwards. It would be fun.'

Evanna thought of her mortgage. *Of her new bathroom.* 'I already have a perfectly good wardrobe.'

'But whenever you meet up with my brother you're either in uniform, because you're working, or you're in jeans, because you're looking after Kirsty. That red top looked fabulous on you, but let's make it a red dress.'

'I wear jeans because they're practical.'

'True. But how about forgetting the practical for once and going for the glamorous?'

Evanna stared at her. 'If I turn up to babysit Kirsty in a tiara and diamonds, Logan will have me locked up.'

'Saturday isn't about babysitting. It's a party and I'm not talking about a tiara and diamonds, just something more sexy and frivolous than you would normally wear. Let's just try it. Anyway, shopping is always fun. I'll pick you up from your house.'

'Kyla—'

'Just try it, and then if Logan still doesn't notice you, I'll back off.'

'He won't notice me,' Evanna said flatly. 'It wouldn't matter if I turned up to the barbecue stark naked. He still wouldn't notice me.'

'Trust me,' Kyla said smugly. 'He's going to notice you.'

Evanna dropped in to check on Lucy on her way home from the surgery and was pleased to see her outside in the garden with the pram.

'I thought she might enjoy being out of doors,' Lucy explained as she walked up the path to meet Evanna. 'I've kept her in the shade but she's been crying a bit and being pushed around seems to soothe her.'

'It often does and I quite agree that taking her outside is a good idea. Janet said you're worried about her cord.'

Lucy pulled a face. 'It looks a bit gooey. Do you mind taking a look?'

'Of course not. That's why I'm here. And I'd like to take a look at you, too. How have you been feeling?'

'Excited. Nervous. Being a mum is scary. Knowing that I'm completely responsible for her keeps me awake at night.' Lucy carefully lifted the baby out of the pram. 'Her eyes are a bit sticky, too. Logan gave me some gauze and told me to use that and boiled water to clean them.'

'That sounds like a good strategy. Let's go inside so that I can have a proper look at her.'

'It's so hot today, I've had all the doors and windows open because none of us can sleep at night. I'm really worried that the baby will overheat.'

'Lay her on her back and keep the window open a crack,' Evanna advised, carefully placing the baby on the couch and undoing the poppers on her vest. 'Hello, you gorgeous thing. Can I look at your tummy?' She spoke softly to the baby and Lucy sighed.

'You're so confident when you handle her. I wish I was like that. I'm all fingers and thumbs and I'm terrified that I'm going to drop her or do something wrong. I feel completely ignorant.'

Evanna's eyes slid to the stack of baby books on the coffee-table and she suppressed a smile. 'You're not ignorant, Lucy,' she murmured, turning the nappy down, 'just naturally apprehensive. Mothers should be mothers.'

'I keep ringing Logan,' Lucy confessed. 'Any day now he's going to scream at me for bothering him with trivia.'

'Logan's never yelled at a worried patient in his life. Her cord looks fine, Lucy. Just keep cleaning it the way I showed you in hospital.'

'It isn't infected?'

'No. But try to fold the nappy over so that it doesn't rub.'

'She's so tiny the nappies swamp her.'

Evanna smiled and closed the poppers on the little vest. 'She'll soon grow. How's the feeding going? Are you feeding her yourself?'

'Yes. I really wanted to, you know that. It's hurting quite a bit, though.'

'Is she latching on properly?'

'I suppose so. I don't know really. We're both amateurs.' Lucy gave a helpless shrug. 'She's due a feed now. Could you watch and tell me if we're doing it right?'

'Of course. You make yourself comfortable and I'll go and fetch you a drink of water. It's important to drink plenty when you're feeding, especially when the weather is as hot as it is today.'

Evanna walked through to the kitchen, fetched a glass of water and returned to the sitting room.

'I'm trying to start on a different side each time, like you told me. Ouch.' Lucy winced as the baby's mouth closed over her nipple and Evanna put the glass down on the table and walked over to help.

'She needs more of your breast in her mouth. What's happening is that she's just playing with your nipple, which is why you're getting sore.' Evanna gently repositioned the baby and watched closely as the little jaws clamped down again. 'There. That's better. Does that still hurt?'

'No.' Lucy gave a smile of relief. 'Will you move in with me? I need you here for every feed.'

'You're doing brilliantly. In a few weeks' time this will feel like second nature. Is she doing plenty of wet and dirty nappies?'

'Oh, yes.'

'And are you bleeding much now?'

Lucy shook her head. 'Just spots, you know? Nothing dramatic.'

'Good. We'll just let her finish feeding and then I'll examine you. I want to feel the height of your uterus just to check that it's contracting properly.'

Evanna stayed another hour, answered a non-stop stream of questions from Lucy, satisfied herself that all was well and then finally made her way back to her cottage.

It was hard not to feel envious of Lucy's happiness. Would

it ever be her? *Would she ever be settled with a man that loved her and a baby of her own?*

Reminding herself that she had a great deal to be thankful for, she let herself into her cottage and walked through to her kitchen to make herself supper.

'That one's perfect.' Kyla stood back with her eyes narrowed and Evanna sighed.

'It's too short.' *And too expensive.*

'Too short for what? You have fantastic legs. Stop hiding them under jeans.'

Evanna stared down at herself self-consciously. 'I'm too old for a dress this short.'

'You're twenty-six! And you still look like a teenager. Stop making excuses.' Kyla was laughing as she grabbed a pair of shoes. 'Try these. They'd look great with that dress.'

'I wouldn't be able to walk in them.'

'You don't need to walk,' Kyla said airily, riffling through the rails again and pulling out a scarlet top. 'You can park right outside and just teeter up the path. All you need to do is turn up and look gorgeous. And these would look nice with your jeans on a different occasion so you'll get plenty of wear out of them.'

Evanna gave up arguing and slid her feet into the shoes. 'I'll break my ankle.'

'Don't be so negative. Take a look at yourself in the mirror.'

Evanna stepped forward with a sigh. 'I just don't feel comfortable in anything this short. I'm going to spend my whole evening tugging the—' She broke off as she stared at her reflection. 'Oh.'

'Yes, oh.' Kyla's grin was triumphant as she stretched out a hand and removed the clip from Evanna's hair. 'And you don't need that. Time to let your hair down, Cinderella.'

Evanna's dark curls tumbled over her shoulders. 'I look a mess.'

'You look sexy,' Kyla breathed. 'Incredibly sexy. If Logan doesn't notice you as a woman dressed like that, I'm willing to admit defeat.'

Evanna stared at herself, forced to admit that she did look good. In fact, she looked better than good. The dress skimmed her figure, hinting at curves rather than clinging, and it suited her colouring. She smiled and shook her head. 'This is far too glamorous for a barbecue in the garden.'

'It's perfect. Why are you inventing excuses?'

Evanna was silent for a moment and then she let out a long breath. 'Because I'm scared?' She turned to look at her friend and the smile on her face faltered. 'I'm scared that I'm just setting myself up for yet another knock.'

'You're perfect for each other,' Kyla said softly, all the humour gone from her face. 'Any day now he's going to wake up and realise that.'

Evanna slipped back into the changing room and wriggled out of the dress.

The dress made her feel good. Feminine. But it was an extravagance she couldn't afford.

Wearing her jeans and T-shirt, she stepped out of the changing room with the dress over her arm and the shoes dangling from her fingers. 'It's too expensive, Kyla.'

'It's in the sale.' Alison, who owned the boutique, strolled up to them and named a price that made Evanna stare.

'But it can't possibly be that cheap. I saw the tag.'

'I haven't forgotten what you did for Mum when she was ill,' Alison said gruffly, removing the tag and taking the dress and shoes from Evanna. 'Call it a thank-you from me.'

Evanna was embarrassed. 'You really don't have to—'

'I want to,' Alison said gruffly, folding the dress around tissue paper and sliding it into a bag. 'My mum always said you were an angel. You deserve to look like one.'

CHAPTER THREE

'THIS is an emergency and I have private health care,' boomed a man's voice. 'Just get me a doctor. Call the helicopter or whatever it is you do around these godforsaken parts!'

Evanna heard the commotion in the reception area from her room and hurried out at the same time as Logan.

It was two days after her arrival home and she'd been working non stop to catch up with everything that she'd missed while she'd been away.

The man was looming over the desk, his expression threatening. Sweat beaded on his brow and his stomach bulged against a T-shirt that was too tight. 'We're only here for a week. If I waste a morning, that's a chunk of my holiday gone!'

'Obviously we're doing our best to see everyone,' Janet said smoothly, 'but Dr Walker was called out on an emergency and Dr MacNeil is seeing his patients, too, and that means that—'

'I keep telling you I have private health care! I can pay.' The man pulled a fat wallet out of his back pocket and lifted an eyebrow. 'How much to jump the queue?'

Logan stepped up behind him. 'We don't offer private health care,' he said calmly, his ice-blue eyes narrowed and assessing as he looked at the man. 'Here on Glenmore, it isn't necessary.

People get seen according to need. If there's no urgency, they wait in line.'

'Well, then, you need to organise yourselves a bit better,' the man spluttered, 'because the line is too long!'

'My partner has had to attend a sick patient,' Logan explained, his voice reasonable, 'so I'm running two lists at the moment. We're seeing patients in the order they arrived, unless someone has an urgent condition.'

'That girl—' the man pointed a finger at little Nicola Horsfield, who shrank closer to her mother '—came in after me and she's going in next.'

'Nicola is severely asthmatic and the heat is bothering her. She's six years old. Do you feel that your medical condition requires you to go in front of her?'

Evanna watched from the doorway but not because her presence was needed. *Just because she couldn't help herself.* Logan was such a master at dealing with difficult people that watching him was a pleasure.

He managed to sound pleasant and reasonable while staying in complete control of the situation.

The man frowned. 'It isn't about queue jumping—'

'There's one doctor and a line of people. That's generally called a queue.'

'You could get me a helicopter to the mainland.'

Logan lifted an eyebrow. 'Are you bleeding, suffering severe chest pains or having breathing problems?'

'No, but—'

'Are you in imminent danger of death or collapse?'

'No, but—'

'Then I'm not ordering the helicopter.'

'I'll call it myself.'

'As island doctor, it requires my authorisation.' Logan glanced at his watch. 'In the time I've taken having this discussion, I could have seen another patient. Do you want to carry on talking or would you rather go outside, breathe in some fresh Glenmore air and cool down? Janet will call you when it's your turn.'

The man inhaled sharply, tightened his mouth and then stomped out of the door.

Logan gave Janet an encouraging smile. 'I'm ready for my next patient. If he gives you any more problems, buzz me.'

Janet leaned forward. 'He's only here because he forgot to bring his tablets on holiday. He wants a prescription.'

'People get cross when the weather heats up.' Logan turned away and caught sight of Evanna. 'What are you doing standing there, Nurse Duncan?' His blue eyes gleamed with humour. 'Getting ready to defend me?'

'You don't need any help. But I was ready to pick him up after you floored him.'

'As if.'

She grinned. 'Logan MacNeil, you were always knocking people flat in the school playground. You were always in Ann Carne's office.'

At the mention of their old headmistress, Logan laughed. 'Well, they all deserved it and I wasn't a doctor then. Now I try not to knock people down because it just makes more work.' He strolled back towards his surgery. 'Ethan should be back soon and then we can start clearing everyone from the waiting room.'

Evanna went back into her own consulting room and buzzed for her next patient.

'He almost fell off the quay into the water!' The young mother cuddled the toddler on her lap. 'He gave me a heart attack. My husband was buying ice creams so he didn't even see it happen. I caught him by instinct, but now he isn't using his arm and I'm worried I've done something awful to his wrist.'

Evanna scribbled a note on her pad and then reached for the

fox puppet that she kept on her desk. She slid her hand inside and made the fox move.

The toddler smiled and reached for the puppet. 'Mine.'

'He likes to be stroked,' Evanna murmured, noticing that the toddler favoured one arm. She glanced back at the mother. 'How did you catch him?'

'I caught his wrist and jerked him up to stop him falling.'

'So his weight would have been on his arm?'

'Yes.' The mother bit her lip. 'Have I broken his wrist?'

'From the sound of it, you did what needed to save him from falling into the water. Looking after an inquisitive toddler is never easy,' Evanna said steadily, thinking of the number of times that little Kirsty had surprised her with her antics. She wiggled the fox and smiled at the child. 'Can you stroke foxy with your other hand, William?'

The toddler ignored her request and kept one arm firmly in his lap.

Evanna put the fox down on her desk. 'He obviously doesn't want to use that arm so I think we do need to ask one of the doctors to check him out. I'll just nip across the corridor and see if one of them is free to take a look.'

'You think he's broken his wrist? Oh, no, and we're on holiday here in the middle of nowhere.'

'I think he may have injured his elbow,' Evanna said gently. 'And Glenmore may be remote but we have a surprisingly large population and two excellent doctors who are used to dealing with all sorts of injuries. Try not to worry.'

The red light was showing outside Ethan Walker's consulting room, which meant that he was back from his house call and busy catching up with his patients. She hesitated outside Logan's door, rapped sharply and then entered when she heard his voice. 'Sorry to bother you. I know we've got a backlog, but I've a toddler in my room who looks as though he might have a pulled elbow. His mother caught him by the arm to stop him falling off the quay.'

Logan sat back in his chair. 'You've taken a look at him?'

'He isn't moving the arm.'

'I'll examine him in your room. Ethan's back now anyway, so things are calming down.' He rose to his feet in a fluid, athletic movement and strode across to her, strands of dark hair flopping over his forehead. His skin was bronzed from the summer sun, his eyelashes thick and dark, and Evanna quickly turned and opened the door, trying not to look at him.

She felt awkward and self-conscious in his company and despair rose inside her. Being full of good intentions was one thing, but somehow she had to communicate her new resolve to her body. She needed to stop her knees shaking and her stomach spinning.

'I'm Dr MacNeil.' He shook hands with the parents and then dropped into a crouch and smiled at the little boy. 'What have you been up to, William? Trying to dive off our quay?'

'Fox.'

'You like Evanna's fox, do you?' Logan carefully examined the child's hand, wrist and shoulder. 'There's no obvious swelling. Does this hurt, William?'

'Ow.' The toddler jerked and his face crumpled.

'Obviously the answer to that question is yes. Sorry to hurt you, little chap,' Logan murmured apologetically, stroking a hand over the toddler's head and reaching for the fox puppet. He waggled it around, made the child smile and then glanced at Evanna. 'He's tender over the radiohumeral joint. He's comfortable until you try and move the elbow. It's all consistent with a subluxation of the head of the radius. I'll reduce it here.'

'Here?' The mother tensed. 'Doesn't he need an X-ray or anything?'

'If there was any suspicion of a fracture, I'd arrange for an

X-ray,' Logan said easily, standing up and crossing the room to wash his hands, 'but all the signs are that your son's elbow is slightly out of place and I'm sure I can correct that. It will hurt for a few moments and then hopefully he'll be fine. If this doesn't do the trick, yes, I'll consider an X-ray as the next step.'

Evanna stepped forward. 'Can you hold him on your lap? Like that—perfect.' She settled the child while Logan ripped a paper towel out of the dispenser and dried his hands.

'All right, William, let's do this so that you can get on with your holiday. Have you tried the ice cream at Meg's Café yet?' He put his thumb over the head of the radius and pressed down while he smoothly extended the elbow. 'It's the best ice cream in the world.'

Evanna watched while he moved the arm and then flexed the elbow, keeping his thumb pressing against the radial head.

The toddler screamed loudly and the mother inhaled and covered her mouth with her hand, but Logan gave a satisfied nod.

'Sorry about the pain but I think that should have done the trick. I felt a click against my thumb. I'd like you to hang around here for about ten minutes, if that's all right, then I'll take another look at him.'

'That's it?' The mother was cuddling William but he'd already stopped crying and was watching, fascinated, as Evanna made the fox puppet perform a series of elaborate tricks. 'Does he need a plaster or a sling or anything?'

Logan shook his head. 'I think he's going to be fine. Let him play with the toys in the waiting room and then I'll give you a shout and take another look. Good boy, William. You were very brave.'

The mother let out a sigh of relief. 'I thought I'd broken his wrist.'

'A sudden jerk on the arm can be enough to pull the elbow in a child of this age.'

'I'll remember that. I have a set of reins in the car but he hates them.'

'He'll probably like them more than having me manipulating his arm,' Logan said gently. 'Use them, at least when you're near the water.'

The mother nodded. 'Thanks very much.'

Logan smiled and walked towards the door. 'I'll see you in ten minutes.'

Evanna showed the couple into the waiting room, settled William with some toys and then returned to her room.

It would help if Logan weren't such a good doctor, she thought wearily as she completed her notes and buzzed for her next patient. It would be so much easier if she didn't admire him so much. She needed to work hard at finding something significantly wrong with him.

'Keep the dressing on over the weekend, Mrs Keen,' she said ten minutes later as she secured the bandage and helped the old lady to her feet. 'Make an appointment with Janet to see me on Monday and I'll look at it then, but it's healing nicely.'

'What are you doing this weekend, dear?' The old lady reached for her bag. 'Anything nice?'

Evanna thought of the barbecue and the new dress hanging in her wardrobe. 'I'm not sure. Possibly.' It would probably depend on the outcome of her new outfit. Would Logan notice a difference in her? And would he even care?

She walked Mrs Keen to the waiting room and brought William and his family back to Logan.

'He seems fine now.' The mother was smiling. 'He's using the hand quite happily. I can't quite believe the difference. I was imagining that we were going to have to go back to the mainland for treatment. Thank you so much.'

'You're very welcome.' Logan smiled and checked the child's arm carefully, satisfying himself that an X-ray wasn't necessary. 'I think he's fine, but if there are any more problems just come back to us and we'll take another look. If he seems reluctant to use it, I want to know. Otherwise, enjoy the rest of your holiday! And don't forget to try that ice cream.'

The toddler gave him a faltering smile and Logan ruffled his hair. 'And don't go near the edge of the quay.'

'He almost gave me a heart attack.' The mother smiled her thanks again and left the room.

'Are we nearly done here?' Logan glanced at his watch. 'I want to have lunch with Kirsty. Why don't you join us? You haven't seen her since you arrived back. She misses you.'

Evanna felt something twist inside her.

What should she say? That she was trying to gradually distance herself from his family to make the whole thing easier to live with?

No, to say that would trigger a full confession and she couldn't think of anything more embarrassing. And, anyway, she didn't really want to distance herself from Logan and Kirsty. She enjoyed their company. She just wanted to feel differently about him.

'I've been away for a month, Logan,' she said quietly, picking up two empty mugs from his desk. 'I've had things to do in the cottage.'

'Yes, of course you have.' His gaze was searching. 'It's just that you usually spend a lot of time with Kirsty.'

Oh, what the heck! 'I'd like to see her,' she said weakly, cursing her lack of self-discipline. 'I'll make us all a sandwich.'

After all, what difference was it going to make? She couldn't possibly love Logan more than she did already and she couldn't possibly feel any worse than she did already. So she may as well just make the most of the time she had with him.

'Good.' He was still watching her. 'Are you sure you're all right? You seem a bit...edgy. Is something the matter?'

Yes, Evanna thought to herself as she walked towards the

door, clutching the mugs. *I'm in love with a man who doesn't know I exist.* 'Nothing's the matter. I've finished my clinic so I'll go through to the house and get lunch on the table. Join us whenever you're ready.'

Something was the matter with Evanna.

Frowning to himself, Logan closed the door of his consulting room, handed a pile of letters to Janet and walked through the door that connected with his house.

It was unlike Evanna to be distracted and yet ever since she'd returned from the mainland she seemed really…jumpy?

Perhaps it was his imagination. It was just that he wasn't used to having to wonder about her. Unlike his sister, who wasn't above throwing something at him when he annoyed her, Evanna was always steady and consistent.

In fact, if he'd been asked to find one word to describe Evanna it would have been predictable. Reliable. Kind. That was more than one word, he acknowledged with a faint smile as he followed the sound of laughter and walked into his kitchen.

Evanna was sitting at the huge table, gingerly wiping blobs of strawberry yoghurt from her dark hair. Kirsty was gurgling with delight and banging her spoon on her high chair.

'Yes, yes,' Evanna was saying in that soft, breathy voice that always soothed anxious patients, 'your aim is fantastic.'

'Sorry.' Logan laughed as he walked over to her and handed her some more kitchen roll. 'I should have warned you about her new throwing technique. I think she might be a cricketer when she grows up. She's quite good at bowling food.'

'I noticed.' Evanna leaned forward, undid the harness and lifted the little girl out of her high chair. 'Come on, then, monster. Let's have a cuddle.'

All smiles, Kirsty wrapped her arms round Evanna's neck and kissed her on the cheek.

Logan felt an aching sadness rise up inside him.

'Are you all right?' Evanna stood up, lifting the child onto her hip. 'Logan?'

She was watching him with dark, solemn eyes and he pulled himself together. 'I'm fine.'

'No, you're not.' Her voice was gentle as she sat the toddler down on the floor next to a pile of toys. 'You were thinking about Catherine. You don't have to pretend with me, Logan. You spend most of your life putting on a brave face in public, you're allowed to let it slip when you're with friends.'

She was so astute. She always saw through to the real emotions. It was what made her such an outstanding nurse. It was why everyone on the island loved her. Evanna cared. Deeply.

Wondering why he always talked to Evanna about things that he never usually talked about, Logan stared at his daughter. 'It's just hard not to worry about her. She needs a mother,' he said gruffly, and Evanna walked over to him and touched his arm.

'Kirsty is a lucky girl.' Her voice was husky with emotion. 'She has an amazing father who adores her. Don't underestimate that. You're doing a good job, Logan.'

'Am I?' His expression was bleak and for a moment he felt empty inside. 'I'm not sure that I have the skills to be a mother and a father to a child.'

'Kirsty has plenty of loving females in her life. She's surrounded by family. What with Kyla and all the aunts and cousins— your parents—' Evanna broke off and sighed. 'I'm sorry. I'm trying to make you feel better. Human instinct. The truth is it's a vile situation that no one should ever have to find themselves tackling. Life is hideously unfair. Feel free to scream, swear and complain as much as you like. I'm always here, you know that.'

He did know that. Evanna was rock-solid and dependable. Always there when he needed her.

And she had the lightest of touches when it came to awkward

situations, Logan thought, watching as she turned away to make them both a sandwich. Other people offered empty platitudes or just ignored the subject altogether because it was just too uncomfortable. Evanna never ignored things. She was happy to listen or to talk, depending on his mood. It was one of the reasons he felt so comfortable with her. There were never any awkward moments with Evanna. 'People keep telling me that I'll find someone else. It's just one of the things that people say to you when someone dies. "You'll find someone else." As if people you want to spend a lifetime with are waiting round every corner.' He saw the sudden stillness in her frame.

'I suppose they're just trying to help. People love you and care about you,' she mumbled, keeping her back to him. 'I'm sure that one day you will find someone else, even if it doesn't feel that way now.'

'Do you? Do you really believe that?'

Her hesitation was so brief that he wondered if he'd imagined it. 'Yes. What would you like in your sandwich?'

'Anything. But love doesn't happen that often, does it? Look at you, Evanna. You're beautiful and sweet-natured and you'd make someone an amazing wife, but you're still single.'

Her head was in the fridge so he could barely hear her reply, but he thought she said, 'That's right. I am.'

After what seemed like an age she turned with a bag of salad in her hand. 'This is soggy and horrible.' Her voice sounded strange. 'When did you last shop?'

'Meg filled the fridge last weekend but I've been too busy to do much with it.'

She gave a faint smile of understanding. 'It's always the same in the summer, isn't it? Tourists double the workload and, goodness knows, you work hard enough as it is. I'll do a quick shop for you later and make a couple of casseroles for your freezer.' Evanna dropped the salad in the bin and added a carton of tomatoes and a soft, liquid cucumber. 'This is vile, Logan. Most of the food in your fridge died at least a century ago. You're going to poison yourself and Kirsty.'

'She's OK. She's still eating the stuff you left in the freezer for her and I've lived on take-aways all week,' he confessed, watching absently as she swiftly stripped his fridge of dubious food and tidied the rest neatly. She was so methodical and efficient. 'Or else I go down to Meg's and eat at the café.'

Evanna peered at the date on a packet of ham. 'Miracles do happen. This is still all right.'

'It's so good to have you home. We missed you when you were away,' he said gruffly, and she turned to look at him, a strange light in her eyes.

There was something about the expression on her sweet face that made him uneasy.

Why did he constantly have a niggling feeling that there was something the matter with her?

Logan shook himself mentally and decided that he was imagining things.

Having been away for a month, it was bound to take her a little while to get back into the swing of island life.

'How's it been going with Amy Foster?' She turned back to her sandwich-making. With a minimum of fuss she buttered bread, layered the ham, added a dab of mustard and handed him the sandwich. 'She seems sweet with Kirsty. Is it working out, her helping you out?'

'I've no problem with the way she cares for Kirsty.' Logan bit into the sandwich, wondering how she'd managed to make something so delicious from the limited contents of his fridge.

'But you have a problem with something else?' Evanna sat down opposite him and Logan gave a weary smile.

'Only the usual. She's obviously one of the many people who think that I should get married again. Soon. Preferably to her.'

Evanna cut her sandwich in two. 'Oh, dear.'

'I'm a widower.' Logan rubbed a hand over his brow and then gave a bitter laugh. 'Do you have any idea how much I hate that word? It sounds so pathetic.'

'Pathetic?' Evanna frowned and put the knife down. 'You're the strongest man I know, Logan. And it's natural that women are going to fall for you.'

'Why?' It didn't make sense to him. 'Because I'm single and well off with a child who needs mothering?'

She stared at him for a moment and he had a strong feeling that she was about to say something. Then she blushed slightly and lifted her sandwich. 'I've no idea why.'

'Well, of course you haven't.' He laughed. 'That's why we're such good friends. In fact, I think you're the only woman on this island, apart from my sister and cousins, who hasn't made a pass at me in the last year. Our relationship is wonderfully platonic. Perhaps what I really need is a male nanny. Anyway, I've tactfully fired Amy. I told her that you were back from the mainland and that I wouldn't need the help any more. One of the cousins is going to look after her during the day when Meg is busy at the café, but I worry about Kirsty having so many different carers.'

Evanna nibbled at her sandwich. 'They're mostly family,' she muttered, apparently absorbed by what was on her plate. 'Kirsty will be fine.'

'You're not eating much.'

She put the remains of her sandwich down and stood up. 'I'm not that hungry. I'll clear up here and get back to the surgery because I still have some paperwork to catch up on before the immunisation clinic this afternoon.'

'You've had less than half an hour.' He frowned at her. 'I know we're busy but don't overdo the work, Evanna.'

'It's fine. I'm fine.' She gave a quick smile and backed towards the door.

If he hadn't known better, he would have said that she was anxious to get away from him and he couldn't shake the feeling that something was wrong with her.

Pushing away thoughts of that entirely disturbing conversation over lunch, Evanna tried to concentrate on her work.

Her first patient of the afternoon was Sonia, who was thirty-four weeks pregnant. Evanna noticed that she looked hot and bothered. 'How have you been?'

'All right.' Sonia sank into the chair and rubbed a hand over her swollen abdomen. 'I wish it wasn't so hot. This is Glenmore. We don't normally have heat waves. Suddenly I'm longing for a good old storm to clear the air. I brought you a sample. I assume you wanted one?'

Evanna nodded and took the sample. 'I'll just test this quickly and then check your blood pressure.' She used a dipstick and checked that there was no protein in the sample. Then she checked Sonia's blood pressure. 'That's a bit on the high side, Sonia. Why don't you lie down on the couch and I'll feel the baby and then I'll check it again.'

She skilfully palpated Sonia's bump, feeling the lie of the baby, and then she used her tape measure to check the size. 'Well, that's all as it should be.'

'Apart from the blood pressure.'

'I'm going to try that again now that you've sat down for a few minutes.'

Sonia watched anxiously while she checked it. 'Well?'

'It's still a bit high, Sonia.' Evanna recorded the result. 'I'm going to mention it to Dr MacNeil and I'll pop round to your house on my way home and check it again.'

'Will it be different in my home?' Sonia sat up and wriggled off the trolley.

'It might be.'

Sonia bit her lip. 'Will I have to go to the hospital?'

'I hope not. We certainly need to keep an eye on that blood pressure but there's nothing to worry about so far. Are you feeling plenty of movements?'

Sonia picked up her bag. 'Oh, yes. I'm definitely having a footballer. It kicks and moves all the time.'

Evanna smiled and slipped her pen into her pocket. 'That's good. I'll see you later, Sonia.'

'I'll make sure to have the kettle on.'

Evanna watched her go and then walked across to talk to Logan, who had just finished his afternoon surgery.

'I'm taking Kirsty down to the beach for a paddle. Do you want to come?' His hair was rumpled, his jaw slightly darkened with the beginnings of stubble, and he gave her a sleepy, sexy smile that made her breath catch.

She gazed at him wistfully and then reminded herself that playing happy families was not a good idea. 'Actually I can't,' she said truthfully. 'I have a few things to do here and then I have to call on Sonia.'

'She was just in surgery.' He pushed some papers into his bag and closed it. 'Why would you be calling on her?'

'Because her blood pressure is up a bit. It's one-forty over ninety.'

The smile left his face. 'Did you test her urine?' His voice was terse and Evanna wondered how long it would take him to stop treating pregnant women as if they were unexploded bombs.

'Of course. It was negative and her fundal height measurement was fine—thirty-five centimetres.'

'Is the baby moving around?'

'Yes. Plenty of movement. I've arranged to call with her later to check her blood pressure again, but I just wanted to let you know.'

Logan nodded. 'If her blood pressure is still up, ask her to come to surgery tomorrow so that we can take some blood. We'll do a single estimate serum urate, urea and electrolytes, full blood count and platelets, and repeat blood pressure recording and urinalysis.'

Evanna gave a soft smile. He was the most thorough, dedicated doctor she'd ever worked with. He let nothing slip past him. 'All right.'

'And Evanna—' he picked up the case and walked towards the door '—don't forget about the barbecue on Saturday.'

Evanna thought of the dress in her wardrobe. The *new* dress. 'I won't forget.'

'Good.' He gave a nod of approval and reached for his car keys. 'See you tomorrow.'

Evanna called in at Sonia's on the way home to check on her and found her blood pressure was still slightly high. Evanna felt a flicker of unease as she closed her bag and thought carefully about the best course of action.

'Dr MacNeil wants you to come to surgery tomorrow and have a blood test,' she said as she walked towards the door. 'And can you bring another sample?'

'Of course.' Sonia winced slightly and rubbed her bump. 'I must admit I'm starting to find it quite uncomfortable. It's the heat, I suppose. Next time I'm going to make sure that I'm pregnant in the winter. Glad I'm not having triplets.'

Evanna smiled. 'I'll see you tomorrow, Sonia.'

She climbed back into the car, lining up the facts and deciding on the best course of action. Tests tomorrow and then careful monitoring. And, if in doubt, she'd send Sonia to the hospital for a check. She wouldn't take any chances.

Suddenly she felt excited about Saturday. Maybe Kyla was right. When had she ever really dressed up for Logan? The answer was never. Yes, they sometimes went to social events at the same time, but she'd never dressed to attract his attention.

He obviously liked her company and there was no doubt that Kirsty loved her.

Perhaps it was just a question of showing him that she was interested—of showing him that, as well as his friend and colleague, she was also a woman.

CHAPTER FOUR

SATURDAY evening arrived and Evanna hovered outside Logan's house, feeling ridiculously self-conscious. She'd walked through his garden gate at least a thousand times in her life and never even hesitated. So why should a glamorous dress and a pair of high heels suddenly make her nervous?

The answer, of course, was because she felt...different.

Normally, when she joined Logan for one of the frequent barbecues at his house, she pulled on her oldest pair of jeans and pushed her feet into a pair of trainers. It was true that occasionally she'd worn a dress in the hope that he'd notice her, but it had never worked. *But she'd never worn a dress as glamorous or feminine as the one she was wearing now.*

Lifting a hand to her hair, she drew in a breath and opened the gate.

'Evanna, you look wonderful!' Meg, Kyla's aunt who owned the café on the quay, stepped forward, a drink in her hand. 'I've never seen your hair down like that! It looks amazing.'

'I—I thought I'd have a change from curls.' Evanna's eyes slid nervously around the garden, which was already crowded with Logan's friends and family. 'Where's Kirsty?'

It was ridiculous, she thought to herself, *hiding behind a child.* But suddenly that was what she wanted to do.

'Last seen clinging adoringly to her father, but you don't want to hold her while you're wearing that gorgeous dress. She was squashing raspberries into her mouth a moment ago and most of the juice was stuck to her.'

Evanna laughed. 'She loves fruit.'

'There she is.' Meg smiled benignly across the garden. 'And Logan is looking well, don't you think? That blue shirt with his eyes—it's no wonder the girls all trip over themselves when he passes. He's not going to be on his own for long, that's for sure. Someone is going to snap him up really soon.'

Were they?

Wondering how she'd cope with that, Evanna kept her smile fixed firmly in place, relieved to see Kyla walking across to them, her hand in Ethan's.

'Good to see Kyla so happy, too,' Meg said, nodding approvingly as Ethan paused to kiss his new wife on the lips. 'Ethan may not be an islander born and bred, but you wouldn't know it to look at him. He fits right in.'

Evanna nodded. It was true that Ethan fitted in. He'd arrived as a locum GP to help Logan and had fallen in love with Kyla and stayed. It was a situation that suited everyone. 'He was always meant to come here.'

'You mean because he's Kirsty's uncle?' Meg lowered her voice. 'I must admit I wasn't surprised when he revealed that he was actually related to Logan's late wife. Her brother, imagine! There was always something secretive about him. And about her, come to that. She certainly never mentioned a brother.'

'They weren't close. That's why Ethan took the job here. To try and learn more about her. I'm sure that if she hadn't died, they would have developed a relationship.' Kyla hadn't shared much of it with her, but Evanna knew that Ethan and Catherine had shared a difficult family background.

Meg sniffed. 'Well, he's a good doctor and that's what

matters. Oh, look at that.' She waved a hand. 'Kirsty has spotted you. And Logan.'

Evanna felt her heart rate double. 'I'd better go and say hello.'

'You do that. And watch that dress.'

Evanna caught Kyla's whispered 'Nice cleavage', took a deep breath and plucked up courage to walk across the lawn.

'Hello, Kirsty,' she said, clasping the raspberry-stained fist in hers and giving it a swift kiss. 'No need to ask what you've been eating.'

Kirsty chortled with delight, a huge smile on her plump cheeks.

'I've given up trying to keep her clean,' Logan murmured, dropping a kiss onto his daughter's silken blonde curls. 'It's a losing battle. I've decided that I'm just going to turn the hose onto her before she goes to bed.'

'It's a good job I know you're joking.' Evanna felt her heart hammer against her chest as he turned to look at her. His blue eyes were shielded by thick, dark lashes and her stomach flipped as she fell into that sleepy, masculine gaze.

Suddenly she felt agonisingly nervous.

What if he hated the way she looked? What if he thought she looked ridiculous? What if—?

He smiled at her. 'I'm glad you came early.'

Didn't he notice anything different about her? Evanna shook her head gently, allowing her smooth, shiny hair to spill over her shoulders.

Kirsty gave a delighted gurgle and immediately reached out and grabbed a handful.

'Don't pull Evanna's hair,' Logan drawled, prising the little girl's fists open and giving Evanna an apologetic smile. 'You know what she's like with hair. Leaving it down was asking for trouble. You should have worn it in a ponytail, like you usually do.'

Evanna swallowed back her disappointment.

That was it?

That was all he was going to say?

That she should have worn her hair in a ponytail? 'Yes,' she croaked, 'I probably should.'

Kyla stepped up to them, a bowl of plump, glossy black olives in her hand. 'Olive, anyone? Doesn't Evanna look fantastic with her hair like that, Logan? It's stunning, Evanna. Really stunning. You should wear it down more often.'

'Well, it certainly makes it easier for Kirsty to pull,' Logan said absently, stretching out a hand and helping himself to an olive. 'I'm going to put the baby to bed now. Then I'll come down and cook. Did you know that Meg has offered Fraser free ice creams for the whole of the summer as a reward for his quick reactions last week?'

'That's a bit rash, isn't it? I've seen how much that boy can put away.' Kyla grinned and held out her arms to Kirsty. 'Come to your Aunty Kyla. I'll put her to bed. You chat to Evanna. You two never have time to talk properly and I'm sure you have lots to catch up on.'

Logan looked surprised. 'All right, thanks. But I'm going to talk Evanna into making a salad while I get the barbecue going.'

'Evanna is not making salad while she's wearing that dress,' Kyla said firmly, and Logan frowned slightly.

'She could wear an apron.'

Kyla gritted her teeth. 'Ethan is going to finish off the cooking. You two just spend a bit of time together.' She walked off with the toddler in her arms and Logan watched her go.

'Well, perhaps we should take her up on her offer. To be honest, I was trying to work out a way of getting you on your own before everyone else arrives. This seems like as good a time as any.' He closed a hand on her arm and pulled her across the grass to the weeping willow. Green tentacles spilled downwards, providing shade and privacy.

His touch was firm and purposeful and Evanna felt her heart start to pound. What could he possibly want to say to her?

He pushed aside the soft curtain of leaves and led her into the cool, shaded centre of the tree. Although they were still in the middle of the garden, it felt secluded and private and suddenly Evanna started to shiver. Trapped in such an intimate atmosphere, she was acutely aware of him and she couldn't look away. He was a strong man in every sense and that strength showed in the rugged planes of his handsome face and the easy, confident way he dealt with everyone on the island.

'L-little Jason is d-doing really well,' she stammered. 'I called in to see them in their holiday cottage. The hospital kept him in for a few days and then sent him home so they were able to continue their holiday. I gave them some advice on the baby. I think she was just hot and uncomfortable, that's why she was crying so much. They were putting too many layers on her and not giving her enough fluid.'

'You're a genius.' Logan leaned his shoulders against the wide trunk of the tree. 'It always amazes me how little thought people give to the weather. I stopped the car this morning to tell a couple to put sun cream on their baby.'

'What did they say?'

He grinned. 'I think their comment was, "Who do you think you are?" To which I replied, "The guy you're going to see when she's burnt and miserable."' He lifted his beer to his lips. 'Funnily enough, that seemed to shut them up. I saw them in the shop later, buying sun cream by the bucketload.'

Evanna laughed. She'd always liked that about him. The way he wasn't afraid to speak up when he saw something that he didn't agree with. 'I've never understood why people insist on putting small babies in the sun.'

'Ignorance. I really do need to talk to you,' he drawled softly, lifting a hand and removing a leaf from her hair. 'And I honestly don't know how you're going to react to what I'm going to say. You're probably going to refuse.'

Refuse?

When had she refused him anything?

Her legs were shaking so badly that she stepped backwards and leaned against the broad trunk of the tree for support. 'Just say it, Logan.'

'All right. But if I'm overstepping the bounds of our friendship then I want you to tell me. Do you promise to give me an honest answer?'

Overstepping the bounds of their friendship?

Hope and anticipation made her suddenly dizzy. 'Yes,' she mumbled, her hands fisting by her sides. 'Of course.' The weeping willow provided a lush, delicate screen from the rest of the garden and suddenly the atmosphere seemed impossibly intimate. It was just the two of them, everyone else forgotten.

He took a deep breath. 'I wondered if you'd consider looking after Kirsty for me on Wednesday afternoons. I know it's usually your afternoon off, but it wouldn't be for ever. Just until I find someone to replace Amy Foster.'

Evanna stared at him. The words he'd spoken were so different from the ones she'd longed to hear that it took her a moment from the meaning to sink in. 'You want me to look after Kirsty? That's what you wanted to ask me?'

'Yes. I know it's a lot to ask. You've often looked after her before, but not on a regular basis. Is the answer going to be no?' He strolled towards her, powerfully built and handsome. *The man she'd loved for the whole of her life.*

She looked away for a moment, struggling to compose herself. Then she cleared her throat carefully. 'Logan…' Her voice cracked. 'Can I ask you something?'

'Of course. Anything.'

What do I have to do to make you notice me? 'Why ask me? Why me?'

'Because you're completely reliable, a wonderful cook, incredibly uncomplicated and Kirsty adores you. That's just a start but I could go on for ever.' He gave a shrug and a lopsided smile. 'If I didn't need you in the practice so badly, I'd fire you and employ you to look after Kirsty full time.'

So he was happy for her to care for his daughter.

That was a compliment, of course. But it was so much less than she wanted.

Evanna stood for a moment, thinking of the heat and the passion she saw in Ethan's eyes when he looked at Kyla. Then she looked at Logan. And saw humour and a faint question in his gorgeous blue eyes.

For him, their relationship was all about friendship. Nothing else.

'Evanna?'

She realised that he was waiting for an answer. And how could she refuse? She loved him. She'd loved him all her life. She'd loved him when he'd been a boy at school and she'd loved him when he'd grown into a man and married another woman.

And she loved Kirsty.

How could she refuse to help him? What sort of a friend would that make her? It wasn't Logan's fault that her feelings towards him were entirely more complicated than his were for her.

He deserved all the help she could give him, even if it proved to be torture for her.

With a smile that cost her greatly in terms of effort, she forced the words past her dry lips. 'Of course I'll look after Kirsty on Wednesdays. It would be my pleasure.'

His eyes were on her face. 'I don't expect you to do it for nothing. I'll pay you.'

Employee. Friend. He offered her just about every role

except the one she wanted. 'I don't want to be paid, Logan,' she said quietly. 'I love Kirsty.'

'Well, it's just until I find someone else, then. I don't want to take advantage of you.' He reached out and tucked a strand of hair behind her ears in a distinctly brotherly gesture. 'Better put your hair back up or she'll tug it out by the handful.'

'Yes. That's probably a good idea. I'll put it up.' A ponytail was practical. Sensible. And that was the sort of person she was. Practical. She wasn't designed for grand passion or wild affairs. She was reliable, sensible Evanna. That was how other people saw her and it was how she should start seeing herself. No more dreams. No more fantasies.

He frowned down at her feet. *At her deliciously sexy, wickedly high-heeled shoes.* 'And you should probably wear something flat and comfortable. She can move like lightning now and you'll never be able to catch her in those. You'll twist your ankle.'

Something flat and comfortable. Something that reliable, sensible Evanna would wear. 'Right. I'll remember that, too.'

He reached out and squeezed her shoulder. 'You're a good friend, Evanna,' he said softly. 'The best.'

And then he turned and walked away from her, leaving her staring after him with all the hope lying shrivelled inside her.

She felt numb. Her limbs wouldn't move and for a moment she stood, staring through the curtain of green leaves, wondering what she was supposed to do now. She felt foolish in her dress and shoes and suddenly wished she'd just worn jeans.

That was it then.

Over.

It had been a foolish idea and it had failed.

And now she had to rejoin the group. Wearing her silly dress and her uncomfortable shoes, she had to talk and mingle and do all the things she usually did because if she didn't, everyone would notice. Everyone would know that something was the matter with her and she didn't want anyone to notice. *She didn't want people to know.*

Evanna blinked rapidly to clear the tears that had gathered and walked carefully on her new heels, brushing aside the fronds of the weeping willow, intending to help herself to some food. And then her eyes rested on Logan's broad, muscular shoulders and she found that she couldn't look away. Why did it have to be him? she wondered helplessly. Why him? Couldn't she have fallen in love with someone who noticed her? She stood there, drinking in his strength and masculinity, memorising every single part of him as if it were the last time she'd be allowed to look.

And then she felt Kyla's hand on her arm. 'Well? I saw him drag you into the weeping willow. The dress obviously worked.'

Evanna willed herself to move—*willed herself to act normally.* 'He wants me to look after Kirsty on Wednesdays. That's what he wanted to talk to me about.' Her voice sounded unnaturally formal, even to her own ears, and suddenly she knew she was going to cry. 'So I think we can safely say that the dress didn't impress him and that plan B has just crashed and burned alongside plan A. Will you excuse me? I'm suddenly incredibly tired. I think I'll go home and have an early night.'

'Evanna, you can't just—'

'I'll see you tomorrow, Kyla.' She needed to get away. Fast. Before she made a fool of herself.

Without looking back, she turned and walked quickly across the garden towards the gate. Let them say what they liked, she thought as she fumbled with the gate and walked to her car. She didn't care any more. She just needed to be on her own.

'Evanna, wait!'

Kyla's voice came from behind her but she ignored her and drove off without glancing back.

She drove the short distance to her cottage, parked the car and nearly twisted her ankle on the path that led to her front door. It was the final straw. With a sob of frustration she stooped and slid them from her feet, throwing them angrily on the grass. She struggled with her key, somehow managed to open the door of her cottage, even though her eyes were swimming with tears and she couldn't see clearly.

'Evanna.' Kyla was right behind her and she turned, all the emotions of the evening suddenly released.

'You didn't need to follow me. I didn't want you to. You're my best friend, Kyla, but there are some things that even best friends can't fix.' Her voice was choked. Clogged with tears. 'Leave me alone, please. I just need to be on my own for a bit.'

'But I can—'

'But you can what? *You can what, Kyla?* If you're even *thinking* about coming up with another plan to make your brother notice me, you can forget it because I already feel completely and *utterly* humiliated. He is never going to notice me, and the sooner I come to terms with that, the better for all of us.' She turned and sprinted up the rest of the stairs and into her bedroom.

'Evanna, wait, *please...*'

Evanna was holding back sobs, the breath tearing in her throat as she tried hard not to cry. 'Please, leave me alone. I need to be on my own.'

'No, you don't. You're upset and—'

'Can't you see?' Tears flooded down her face and Evanna gave up the struggle for control. 'Can't you see that this is *never* going to work? Aren't you satisfied? We changed the way I dressed and he simply thought I looked ridiculous! He told me to put my hair back up so that Kirsty wouldn't pull it and to wear something more flat and comfortable on my feet, and do you know what that is?' She ripped the dress from her body so violently that she tore the fabric. 'Because I'm not a flamenco dancer or anyone glamorous. I'm just me and it isn't enough.'

'Don't, Evanna.' Kyla reached out a hand to try and stop her but Evanna brushed her away, stepped out of the dress and reached for her comfortable dressing-gown.

'Enough!' The tears thickened her words as she quickly covered herself. 'You have to let it drop, Kyla, and so do I. When I was on the mainland I promised myself that this wasn't going to happen again. I wasn't going to keep hoping. No more jumping through hoops. No more waving flags that say, Here I am! No more humiliation. And now here I am yet again, crying over a man who doesn't want me. It has to stop. *It's got to stop.*'

Kyla's eyes were swimming with tears. 'I'm so sorry,' she whispered, and Evanna felt herself pulled into a warm hug. 'I'm so, so sorry.'

'Don't be sorry,' she said gruffly, wiping the tears from her cheeks with the flat of her hand. 'It's me who should be sorry for yelling at you. You're a good friend and you were only trying to help. It wasn't your fault. None of this is your fault. It's nobody's fault.'

'Yes, it is. It was me who forced you to dress up for him. I just know you'd be so amazing together.' Kyla's expression was stricken as she wiped the tears from her own face. 'I shouldn't have interfered, but I love both of you so much.'

Evanna reached for a tissue. 'And you can carry on doing that, but you have to love us separately. Logan and I are not a couple and we never will be. We can't be together.'

Kyla sank down on the edge of the bed. 'So what will you do now?'

'I'm going to do my job, help look after Kirsty and be a good friend to your brother.' Evanna blew her nose hard and kept her tone matter of fact. 'It's what he needs from me. It's what he wants.'

'But what about what you want?'

'What I want isn't important at the moment. What's important is Kirsty and Logan. He's been through hell and he needs support. And that's what friends are for.' Evanna looked up with a watery smile. 'You can have those shoes, if you like. I left them in the garden. You're the same size as me and I don't think I'll be wearing them again. Anyway, they pinched my toes.'

'Oh, Evanna...'

Evanna shook her head. 'I'm not a high heel sort of girl. I'm just me and—and he doesn't want me. And that's fine,' she said, blowing her nose for a final time. 'Deep down I always knew that I wasn't the right girl for him. I've just been deluding myself in the same way that all the other women on this island do. But he has no idea how I feel, so that's good. If he knew, that would make the whole situation incredibly embarrassing. As it is, we can carry on as if nothing has happened.'

She almost laughed as she listened to herself. Nothing *had* happened. Except in her dreams. And in her dreams was the only place that Logan was ever going to be.

CHAPTER FIVE

AFTER a sleepless night, Evanna woke with a pounding headache and gritty eyes to find Craig on the doorstep, ready to finalise the details for her bathroom.

'It's not even eight o'clock, Craig.' Her voice was croaky with lack of sleep and she dragged a hand through her tangled hair. 'And it's Sunday. Don't you have a home to go to?'

'I finished up at the Murray place last night so I thought I might as well come down here and get started as soon as possible. Can't get any peace at home, anyway, with our Molly waking everyone up at the crack of dawn.' He was wearing filthy overalls and Evanna led him through to the kitchen and put the kettle on.

'I can't string a sentence together until I've had a cup of coffee,' she muttered, spooning fresh coffee into a pot and adding the water. A delicious aroma filled the kitchen. 'What time does Molly wake up?'

'Five.'

Evanna winced. 'That's a wicked time to start the day.'

'She doesn't think so.' Craig rubbed his eyes with his fingers. 'We take it in turns to get up with her.'

'She's two. She ought to sleep later than that. Have you tried just leaving her?'

'Annie doesn't like to do that.' Craig gave a crooked smile. 'Can't bear her to cry. The moment she hears a murmur, she's in there.'

Evanna lifted two mugs out of the cupboard. 'It might be worth leaving her for a few minutes. She might just go back to sleep. Logan tried that with Kirsty a few months ago and it worked. She didn't even cry much, just whimpered a few times and then drifted off again.'

'Really? So you think that might work for Moll?'

'It's possible, but obviously you have to do what feels right for you. Here. Have some caffeine.' She handed him a brimming mug. 'I'm sure that we both need it.'

'Did I wake you? I assumed you'd be up.'

'I was up.' She hadn't really slept all night. She'd just stared at the ceiling, thinking about Logan, and now her eyes pricked angrily and her head ached. It was going to be a long day. 'Do you want to have another look at the bathroom?'

'That's what I was hoping.'

They walked upstairs and Craig wandered into her bathroom. 'I reckon it will take me and the lads about ten days,' he said, peering around the bathroom and scribbling something on a piece of paper. 'Providing there are no hitches.'

'My life is full of hitches,' Evanna said wearily, 'but we'll aim for the ten days. Will I be able to wash?'

'Yeah. Well, most of the time.' Craig frowned up at the ceiling. 'You want that painted the same blue as the rest?'

'Yes.'

'Nice. Looks like a seaside bathroom.' He nodded approval and then pulled out a tape measure. 'I'm going to cut some wood to fit there. Has all the stuff we ordered arrived?'

'It's blocking my garage as we speak.'

Craig stretched out the tape measure and recorded the length. 'That's a standard size. OK. We'll start tomorrow. I'll try and make sure the bath is only out of action for a few days. You can shower at Kyla's.' He tucked the pencil behind his ear and slid a finger over a pipe. 'We'll box this in for you. It will look better.'

'Whatever you say, Craig.' Evanna wished she could summon up more enthusiasm. 'As long as it looks like the picture I showed you, I don't care how you do it.'

'It's a shame we couldn't have fitted it in while you were on the mainland. Would have meant less disruption for you, but never mind.' He took a closer look at a hairline crack that was running across the ceiling. 'I bet Dr MacNeil is pleased to see you home. He told me Kirsty was missing you.'

Evanna tensed. 'She's growing fast.'

'No doubt about that.' He dropped to his haunches and studied the floor. 'This will have to come up. Those flashy Italian tiles you chose are going to look the business.'

'Thanks, Craig. I'll let you have a key so that you can just come and go while I'm at work.'

He stood up. 'There's going to be some dust and mess while we remove the old stuff, but I'll cover your carpet for you.'

Evanna waved him off and decided that, although it would be fun to have a new, luxurious bathroom, the process was obviously going to be unpleasant.

It wasn't even nine o'clock and suddenly the day stretched ahead of her. Before her trip to the mainland, she probably would have gone to Logan's and spent the day playing with Kirsty but now she was wondering whether that was the wrong thing for everyone.

While it was true that she was able to help with the little girl, it was also true that her constant presence was a disincentive to Logan to find someone else. And he needed to find someone else.

Remembering the look of sadness on his face the day she'd made lunch for them, Evanna resolved to try and think about someone who might suit him. Catherine had been wild and adventurous, so clearly that was the sort of woman who interested Logan and, offhand, she couldn't think of anyone who fitted that description.

Thinking about suitable partners for Logan did nothing for her piece of mind so she drank two cups of herbal tea, ate some fruit and wandered into her garden.

Although it was still early, the sun was already hot and it was obviously going to be another scorching day.

Deciding that the best cure for misery was a good exercise session before the weather became too hot to run, Evanna pulled on an old pair of shorts, slid her feet into her trainers and let herself out of the back door of the cottage.

The air was still, without a breath of wind, and the sea lay calm and quiet below the cliffs.

Forcing herself into a run, Evanna jogged steadily along the path, gradually increasing her pace.

She ran for almost half an hour, feeling the prickle of heat between her shoulder blades and the heat of the sun on her face. To her left the cliffs fell away steeply towards the sea and to her right were fields. Sheep grazed, placidly chewing on parched grass. Further inland was the rugged interior of the island, the province of walkers and climbers.

There had been no rain for weeks and the air smelt of sun and summer. The ground was hard under her trainers but still she ran, determined to chase away her gloom. It wasn't like her to be unhappy. She was, by nature, a happy, steady person. She wasn't given to fits of depression. So why did she feel so down?

Her pulse was thundering, her breath tearing in her lungs, and she pulled up for a brief rest, breathing heavily as she stared at the view. A few lone yachts bobbed on the water, barely moving in the still air. Apart from the occasional shriek of a seagull, it was completely peaceful. A lazy, quiet Sunday.

Later the tourists would crowd onto the beaches with their buckets and spades, but for now it was still too early for all but the most energetic of visitors to be up and about.

And then she glanced along the coast path and saw him.

Logan. And he had Kirsty on his shoulders.

Evanna let out a groan of frustration. Wasn't that just typical? Why did he have to be the one other person up and about? And how had she not realised that she'd run so far?

Kirsty waved her arms with excitement and Logan turned before she had time to vanish discreetly.

Wondering what terrible sins she'd committed to be forced to confront him in such a miserable, sweaty state, Evanna stood still, wishing she could wave a wand and transform herself. If she hadn't been feeling so dejected she would have laughed. Talk about going from one extreme to the other. Last night she'd worn a short dress and high heels and she'd been groomed to within an inch of her life. Today she was wearing her oldest shorts and a T-shirt with a half-faded slogan and her hair was a mess.

But what did it matter?

She'd never looked more feminine or glamorous than she had the night before, and had he noticed her? No. And if he hadn't noticed her in a dress and heels, why would he notice her in her ancient, practical running gear?

Logan just didn't find her attractive.

So she really didn't need to worry about him seeing her in her ancient shorts.

All the same she smoothed her damp hair away from her face as he approached. 'Hi. You're up early.'

'Kirsty hasn't learned to lie in yet. We make it until seven o'clock and that's good enough for me.' He reached up and lifted the toddler from his shoulders with strong hands. 'We thought we'd have an early walk to work up an appetite for a late breakfast.'

'Good idea.' *He looked good in shorts,* she thought. Logan had always been athletic and it showed in his physique. Dark hairs clustered at the open neck of his polo shirt and she looked away quickly, concentrating her attention on Kirsty, aware that he was looking at her.

'You hardly stayed for five minutes last night. Kyla said you weren't feeling that well.' There was concern in his voice. 'Are you sick? Bug of some sort?'

'No. No bug. I just felt a bit— I'm not sure—'

'You're not sure how you felt?'

Oh, for crying out loud, Evanna! 'I was just a bit tired.' She glanced out over the bay. 'It's going to be hot today.' Oh, help, she was reduced to talking about the weather.

'Yes.'

He was still looking at her. She could *feel* him looking at her and she turned to look up the coast path, afraid that he'd see something in her eyes that she didn't want him to see. 'I'm going to spend the afternoon cleaning out my bathroom, ready for Craig. He's starting tomorrow and—' She broke off and frowned slightly, squinting into the distance. 'What's the matter with them?'

Logan turned and looked. 'That couple? I walked past them about ten minutes ago. They're just tourists, out for an early stroll. They had a stack of newspapers in their rucksack. Probably looking for a peaceful spot on the headland to sit and catch up on the news. I can never understand that really, can you? People come to this island to escape from the big wide world and the first thing they do is buy a newspaper.'

'They're waving at us.'

'Why would they wave at us?' Logan lifted Kirsty off his shoulders and winced. 'She always holds onto my hair.'

'Logan.' Evanna caught his arm. 'They *are* waving at us. He's shouting something.'

Kirsty wriggled in Logan's arms and he shifted her back onto his shoulders in a smooth, confident movement. 'All right. Let's stroll back up there and see if there's something wrong.'

'There is something wrong. Definitely.' Evanna suddenly had a bad feeling. 'The woman's on the ground now. Has she collapsed or is she sitting down? I can't see properly from here.' She started to run along the path, aware that Logan was right behind her.

When she reached the couple the woman was on her knees and her hands were at her throat.

The man was right beside her. 'It's my wife, Alison. She's been bitten!' There was panic in his voice as he fumbled with his phone. 'I need to get help. I can't believe this has happened.'

'Bitten?' Evanna was already on her knees beside the woman. 'Bitten by what? Where?' She put a hand on the woman's shoulder in a gesture of reassurance and then closed her fingers around her wrist and felt her pulse. It was extremely rapid.

'It's a hundred and twenty, Logan.'

'Her foot. It's her foot. She trod on the damn thing. Oh, I can't do this.' The man's hands were shaking so much that he couldn't dial the number and the woman's breathing was becoming laboured.

She looked at her husband in blind panic and let out a sobbing breath. 'Pete—do something. My mouth's really dry and I feel dizzy. I didn't see it until I put my foot on it. *Do something.*'

Logan had transferred Kirsty from his shoulders to his arms but he didn't put her down because they were too close to the edge of the cliff. Instead, he held her easily and squatted down beside the woman, his voice calm and steady. 'Alison, try not to panic. I'm a doctor and I can help you but I need to know what happened. You said that something bit you? What was it? Insect?'

Alison turned her head to look at him and there was fear and revulsion in her eyes. 'Snake.' She croaked the word and Evanna frowned, thinking that she must have misheard.

'Snake? Are you sure?' Baffled, Evanna glanced around her but Logan didn't waste time questioning further. Instead, his fingers were on the woman's leg, examining an area that was reddening by the minute.

'Adder. It must have been an adder. Evanna, I want to bandage and splint the leg to stop her moving it around. What can we use?'

Still one step behind him, she stared at him blankly for a moment, tempted to answer, *Fresh air*. And then she saw something in his eyes—something serious—and his voice held an urgency that she didn't often hear. Logan was always calm and relaxed. It was unlike him to show that he was worried. 'I— You need a splint?' She thought quickly, her eyes flitting around her. 'Kirsty's cardigan? That's cotton so it would be fine as a pad. Your socks because they're longer and we can tie them, a folded newspaper as a splint?' Her improvisation clearly met with his approval because his blue eyes gleamed with approval.

'Let's do it.' Handing Kirsty to the woman's husband to hold, he dragged off his socks and thrust them into Evanna's hands. 'You'll be relieved to know that they've only been on my feet for about two minutes. You were reading the Sunday papers.' He turned to the woman's husband. 'Fold a section for me so that I have something rigid to use as support.'

The man dropped the phone, fumbled with the newspaper, cursing as he tried to fold it with hands made useless by nerves. Evanna reached over and took it from him, folded it neatly, placed it on the wound and they strapped the ankle.

Logan had the phone in his hand and was dialling. He made two calls—one to the air ambulance and one to Jim—and Evanna gave a swift nod of understanding. Jim owned the land they were walking on. The sheep in the field were his sheep and he owned a four-wheel-drive vehicle. Travelling cross-country, they could be in the surgery in less than five minutes.

Still holding Kirsty on one arm, Logan made the calls while Evanna glanced nervously around her. She'd lived on the island virtually all her life and she'd never seen a snake.

'What if it bites someone else? Should we look for it?'

'It will have gone. Adders are shy. They've been spotted on the island occasionally but they don't normally bother people. They feel the vibration of approaching walkers and slide away.'

'I think it must have been lying in the sun, warming itself,' the man muttered, dropping to his knees beside his wife. 'She trod on it and she was wearing sandals. It's summer. We didn't even bother with walking boots. We heard this terrific hiss and then she felt a really sharp stinging in her leg.'

'Can't breathe properly,' the woman gasped, lifting her hands to her throat, and Logan glanced across the fields.

'We're going to have you in the surgery in a couple of minutes,' he said easily, standing up and shielding his eyes from the sun. 'There's Jim now. I'm going to help you up, Alison, and we're going to get you into the car.'

Evanna looked at the woman's face, saw her increasing struggle for breath and wondered if they'd make it. Panic, with its sharp, deadly claws, stabbed through her and she looked at Logan, taking reassurance from the fact that he was so calm.

He was watching Alison and clearly working out a plan in his head. As Jim pulled up in his four-wheel-drive vehicle, Logan handed Kirsty to Evanna and lifted Alison inside. The rest of them clambered into the vehicle and Logan slammed the door shut.

'Drive,' he said to Jim, without wasting time on conversation or niceties and, to his credit, Jim rose to the challenge, covering the distance to the surgery in record time.

'I'll keep Kirsty with me,' Jim volunteered, and Logan gave a brief nod of thanks as he and Pete helped Alison out of the car.

Evanna unlocked the door and sprinted through to the con-

sulting room. Without hesitating, she unlocked the drug cupboard and removed the adrenaline.

'Can you do a pulse and blood pressure, please? And let's
give her some oxygen.'

Without hesitation, Logan helped Alison onto the couch,
jabbed the injection straight into the muscle and depressed the
plunger. 'Her pulse is a hundred and forty. I'm going to need
more adrenaline, Evanna, and I want to do an ECG.'

'Her blood pressure is ninety over fifty.' Evanna quickly
fastened a mask over the woman's mouth and nose and adjusted
the flow of oxygen. Then she reached for the ECG machine and
swiftly attached the leads.

'Ninety over fifty? That's low, isn't it? Is she going to be OK?'
The woman's husband was pacing the floor, his hands clasping
his head. 'I can't believe this has happened. I didn't even know
that we had poisonous snakes in the UK. If I'd known, I wouldn't
have let her walk in sandals. But it was hot and—'

'They rarely show themselves and the bite doesn't always
cause such an extreme reaction. She was unlucky.' Logan took
the second syringe from Evanna and injected the contents into
his patient. 'Let's give her some antihistamine and hydrocor-
tisone and I'm going to put a line in, just as a precaution.'

Evanna reached for the IV tray that she kept ready. 'Do you
think she needs antivenin?' She knew nothing about antivenin
but she knew that it existed.

'Possibly. She's obviously absorbed some venom.'

Evanna watched the ECG trace carefully but could see nothing
amiss. 'That seems all right. What exactly are you looking for?'

'Non specific changes—ST depression or T-wave inver-
sion.' Logan frowned and leaned closer. 'That seems all right.
Leave it on until we transfer her to the helicopter. I want to keep
an eye on it.'

'You're sending her to the mainland?' Evanna knew that

Logan never requested a helicopter transfer unless he was absolutely confident that the patient needed hospital help fast. In his years as the island GP, he'd shown himself to have an uncanny instinct for exactly when to call in the air ambulance.

'Yes.' His eyes were still on the ECG trace. 'Can you get the poisons unit on the phone for me? I want to talk to them.'

'Her blood pressure is coming up,' Evanna said, recording the reading and then reaching for the phone. She looked up the number and dialled swiftly, aware that Logan was examining his patient.

It was impossible to work with him and not admire him, she thought as she waited for someone on the other end to pick up the phone. In all the years that he'd been the doctor on Glenmore Island, she'd never seen him panic. *Even that awful night with Catherine, he'd been in control.* He was incredibly skilled and his confidence had a soothing effect on patients who were often anxious at finding themselves ill or injured so far from what they considered to be civilisation.

Logan removed the ad hoc dressing that they'd applied. 'Her leg is swelling up,' he said quietly, 'and I can see fang marks on her foot. So it was definitely a venomous bite. Do you know if her tetanus is up to date?'

'I have the poisons unit on the phone for you.' Evanna held out the phone and Logan stepped towards her and took the receiver.

'Can you clean and dress it, Evanna?' He lifted the phone to his ear. 'It's Logan MacNeil here.' His voice deep and steady, he swiftly outlined what had happened and discussed the best management with the person on the other end.

'Her colour looks better,' Pete said, and Evanna nodded as she checked her pulse again.

'Her breathing seems easier. We haven't even had a chance to take details from you. What's her surname?'

'Winchester. Alison Winchester. I'm Peter. We're staying at the Glenmore Arms. We only arrived yesterday.'

Evanna scribbled down the details and then checked the woman's pulse again and gave a nod. 'It's ninety-five now. Better. I'm just going to clean the wound and splint that leg properly.' She washed her hands, laid up a trolley and quickly cleaned and dressed the wound.

Logan replaced the phone. 'The air ambulance will be here any minute and we're going to transfer her to the mainland. They're expecting her in the hospital. I'll just write a quick letter so that they know what we've given.'

'I feel better.' Still pale, Alison lifted a hand to try and move the mask but Logan stopped her.

'Keep that on for the time being. The drugs I've given you are obviously taking effect and that's good, but we're going to fly you to the hospital on the mainland just in case you need some more treatment.'

'Will they keep me in?'

'It's likely, at least in the short term.'

'Are you going to go with her?' Evanna glanced out of the window as she heard the approaching helicopter.

'I ought to.' Logan's eyes were on the computer screen as he quickly drafted the referral letter. Then he pressed the print key and turned to look at her, and she read his mind.

Kirsty.

'I was just planning to have a quiet day so I'd be happy to have her,' she said softly, and he let out a long breath and ran his hand over the back of his neck.

'I feel guilty asking.'

'Don't. I love her, you know that. We'll have fun.' Evanna checked Alison's blood pressure again. 'That's much better. You go and talk to them, Logan.'

'Will I be able to go with her?' Pete glanced between the two of them and Logan nodded.

'That shouldn't be a problem. Unless you'd rather take your

car over on the ferry and drive. That way, you could pack a few things.'

'Yes, do that.' Alison shifted the mask slightly. 'I need you to bring me my night things and my bag from the bathroom. And I left my jewellery in the drawer by the bed. Better bring that, too.'

Evanna helped them transfer Alison to the helicopter and then went to check Kirsty.

'You might have warned me that she likes to pull hair. I've taught her to drive.' Jim grinned and Kirsty laughed with delight and held out her arms for a cuddle from Evanna.

'You and I are having a girls' day at home, Kirsty.' Evanna slid into the car. 'Jim, do you mind giving Pete a lift back to the Glenmore Arms? He's going to pack a few things, pick up the car and take the ferry to the mainland to be with his wife in hospital.'

'No problem. I'm due at work in half an hour anyway. Do you want to be dropped home?'

Evanna thought of all the preparation she'd planned to do on her bathroom and then dismissed it as unimportant. She could do it later. Her head ached and she didn't want to think about how tired she was. 'No, I'll spend the day here at Logan's. All Kirsty's toys are here. It will be easier to keep her occupied.'

It was mid-afternoon by the time Logan arrived home and Evanna and Kirsty were in the middle of an extremely messy painting session in the kitchen. She'd opened the sliding doors that led to the garden and a breeze cooled the stifling air.

'You put your hand flat, like that,' Evanna was saying as she planted Kirsty's hand in the middle of the paper and rocked it from side to side. 'Great!'

Logan stood in the doorway and watched. He loved the fact that Evanna wasn't bothered about the mess. She'd spread newspaper over the kitchen floor to protect it and then squeezed paint into saucers so that Kirsty could use her hands and feet, and Kirsty was bright-eyed with excitement. 'Whatever happened to reading a book or dressing a doll? I can't leave you two alone for a moment.'

Evanna glanced up, saw him there and scrambled to her feet, her cheeks flushed. She was still wearing the shorts and T-shirt that she'd been running in that morning, but she'd removed her trainers and her feet were bare. 'You know she loves painting. It's her favourite thing and I can't bring myself to say no. I've used plenty of newspaper so I'm hoping you won't be needing a new kitchen.'

'You spoil her,' Logan said softly, dropping his bag onto the nearest chair and removing his jacket. 'Amy used to hate doing anything messy because it meant clearing up, and she was always worried that Kirsty would splatter her with paint.'

'Well, I'm in my ancient running gear and I don't mind clearing up.' Evanna carefully lifted the paintings and put them outside on the table to dry in the sun, anchored by jam jars. 'How did it go with Alison?'

'I think they might give her antivenin. I've left her in their hands. She's in quite a bit of pain but her pulse and blood pressure have stabilised and her breathing has settled down. Hopefully she'll be all right now but they're going to keep her in for a bit just to check on her. Everyone is crowded around her, of course, because it's such an unusual thing to see.'

'I couldn't believe it was really a snake bite. I mean—' Kirsty was still planting her chubby little hands in the paint and Evanna stooped to adjust the newspaper on the floor '—we see a variety of accidents and illnesses on this island, but that was a first.'

'It's pretty rare.' Logan pulled open the fridge and removed a bottle of chilled water. 'And not often fatal in humans, although there are reports of severe allergic reactions and I thought Alison might have been one of those. Frustrating, actually, because you know I always carry adrenaline with me in the summer, ever since that wasp episode a few years ago. But Kirsty and I had only left the house for a quiet stroll so I didn't think of it. I had a nasty moment back there.'

'It didn't show. I think the fact that you were so incredibly calm helped to reassure Alison. Have you finished, sweetheart? That's a lovely painting. Clever girl.' Evanna lifted Kirsty, unconcerned about the volume of paint that was now attached to the child. 'I'm usually quite confident with emergencies, but not that one. I didn't want to speak in case I looked like a complete idiot. I had to stop myself from asking you stupid questions about first aid. I'm sure I read somewhere that you're meant to suck the venom out or something. Or cut the leg and let the blood flow.'

Logan drank the water straight from the bottle and then lowered his arm and smiled at her. 'You've been watching too much TV.'

'Actually, I never get to watch TV because I'm always working,' Evanna said with a pointed look. 'But there's so much myth and you hardly get copious amounts of experience in this country.'

She was so generous with Kirsty, Logan thought as he watched her. So patient. 'Well, these days more and more people keep dangerous snakes as pets and there's still some argument over best management and it does actually depend on the type of snake. But there is a body of medical evidence now and sucking and slashing isn't generally recommended.' Logan lifted the bottle and drank again. 'If you want to know about snake bites, Ethan is your man. He dealt with a few when he was working in Africa.'

Still holding Kirsty, Evanna glanced towards him. 'Really? I don't know how I feel about snakes. Sort of repelled and fascinated at the same time. I think if I'd met an adder on the path, I might have frozen with fright. I'm not surprised Alison felt a bit freaked out. Ugh.' She gave a shudder and Logan smiled, trying to imagine steady, practical Evanna freaking out about anything.

'It probably would have run away long before you saw it. To be honest, adders aren't generally a problem. They're shy.'

'But not this time.'

'She must have surprised it.'

'Well, she was lucky you were there.' Evanna wiped the worse of the paint from Kirsty's hands with kitchen roll and dropped it into the bin.

'I suppose so. I doubt the air ambulance would have made it quickly enough to deliver the adrenaline. That's why I decided that it was safer to take her to the surgery.' Logan threw the empty water bottle into the recycling bin. 'I'll talk to the warden about looking at the path. If they have a nest there, we should try and move it. We don't want a repeat of that, even though it was probably a one in a million chance. Is there anything to eat? I'm starving.'

'I made a chicken salad for your tea, but you could eat it now if you like.' Still with Kirsty on her hip, she walked to the fridge and pulled out a large white dish. 'I probably made too much but I thought you might be starving, having missed break-fast and lunch.'

'I am starving.' He looked at the dish and his mouth started to water. 'Is that your amazing chicken with the honey and lemon marinade?'

'That's the one.'

'My favourite. Have I ever told you that you're a genius in the kitchen, Evanna Duncan?'

A strange expression flickered across her face. 'Thank you.'

'Have you eaten?'

Evanna put Kirsty down on the floor. 'I should be going home. I still need to clear out my bathroom for Craig.'

Why was it, Logan mused, *that he always had the feeling she was trying to escape from him?* 'Share the salad with me.'

She hesitated and then gave a gasp of horror as she saw Kirsty crawling towards the white cupboards. 'No, angel. Not until I've washed your hands.' Smiling, she scooped the toddler into her arms and held her hands under running water, which turned blue and yellow as the splodges of paint faded and then disappeared. 'There. That's better. Now you're safe to have around. Just sit there a moment while I finish clearing up all the mess.'

She popped Kirsty on her bottom on the floor, carefully placed the paintings on the kitchen table to dry and swiftly gathered up the newspaper and disposed of it. Then she turned. 'Oh!'

Something in her voice made Logan look and he saw that Kirsty was up on her feet. While they both watched, she took a faltering step and then sank back onto her bottom with a satisfied grin.

'She walked!' Evanna clapped her hands with delight. 'Logan, she walked! You are a clever girl, Kirsty MacNeil. Let's see if she'll do it again.' She sank onto her knees and held out her hands. 'Walk to Evanna. Come on, Kirsty. Up you get!'

Kirsty scrambled to her feet again, swayed perilously and then took two steps before plopping back onto her bottom with a beaming smile.

'She's so pleased with herself!' Evanna grinned and scooped the child into her arms. 'Clever girl.'

'There'll be no peace for any of us now,' Logan predicted, captivated by the look of delight on Evanna's face. She was such a generous friend, he thought to himself as he picked up the salad and two plates. It was her day off and yet she'd willingly sacrificed it to look after his child.

And now she was eyeing the salad and the plates. 'I really ought to get home.'

'Not until you've eaten. Having given up your entire day for me, the least I can do is feed you, especially as you prepared the food.'

'You're the one who gave up your day, Logan,' she said quietly, opening a drawer and pulling out cutlery. 'I've been playing here with Kirsty. Hardly arduous. You've been working.'

'You have to join us, that's an order.' He winked at her and then watched, intrigued, as colour seeped into her cheeks. Why was she blushing?

'All right. You take the food out, I'll bring the drinks.'

They sat in the garden at the wooden table and Evanna held Kirsty on her lap and gave her breadsticks and chicken to eat. 'She's such a good eater. She loves my chicken.'

'We all love your chicken. That was the other thing about Amy.' Logan forked more salad onto his plate. 'She had a very limited repertoire in the kitchen. All she could cook was fish fingers.'

They ate in silence for a while and then Kirsty started to become fractious.

'She needs an early night,' Evanna murmured. 'I tried to put her down for a nap earlier but she was too wound up to sleep. She's tired.'

'You look tired, too.' Logan studied her face, noticing that her cheeks were paler than usual. 'Is something wrong? Did you have a bad night or something?'

'I'm fine.' She fussed around Kirsty and Logan suddenly had a strong suspicion that she was avoiding eye contact.

'Are you feeling ill? Because if you are then I can—'

'I'm not feeling ill, Logan. I'm fine. Really.' She stood up quickly, brushing a strand of hair out of her eyes and giving him a quick smile. 'If you're all right with Kirsty, I really ought to be going.'

He'd never known her so jumpy. 'Evanna.' He kept his voice

gentle. 'We're friends, aren't we? If there's something that you
need to talk about, I hope you know that I'll always listen. You
listen to my problems often enough. I hope you know that I'm
here for you, too. This isn't a one-sided relationship.'

'I don't have a problem. There's nothing I want to talk
about.' She handed him Kirsty and picked up her little rucksack.
'I'm going to make a move because I need to clear out the
bathroom before Craig comes tomorrow.'

Why was she in such a hurry to leave? 'I'll give you a lift home.'

'You don't need to do that, I can walk. The exercise will be
good for me. I was out for a run this morning when we met that
couple so I didn't exactly finish my session.'

Was she ill?

Was she worried about something?

Seriously concerned, Logan would have pursued the topic
but Kirsty was wriggling in his arms and he lifted her and
decided to have a word with Kyla. She was Evanna's best
friend. If something were wrong, Kyla would know. 'So you're
happy to look after her on Wednesday afternoon?'

'Of course. It will be a relief to escape from all the mess and
banging that will be going on at my house.' Evanna walked
across the garden towards the gate. 'See you in surgery, Logan.'

She couldn't even behave normally around him any more,
Evanna thought helplessly as she lengthened her stride and ran
the distance back to her house.

All her life she'd felt more comfortable with Logan than any
other person, but suddenly she felt awkward and uncomfortable
in his company. It was becoming harder and harder to hide her
feelings and obviously she wasn't succeeding any longer. He'd
guessed that something was wrong. And that was typical of
Logan, because he was extremely intuitive when it came to people.

Had he guessed how she felt about him?

No, of course he hadn't. Not yet.

But if she wasn't careful then he would, and then everything would change. She'd be mortified, he'd feel sorry for her—it would be completely hideous.

She shouldn't have stayed to eat with them. The moment he'd walked through the door she should have handed Kirsty to him and left. Playing house and getting cosy wasn't going to help her rehabilitation one bit. She'd never wean herself off Logan if she carried on spending this much time with him.

On Wednesday, things were going to be different, she promised herself as she let herself into her cottage. She'd stay with Kirsty until he arrived home and then she'd leave. No cosy chats. No supper in the garden.

Dropping her keys on the kitchen table, she went straight up to the bathroom for a shower.

She'd promised herself that she was going to build a life without Logan and that was what she was going to do.

CHAPTER SIX

'CAN you sign this prescription for me? I've changed Ann Carne's inhaler. I think she'd be better controlled on this.' Kyla stuck a prescription in front of her brother. 'I gather you had a busy Sunday.'

'Yes.' Logan signed with a flourish. 'Snake bite.'

'Good job Evanna was there to help.' Kyla took the prescription from him, her movements brisk and efficient. 'Would have been hard handling that on your own.'

'Yes. She was brilliant, as always. And then she took Kirsty for me while I went to the hospital.' Logan tucked his pen back in his pocket and looked at his sister. 'I wanted to ask you about her. Is she all right?'

'Why ask me? Why not ask her?'

'I did. I got the distinct impression that she was hiding something.'

'Like what?'

'I don't know.' Suddenly exasperated, Logan kept his eyes on his sister's face. 'Yesterday she looked pale. Tired. And she left the barbecue early. I just have a feeling that something is not right. She seems different. Jumpy.'

Kyla's gaze was direct. 'Well, you're the genius with women. I'm sure you'll figure out what's wrong.'

'That's why I'm asking you,' Logan said patiently. 'I thought you'd probably know. She's your best friend after all.'

'And best friends don't betray confidences.'

So there *was* something wrong. Logan sat back in his chair, genuinely concerned. 'If you know something, tell me. You have a duty to the practice to inform me of anything that affects my staff.'

'Your *staff?*' Kyla gave him a look of ill-disguised impatience. 'For goodness' sake, Logan, don't be so high and mighty! And try thinking about something other than work for five minutes, will you?'

He felt his shoulders tense. 'I'm not in the mood for a row, I just care about Evanna.'

'Do you?' Kyla looked at him, her gaze disturbingly direct. 'Really?'

Logan felt his own temper rise. 'Well, what sort of a question is that? Of course I care about her. Evanna has lived on this island all her life. She's a fantastic nurse and a really good friend. Frankly, I'm surprised you're not more worried about her yourself.'

'I'm worried,' Kyla said flatly. 'I'm very worried.'

'So you *do* know something.' Logan leaned forward, his voice a low growl. 'Tell me what's going on.'

'I dare say if Evanna has something she wants you to know, she'll tell you in good time. Thanks for the prescription.' Kyla walked towards the door and Logan stood up, his expression grim.

'Don't you dare say something like that and then leave the room.'

Kyla paused with her hand on the doorhandle. 'There's nothing I can tell you, Logan.'

The week flew by and by Wednesday afternoon Evanna was ready for a rest.

'I can't believe he's asked you to look after Kirsty,' Kyla grumbled as they exchanged notes after a busy clinic. 'What a nerve.'

'It isn't a nerve,' Evanna said calmly, dropping a soiled dressing into the correct bin. 'He needs someone that she's comfortable with. And, frankly, looking after Kirsty will be a pleasant change from looking after the rest of the population of this island. My feet are killing me and if I have to look at another case of sunburn I'm going to scream. It's the middle of August and it's blazing hot! Why don't people use sun block?'

'Because they're stupid,' Kyla said cheerfully. 'I've told Nick Hillier to arrest anyone who isn't wearing at least a factor twenty-five and lock them up until the sun goes down. And stop changing the subject. You're letting my brother take advantage of you.'

Evanna washed her hands and dried them. 'That's not true,' she said quietly, turning to face her friend. 'Logan and I have been friends for as long as you and I. He needs help and that's what friends are for. And anyway, if you saw the state of my house at the moment you'd understand why I'm only too happy to spend that afternoon at someone else's place.'

'You're too generous.'

'It isn't Logan's fault that I feel the way I do about him.'

'He asked me what was wrong with you.'

'Really?' Evanna stopped what she was doing. 'And what did you say?'

'Relax, I didn't tell him the truth, if that's what's worrying you, although I was very tempted. I told him that he should work it out himself. But obviously we're not going to hold our breath on that one because you've been in love with him for twenty-six years and he hasn't worked it out yet.' Kyla suppressed a yawn and made for the door. 'I'm still thinking about plan C.'

'What's plan C?'

'Hitting him over the head with an extremely hard object. I thought it might bring him to his senses.'

Evanna managed a smile. 'I'm relieved he doesn't know. Can you imagine how awkward it would be if he found out how I felt?' She gave a shudder and Kyla looked at her thoughtfully.

'Maybe it would just be a relief.'

'I don't think public rejection could ever be a relief,' Evanna said flatly. 'It's bad enough loving him, without him knowing. At least spare me that.'

'But if he knew, maybe he'd—'

'Don't.' Evanna interrupted her with a lift of her hand. 'Just don't even go there! You can't change a man's feelings. I'll see you tomorrow.'

She let herself through the door that connected with Logan's house and relieved Meg, who had been looking after Kirsty all morning.

The weather was stifling and Kirsty hot and short tempered and they spent the afternoon playing and reading books under the shade of the weeping willow.

Once Logan arrived home, Evanna made for the door, ruthlessly squashing the temptation to linger and chat. *And be with him.*

'Craig is tearing my bathroom to pieces so I need to go and scowl at him just to be sure he doesn't get too carried away. Looking at the mess at the moment, I can't believe it's ever going to look even half-decent.'

She arrived home to find her cottage in chaos. The front door was open and half her old bathroom was lying in the front garden.

'Remind me never to contemplate having anything more adventurous than the bathroom done.' She picked her way through a pile of dust and rubble. 'Craig, tell me that this is going to look good when you've finished. Please, tell me that.'

He pushed his hair out of his eyes with a grubby hand and

grinned. 'It's going to be stunning. The taps arrived today. They're great. You've got good taste, Nurse Duncan.'

Evanna sighed and tried not to look at the mess. 'So how long am I going to be without a bath?'

'A few days. I hear the helicopter was out twice on Sunday.'

'Yes.' Evanna tried not to look at the mess. 'Typical August, really.'

'And you've been helping Dr MacNeil with the little one.' Craig rubbed his forehead with the back of his hand. 'The man needs a wife. I dare say he'll meet someone else soon enough.'

Was it her imagination or was he giving her a funny look? 'Very possibly, but in the meantime he's managing perfectly well on his own.' Evanna remembered what Logan had said about everyone telling him he'd meet someone else. 'He's doing fine.'

'Still—nice of you to help him.'

'I've known Logan since I was born,' Evanna said evenly. 'He's one of my closest friends.'

'Of course he is. And you and Kyla have been thick as thieves since you were both in nappies.' Craig stared out across her garden. 'Sometimes you don't notice something when it's been in your face all your life.'

Was it that obvious to everyone? 'Craig—'

'He's single. You're single. Seems perfect to me.'

Evanna stared at him with a mixture of exasperation and embarrassment. Was everyone thinking the same as Craig? 'Anna Brice is single, too, Craig,' she said in a tart voice. 'Why not just pair her up with him.'

'Possibly because she's eighty-six on her next birthday.' Craig scratched his arm. 'It isn't just because you're both single that I think you'd be good together. You're friends. Everyone can see that.'

'Marriage is about far more than just friendship,' Evanna said briskly, and Craig gave a nod.

'Perhaps. But it's a good start.'

Evanna thought of the passion that Kyla and Ethan shared. She thought of the looks they exchanged and the way that they touched all the time. It was as if they couldn't be near each other and not be joined.

She wouldn't settle for less.

'I need to get on, Craig.'

'Of course you do, what with a busy morning in the surgery and a busy afternoon at Dr MacNeil's. I'll just finish up here and get out of your way.' He beamed at her. 'Is seven too early to start tomorrow? I like to get the heavy stuff done before the sun comes up.'

'Seven is fine. Thanks, Craig.'

One of the problems of living in a small community, Evanna reflected as she stepped over the rubble and walked into her kitchen, was that everyone was far too interested in everyone else.

She just hoped that no one said the same thing to Logan.

The next week passed in a blur as the surgery handled an unprecedented number of tourists.

'I feel as though I'm running an A and E department,' Logan grumbled as he and Evanna cleared up after stitching yet another child who had slipped on the rocks. 'That was a nasty cut.'

'He was rock-pooling and he should have been wearing shoes and not flip-flops. I suppose he just didn't have any grip, which was why he slipped.' Evanna dropped the stitch cutter into the sharps box. She'd been making a supreme effort to behave naturally with Logan and it seemed to be working. At least he'd stopped asking her if anything was wrong.

'People leave their brains behind when they're on holiday. I heard from the hospital today about Alison Winchester. They kept her in for a night and then followed her up before she went back down to London. She was still suffering aches and pains but no other effects that they can see. They've written to her GP.'

'That will be a first for him. I bet a GP in London would know even less about an adder bite than I did.' Evanna walked across the room and washed her hands. 'Did they manage to find the snake, by the way?'

'Funnily enough, yes. The park ranger rang me last week. They've relocated the family.'

'Mr and Mrs Adder.' Evanna laughed, yanking paper towels out of the holder. 'Somewhere homely with a nice view, I hope. Hot and cold running water.'

'Somewhere that no one is going to tread on them again, I hope,' Logan said dryly, sitting down and hitting a key on the computer. 'Am I finished here?'

'For now. Janet told me that you have three house calls. Doug is feeling really dizzy and wondered if you'd call on your way home. I suspect it's the heat or maybe his tablets, but it's worth checking. You know how worried he's been since they discharged him from the hospital.'

'Patients are always worried after a heart attack and it's still relatively early days for Doug.' Logan picked up a set of results and scanned them. 'How's Sonia's blood pressure at the moment?'

'It's still on the high side but her urine is fine and she has no swelling.'

Logan pulled a face and leaned back in his chair. 'I still feel uneasy about her, Evanna. I'd rather she was in hospital.'

Evanna felt a twist of sympathy. 'It's natural that you'd worry after what happened with Catherine, but so far there isn't an indication to admit her. I'm calling on her every day and if there's any change, we'll transfer her to the mainland in plenty of time.' Her eyes met his and she knew what he was thinking. That night, the horrible storm, losing Catherine because the helicopter hadn't been able to reach the island.

'Logan…' She hesitated, unsure whether to speak or not. 'You know that there was nothing else you could have done, don't you?'

'Yes.' His voice was harsh. 'But knowing that doesn't make it any easier to live with.'

'I know that. I was there, too.' Evanna swallowed, remembering the night with a shudder of cold panic. 'And I ask myself every day whether I could have done something different. Whether I should have spotted something.'

He ran a hand over his face and let out a long breath. 'There was nothing, we both know that. Catherine had an undiagnosed cardiac problem. Even if she'd been in hospital, the outcome would have been the same.'

'You were amazing, Logan.' She bit her lip, desperately wanting to comfort but not knowing how. 'You saved Kirsty and look how bonny she is.'

'Yes.'

Evanna hesitated. 'You should go out more, Logan. I'll babysit for you so that you can have dinner or something.'

He lifted an eyebrow, a flicker of humour in his blue eyes. 'With whom, exactly?'

'I don't know.' Evanna blushed, wishing that she'd never brought the subject up. It was bad enough thinking of Logan with another woman, without actually putting a face and name to someone. 'I just think you need to get out. Have a social life.'

He frowned. 'I have a social life. I see Kyla and Ethan. Meg and the cousins. You. We're always eating together and spending time on the beach.'

Her heart skipped. 'I know that. I was talking about… romance.'

'I'm not interested in romance.' His gaze was steady. 'Maybe I will be one day, but not at the moment.'

'Then that's fine. I'm not pushing you. I'm just saying that whenever you're ready, I'll help. I just want you to know that I'll babysit.' She decided that it was time to change the subject. 'You've been great with Lucy. She tells me that she's always ringing you in a panic about something and that you're incredibly patient.'

'She's a new mother. It's natural to worry. I keep meaning to pop in and see her but Ethan and I have just been too busy.' His eyes lingered on her face for a moment. 'How's she getting on?'

'Fine.' Evanna nodded. 'Sweet, actually. She's so in love with that baby.'

'Lucy is a nice girl. No problems, then?'

'No. The feeding is going well, the baby is starting to sleep a bit longer and I've seen Lucy out and about, pushing her in the pram, several times this week.'

'Good.' Logan glanced at his watch and stood up. 'Right, then. I'll get on with my house calls. It's Wednesday.' He frowned as if he'd only just realised that fact. 'Are you all right to look after Kirsty again this afternoon?'

'Of course. It's what we agreed. I hadn't forgotten. Believe me, it's a relief to escape from the banging and the blaring radio in my house. Why do builders always need the radio on full blast? I've eaten my way through two packets of paracetamol since they started and I'm sick of making bacon sandwiches for hungry men.'

Logan picked up his bag. 'You spoil people, that's your problem. Most builders are lucky to be given a dry biscuit.'

'I suppose I always feel that they'll do a better job if I've fed them properly,' Evanna said gloomily. 'I still can't quite believe that this bathroom is going to look nice when it's finished. There's dust everywhere and the walls are full of holes.'

'Craig is a reliable guy. And if he messes up your bathroom, I won't sign his repeat prescriptions.' Logan walked towards the door and then turned. 'By the way, the cleaner cancelled this morning so my house is going to be a complete mess, but just ignore it. Hopefully she'll be able to make it tomorrow. Anyway, by the time Kirsty has finished throwing her toys around, you'd never know a cleaner had been near the place. It always strikes me as a complete waste of money.'

'Spoken like a true man. I've bought a couple of new books for her. I thought I'd take her down to the beach for a picnic tea once it gets a bit cooler.'

'Good idea. If I finish my surgery early enough, I might join you down there.' He glanced at his watch. 'I'd better dash. Thanks, Evanna.'

'You're welcome.'

She watched him go and then lifted a hand to her ponytail. It was a good job he didn't notice her as a woman, she thought wryly, glancing at her reflection in the mirror. She hadn't been able to wash her hair for two days because Craig had turned the water off and now there was some problem with the plumbing that wasn't likely to be fixed for at least another day.

She was desperate for a shower or a bath but Kyla had a houseful of guests so she hadn't liked to ask.

And then a thought occurred to her.

What was stopping her having a shower at Logan's? She had a change of clothes in her bag ready for the afternoon, and Kirsty would be perfectly happy to play in the bathroom for five minutes while she washed her hair and scrubbed off all the dust and dirt that seemed to have stuck itself to her during the bathroom renovation.

She walked through the door that connected the surgery to Logan's house and smiled at Meg. 'My shift.'

'I don't know how you manage her,' Meg said wearily, handing over a wriggling Kirsty. 'All I do is spend the morning pulling her away from danger. I had all sorts of plans for cleaning and ironing and I've done nothing except wrestle with her. And as for feeding her—I'd swear that girl doesn't know where her mouth is. I had to change her twice during breakfast. There was porridge on the walls and the ceilings.'

'Have you been a handful?' Evanna kissed Kirsty's cheek and popped her down on the floor. 'Don't worry about the house, Meg. She'll probably have a nap in a minute. I'll try and catch up on a few things while she sleeps.'

'Don't you go doing Logan's cleaning.' Meg frowned her disapproval as she gathered her things together. 'It's good of you to look after Kirsty, without sorting out his mess.'

'I'm happy to help, Meg,' Evanna said softly, smiling at Kirsty who giggled and clapped her hands. 'I know it isn't very fashionable to admit it, but I love cleaning and keeping house.' Only she didn't have anyone to do it for, except herself.

'Well, if Kirsty lets you so much as lift a teatowel, it will be a miracle. I need to dash because apparently the café is heaving with tourists.' Meg leaned towards Kirsty and waved a finger. 'Now, you be a good girl!'

Kirsty beamed and waved. 'Byee-ee.'

'Oh!' Evanna gasped with delight. 'I didn't know she'd learned that!'

'Now, don't you go being soppy about her—she's a cheeky monkey. And she knows exactly how to get round you.' Meg slipped her bag onto her shoulder and made for the door. 'Have a good afternoon. Pop in for an ice cream if you feel like it. I'll make her one of my specials.'

Evanna waited for the door to close behind her and then settled down on the floor next to Kirsty, who was rubbing her eyes. 'You've had a busy morning. Are you tired, pickle? Where's your blanket?' She looked around for the little pink blanket that Kirsty always slept with and spotted it lying over the back of a chair. 'Let's take you up to bed and see if you feel like a nap.'

She changed Kirsty's nappy, gave her a drink of milk and then settled her in the cot with her blanket. Immediately Kirsty's eyes drifted shut.

'Creating trouble for Meg obviously wore you out,' Evanna murmured with amusement, creeping out of the room and leaving the door open a crack.

She glanced longingly at the bathroom but then decided she may as well tidy the house before she finally had the wash she'd been fantasising about for hours.

For the next hour she worked like a demon. She neatly stacked all Logan's medical journals, she scooped clothes from the floor and put them in the washing machine, she tidied and scrubbed the kitchen until all the surfaces were gleaming, she mopped the floor, ran the dishwasher and emptied all the bins.

Then she threw open all the doors and windows to air the place. Logan's house was lovely, she reflected as she plumped the cushions on his soft, comfortable sofa. So airy and light. It was a little further from the beach than hers, but she loved the space and all the windows and she adored his garden. As well as the weeping willow there were four huge apple trees that provided plenty of dappled shade. A large white hammock was strung between two of the trees and a children's book and several toys were lying abandoned on the grass. Logan had obviously been out there with Kirsty. Evanna looked at the hammock longingly. *Later,* she promised herself. Maybe she and Kirsty would curl up in the hammock to read books.

She chopped vegetables ready to add to the casserole that she planned to make later and then looked at the clock. Kirsty had been asleep for an hour and a half.

Feeling horribly hot and sticky after her efforts on the house, Evanna dragged her forearm over her forehead and decided to check on the child.

She crept upstairs and peeped around the door but the little girl was still fast asleep, the tip of her thumb in her mouth.

Evanna closed the door again and decided that she just about had time for a quick shower before the toddler woke up. Then she'd make the casserole for supper. She could give it to Kirsty for tea and Logan would be able to eat the remains when he finished work.

She walked into the bathroom that she'd cleaned earlier. Oh, the bliss of not having to pick her way through rubble! Swiftly she stripped off her clothes and stepped under Logan's state-of-the-art power shower. Five minutes. That was all it would take. And, by then, Kirsty should be ready to wake up.

Logan opened the front door and walked into his house. Bracing himself for the usual noise and activity, he was surprised to find the house silent. Then he remembered Evanna mentioning that she might take Kirsty to the beach.

The morning post was neatly stacked on the hall table and he could see at a glance that both the kitchen and the living room were immaculate. Meg had already called him to apologise for the fact that she hadn't managed to touch any of the housework, thanks to the demands of his daughter, so he knew that only one person could be responsible for the sudden transformation of his house.

Evanna.

She must have cleaned for him. She was a born nurturer, he thought as he noticed the polished kitchen floor and the vegetables chopped ready for a casserole. Always caring for people whether she was on or off duty. Feeling a twist of guilt, he ignored the post and walked upstairs towards his bedroom. He'd just find the textbook he needed, make himself a cup of tea and then get back to the surgery and tackle the mountain of paperwork that awaited him.

As he reached the top of the stairs, the bathroom door opened and Evanna walked out.

Naked.

And dripping wet.

Logan stared and then he almost swallowed his tongue.

Her legs were long and slender, her hips wonderfully curved and her breasts full and crowned by rosy pink nipples which glistened with drops of water from the shower.

'Evanna!' He croaked out her name and she froze to the spot and her eyes widened and locked with his.

For a long, pulsing moment they both stood. Staring.

The atmosphere crackled with tension and then she came to her senses, gave a squeak of horror and looked around desperately for something to cover herself up with, but there was nothing. 'I forgot to grab a towel—I—I was—You can't look—*Logan!*' Her voice was tortured with embarrassment as she glared at him. '*Stop* looking at me! It's not very gentlemanly.'

Gentlemanly?

At any other time Logan would have laughed at her use of such an old-fashioned word but he was too busy being thoroughly ungentlemanly to respond. In fact, he didn't really know what he was doing. His brain had ceased coherent thought and his eyes were definitely under independent rule. It wasn't until she moved her hands down to cover herself that he realised his gaze had been firmly fixed on the tempting shadows between her legs.

All the oxygen seemed to have been sucked out of the air and Logan suddenly couldn't breathe properly.

She was still trying to shield herself with her hands but he already had an all too clear image of her lush feminine curves imprinted on his brain.

He'd known Evanna for his whole life and he'd thought that he knew everything there was to know about her. He knew that she was kind, endlessly patient and had a good sense of humour.

He knew how she liked her coffee, he knew that she liked to run and swim. He knew that at school she'd been top in English but hopeless at maths. She was his sister's best friend and he knew her well. Really, really well. Up until today he would have said that there was nothing about Evanna that he didn't know.

So why hadn't he known that she had a body straight out of a hot male fantasy?

Gripped by lust, he closed his eyes briefly to try and erase the image and dragged a towel from the cupboard.

'Here…' His voice hoarse, he clutched the towel, intending to hand it to her and move away, but he couldn't prevent himself from taking one more look and then found he couldn't stop looking. The creamy skin of her shoulder and the tempting swell of her breasts were more addictive than any drug.

She had fantastic breasts.

Had she always had those breasts or had she suddenly grown them?

Why had he never noticed her breasts before?

Jabbing his fingers through his hair, he tried to look away but his eyes just wouldn't obey his brain. Her hair was soaking wet and hung halfway down her back, and she was deliciously slippery and gleaming wet after her shower. His mouth dried and he realised that any moment now he was going to power her back against the wall and take her. Hard. 'I— You—'

'For crying out loud, Logan, *stop staring!*' Her voice sounded strangled and her expression was horrified as she snatched the towel and held it in front of her. 'You've seen me in a bikini a million times so I don't see why seeing me naked is such a big step.'

Had he seen her in a bikini? His mind dulled by lust, Logan struggled to think. Yes. He *had* seen her in a bikini. So why hadn't he ever noticed her body before? Was he blind? Stupid? *Both?* Lost in an explicit fantasy involving his hands and mouth on those delicious curves, it took him a minute to realise that she'd asked him a question. 'What? Sorry?'

She stared at him in exasperation. 'What is the *matter* with you? I asked you what on earth you were doing here, anyway.'

Taking a fast ride to paradise? 'I live here. I think.' He wasn't sure of anything any more.

'Well, I know that you live here. I'm not stupid.' She tightened her grip on the towel, trying to hold it in place. 'But I wasn't expecting you home. You're *supposed* to be working.'

He'd never heard Evanna snappy before but she was decidedly snappy and he found her efforts to maintain her dignity and privacy incredibly endearing. Water clung to her dark lashes and her cheeks were pink with embarrassment.

'I was working,' he drawled softly, 'but I wanted—I needed…' He couldn't remember what he wanted or needed because it had been superseded by something else entirely. *Her.*

'Oh, forget it! It doesn't matter now.' She interrupted him and backed into the bathroom, glaring at him as if he'd committed a terrible sin.

And he hadn't. Not yet.

But in another moment he might do just that.

The temptation to just grab her and bring his mouth down on her soft, pink lips was so overwhelming that he clenched his fists by his sides, just to make sure that he wasn't tempted.

'Oh, this has got to be the most embarrassing moment of my life,' Evanna muttered, pushing the door closed between them and leaving it open just a crack. 'Stop staring and pass me my clothes.'

'Clothes?'

'Yes, Logan,' she snapped. '*My clothes!* They're in a pile on the floor outside the bathroom door. Get a grip! Did you leave your brain behind at work?'

In all the years he'd known her, he'd never heard Evanna irritable before. She was the most tolerant, patient person he'd ever met but suddenly she was behaving as though he'd done something grievously wrong.

'Evanna.' He tried to keep his tone mild. *Tried to sound indifferent.* 'There's no need to be embarrassed. I've known you all my life.'

And he'd obviously been walking around with his eyes shut!

'Well, that doesn't mean I want to stand in front of you stark naked! My clothes, Logan! They're in the bag by your feet. And don't you *dare* ever breathe a word of this to anyone. If I am on the receiving end of a single knowing wink when I walk into the pub, you'll be finding yourself a new practice nurse.'

Logan dutifully found the bag and handed it to her. She virtually dragged it from his hand and closed the bathroom door firmly in his face.

Logan stared at the wood. He could have told her that it didn't make any difference, hiding behind a door or a towel. He could have told her that the image of her lush, naked body was now firmly fixed on his *extremely* over-heated brain. But he thought that in her current mood she just might hit him so he stayed silent and tensed slightly when she dragged open the door and faced him.

She was wearing skimpy shorts and an ancient T-shirt in a washed-out, faded blue and her long, damp hair was caught up in a ponytail.

She looked like the old Evanna. Except that she didn't. Because now he knew.

He knew what was underneath the clothes.

'I'm dressed,' she said through gritted teeth, thrusting the damp towel into his hands, 'so you can stop standing there, gawping.'

'Evanna—'

'Oh, grow up!' Her cheeks flushed a deep shade of pink and she scurried into Kirsty's room, leaving Logan staring after her.

Aware that he needed to pull himself together, he drew in a deep breath and tried to think about something boring and inconsequential. Anything that would take his mind off the vivid image of Evanna's naked body. Since Catherine's death he hadn't thought about a woman—*hadn't wanted a woman.*

Until now.

Frustrated and taken aback by the strength of his own reaction, he suddenly knew that he had to get out of the house before he did something that would embarrass both of them. This was Evanna. They were friends, for goodness' sake. Somehow he had to erase that image from his mind and go back to the way he'd seen her previously—as a colleague and a lifelong friend. *The best friend he had.* Thoughts of sex had never intruded on their relationship before and he couldn't let it now.

If she knew just how much she'd affected him, she'd feel awkward. Their entire relationship would change. They wouldn't be able to work together properly. They…

Swearing softly, he retreated back downstairs, pushed open the door that connected his house to the surgery and walked back to his consulting room without any hope of being able to concentrate.

Evanna held her head in her hands and tried not to scream.

How could she have been so *stupid?*

Wasn't it perfectly obvious that he'd come home the minute she'd chosen to take a shower in his bathroom? Wasn't life always like that?

Tortured by embarrassment, Evanna resisted the temptation to hide under Kirsty's cot and never come out again.

The little girl was wide awake, lying on her back, hugging her blanket and sucking her thumb, oblivious to the turmoil that Evanna was suffering.

Why hadn't she at least remembered to take a towel into the bathroom with her?

What had possessed her to walk out of the bathroom, naked?

And why hadn't he just done the gentlemanly thing and looked away? Why hadn't he given her one of his cheeky smiles and covered his eyes?

It didn't even help to tell herself that he'd seen her in a swimming costume a million times because never, when he'd seen her on the beach, had he ever reacted with such stunned amazement.

Did she really look that awful?

Anyone would think he'd never seen a naked woman before, she thought crossly, lifting Kirsty from her cot and giving her a hug. Which was nonsense, because everyone knew that Logan Alastair MacNeil had had a fearsome reputation with women until he'd met and married Catherine. There were some on the island who'd thought he'd never settle down. So, for him to stand there with his mouth open as if he were shocked to see a naked woman was ridiculous, because she happened to know that he'd seen more than his fair share of naked women in his time.

'Oh, Kirsty, I've never been so embarrassed,' she whispered, delaying the moment until she had to leave the safety of the bedroom. But Kirsty was full of energy after her sleep and dying to play so she had no choice but to take her downstairs.

Determined to behave as though nothing had happened, Evanna lifted her chin and carried the toddler into the kitchen.

But there was no sign of Logan.

Unnaturally jumpy, Evanna looked around, called his name and then peeped out of the front door, but there was no sign of his car.

He'd gone.

Without even saying goodbye.

'Nice to know that seeing me naked had such an amazing effect on him,' Evanna grumbled as she pulled a fromage frais out of the fridge for Kirsty. 'Did he grab me and kiss me senseless? No. Was he so overwhelmed by the sight of my wet, naked body that he couldn't keep his hands off me? No. What does he do? He just stares, stammers like an idiot and then walks off without even bothering to say goodbye. I tell you, Kirsty MacNeil, you should have been born a man. It's a lot easier than being a woman, believe me.'

CHAPTER SEVEN

'SONIA'S blood pressure is still high. She's made an appointment to go to the hospital on Monday for a check.' Evanna put some forms on the desk in front of Logan, not meeting his eyes. But he was watching her.

She could feel him watching her.

'Good. I don't mind admitting that I'd be far happier if they kept her in.'

It was two days after what Evanna now called 'the bathroom incident', and every time they came into contact with each other, they skirted round the issue, each of them incredibly formal with the other, and Evanna was starting to despair that she'd ever be able to behave naturally again.

And he wasn't behaving naturally either.

It would have helped if he'd laughed or made some sort of light-hearted comment, but he hadn't referred to it. Not only that, but he hardly looked at her when she walked into the room.

It was enough to make a girl lose every scrap of confidence. 'Janet wanted to know if you'd like some more coffee.'

'Yes, please.' His voice was terse. 'I need the caffeine to keep me awake. I had a terrible night. Again.'

Evanna hesitated. Two days ago, *before the bathroom incident,* she would have been concerned enough about that statement to question him further, but now she didn't dare because she was suddenly horribly aware of everything about him and the effect he had on her was incredibly frustrating.

She just didn't know what to say or do. And clearly he felt the same way because he made no effort to detain her when she scurried towards the door.

'I'll ask Janet to bring you some coffee.' She delivered the message to the kindly receptionist and retreated to the safety of her own room, finished her clinic and then restocked and tidied until she could be sure that Logan would have left on his house calls.

'Logan's looking terrible,' Janet clucked as she locked the surgery door. 'Four cups of coffee he's asked for this morning. It's a wonder his hands aren't shaking too much to hold his stethoscope. And the same yesterday.'

'Kirsty's probably keeping him awake,' Evanna mumbled, as she returned a set of notes she'd borrowed. 'Disturbed nights.'

'Well, you can tell from the shadows under his eyes that he's having disturbed nights, but I don't think Kirsty is the culprit.' Janet checked the clinic list for the afternoon. 'He told me only yesterday that she goes right through the night now, bless her.'

'So what's keeping him awake?' Evanna delved into her bag for her keys and Janet gave a sigh.

'I don't know, but I was hoping you did. You're the one he talks to, Evanna. Through all of last year when he was struggling to keep everything going, you were the only one he really talked to.'

Evanna stilled. It was true. Logan had found her easy to talk to. But since she'd stripped naked in his bathroom, he'd hardly spoken a word to her that didn't revolve around patient care.

Which meant only one thing. Clearly he felt as awkward about the whole incident as she did, which was entirely ridiculous, she told herself as she waved goodbye to Janet and made for the door. They'd known each other all their lives. Surely they could get themselves past one embarrassing incident?

If he wasn't going to tackle the subject then she would. She'd mention it and dismiss it as if the whole incident had been nothing more than a laugh.

Logan kept the top down on his sports car, hoping that the breeze might clear his head.

Four cups of coffee and a splash of cold water on the face had done little to revive him and he vowed to have an early night.

Then he remembered that an early night was going to make no difference whatsoever. It wasn't going to bed that was a problem, it was sleeping when he got there. Eyes open or eyes shut, he saw Evanna. Naked. Her creamy, smooth skin still glistening and damp from the shower, her hair trailing down her back. It had been two days since he'd walked in on her but he couldn't erase the image from his brain.

He felt himself grow hard and cursed repeatedly, jabbing the car into gear more viciously than was necessary.

He was afraid to stand up when she walked into a room in case she noticed the effect she had on him.

What was the matter with him?

Why was his reaction so extreme?

Was it just because he hadn't had sex since Catherine's death? And so what if it was? What could he do about it? He was hardly likely to go up to Evanna and suggest that they spent a steamy night between the sheets together, was he? What was he supposed to say? *Oh, good morning, Nurse Duncan. Doug McDonald's blood pressure has come right down on his new drug regime and, by the way, do you fancy stripping naked and sleeping with me because I can't get your body out of my head?*

Suffering from an intense bout of male frustration, Logan pulled the car to the side of the road and switched off the engine.

He sat for a long moment just staring out across the sparkling sea while he sifted through the options.

Forget the whole thing, that was the obvious option. But he'd just spent an extremely frustrating two days trying to do exactly that, and it hadn't worked. So forgetting her wasn't an option.

But what was the alternative?

Tell her how he felt? Ask her out?

He almost laughed as he anticipated her reaction. He'd known Evanna all her life. If he asked her out, she'd laugh and, anyway, they already spent a great deal of time together. She was in and out of his house, helping him with Kirsty and joining his extended family for meals. She was his sister's best friend. How was he supposed to make it clear that he wanted the time they spent together to be different? How was he supposed to let her know that when he asked her to spend time with him, it wasn't a platonic invitation.

How did you turn a deep and lasting friendship into a love affair?

The answer was that you didn't.

If anything were going to happen between them, it would have happened years ago. When they'd been teenagers, fooling around on the beach. When she'd had sleepovers with Kyla. When they'd started working together. They'd had so much opportunity.

And if Evanna had felt anything for him at all, why would she have been so appalled that he'd seen her naked?

There was no way she could have failed to be aware of his reaction to her.

And yet she hadn't flirted or even laughed. She'd been shocked. Embarrassed. Unable to hide herself quickly enough.

Hardly the reaction of a woman keen to alter the status of their relationship.

If he showed her how he felt and she rejected him, it would make their working situation intolerable.

Which meant that somehow he had to get his feelings under control.

Somehow he had to behave as if nothing had happened.

As if he wasn't constantly fantasising about her body.

It was impossible to miss the irony of the situation, he thought to himself as he ran a hand over his face and breathed out heavily. *Finally,* he was interested in a woman again. For the first time since Catherine's death he wanted to get out there and *live,* instead of just surviving from day to day. But the object of his attentions was just about the only woman on the island who had never made a pass at him.

'Evanna? Have you been listening to a word I've been saying? Hello? Is anyone in?'

Evanna gave a start, a far-away look in her eyes as she focused on her friend. 'Sorry. Did you say something?'

'No, I'm just chatting to myself for entertainment really. I love the sound of my own voice,' Kyla quipped, rolling her eyes to the ceiling. 'I've been talking to you for *ten minutes* and you've been staring out of the window with a glazed expression on your face. If I didn't know better, I'd think I was boring.'

Evanna shook her head and gave a guilty smile. 'Sorry. I was thinking about…something.'

'Humph.' Kyla threw her a penetrating look. 'I don't suppose that *something* is six foot two, has blue eyes and shares my DNA?'

Evanna ignored the question. 'So, what were you telling me about?'

'Well, I don't have a lifetime to repeat it, so I'll just summarise,' Kyla said dryly. 'Are you going to the beach barbecue next Saturday?'

Evanna frowned. 'I'd forgotten about it.'

'How could you possibly have forgotten the highlight of the Glenmore social calendar?' Kyla sat back as Meg placed a towering ice cream in front of her. 'Thanks. I've been fantasising about this all day.'

Evanna shook her head in disbelief. 'How you can consume so much ice cream and still fit into your clothes is beyond my understanding.'

'Life is to be lived,' Kyla said airily, sticking her spoon into the ice cream. 'So—are you coming?'

Would Logan be there? Probably not, Evanna decided. He never went. And she needed to get out. *She needed the distraction.* 'I'll be there.'

'Good. Ethan and I will meet you on the beach. They're going to do a lifeboat demonstration at six.'

'Well, I refuse to be a volunteer victim.'

'We probably won't need a volunteer,' Kyla said cheerfully, finishing her ice cream in record time. 'The tourists are so reckless, one of them is bound to be drowning at the right moment.'

'Kyla, that's a terrible thing to say!'

'It's the truth. Ask the lifeboat crew. They've never been as busy as they have this summer. Is that your phone ringing?'

Evanna dug into her pocket and removed the phone. 'Missed call. I wonder who it was.' She checked the number and frowned. 'That's Sonia. I wonder what she wants. I called on her yesterday.'

'You gave her your mobile number? You're a soft touch, Evanna Duncan.' Kyla waved the spoon in her direction. 'Why don't you just let the patients move in with you? Save them having to make appointments or ring you at all.'

Evanna was too busy calling Sonia to respond. 'She isn't answering the phone.' She tried the number again but it was busy.

'She's probably busy ringing you!'

'She's supposed to be going to the hospital on Monday for a check. Her blood pressure has been giving Logan nightmares.'

Kyla's smile faded. 'Yes, well, obviously heavily pregnant

women aren't his favourite thing after what happened to Catherine.'

'I know that. But we can hardly send everyone to live on the mainland the moment they become pregnant.' Evanna glanced at her watch and stood up. 'If I go now, I've time to call in before my afternoon surgery. Thanks for the coffee. Meg?' She called across the café. 'I'm off.'

Meg was cutting a large chocolate cake into generous slices, ready for the afternoon rush. 'Will we see you at the beach barbecue, dear?'

'Yes. I hope so.' Evanna was distracted. Why was Sonia calling? Was she in trouble?

'It's going to be a fantastic night. Ben and Nick have planned the most fantastic firework display.'

'I'm looking forward to it. I'll call you, Kyla!' Evanna hurried out of the café and onto the quay. It was mid-afternoon and the sun was blazing. Tourists ambled along the pavement next to the harbour, legs and shoulders bared, feet tucked into flip-flops. They queued for boat trips and crowded into the ice-cream shops in an attempt to cool down.

'Good afternoon, Nurse Duncan!'

Spotting the headmistress from the local primary school, Evanna quickly crossed the road to talk to her.

'Hello, Miss Carne. Everything all right?' Immediately she felt ten years old again and to cover her awkwardness she stooped to pat the little dog that was panting in the heat. 'Are you enjoying the school holidays?'

'Yes. I'm off to Venice next week with my friend Diane from Glasgow. We're having a city break.'

'Well, that will be a change from island life. You have a good time and don't forget your inhalers.' She blushed, always un-comfortable discussing health topics with her old headmis-tress. Usually she left it to Kyla, who was much bolder.

'I won't. I had a long chat with Kyla about what I should be doing with them on holiday and Dr MacNeil wrote me a new prescription. What about you, dear? Are you getting away?'

'No. I've just had my bathroom done and it's left a hole in my bank balance.' Evanna laughed as she straightened up. 'Does that sound sad?'

'Not at all. Very indulgent. You'll be able to enjoy it the whole year round.'

'It doesn't feel indulgent at the moment when I'm stepping over dust and rubble. Still, I hope it will be finished soon.' It didn't matter how old you were, she reflected, your headmistress was always going to be your headmistress.

Miss Carne adjusted her glasses, as she'd always done at the beginning of every lesson. 'Are you going to the beach barbecue on Saturday?'

Why was everyone suddenly so interested in whether she was going? 'Yes, I think so.' Evanna brushed a strand of hair out of her eyes and tried to remind herself that she was an adult now, with a responsible job. 'Well, I'd better go. I have afternoon clinic starting soon and I want to call in on Sonia on the way.'

Miss Carne gave an indulgent smile. 'Little Evanna. You were always such a star at English.'

'But hopeless at maths,' Evanna murmured, and the other lady smiled.

'You would have done a great deal better if that little monkey Kyla hadn't always been talking to you instead of letting you concentrate! I always knew you'd be a wonderful nurse. If someone fell in the playground, you were always there, patching them up, delivering a hug.'

Evanna blushed. 'Well—it's good to see you, Miss Carne.'

'You take care, dear. Oh, Evanna—I've been meaning to ask you.' She frowned. 'Do you know the little Price girl? Helen.

She moved here in the spring with her family. She joined my reception class.'

Evanna recalled Kyla pointing out a little girl on the beach earlier in the summer. 'Vaguely. I haven't actually met them. Why?'

Ann Carne looked thoughtful. 'She just seems quite a delicate child. And I noticed during sports day that she was terribly out of breath. I thought she might have asthma.'

'Have you mentioned it to the parents?'

'Well, the father's hardly ever around. He's a journalist, I think. Travels all the time. And the mother is quite shy. Not mixing that well.'

'To my knowledge she hasn't been to see us, but obviously I was away for a month so I can't be sure. I'll dig out her records and have a check. And I'll have a word with Logan.' Evanna dodged a group of tourists and slid into her car. 'Bye, Miss Carne.'

'You shouldn't be parking there, Nurse Duncan.' Nick Hillier, the island policeman, stuck his head through her open window. 'I ought to book you.'

'Now, why would you do a thing like that when you've so many other better things to be doing?' She smiled at him, wishing that she could find him attractive. Kyla always said that it was because he'd tied their plaits together in school but Evanna knew that wasn't true. At least, not for her. The reason she couldn't find Nick Hillier attractive was because she was crazy about Logan and always had been.

'Nick, can I ask you something? When you see Miss Carne, does she make you feel as though you're back in primary school?'

He grinned. 'Every time. Even when I have her in a cell in handcuffs.'

Evanna laughed at the ridiculous image that his words created. 'I always feel very uncomfortable with her.'

'I don't know why because you were always her favourite.

In fact, you were pretty much everyone's favourite,' Nick said gruffly, and Evanna looked at him, startled.

'Nick—'

He lifted a hand and gave a rueful smile. 'I'm not going to ask you on a date because I know you'll only refuse me, and there's only so much rejection a guy can take, but are you going to the beach barbecue on Saturday?'

'Yes.' Evanna fastened her seat belt and started the engine. 'Although why everyone is so interested in whether or not I'm going is a mystery to me.'

'I suppose we're all hoping you're going to make an extra-big batch of your double chocolate brownies.' Nick grinned and stood up. 'If you don't, I just might have to give you a night in the cells handcuffed to your old headmistress.'

'If you saw the current state of my house you'd realise that the cells are currently an attractive option. I have to go, Nick. I want to call on Sonia.'

Nick frowned. 'I saw her earlier. She looked pale.'

'I'm going to check on her now.' Evanna felt a flicker of unease. 'I really have to go. Take care of yourself and make sure you arrest anyone who isn't using sun cream. We're fed up with treating burns.'

He laughed and stood back so that she could pull out.

Evanna drove away from the harbour and took the turning that led inland to Sonia's house. She should just have time to call in, reassure herself that everything was all right and that the call had been about something trivial, and still make it in time for her afternoon clinic.

And then she saw another car close behind her. An open-topped sports car with a dark-haired man at the wheel.

Logan. And he was flashing his lights.

She pulled up outside Sonia's house and hurried out of her car. 'What are you doing here? Sonia tried to phone me and—'

'Her waters have broken.' Logan's tone was grim. 'Steve called me five minutes ago. There's a ferry leaving in ten minutes. Damn it, Evanna, we'd better get her on that boat because I am not delivering another baby on this island.'

'Calm down,' Evanna said softly, reflecting on the fact that she'd never had to use those words to Logan before. In all the years they'd worked together, she'd never seen him panic. 'It's her first baby so I'm sure there's plenty of time. Given that she's only thirty-six weeks, I agree that we should transfer her to the mainland. Is she having contractions?'

'Not according to Steve.'

Evanna looked at his face and saw the tension. She put a steadying hand on his arm. 'It's going to be fine, Logan.' And then she realised what an utterly stupid thing that was to say because it hadn't been fine for Catherine. 'I'm sorry.'

'Don't be.' His voice was harsh. 'And I'm sure it will be OK but I'd rather it was fine on the mainland and not on this island. I'm not delivering another baby here, Evanna. Unless the head is actually showing, she's going on that ferry. And if the head is about to be delivered, I'm calling the helicopter.'

'Logan…' It was so unlike him to be anything other than entirely relaxed that for a moment she didn't know how to respond and she wasn't given a chance to work out the right thing to say because Steve appeared in the doorway, the phone in his hand.

'Thank goodness you're here. She's having contractions.' He spoke rapidly and there was panic in his voice. 'Strong ones. Every minute.'

Evanna grabbed her bag from the car and sprinted down the path. 'Where is she?'

'Up in the bedroom. She was having a lie-down when it all started. She stood up to go to the toilet and her waters broke. Then nothing for a while and then suddenly all this pain and she keeps yelling at me and telling me she feels sick.' Steve jabbed his fingers through his hair. 'Her bag's packed and everything. Should I take her to the hospital?'

'Yes. Get the car out of the garage,' Logan said tersely, but Evanna intervened.

'We'll just look at her first,' she said quickly, catching Logan's eye to prevent him from arguing with her. It wouldn't help Steve to know that Logan was worried. 'Can I go up?'

'Of course. You know where it is. First on the right.'

Evanna ran up the narrow staircase and pushed open the bedroom door. 'Sonia?'

She was on the floor, kneeling, her elbows on the bed. Her hair was sticking to her forehead and her eyes were scared. 'Nurse Duncan. Thank goodness. I tried to call you.'

'I know. I had a missed call and then you didn't answer. But I'm here now. Goodness, you look hot. Let's get a cool flannel on your head.' Evanna dropped her bag on the floor and knelt down next to Sonia. 'You're going to be fine, I promise. I just need to wash my hands and then I can take a look at you and we can decide what to do. Can I use the bathroom?'

'Through there.' Sonia waved a hand and then gave a howl of pain and buried her head in her arms. Steve came thundering up the stairs and slid an arm round her.

'There, love. You're doing well,' he said in a bracingly cheerful tone.

Evanna emerged from the bathroom in time to hear Sonia snap, 'Get away from me.'

Seeing the hurt and confusion on Steve's face, she put a hand on his arm. 'Women in labour always say things they don't mean,' she said softly, kneeling on the floor next to Sonia and rubbing her shoulders.

'I just want to help,' Steve said helplessly, and Evanna nodded.

'Could you fetch a jug of iced water? And a cool flannel would be welcome, I'm sure. This heat is stifling.'

'I put the fan on her but it seemed to make her cross.'

'Don't tell the whole island I'm moody!' The contraction eased and Sonia groaned. 'This is agony. Why don't any of the books tell you that it's this painful? There's all this rubbish about breathing through the pain and when it hits it's so bad I can't breathe at all!'

'How often have the pains been coming?'

'It feels continuous,' Sonia groaned. 'My waters broke and there was nothing and then suddenly, wham. Agony.'

'Evanna.' Logan's tone was sharp and Evanna looked up to see him standing in the doorway, his knuckles white as he held onto his phone. 'We need to get her to the hospital. Jim is holding the ferry.'

'I'll go and get the car,' Steve began, but at that moment Sonia turned her head and was violently sick into the bowl that Steve had left by her side.

'She can't go on a ferry like this, Logan,' Evanna remonstrated softly, sliding a hand over Sonia's shoulders to support her, 'neither can she go on a helicopter. I need to examine her, but I think she's in transition.'

'Transition?' Logan repeated the word as if he'd never heard it before, and Evanna felt a twist of unease deep inside her.

Since the death of his wife in childbirth, Logan had always been careful to transfer every woman to the mainland in time for delivery.

Was he going to be able to cope with this?

'She's not going anywhere, Logan. She's going to have the baby here, and that's fine.' For everyone's sake, Evanna kept her voice calm and steady. She didn't want to frighten Sonia. Logan's jaw tightened and he glared at her as if she were personally responsible for the fact that Sonia had gone into labour a month early while still on the island.

Understanding the reason for his tension, Evanna wanted to

reach out and hug him. *She wanted to tell him that she understood.* She wanted to reassure him and talk it through with him, but Sonia gave another groan and writhed in agony.

'Breathe in now, Sonia,' Evanna instructed, her eyes still on Logan's face as she coached Sonia through the contraction. 'That's good. Well done. Just as we practised in class.' She was talking and encouraging but her attention was on Logan.

His face was white and drawn and suddenly she felt tiny fingers of panic slide down her spine. If this turned out to be a normal delivery then there would be no problem, but if she needed a doctor, would Logan be able to help?

She'd never known him like this before—*never known him anything but completely calm and in control.* Normally it was Logan who led everything. The time Michael King had crashed his tractor and suffered a severe head injury, it had been Logan who had managed to keep him alive. When Barbara Mullond's baby had developed meningitis, it had been Logan's quick actions and incredible instincts that had prevented a disaster. He was never anything less than confident and skilled and she was used to turning to him.

As Sonia's contraction eased, Evanna rocked back on her heels and snapped on a pair of gloves.

Was it her fault? Should she have sent Sonia into hospital sooner? But even as she asked herself the question, she knew that the answer to that was no. She'd looked at the guidelines, she'd discussed Sonia's case with the hospital and she'd monitored her regularly. She'd done all the right things, but the truth was that, no matter how careful they were, childbirth was occasionally unpredictable. They couldn't transfer everyone just because they lived in a rural area.

But Logan certainly didn't need this particular outcome.

Why did life have to be so complicated? Why couldn't Sonia's delivery have been straightforward? Logan's face was white and drawn and Evanna felt awful for him, hardly daring to imagine what he must be thinking. After what had happened with Catherine, he didn't need this. And she wasn't in a position to offer the support he deserved because she had a labouring woman to deal with.

Afterwards, she promised herself, forgetting the awkwardness that had suddenly emerged between them. After this was over she'd make sure he had the opportunity to talk.

Before she could examine Sonia, another contraction consumed her and suddenly Evanna was in absolutely no doubt that the arrival of the baby was imminent. There was going to be no time to get her to the mainland. No time even to track down Ethan, the other island doctor.

Somehow she was going to have to do this by herself but make it look as though Logan was helping. *She didn't want the inhabitants of the island gossiping.*

'I don't want to do this any more! I've changed my mind.' Sonia started to sob and thump her husband. 'This is *all* your fault. All of it. I hate you. I *really* hate you. You were the one who wanted children!'

'You said you wanted them, too. Sonia…' Stricken and helpless, Steve tried to take her in his arms but she thumped his chest and pushed him away.

'Get away from me! *Don't touch me!* I hope you wanted an only child because this is the last baby we're going to have!' Sonia gave a gasp and then leaned over and vomited again.

'You poor thing,' Evanna soothed, holding the bowl and gently stroking Sonia's damp hair away from her face. 'You're in transition, Sonia. Do you remember that we talked about that stage? This is often the most uncomfortable bit of the whole process, but you're nearly there. When this contraction passes I'm going to examine you and I'm willing to bet that you're almost fully dilated and ready to push.'

Sonia's face was blotched with tears and she clutched at Evanna's hand. 'I'm scared,' she confessed, her face crumpling. 'It wasn't supposed to be like this, was it? I know it's dangerous—'

'It's not at all dangerous,' Evanna soothed, her voice calm and level. 'People have babies at home all the time. It's perfect.'

'But they don't have babies stuck on Glenmore Island! You didn't want me to have this baby at home. Dr MacNeil didn't want me to have it at home.'

'Doctors never do, but that doesn't mean that Dr MacNeil isn't perfectly capable of assisting in a delivery if he has to,' Evanna said firmly, hoping that Logan wouldn't contradict her. She slid a hand over Sonia's abdomen, feeling the tightening. 'You've got another contraction coming now, Sonia. Lovely deep breath for me.'

'It's all going wrong...'

'Everything is completely normal. Nothing is going wrong.' Evanna glanced towards Logan, willing him to say something to support her—something encouraging—but he was frozen to the spot, his face an expressionless mask. She felt her insides twist in sympathy. She could only imagine just how terrible this situation must be for him. It must bring everything back.

Perhaps some fresh air would do the trick. 'Logan.' She kept her voice light and confident. 'Can you go to the car and fetch the delivery pack from my boot, please?'

For a moment he didn't respond and she wondered if he'd even heard her. What should she do? Uneasily, she repeated her question.

'Logan—the boot's open. Can you fetch the delivery pack, please?'

'I've called the helicopter.' His voice was hoarse and Evanna gave a nod and a smile, trying to look as though they were having a routine conversation.

'That's great. Good idea. But I do need the delivery pack from my boot.' *Please*, Logan.

'Dr MacNeil?' Sonia's voice faltered and she looked pleadingly at Logan. 'Is everything all right? You look a bit funny.'

Evanna discreetly slid a hand into her pocket and removed her mobile phone. This wasn't going to work. She was going to have to call Ethan. She needed medical back-up and Logan obviously wasn't able to give it. His face was grey with strain and she hadn't seen him look so drawn since Catherine's death.

Sonia must have seen it, too, because she gave a whimper of panic. 'Dr MacNeil?'

The fear in her voice must have penetrated Logan's brain because he suddenly stepped forward. 'It's all right, Sonia.' His voice gruff, he moved across to them and sat on the edge of the bed.

Sonia's eyes were terrified. 'You don't want me to do this here, do you? You're afraid that…' The words lay unspoken in the air and Logan hesitated for a moment and then took her hand in his.

'I'm not afraid of anything,' he said roughly. 'Of course I would have rather you had the baby in hospital because I'm a doctor and we're only ever comfortable if we're surrounded by technology that beeps at us. Ask Evanna. Midwives despair of us doctors because we always try and turn childbirth into something medical because that's all we understand. But women have been having babies successfully by themselves for centuries. And Evanna is the best midwife I've ever worked with. You don't need to worry.'

Almost weak with relief, Evanna slid the phone back into her pocket without making the call. 'Well, luckily for you, I'm here to show you how it's supposed to be done, Dr MacNeil,' she said lightly. 'But in order to do that, I need some equipment.'

'Of course. The delivery pack from your boot.' Logan gave Sonia's hand another squeeze and rose to his feet. 'I'll fetch it.'

He left the room and Sonia screwed up her face. 'Oh, here we go again. Oh, my…' She swore fluently and her husband blinked several times and then glanced at Evanna, embarrassment on his face.

'I've never heard her use language like that before.'

'Don't worry about it.'

'My feet are tingling. Something's the matter.'

'You're breathing too fast, that's what's the matter,' Evanna said calmly. 'Just try and slow everything down. That's better. Good. Here's Dr MacNeil now. I'm going to wash my hands, then I'm going to examine you.'

'Don't leave me!' Sonia's voice was sharp with panic. 'Please, don't leave me!'

'I'm just going to—'

'I want to push.'

Logan opened the pack swiftly, his hands steady. 'She can't possibly have dilated that quickly,' he muttered to Evanna, and she cast a wry smile in his direction.

'Babies don't always perform according to the textbook. Don't push, Sonia, because if you're not fully dilated you could damage your cervix. Steve, can you fetch clean towels and spread them over the floor?' Swiftly Evanna washed her hands and pulled on a pair of gloves.

Sonia was trying to breathe steadily. 'My back hurts so much. I'm so uncomfortable.'

Evanna looked at Steve who had returned with armfuls of towels, which he placed at Sonia's feet. 'If you could just rub her lower back, that might help.' She quickly checked her equipment and prepared for the delivery. A swift examination told her that there was no time to move Sonia even had she wanted to. Her perineum was distended and the head was clearly visible. 'This baby is certainly in a hurry. I can see the baby's head, Sonia, so I don't need to examine you. Try and relax between contractions. That's good. Now pant. Don't push. Pant.' As she delivered the baby's head she was aware of Logan beside her and felt relieved to have him there.

'Cord,' he said quietly, and she gave a nod and gently freed the loop of cord that was round the baby's neck. 'I'll give the syntometrine. I don't think we should risk a physiological third stage. Do you agree?'

It was typical of Logan to confer with her rather than just dictating, as so many other doctors would have done in the same situation. Evanna nodded agreement, knowing that to leave the placenta to be delivered naturally increased the chances of post-partum haemorrhage. And they had no facilities to deal with haemorrhage.

'One more push and the baby should be born, Sonia,' she said huskily, hoping and praying that this was one delivery that would be straightforward from here on. *Please, don't let there be any complications.* Not this time. Not again. Glenmore Island had already had its fair share of obstetric emergencies.

The baby shot out into her waiting hands and Evanna let out a delighted laugh that was full of relief. 'Oh, Sonia, she's beautiful. A little girl.' The baby yelled furiously and Sonia gave a sob as she turned onto her bottom and took the baby from Evanna.

'Oh, Steve.' Sonia's voice was choked and tears poured down her face as she held her daughter. 'She's beautiful. Perfect.'

Evanna looked at Logan, saw him dispose of the syringe and close his eyes briefly. Then he caught her gaze and gave a faint smile and a nod.

'OK.'

'OK,' Evanna agreed quietly, as she clamped the cord. 'A perfectly straightforward delivery. Thank you, Dr MacNeil.'

'I didn't—'

'You were great. Sonia, I think you'd be more comfortable up on the bed now. You can have a proper cuddle with her.'

Kyla appeared in the doorway. 'I gather we're having a drama. The helicopter is here. Oh, my goodness, they're obviously a bit late.' She watched as Evanna delivered the placenta and then she grinned at Sonia. 'You were always determined to have your home birth, weren't you?'

Sonia shook her head, her eyes misty. 'It was perfect. I wouldn't have missed a moment of it.'

'Perfect? Are you kidding?' Steve stared at her in confusion. 'You were yelling like a madwoman. And telling me we were never having any more children. And swearing.'

'Was I?' Placid and calm now, Sonia gently stroked the baby's head. 'She needs a bath. And so do I. It's so hot in here. Why did I have to have a baby in August? Next time I'm going for January.'

Quietly, and with a minimum of fuss, Evanna helped Sonia attach the baby to the breast, skin to skin, and then covered her. 'It will help your uterus contract,' she explained, 'and also keep the baby warm.' She looked at Logan. *Saw the lines of strain around his eyes.* 'She needs to go to the hospital anyway, given that her blood pressure was up and the baby is four weeks early. We may as well use your helicopter.'

He nodded agreement. 'I'll go and speak to them. Will you get her ready?'

'She's a month early.' Sonia was watching the feeding baby with wonder and awe. 'Will she be all right?'

'Well, if her appetite is anything to go by, she's going to fit right into this island. We'll have her gorging herself at Meg's in no time,' Kyla said with a grin, helping Evanna to clear up. 'What are you calling her?'

'Oh…' Sonia glanced at Steve, her eyes shining. 'We couldn't agree, could we? It was a battle between Emma and Rachel.'

'You wanted Rachel and I think she looks like a Rachel,' Steve murmured, his voice gruff. 'What do you think of Rachel Evanna?'

Touched, Evanna glanced up from her preparations. 'You don't have to do that.'

'We want to.' Sonia smiled at her husband and then looked at Evanna, gratitude in her eyes. 'We're so grateful to you and Dr MacNeil. You were both amazing.'

'Just don't call her Logan,' Kyla advised cheerfully, folding a towel neatly. 'One of those is more than enough on an island this size. I'll go and tell the helicopter lads what's happening. Which one of you is going with her?'

'Me,' Evanna said immediately. 'Logan has to get back to surgery and then there's Kirsty to think of. Can you cover my clinic, Kyla? Ask some of them to come back tomorrow.'

'I don't think they'll mind doing that, given the reason.' Kyla took a last peep at the baby and sighed. 'Maybe I'm broody after all.'

Evanna laughed and ignored the painful twist of her heart. 'I'd better warn Ethan.'

CHAPTER EIGHT

LOGAN'S house was in darkness.

Could he already be in bed? She was later than she'd planned, but by the time she'd sorted Sonia out and completed all the paperwork, several hours had passed. Reluctant to knock on the front door in case she woke Kirsty, Evanna walked round the back of the house and opened the garden gate.

She'd just take a look. If there were no lights on then she'd give up and go home. But she wasn't comfortable about just going home.

Not until she'd checked on Logan. The whole experience must have been completely harrowing for him and she wanted to give him a chance to talk about it. But there was no sign of life in the house. Just one small light burning in the hall.

Could he be out?

Perhaps he'd found a babysitter and gone down to the pub to celebrate the birth of Rachel Evanna, along with the rest of the locals.

She walked into his garden, intending to look through the back door, but then she spotted him sprawled in the hammock at the end of the garden. The moon provided just enough light for her to see that he was holding a bottle of beer in his hand.

'Logan?' Perhaps he didn't want to be disturbed. It was a

stiflingly warm summer's evening, but his garden was cooled by a breeze drifting in from the sea. It was peaceful and tranquil and the perfect setting for quiet contemplation. And she was fairly sure that she knew what he was thinking about. Or who.

Catherine.

Feeling like an intruder and wishing she'd never come, Evanna was just wondering whether to melt back through the garden gate and into her car when he spoke.

'I thought you'd be in the pub with the others.' His voice was low and impossibly sexy and she walked across to him on shaking legs, wondering why she continued to torture herself like this.

'I wasn't in the mood for celebrations.'

'Why not?' He lifted the bottle and drank. 'You did a good job.'

'So did you.'

'Me?' His mouth twisted into a smile and his blue eyes glittered with an emotion that she didn't recognise. 'You did all the work, Evanna.'

'I'm the midwife. I'm supposed to do all the work. If you'd taken over, I would have resigned on the spot. Goodness knows, I get little enough opportunity to deliver babies on this island—that's why I go to the mainland once a year. Otherwise I'd forget how to do it.' She kept her tone light and then sighed. 'All right, let's stop being tactful and be honest. I was worried about you. That's why I'm here. It must have been completely hideous to have to cope with that. I can't even begin to imagine—and I wasn't able to give you any support because of Sonia, and all the time I knew that you were in agony and I just wanted to give you a hug. So I'm here to check you're all right.' The words tumbled out of her and she felt horribly self-conscious. They hadn't had a proper talk since he'd caught her coming out of the shower and their whole relationship seemed to have changed since then. What if he didn't want to talk to her any more?

What if things were different?

He stirred and the hammock swung gently. 'I'm sorry if I gave you a fright back there. You needed support and I wasn't any help at all.'

'That's not true,' Evanna said quickly. 'You were great.'

He gave a twisted smile that was loaded with derision. 'I froze. If you hadn't given me that look, I probably would have just turned and run. Yesterday was the first time in my entire medical career that I panicked.'

'And is that really so surprising? No one who had been through what you went through would have found that situation anything other than difficult.'

There was a long silence and then he put the empty bottle down on the grass and stretched out a hand. 'Come and sit down.'

Evanna eyed the swaying hammock. 'In that?'

'Of course. There's plenty of room for two.'

'That's when one of the two is a toddler.'

'Just be careful how you climb in or you'll tip me out.' He closed his fingers over her wrist and gave her a gentle tug so that she tumbled off balance and landed on top of him.

'Logan!' Thoroughly embarrassed, she rolled off him and lay on her back in the hammock. They were hip to hip, shoulder to shoulder and, for a moment, she couldn't breathe. Then she looked up and gave a murmur of delight. 'Oh—the stars are amazing.'

'You've never lain in this at night?'

'You know I haven't.'

'It's so hot indoors that I'd sleep here at the moment if it weren't for Kirsty. So why did you come, Evanna?'

His quiet question flustered her. 'I wanted to check on you.'

'I'm not one of your patients.'

'I—' *What did he want her to say?* 'I know that. But I care about you.'

'And that's why you wanted to hug me?' He turned to look

at her, a dangerous glitter in his blue eyes. 'Because you care about me? You care about everyone, Evanna. You always have. At school you were the one who broke up fights, smoothed everyone's feathers. You always hated conflict. Caring is part of your personality.'

His face was close to hers. *So close.* Evanna's heart lurched. Had he guessed how she felt about him? Had she failed to hide it? 'Of course I care about you.' Her voice came out as a whisper, as if anything else would have punctured the perfect stillness of the garden. 'We all care about you, Logan.'

For a moment he didn't respond and it seemed to her that the air around them thickened with tension. 'So the whole community is still keeping an eye on me.'

'You make it sound patronising, but it isn't like that.'

'Isn't it?'

'No.' *His eyelashes were really long.* And dark. Such a contrast to his blue eyes. 'You're not an object of pity, if that's what you mean. No one could ever pity you because you're so strong, but that doesn't stop them feeling sad for you or wanting to protect you from any more pain. The situation with Sonia this afternoon must bring it all back and that must be hard.' She felt the hard muscle of his leg brush against hers and felt crazy flutters of excitement in her stomach.

'What's hard is realising that I'm nothing like people's image of me.' There was a harshness in his tone that disturbed her.

'What do you mean?'

He gave a faint smile. 'People look at me and see a dedicated doctor. Grieving widower. Single father. Doting dad.'

'I suppose. Maybe. Aren't you all those things?'

He stared at her for a long moment and then dragged his eyes away and stared up at the sky. 'Am I?'

He was frustratingly uncommunicative. 'What are you

thinking? You're obviously upset. Talk to me,' she urged, and he gave a cynical laugh.

'You know that men aren't great at talking.'

'But you are. When you want to be. I've seen you spend hours with patients who are worried about something. You're amazingly intuitive and a fantastic listener.'

'Not such a great talker.'

Evanna swallowed. 'You've always talked to me.'

'That's true. Funny, that, isn't it? I've said things to you that I've never said aloud before.' There was a long, throbbing silence and then he turned to look at her again. 'The truth is that I'm not feeling what I'm expected to feel.'

'I don't think anyone expects anything, Logan.'

'Don't they? I'm supposed to be devastated and far too grief-ridden to even contemplate—' He broke off, swore softly and ran a hand over his face. 'I think of Catherine, that's true, but lately...'

'Lately?'

He paused and then reached across and took her hand in his. 'Lately—well, let's just say that lately a lot of things have changed.'

Evanna didn't know whether to snatch her hand away or hold on tight. It felt impossibly intimate to be lying together in the dark, touching, even if she knew that, for him, that touch was only a symbol of friendship.

The air around them was still and the heat was stifling, despite the lateness of the hour. They were enclosed by the garden and the silence of a summer evening, disturbed only by the faint barking of a dog from the farm across the fields.

Reminding herself that the whole point of coming up here that evening was to listen to him, she forced herself to ignore the firm press of his fingers against hers. 'What's changed, Logan?' She struggled to sound casual and Logan gave a short laugh.

'I have. I've changed.'

'Well, I'm sure that's to be expected. No one could go through what you went through and not change. And I don't think that there's a right and a wrong to cope with anything. You just have to do what feels right for you. We all struggle through life in the best way we can, and you do brilliantly.'

'Do I? Tell me, Evanna, what is the required time for remaining celibate after the loss of a wife? A year? Two years? More?'

'I've never thought about it.' Startled by the question, she hoped that the darkness hid the sudden rush of colour to her cheeks. 'I suppose it depends on the individual. You're a normal, healthy guy, Logan, and surely it's to be expected that you'd— I mean of course eventually you're going to— It's natural to—'

'Want sex?' He didn't let go of her hand. 'Is it? Is it natural to be interested in another woman? To be honest, the feeling took me by surprise.'

Was he telling her that he wanted to have sex with someone?

Her heart flipped and she struggled to squash down the sick feeling of disappointment that rose up inside her. This wasn't about her, she reminded herself swiftly, this was about him. Of course he was going to want sex. He was a healthy adult male in his prime. 'You're telling me that you're interested in other women? I think that's…' She hesitated over the word. 'Great,' she said firmly. 'Really great. It means you're moving on.'

'Does it?'

'Of course.'

He turned his head to look at her. 'You're not shocked?'

'That you want a relationship? Of course not. I'm thrilled for you.'

His mouth moved into a slow smile. 'I didn't say I wanted a relationship,' he murmured softly. 'That might be more complicated. I'm just talking about sex.'

'Oh—yes, of course.' Suddenly flustered, Evanna struggled

for the right thing to say. 'Well, I think that—that it's fine. Whatever works for you. More than anyone, you deserve happiness, Logan.' Despite the darkness, she could feel him watching her.

'You're so sweet. And generous.' His voice was soft and his hand held hers firmly. 'You never judge, do you?'

She mustn't mind that he thought she was sweet. Sweet was a compliment, she told herself firmly. 'What is there to judge?'

'Plenty of people would.'

'And does that bother you?'

He gave a soft laugh. 'What do you think?'

'I think that you've never minded what people say about you. You've always done your own thing and, frankly, that's the only way to be able to live on an island this size. So what's the problem?' She tried to put her own feelings aside and respond in the way that she would have done had she not been emotionally involved. 'Is there someone you like? Someone special? Obviously there must be, or you wouldn't have suddenly started thinking about...sex.' She tried to sound relaxed, as if conversations about sex were an everyday occurrence for her. He wanted to talk about it, she told herself, and she should allow him that. It was the least she could do.

The darkness of the garden folded over them, creating an atmosphere of intimacy that seemed to mock her. Here she was, lying in the darkness, on a perfect summer's evening, holding hands with the man she loved while he told her about another woman that interested him.

'Maybe. I don't know. I'm in dangerous territory.'

'Because you feel guilty about Catherine?'

'Strangely enough, no. I don't feel guilty. I probably should, but I don't. If there's one thing that I learned from Catherine, it's that life is to be lived.'

'That's true.' Evanna smiled. 'She was a very adventurous

person. A bit wild. If she were standing here now, she'd probably just want to know why it's taken you so long. So, if you don't feel guilty and you're not worried about what anyone thinks, why is it dangerous territory? What's holding you back?'

He was looking at her and he still hadn't let go of her hand. 'Because I'm not sure that the woman in question is interested in me.'

'Logan MacNeil, I never heard such nonsense! Women have been falling over you since you first learned to walk. And you've never been one to hold back! Just ask her!'

'You think I should ask a woman for sex?'

Evanna laughed to hide her embarrassment. 'I think you might need to be a little more subtle than that or someone might slap your face.'

'So what should I do?'

Just smile, she wanted to say. That's all it would take in her case. One smile and she'd be his for ever. 'Give her one of your hot looks! I don't know, you're the expert,' she mumbled. 'If ever a man knew how to put the moves on a woman, it was you. There were more broken hearts in our school than in a coronary care unit.'

He smiled at her analogy. 'That was a long time ago. In my wild, reckless youth.'

Despite the humour in his tone, she decided not to point out that he'd still been breaking hearts up to the day before he'd met Catherine, which had only been two years previously. 'Well, I'm sure it's like riding a bicycle,' Evanna joked weakly. 'Just get back out there. Go for it. There are no end of possible candidates. Loads of women who aren't your patients. Polly in the pub. She's very pretty. Or Mary Simon, who helps Meg in the café. Any woman would want to be asked out by you.'

He didn't release her hand. 'Would they?'

His thigh was pressed hard against hers.

'Of course.' His features seemed dark and unfamiliar and she swallowed hard. 'What do you think?'

It was a moment before he answered. 'I think that sometimes when something is incredibly familiar, we don't always notice it. We think something is a certain way and then suddenly we discover that we were entirely wrong. And that takes some adjustment.'

He was talking in riddles. Her eyes slid to the empty bottle on the ground but it was a small bottle and there was only the one so it couldn't be that. And, anyway, she hadn't known Logan to drink to excess since that one occasion on the beach on his seventeenth birthday when she and Kyla had spent an entire night holding his head over a bowl while he'd been sick. 'You think Polly and Mary don't notice you? Because I can tell you now that they—'

'I'm not talking about Polly or Mary.' His gaze was steady on hers and her stomach performed a series of elaborate acrobatics.

Determined not to read something into his words that wasn't there, she kept her tone matter-of-fact. 'Well, if you're suggesting that people see you as a widower and not as a man, I don't think that's true, Logan. If you're interested in someone then you should just go for it.'

'You think so? You think I should go for it?'

'Definitely.' She ignored the new surge of misery that flooded through her veins. Here she was, advising the man she loved to go out and find another woman. But he deserved happiness and so did Kirsty. And he deserved a sex life. But it was impossible not to feel envious of the woman who was going to find herself burning up the sheets with Logan. 'Find the right moment and go for it.'

His eyes dropped to her mouth and for a wild, crazy moment she really thought he was going to kiss her. She even found herself leaning towards him.

And then she remembered her promise to herself, snatched her hand from his and struggled out of the hammock, almost twisting her ankle and landing flat on her bottom in the process. 'It isn't easy to stand up from one of these with dignity,' she said in a strangled voice, horrified to realise just how close she'd come to kissing him.

'Evanna, you don't have to—'

'I should really be going,' she said in a bright voice. 'I mean, I just came to check up on you. And you should be going. Inside, I mean. Because you can't go anywhere because you're already here. Obviously.' Nerves made her babble incoherently and she almost groaned as she listened to herself.

What must he think of her?

No wonder he didn't find her sexy. She didn't have the first clue about seducing men.

Logan simply watched her, his handsome face unsmiling. 'So that's it? You're leaving?'

What did he expect? Did he want her to pull out a pad and pen and start drawing up a list of possible candidates for his sexual pleasure?

'It's late.' She waved a hand in the vague direction of the gate. 'I should be going, and you should be—'

He scooped up the empty bottle and stood up in a smooth, athletic movement that was a complete contrast to her own tumbled exit from the hammock. 'I should be getting back to the woman in my life. My daughter.'

There was an awkward silence and Evanna chewed her lip, wishing that she was better at talking about sex. Kyla would have lain there and chatted quite comfortably about any topic of his choice, but she'd been gauche and stiff.

'I haven't helped much, have I?' she mumbled, and for a long moment Logan didn't answer.

Then he gave a sigh. 'You always help. Thanks for coming

round, Evanna,' he said gruffly, and she gave a helpless nod as she backed towards the garden gate.

'You're welcome. I'm sorry I didn't— I mean, I hope it works out the way you want,' she muttered, and then gave up trying to say the right thing and just made for her car.

Find the right moment.
Find the right moment.

Logan paced the floor of his bedroom, battling with a growing frustration. Hadn't that been Evanna's advice to him? But when exactly was the right moment to tell a woman that you wanted to strip her naked and have wild, abandoned sex with her?

Evanna's life was so tidy and neat. Everything planned. He'd seen the way that she'd blushed when he'd mentioned sex. How much deeper would that blush have been had she known that the woman he was interested in was her?

Any other woman would have picked up his signals, but not Evanna.

Evanna didn't do wild love affairs and she never had.

She was sweet and conservative and a bit shy. The sort of woman who blushed when she was caught coming out of the shower.

And, as far as he was concerned, that just made her all the more appealing.

They'd been sitting in the dark in his garden, talking about life. Talking about the future. Surely there would never be a better moment to tell a woman that you were interested in her, and yet had he spoken up? No. He'd lain there like a tongue-tied, hormonal teenager on a first date. Dropping hints. Skirting around the subject.

Logan walked over to the window and stared out over the garden.

He hadn't really thought about sex for a year and suddenly

he couldn't think about anything else. But there was only one woman that interested him. And he had absolutely no idea how to go about telling her. And this lack of confidence with the female sex was an entirely new experience for him.

Never in his life could he recall being anything less than confident with a woman. He'd seen. He'd wanted. He'd taken. It had all come so easily to him.

But Evanna was different.

He ran a hand over his face and sat back in his chair. There was so much more at stake than rejection and damage to his ego. If he got this wrong then a lifelong friendship would be damaged. Glenmore was a small, close-knit community. If it all went wrong, they wouldn't be able to avoid each other. It could be hideously awkward.

Was it really worth the risk?

Given the choice of Evanna as a friend or Evanna out of his life, which would he choose?

Without question, he'd rather keep her as a friend than lose her. Which meant that he now found himself in an extremely delicate situation.

He'd just have to work harder at forgetting her, he promised himself, sprawling on the bed without any expectation of actually sleeping.

Somehow, he'd get their relationship back to the place where it had always been.

'I've got Jenny Price in Reception with Helen.' Janet's voice was crisp and efficient on the phone. 'Can you fit her in?'

Helen Price. 'Well, that's a bit spooky because I promised Ann Carne I'd take a look at her notes this week.' Evanna ran through the conversation in her head. 'Send them in, of course. Do you know what the problem is?'

'No. But Jenny Price is very quiet. Shy. Keeps herself to

herself. But she looks worried and there's something about that child that doesn't seem right to me.'

Evanna tucked the phone between her shoulder and her ear so that she could finish printing off the letter she was writing. 'What's that?'

'That child is small.'

Evanna took the paper out of the printer and sighed, remembering Ann's concerns. 'She's five years old, Janet. Little girls of five are often delicate.'

'Maybe. Maybe not.'

Evanna smiled. 'OK, I'll take a look. If I'm worried, I'll get Logan to examine her. Is he still around or has he gone out on calls?' She'd successfully avoided him all week and buried herself in work, trying not to think that he might be out there seducing one incredibly lucky woman.

'He's just finishing his list.'

'Send in Jenny and Helen whenever they're ready.' They appeared at her door only moments later.

Jenny was a slender, nervous-looking woman with mousy hair caught up in a clip at the back of her head. She looked pale and harassed. 'Nurse Duncan, I know I should have made an appointment, but—'

'It really doesn't matter at all, Mrs Price.' Evanna interrupted her apology with a dismissive wave of her hand and a friendly smile. 'We try to be quite informal on Glenmore if we can.'

Jenny pulled a face. 'Where I was living last you were lucky to be able to get an appointment within a fortnight.'

'By which time you're either dead or cured.' Evanna smiled with understanding and brought up Helen's notes on the computer. 'How can we help you today?'

Jenny hesitated and then glanced towards her daughter. 'It isn't anything specific. Well, I suppose it is in a way. I mean, she gets incredibly breathless when she runs around and that's starting to worry me because a young girl of her age surely shouldn't be that unfit.'

'So she's breathless. Anything else?'

'Well, we had a terrible winter with chest infections.' Jenny bit her lip. 'I'm wondering whether it could be asthma. That's why I came to see you because Miss Carne, the headmistress, told me that you and the other nurse see patients with asthma.'

'Yes, we do, although in the first instance patients are diagnosed by one of the doctors. Then we usually do the follow-up and make any adjustments to medication.'

Helen wandered over to Jenny and tugged at her sleeve. 'Mummy, I'm thirsty.' She was a small, pale girl with soft blonde hair and delicate features.

Evanna watched her for a moment, remembering what both Ann and Janet had said. 'I'll fetch you a glass of water, Helen,' she said gently, walking over to the brightly coloured paper cups she kept for children. 'Can you just step on the scales for me?'

She weighed Helen, recorded the result and then handed her a cup of chilled water. Then she questioned Jenny in more depth, asking her about Helen's medical history.

'She was a normal delivery. No problems. Since then she's had chest infections. Every winter she starts. Nasty cough.'

'Does she cough at night?'

'Not in the summer. Only when she has an infection.'

'And have you ever seen a doctor about her infections?'

'Every winter we end up at the doctor's but they just say that chest infections are normal in winter.' She gave a shrug. 'But I know there's something wrong. When you're a mother you have a sense about these things. An instinct.'

Evanna glanced towards the little girl but she was playing happily with the basket of toys in the corner of the room, apparently oblivious to the conversation. 'And you say that she's out of breath the whole time.'

'I've watched her playing with other kids. She's different. She's just so out of breath when she runs around,' Jenny said quietly. 'And it seems to be getting worse.'

Could it be asthma? 'Has she ever suffered from eczema?' Evanna asked a series of questions and then stood up. 'I'm going to see if one of our doctors is available to see her.'

She lifted the phone and spoke to Janet who told her that Logan was with his last patient. She waited for his light to flash on and tapped on his door.

'I wondered if you could see a patient for me.' She was trying desperately to think of him as a doctor and not as a man. *A man who was currently fantasising about some unknown but incredibly fortunate woman.*

'Who is it?'

'Helen Price. They moved into the Garrett property in the spring. She's extremely breathless on exertion. Funnily enough, Ann Carne mentioned her to me. She wondered if she was asthmatic and the mother thinks that, too, but—'

'But you don't think so.'

'Well, obviously you need to take a look at her but, no, I'm not sure about asthma. There's no family history of atopy, no wheezing and no night cough. On the other hand, she is getting chest infections every winter.' Evanna broke off and gave an apologetic smile. 'Look, you're the doctor. I just have a funny feeling about her.'

'Then I'll see her, of course. Send her in.' His eyes lingered on hers. 'Why don't you stay while I examine her?'

Evanna nodded. 'I'll do that. And I think we ought to invite Jenny, the mother, to the beach barbecue. Her husband works away a lot and I think she's a bit lonely. Janet doesn't think she's really settled into island life.'

'Invite her. Good idea.'

'Are you going?' She didn't know what made her ask the

question. He didn't usually go. And she shouldn't care whether he was going or not.

He studied her face, his blue eyes speculative. 'Probably.'

And suddenly Evanna wished that she hadn't asked the question. Of course he'd be going. Why hadn't she thought of that? The beach barbecue would be the perfect opportunity to deepen his relationship with the woman he fancied. And that was good, she told herself firmly. Last year he hadn't attended and she'd spent the entire evening worrying about him, alone in his beautiful big house with a six-month-old baby for company. She'd left early and taken him a plate of food and they'd sat in his garden, chatting about all sorts of things. Normal things. *Things designed to distract him from the death of his wife.*

'I'm glad you're going.' She braced herself and smiled. 'Everyone will be thrilled to see you there.' She backed towards the door, wondering why he was studying her so intently. 'I'll just fetch Helen and her mother.'

When she returned, Logan was thorough and professional, questioning Jenny in detail and then examining the little girl.

Finally he unhooked the stethoscope from his ears and gave a brief smile as he handed Helen a colouring book and crayons. 'Do you want to colour that for me, Helen? I just need to talk to your mum.'

Helen grabbed the book with a delighted smile and a mumbled, 'Thank you,' and immediately lay on her stomach on the floor and started colouring.

Logan sat back down at his desk. 'Has anyone ever mentioned to you that she has a murmur?'

'A murmur?' Jenny stared at him. 'You mean a heart murmur?'

'That's right.' Logan's voice was quiet as he tucked the stethoscope into his pocket. 'When I'm using the stethoscope on her chest I'm listening to the sounds that her heart makes. A heart murmur is basically an extra sound.'

'Are you telling me that you think she has something wrong with her heart? Oh, my gosh.' Jenny's face drained of colour and she lifted a hand to her mouth. 'How can you possibly know that from just listening?'

'I don't know, for sure. And a number of young children would be found to have heart murmurs and yet have structurally normal hearts. But given her history of breathlessness and the fact that her weight is lower than average for her age, I'd like to refer her for some more tests. I think we do need to check this out further.'

'I thought it was asthma,' Jenny whispered. 'She gets all these chest infections.'

'Yes. I read that in her notes.'

'No one ever mentioned her heart before. Are you saying that chest infections can be linked to heart disease?' Jenny's eyes were wide. 'What exactly do you think is wrong?'

Logan hesitated. 'It's impossible for me to give a definitive diagnosis just by listening to her chest. I'd like you to go to the mainland and see the paediatric cardiologist. He'll do an echocardiogram, which will allow him to look at the structure of the heart. He'll also probably do a chest X-ray and an ECG, to see how the heart is working. All of that is non-invasive and won't hurt Helen at all.'

'I can't believe this.' Jenny ran a hand across her face and took several deep breaths. 'I…' She struggled with tears and Evanna reached across to borrow Logan's phone.

'Janet?' She quickly spoke to the receptionist. 'Can you come and take Helen and show her some interesting toys, please? It's very boring in here for her and she's finished the colouring Logan gave her.'

Jenny shot her a grateful look and moments later Janet appeared, a wide smile on her motherly features. 'You come with your Aunty Janet. I've all the plants to water and I really need some help,' she said happily, holding out a hand to Helen, who scrambled to her feet and glanced towards her mother doubtfully.

'You go, sweetie,' Jenny breathed, her smile just a little forced. 'Help Janet with the plants. Then Mummy will come and get you.'

Helen slipped her hand into Janet's and went without protest.

Jenny reached into her bag for a tissue. 'That was kind of you,' she whispered, blowing her nose hard. 'You try so hard to protect them, don't you? And then something like this happens. I'm sorry to be a baby, but it's such a shock.'

'I can understand that.' Logan's voice was kind, his gaze sympathetic. 'But I'd really like you to try not to worry until you know exactly what there is to worry about. That's easier said than done, I know, because once you're a parent all hope of being calm and rational goes out of the window.'

'Do you have children?'

Logan gave a crooked smile. 'Little girl. Thirteen months. So I know all about parental worry.'

'Oh. Yes.' Jenny blew her nose again. 'So what happens now?'

'I'd like to ring a good friend of mine who is a paediatric cardiologist. He'll arrange for you to have those tests that I described. Then you come back to me and we'll talk.'

'But you definitely think there's something wrong with her heart.'

'Yes, I do,' Logan said quietly, 'and I'm not going to lie to you about that. But she's a bonny little girl who has obviously done very well up until now. This may be something that is easily solved. They may even decide to wait and do nothing.'

Jenny was still struggling with tears. 'My husband, Bobbie, is away so I can't even talk to him.'

Logan leaned forward and covered her hand with his. 'You can talk to us,' he said gruffly, glancing towards Evanna. 'Anything. Any time.'

EVANNA

Jenny gave a dismissive laugh. 'You're suggesting I make an appointment just to discuss how worried I am about my daughter's heart?'

'Yes. Why wouldn't you? Being a GP is about caring for the whole family.' Logan's eyes were kind. 'Let's have those tests done and then talk again. If there are any decisions to be made, I'll help you weigh up all the pros and cons.'

'You're incredibly kind.' Janet shook her head. 'I—I'm just not used to having a GP who encourages me to come back. The practice we were in before had eighteen GPs. I never saw the same person twice and they were never interested in anything other than hurrying me out of the door as fast as possible.'

Logan nodded. 'Different pace of life,' he said easily, 'and different priorities. Glenmore is a small community, Jenny. And when you moved here, you became part of that. I'm going to call the cardiologist now and I'll phone you with an appointment time. Will you be able to get her to the mainland?'

'Oh, yes, I have a car and I travel across once a week anyway, to see my sister.'

'Good. Here's my home number and my mobile.' Logan scribbled on a piece of paper. 'Call me if you need to. Otherwise I'll see you when we have some results.'

Jenny slipped the piece of paper into her bag and stood up. 'Thank you.' She looked at Evanna and gave a faltering smile. 'And thank you, too.'

'You're very welcome.'

Evanna took Jenny to find her daughter and then returned to Logan. 'You really think she has a heart defect?'

'Yes. But obviously it needs to be confirmed by the cardiologist. She needs an echo.'

Evanna looked at him. 'But now that it's just you and me— tell me what you think.'

He didn't hesitate. 'I think she has an ASD. Atrial septal

defect.' He was sure and confident. 'The second heart sound is split. It's fairly characteristic.'

'But why hasn't it been picked up before now?'

'There are often no symptoms in early childhood. But in Helen's case I'm fairly sure that her breathlessness, the chest infections and the fact that her weight is below the tenth percentile…' He shrugged. 'I could be wrong.'

'You're not usually wrong, Logan,' Evanna murmured, and he studied her for a long moment.

'Are you leading my fan club?'

'You're a good doctor. You don't need me to tell you that. So what will they do? Surgery? Or did I read somewhere that they sometimes close on their own?'

'It's unlikely that Helen's will close on its own. By the time a child has reached the age of three it's extremely unlikely that it will sort itself out, and she's five and a half.'

'Which means surgery, then.'

'Not necessarily. There are some new techniques that can be done by an interventional cardiologist, rather than a surgeon. Basically they attach a device to a catheter and they can put it in place without having to stop the heart.'

Evanna pulled a face. 'Which still sounds scary when it's a child. Poor Jenny. And her husband away, too. How quickly can you get her an appointment?'

'I'm going to call him now.' Logan opened a file on the computer and scrolled down a list of phone numbers. 'We worked together in London and he's a really bright guy. I'm hoping he can fit her in this week. Did you call the hospital about Sonia?'

'Yes. They're very happy with her. Baby is a bit jaundiced so they're going to keep her in for a few days but they hope she'll be home by the middle of the week.'

'A good outcome, then.' Logan reached for the phone and

then looked at her. 'You asked me about the beach barbecue, but what about you? Are you going?'

Did she want to spend the evening watching him with another woman? The answer was very definitely no, but to not go would draw attention to herself. And anyway she lived on an island. No matter how she felt about Logan, she had to get on with her life. 'I'm going.'

The beach was big enough, she reassured herself. There would be volleyball and football and a barbecue going, not to mention swimming. It should be easy enough not to have to stand staring at him.

CHAPTER NINE

EVANNA spent Saturday afternoon getting ready for the beach barbecue in her new bathroom. She opened the windows and lay in a deep bubble bath, soaking away the stresses of the week and enjoying the view of the sea. There couldn't be many people lucky enough to have a view of the sea from their bathroom, she thought to herself when she finally eased herself out of the suds and reached for a towel.

She dried her hair and put on her bikini, knowing that the evening usually began with a swim. The she pulled on a halter-neck sundress in a deep shade of blue and slid her feet into pretty flip-flops. There was no point in considering elaborate footwear when she knew from experience that she'd be spending most of the evening barefoot.

Her doorbell rang just as she was pushing a towel into a raffia bag.

It was Kyla. 'Ethan and I thought we'd give you a lift.'

Evanna picked up her key and pulled the door closed. 'How many people are coming, do you know?'

'Everyone. How's Sonia—have you heard?'

They walked to the car and Evanna smiled at Ethan who was lounging in the driver's seat, a pair of dark glasses shielding his eyes. 'Sonia is doing very well.' She squashed into the back seat of Ethan's sports car. 'She came out on Wednesday and I've already seen her in Meg's, chatting to Lucy and feeding the baby.'

'Those two will have a lot in common. Quite nice, really.' Kyla checked her lipstick in the mirror. 'A sort of ready-made support group. And how was Logan? I expected him to be traumatised but he's actually seemed quite buoyant all week.'

Evanna fastened her seat belt. And she knew why that was. He was thinking about a woman. 'He seems fine. He looked pretty grey to start with but then he seemed to pull himself together and he was fine during the delivery.'

'Really?'

'He's fine,' Ethan drawled, pulling up in a vacant parking space. 'You girls worry too much.'

They arrived at the beach, parked in the car park and then made their way down the steps to the sand. A delicious smell of charcoal and cooking floated through the air and a group of teenagers were playing an extremely noisy game of volleyball on the sand.

Automatically, Evanna wandered over to help with the food.

'We're all under control,' Meg said firmly, giving her a gentle push. 'You go and have a swim, dear. It's so hot, I'm sure you need it.'

'I must admit, I do fancy a swim. Are you sure you can manage here?'

'Absolutely. If I need help, I'll yell. Kyla and Ethan are already in, look.' She adjusted her sunglasses. 'Go and join them.'

Deciding that it was too hot to argue, Evanna wriggled out of her dress, folded it neatly and placed it on top of her bag and then sprinted towards the water's edge to join the others.

Kyla and Ethan were fooling around, splashing and ducking each other, and she waded cautiously into the water, shivering slightly as it surged above her knees. 'I don't know how you two can be so brave. It's freezing.'

'Fresh is the word you're looking for,' Kyla yelled, splashing Ethan and finding herself ducked as a result.

Smiling at the two of them, Evanna gingerly eased herself into the water.

She swam with them for about ten minutes and the cold water was deliciously refreshing against her hot skin. Despite the fact that it was late afternoon, the heat of the sun was relentless.

'All right. That's quite enough exercise. I'm starving.' Kyla rubbed a hand over her face to clear her vision and squinted towards the shore. 'Do you think the food is ready yet?'

'I expect there will be sausages because they always feed the children first.' Evanna dived under the water again, enjoying the cool rush of water through her hair. When she emerged, dripping, Logan was standing in front of her.

Instantly her legs weakened. 'Logan!' Her voice was a shocked squeak. She hadn't expected to see him. Not yet.

More beach bum than doctor, she thought to herself, trying to catch her breath. He was wearing a pair of blue surf shorts and his shoulders were bare.

'Hi, Evanna.' His voice sounded unusually strained and she wiped the water from her eyes and studied him closely.

Something was wrong, she could sense it.

'I— Is everything all right? Where's Kirsty?'

'One of the cousins offered to babysit. I decided to take your advice and have a night out.'

'Oh. Great idea.' He was staring at her. Why was he staring at her? Feeling self-conscious under his steady blue gaze, Evanna lifted a hand and squeezed the water out of her hair. It trailed over her shoulder in a thick, wet rope. 'I tried to call you this morning.'

'You did?' His eyes were on her hair. 'Why?'

She felt hideously flustered, not least because Kyla gave her a wink and started to swim towards shore, leaving her alone with Logan. 'Why did I call you?' She turned away from Kyla, found herself looking at his chest and backed away, flustered. 'Because I wanted to ask about Helen Price. Do you know if she saw the cardiologist?'

'Yes. He confirmed my suspicions. She has an atrial septal defect.'

'Oh, poor thing.' Evanna took another step backwards. 'So what happens now? Open-heart surgery?'

He shook his head. 'They're going to have her in as a day case and operate using a catheter. It should be relatively straightforward.'

'Well, that's progress for you,' Evanna croaked.

He watched her for a long moment and then his eyes slid to her mouth. 'Evanna—' He broke off and lifted his gaze to hers.

For a long moment they stared at each other and she felt her heart hammering rapidly against her chest. There was something in the atmosphere. Something—

No.

She was doing it again! She wasn't going to start imagining something that wasn't there! She wasn't going to start dreaming again!

Anxious to get away from him, she turned towards the shore, her voice bright and breezy as she spoke. 'Well, I've finished my swim so I think I'll go and eat something.'

There was a long, aching silence and then he cleared his throat. 'Go ahead. If you're hungry.'

See? She spoke firmly to herself as she waded to shore. He hadn't even tried to detain her. And what had they spoken about? Work. As usual. It didn't matter whether they were in uniform or swimming gear, their relationship was the same as ever. Professional friendship.

Determined not to wallow, she pulled the blue sundress on top of her damp bikini and left her hair loose. And tonight she wasn't going to spend her evening staring at Logan. She was going to socialise. Mingle. Allow him the space to find the woman he wanted to move on with.

Determined to enjoy herself, she talked to everyone she knew and at least a dozen people who she'd never met before. She spoke at length with Janet Price who was there with Helen, she helped Meg serve the food, she laughed with Kyla as they shared a delicious hamburger, trying not to drip ketchup on their clothes. Then the music started and she kicked off her flip-flops and danced barefoot in the sand with Ethan and then with Nick.

But no matter how much she talked, laughed or danced, she was always aware of Logan standing in the shadows. He danced with no one. Occasionally he exchanged a few words with someone but only when they'd made the effort to approach him. Other than that he stood alone. Apart.

And as midnight approached and lots of families started gathering their things together, Evanna couldn't stand it any longer.

He'd said that he'd forgotten how to approach a woman but surely that couldn't really be the case? Out of the corner of her eye she spotted Polly from the café, laughing at one of Nick's terrible jokes.

Pretty Polly. Wasn't that what all the boys had called her at school? Evanna knew that she'd be only too thrilled to be approached by Logan, so why was he hesitating?

Part of her wanted to leave for her own self-protection but a bigger part of her wanted to see Logan happy.

She walked over to him. 'All you have to do is ask, you know.'

'Ask?'

'You say something like, "Do you fancy joining me for a walk on the beach?"'

'Oh.' He put his drink down on the upturned crate that had been placed on the sand. 'In that case, do you fancy joining me for a walk on the beach?'

Evanna giggled. 'Not me, you idiot. Polly. She's standing there, looking hopeful. If you want to approach her, this is a really good time.'

'But I've already asked you.'

'W-we were j-just practising,' Evanna stammered. 'Role play.'

'All right. In that case, I want you to walk along the beach with me. Call it role play, if you like. It's been so long since I've walked along the beach with a woman, I've forgotten how to do it. I might put my feet in the wrong place.'

There was a dangerous glint in his blue eyes that made her feel strangely uncertain. She couldn't read his thoughts. She really had absolutely no idea what he was thinking. 'Logan, you should be asking Polly.'

'I'm asking you.'

He was obviously still afraid to approach Polly. Deciding that he clearly had no idea just how attractive he was to women, Evanna smiled. 'All right, then. Let's walk. Towards the road or towards the cliffs?'

'The cliffs.' He'd pulled on a loose linen shirt over cut-off shorts but his feet were bare.

'Is it so hard, Logan? Approaching another woman. Is it because you're thinking of Catherine? Does it feel strange? Wrong?' She wanted to understand. *She wanted to help.* Despite the late hour, there was still enough light for her to make out his features.

'I'm not thinking of Catherine. Not at the moment. Should I be?'

'No. I think it's good. But I don't understand why you were reluctant to approach Polly.'

They moved closer to the water's edge and the sea rushed in, swirled around their ankles and then retreated with a gentle hiss.

She glanced back and suddenly realised how far they'd walked. 'I can't see the others.'

'Does that matter?'

'No. I just thought you might want to be getting back so that you can—'

'Are you afraid of the dark?' He gave her a lazy smile and took her hand in his. His fingers closed over hers, his grip strong and firm.

'I'm not afraid of the dark.'

Without announcing his intention, he gave her a gentle pull and started walking away from the sea in the direction of the dunes.

What was he doing? 'Logan—'

'Don't say anything.' His voice sounded strained and suddenly her heart was beating so rapidly that she felt dizzy. This was ridiculous. She was walking hand in hand along a beach with a man she adored. And she didn't have a clue what was going on. *She just didn't know what to say or do.*

They crested the first dune and then slithered and slipped down into the dip. The sea breeze immediately faded away and they were enclosed, cocooned by the gentle swell of sand that created an intimate atmosphere.

'Logan, I really think we should—'

His mouth came down on hers with a hunger that knocked the breath from her body. For a moment Evanna just stood still, so shocked that she couldn't move. She felt the firm pressure of his hand behind her neck, felt his other arm slide round her waist, dragging her hard against him. And then she felt the tip of his tongue demanding an entry and excitement devoured her like a ravenous beast.

Her lips parted against his and she melted into the heat of his kiss, her senses stirred and tumbled as she closed her eyes and sank against him. Shock and surprise melted into frantic excitement. She tried to speak. Tried to reason with him. But his kiss was fierce and greedy and he clearly had no interest in conversation.

With a swift, purposeful movement he undid the tie at the back of her neck and pushed the sundress down over her hips, leaving her in only her skimpy bikini. The air was warm and yet she was shivering uncontrollably and he dragged her closer still, murmuring something incoherent against her mouth.

'Logan…' She didn't know what he was saying. She didn't know what he was thinking. Or what he was doing.

'If you want to stop me, do it now,' he breathed, pulling away from her just long enough to allow him to remove his shirt. He dropped it onto the ground, gently pulled her off balance and lowered her onto the soft mattress of sand. 'Are you going to stop me, Evanna?'

Evanna opened her mouth to suggest that they talk, but he kissed her again and all she was aware of was the hard, male press of his body against hers. Her head was spinning, her thoughts were jumbled and speech suddenly seemed impossible.

'Evanna?' His voice was low and deep and he trailed his mouth over her collarbone, down to her breast.

She felt his fingers pull aside the fabric of her bikini, felt the cool night air touch her exposed nipple and then gasped with shock and agonising pleasure as he took her in his mouth. The skilled flick of his tongue drove hot flashes of fire down her body and she writhed under him in an instinctive attempt to get closer to him. Her hips lifted in an unconsciously feminine gesture of desire and she felt the rigid length of him pressing against her. Hard and ready. He wanted her. Logan wanted her. And she couldn't believe that it was actually happening because although she'd lived this precise moment so often in her dreams, she'd never once allowed herself to believe that it might become reality.

Then he turned his attention to the other breast and all thoughts of reality vanished as the excitement levels became almost unbearable.

She needed him to touch her. Properly. And he obviously knew that because she felt the smooth slide of his hand over her heated flesh and then the subtle movement of his fingers as he removed the final item of her clothing, leaving her naked and exposed.

His fingers cupped her and he paused for a moment, his breathing fractured as he struggled for control. His mouth hovered above hers, their breath mingling as he murmured her name, and then he lowered his head and kissed her again, his fingers moving gently and skilfully until he found that one secret place that was waiting to be discovered.

'Logan, please...' she sobbed against his mouth, and reached down to fumble with his zip, driven by an emotion far more powerful than common sense.

She forgot that they were on a public beach and that others might chose to walk the way that they had walked. For Evanna, the world began and ended with Logan. No one else existed.

'Evanna—my beautiful, gorgeous, Evanna.' His voice was a deep, husky caress and she was so dizzy with excitement that her only response was a shake of her head.

She wasn't his Evanna. Neither was she beautiful or gorgeous, but she didn't even care. All she cared about was now. What he was doing to her. *And what she wanted to do to him.*

Her fingers were on his zip again but he shifted away from her and slid down her trembling, excited body, tasting and touching, using his lips and tongue to expose all her secrets. And he wouldn't let her hide. When she tried to pull him back up her body he gently resisted, pulling away from her seeking fingers, and she felt the rough scrape of male stubble as he moved his lips across her stomach. Then came the gentle nip of his teeth on the inside of her thigh, and finally the skilled flick of his tongue against the nub of her womanhood. And the heat of his mouth and the damp stroke of his tongue felt so maddeningly good that all thoughts of protest evaporated before

they'd even formed in her head and she allowed him intima-
cies that she'd never allowed another man.

And then, when she thought she couldn't stand it any longer,
when she thought she was going to have to beg, he moved back
up her body and slid a strong arm under her hips, raising her
slightly. She felt weak and drugged under the skill of his assault
and when she felt the blunt tip of his erection brush against her
she gave a sob of delicious anticipation. Stopping him was not
an option. Instead of stopping, she encouraged him, opening
for him, breathing his name against his mouth until he finally
thrust into her, entering her by degrees until she was aware of
nothing but him, the hardness and the fullness, and she closed
her eyes, overwhelmed by the feelings that erupted as he
deepened his possession.

For a moment it felt like too much and she ceased to breathe,
her body held tense against the fullness and pressure of his.

And then he stilled.

For a moment everything was suspended. Her body was
humming with excitement and his elusive male scent made her
dizzy with longing.

He lifted his head just enough to speak. 'I just had to be
inside you.' As if that were all the explanation that was needed
and she didn't even need to question his explanation because
she understood.

He gave her time to adjust, allowed her body time to accom-
modate him, and then he slid a hand through her hair and
lowered his mouth to hers in a kiss so possessive that her head
spun and excitement spurted. Unable to help herself, Evanna
moved her hips and he gave a low grunt of masculine satisfaction and anchored her against him, taking back control.

She slid her hands down his back, over satin-smooth skin
and hard male muscle, drawing him still deeper inside her. And
still he moved, occasionally withdrawing and then sheathing

himself again until his movements became more demanding and he drove them both hard towards completion.

She felt her body explode and tighten around his, heard him mutter something against her mouth and then felt the spasms consume his own body.

And then, finally, peace descended on them.

Lying there in the semi-darkness, Evanna gradually became aware of her surroundings. She heard the soft hiss of the sea and the distant laughter of people enjoying the last moments of the beach barbecue. She smelt sea and sand and healthy, sexy man.

And she couldn't believe what had happened.

She kept her eyes tightly shut, unwilling to open them in case looking somehow broke the spell and returned her to her old life. Because she could never go back, she knew that now.

She'd had so many dreams and none of them had ever come close to the reality of making love with Logan. She'd always thought that she understood what it meant to be close to someone, but suddenly she realised that she hadn't understood at all. She'd been entirely ignorant of the depth of connection that was possible between a man and a woman.

She was aware of him deep inside her, of the fact that he was still hard, and she shifted her hips slightly, enjoying the intimacy.

'Evanna…' His voice hoarse, he lifted his head and brushed his fingers over her cheek. Then he gave a soft curse and moved deeper into her, triggering another set of fireworks in her head. 'I can't let you go. Not yet.'

Why would he want to? She slid her arms round his neck and moved her hips, feeling his instant response.

'We should stop,' she murmured, groaning softly as he moved deeper inside her. 'Someone might walk past.'

'I'm not stopping. No way.'

And she had no real desire to persuade him. 'Then we should move,' she whispered softly, 'somewhere more discreet.'

He didn't reply and she wondered whether he'd even heard her. And then he lifted his mouth from his determined seduction of her breast. 'All right. Your house. It's closer and we don't need the car.'

How they got there she didn't know.

He pushed her bikini in his pocket, pulled her dress over her head, zipped his shorts and slung his shirt over his shoulders. Then he took her hand and propelled her up the path that provided a short cut to her house.

Once inside he barely closed the door before he brought his mouth down on hers again.

Evanna felt her head swim and clutched at his shoulders. 'Logan—the bedroom.'

'Too far.' He scooped her into his arms, carried her into the living room and laid her on the sofa. 'Kiss me.'

And she did.

She wrapped her arms round his neck and felt his hand slide her dress upwards and then he thrust hard inside her and she cried out because it was so perfect.

CHAPTER TEN

WHEN she woke up he was gone.

Evanna sat up slowly, aware that her entire body was aching in a way that it had never ached before. But no one had ever made love to her like that before.

Where had he gone?

When had he gone?

Now that the storm had settled she had so many questions that needed answering, but the biggest was why. Why had he made love to her?

She wanted to believe that what they'd shared was unique and special.

He'd been tender and caring, passionate and demanding all at the same time. Could a man make love like that, *give so much,* and yet feel nothing? Was that possible?

And then she remembered what he'd said that evening she'd talked to him in the garden. He was ready for sex. He'd wanted to have sex with a woman.

And she was that woman.

It hadn't meant anything to him except another step forward in the recovery process. Hadn't he told her that he wasn't interested in a relationship? Hadn't he told her that he wanted sex? Well, finally he'd slept with another woman.

She took a deep breath.

The fact that he'd left before she was awake said everything there was to be said. He was obviously wondering how on earth he was going to deal with the fallout of their night of passion.

Evanna bit her lip and swallowed back the lump in her throat. She needed to let him know that she understood. That she wasn't going to demand anything of him. She'd given him what he'd needed and that was fine.

Except it wasn't fine, was it?

For her, everything had changed.

She'd loved Logan all her life. Lived alongside him. Shared his life. But this was entirely different. What they'd shared couldn't be ignored.

They couldn't just go back to the way they'd been before.

She walked towards the kitchen, stepping over her discarded dress, a cruel reminder of the wild passion of the night before.

In the kitchen, she flicked on the kettle and then stood staring out at the sea.

And suddenly she knew. She knew what had to be done.

She'd deal with Logan and then she'd leave.

She'd leave her beloved Glenmore.

What choice did she have?

Logan was moving on and it was time for her to move on, too. Somewhere else. Somewhere without Logan. She needed to build a new life. While she'd been working on the labour ward in the hospital, they'd made it clear that they'd give her a job any time. She'd call them. Accept the offer.

She glanced around her, realising that moving away would mean selling her precious cottage by the sea.

Change, she reminded herself. Things changed, whether you wanted them to or not. And you had to ride the wave or drown.

* * *

I love you, Evanna.

Slumped in the hammock in the garden, Logan rehearsed the words in his head.

He was stunned by the strength of his feelings. Nothing in his past had prepared him for what he'd felt when he'd made love with Evanna.

So much for all his resolutions about staying away from her. He'd taken one look at her in her bikini and had had red-hot thoughts. So red-hot that he hadn't even been able to look at anyone else all evening, let alone dance with them. Women had approached him, dropping hints, but he'd brushed them all aside as politely as possible. For him, Evanna had been the only woman there. No one else had existed.

Even now his body tightened at the memory of how she'd looked. Her hair had been damp from the water and had hung, glossy and dark, over her bare shoulders. Her eyes had been as dark as sloes, her lashes thick and unbelievably long. And then there had been her mouth.

Logan groaned and closed his eyes.

Her mouth.

Her mouth, curved and laughing at something he'd said. Her mouth parting in shock under his. Her mouth responding, greedily to his demands. *Her mouth touching him...*

He'd been celibate for over a year but he knew that what he'd shared with Evanna had been so much more than just a physical release.

So much more than sex.

They hadn't just shared their bodies. They'd shared *everything*.

And that sharing, *that giving of everything,* had somehow cleared his thoughts and he'd realised at the moment of deepest intimacy just how much he loved Evanna. Just how much he needed her. How much he'd always needed her. Her warmth, her kindness, her endless compassion.

Her gentle hands, her soft mouth and her warm, amazing body.

He'd always thought that what they'd shared had all been about friendship, but he realised now that it was so much more than that.

So much more than he'd imagined possible.

A smile touched his lips. He wished now that he'd called the babysitter and asked her to stay the night. Then he would have been there when Evanna had woken up. He wouldn't have had to wait to tell her that he loved her and he wouldn't have had to wait to look into her eyes and seen that love returned. And he had no doubt that it was returned. Why else would she have responded to him with such unrestrained passion?

Evanna was an old-fashioned girl. She didn't do one-night stands or casual flings. She never had. There was no way she would have allowed him to make love to her unless she had strong feelings. True feelings.

All he had to do now was give her the chance to tell him how she felt.

'Logan?'

Her soft, breathy voice came from right beside him and he felt his body's immediate response.

'Evanna?' He swung his legs out of the hammock and stood up, seeing immediately how nervous she was.

Her hands were clasped in front of her, she was wearing a simple white shirt with a linen skirt and her dark hair was pulled back in a ponytail. Her eyes were shy and there was more than the usual amount of colour in her cheeks.

Her smile faltered, as if she wasn't entirely confident of her reception. 'You were gone when I woke up and I thought we ought to talk.'

She really was nervous and he frowned. 'Evanna—'

'No, wait.' She lifted a hand to cut him off, her smile slightly shaky. 'There are things I have to say and I won't be able to say them if you interrupt. I know you must be worrying about what to say but you really don't need to. Last night was very special to me.' She stumbled over the words and he found himself wondering yet again how he could have taken so long to discover just how much he loved Evanna. She was gorgeous. Incredible.

'It was special to me, too.' He held out a hand but she took a step backwards and gave a little shake of her head, as if to warn him off.

'Don't touch me. Not for a minute. I have to say this and I won't be able to if you touch me.'

With a dark sense of foreboding Logan let his hand drop to his side. 'Have to say what? What is it you have to say, Evanna?' Why wouldn't she let him touch her when they'd spent almost all of last night touching? *Intimately.*

'Last night was a really big step for you. Something you needed to do. And I'm pleased that you chose me.' She stumbled slightly over the words. 'Really pleased that you turned to me. After everything that's happened—it was a really big thing for you. Important. I understand that. A big step in the recovery process. And that's fine.'

He frowned. Recovery process? What was she talking about? She was making an incredible, mind-blowing night of passion sound like some sort of therapy. 'Evanna—'

'We've been friends a long time, Logan. A very long time.'

And he didn't want to be friends any longer. *He wanted so much more than that.* And he'd assumed that she did, too. 'I'm glad you came because I wanted to talk to you. There are things I need to say, too.'

'You don't need to say them, Logan,' she said quickly, her eyes sliding from his. 'We both know how things are. One steamy night isn't going to ruin our friendship. Nothing is going to change. Our friendship is precious and nothing is going to damage that. So we're just going to forget it.'

'Forget it?' He stared at her, stunned by just how sick her words made him feel. He wanted things to change. He wanted everything to change. *He wanted them to be together.* And he certainly didn't want to forget it. 'You want to forget it?' Her fingers were clasped in front of her and he saw that her knuckles were white.

'Of course. I think we should both see it as what it was. An interlude. Hopefully now you'll be able to start going out more. And eventually you'll find someone that you can share you life with.'

So she didn't care for him.

All that giving—*all that loving*—it had been about therapy, Logan thought dully, feeling as though someone had hollowed him out with a sharp knife.

She hadn't slept with him because she loved him but because she cared about his rehabilitation. She felt sorry for him and wanted to help him get over Catherine. What they'd shared had been a sacrifice on her part.

Not love.

Somehow he made his lips move. 'So, that's it, then?'

'Of course. We should just forget it ever happened and you should get out there and start seeing other women. No guilt. No regrets. You know it's what Catherine would have wanted. Life is so fragile, Logan, you should snatch happiness whenever it presents itself.'

He had.

Last night.

'Yes.' He watched as his fresh chance at happiness melted away in front of him. 'Evanna—'

'I really have to go.' She backed away and waved a hand. 'I just didn't want you to feel awkward or embarrassed or anything—I wanted you to know that everything's fine. Fine. No problems.'

She was babbling again, the way she always did when she was nervous, and Logan wanted to drag her into his arms and tell her to stop talking and just kiss him the way she'd kissed him the night before.

But before he could move she turned and walked quickly towards the gate, leaving him staring after her.

Now what?

Now what was he supposed to do?

She'd kept saying that everything was fine. Fine. When everything was far from fine.

After two nights without sleep and a ridiculously busy day during which she'd successfully managed to avoid Logan, Evanna was sitting in her kitchen, wondering whether she even had the energy to drag herself to bed, when the back door flew open and Kyla marched in.

'Is it true?'

Tired and jaded by the events of the weekend, Evanna looked at her warily. How much did she know? 'Is what true?'

'That you're selling the cottage.' Kyla slammed the door shut behind her and glared. 'When did you put your house on the market?'

'Oh.' Evanna blinked several times, surprised at how fast the news had travelled. 'How did you find out?'

'Ed Masters is the only estate agent on the island so it wasn't hard,' Kyla said, her tone sarcastic. 'And I happened to be taking bloods from him today.'

'Word travels fast. I only saw him a few hours ago.'

'He was my last patient of the day. So it's true? You spoke to Ed before you told me?' Kyla put her hands on her hips. 'You're selling your cottage and you didn't think it was worth mentioning? Buy a new lipstick or a pair of shoes, fine. That's information that I don't need to know for a couple of days. But *selling your house? What's going on?'*

'Well, of course I was going to tell you, but—'

'When? After you'd moved?'

Evanna lifted a hand to her forehead, which throbbed and pounded with relentless ferocity. 'Kyla, I don't need this. I'm tired and I'm…' *Miserable, lost, confused.* Her hand dropped to her side and she closed her eyes briefly, blocking out the reality. She still couldn't really take in what selling the house really meant. *She was leaving Glenmore.* 'Yes, I'm selling the cottage.' Saying the words aloud had a finality that unlocked the misery inside her.

'Why? What's happened? You *love* Glenmore. You love your cottage.' Kyla waved a hand and her long blonde hair bounced around her shoulders. 'You've done up every inch of this place exactly the way you like it. It's taken every penny of your salary.'

'Yes.' She didn't need to be reminded exactly how much of herself had gone into this house.

'So why are you selling your house. Your *home?'*

'Because I don't need a home,' Evanna croaked. 'At least, I don't need a home on Glenmore. Not any more.'

Kyla stared. Then she took a deep breath. 'Run that past me again.'

'I'm leaving, Kyla. I've spoken to the Royal Infirmary today and they're going to give me a job on the labour ward. I'm moving to the city. I can start as soon as Logan and Ethan agree to let me go.'

'They'll never agree to let you go and neither will I.' Kyla's voice sounded scratchy and she plopped down onto one of the kitchen chairs. 'Why? Why would you leave Glenmore? You love the island. Why would you go?'

'Because I can't breathe the same air as Logan any more,' Evanna whispered, her expression stricken. 'I have to move on and I've realised that I can't do that when I'm rubbing shoulders with him all the time.'

Kyla was silent. 'Has something happened?'

Evanna hesitated. There were some things too personal to share even with her best friend. 'I just made a decision, that's all.' *After they'd made love for almost all of the night.*

'Does he know?' Kyla's voice was gruff. 'Have you told him?'

'Not yet.' But she was sure he'd be relieved. He wouldn't want her hanging around. It would be too awkward. Evanna walked to the kitchen table and picked up the letter that she'd typed earlier. 'I've redone this a thousand times and I still don't know if it's right.'

'What is it?'

'My letter of resignation.'

'Then it isn't going to be right.' Kyla took it from her and read it swiftly. Then her shoulders sagged and her eyes filled. 'Evanna, don't do this. You're my best friend. You've been my best friend since we pulled each other's hair in toddler group.'

'You pulled my hair,' Evanna mumbled, looking away so that she couldn't see the tears. 'I never touched yours.'

Kyla gave a smile that wasn't entirely steady. 'Yes, well, you always did hate confrontation. You're hopeless at rows because you just want everyone to be friends and love each other. Oh, heck, you're making me cry, and you know I never cry.' She scrabbled in her pocket for a tissue and blew her nose. 'I know I drive you mad but I love you. You're my best friend. What would I do without you?'

'You're married now,' Evanna said softly, blinking back her own tears. 'Everything's different.'

'Being married doesn't alter our friendship.'

'Maybe not. But loving Logan alters everything.'

'Have you told him how you feel about him? Surely it's

worth it before you take such a drastic step? If you're leaving anyway, what does it matter?'

'He knows.' She hadn't told him, but she'd shown him. With her body. *She'd given him everything.* And he hadn't wanted it. Not in the way that she wanted him to want it. He hadn't said a word. Just left while she'd still been sleeping.

'You've spelt it out?'

'We've been here before, Kyla,' Evanna said patiently. 'You can't force someone to love you. Anyway, I don't know why you're being so tragic. You can come and visit me.'

'I'm hopeless in cities,' Kyla muttered, blowing her nose again. 'I get lost and I feel crowded and hemmed in. So do you, you know you do. You've never been a city person and you never will be.'

Evanna took a deep breath. 'You won't change my mind, Kyla,' she said quietly. 'I've been over and over it in my head and I know it's the right thing to do.'

Kyla watched her for a long moment, her eyes swimming with tears. 'Ethan might just beat you up. He hates seeing me cry.'

'I hate seeing you cry, too.' Evanna stood up and held out her arms and Kyla walked into them, hugging her tightly.

'I need Cupid to visit the island and stab my brother. Hard.'

'Yes. It's time he fell in love.'

'I want it to be with you.' Kyla squeezed her hard and then released her. 'I really wanted it to be with you.'

Evanna gave a helpless shrug. 'Life doesn't always turn out the way we want it to. You know that as well as I do. We just have to get on with it. Play the hand we've been given.'

Kyla wiped her face with the palm of her hand and managed a smile. 'You're always so sensible, do you know that? What am I going to do without you? Who is going to stop me eating Meg out of ice cream and chocolate flakes?'

'I never manage to stop you, anyway.' Evanna gave a shaky smile. 'I'll call. And e-mail. We'll stay in touch. I promise.'

'But it won't be the same.'

'No.' Evanna felt her heart twist for everything she was losing. 'No, it won't be the same. But life doesn't stay the same, Kyla. No matter how much you want it to, it doesn't stay the same. We all have to keep moving forward.'

She kept telling herself that.

Keep moving forward.

Logan was just finishing surgery the next morning when his sister marched into the room. One look at the flash in her blue eyes warned him that she was about to pick a fight.

He sighed and sat back in his chair. 'If this is one of your explosions, make it quick. I have house calls.'

'I know. Ellen McBride and Gail Forster. I spoke to Janet. They can both wait.' She slammed the door shut and strode across to his desk. 'Are you seriously going to let her go? She's part of this practice—part of this island—and you're going to let her walk away? Are you nuts?'

Logan blinked. There was nothing quite like his sister in a seething temper. 'I have absolutely no idea what you're talking about,' he drawled softly, and she glared at him.

'Well, of course you haven't. You're obviously *completely* stupid.'

He lifted an eyebrow. 'And your evidence for that assessment would be—?'

'The fact that you're letting Evanna leave! How could you do it? How *could* you let her resign? She belongs here. She belongs with us. She's part of Glenmore Island. Part of the practice. You'll never find another nurse like her if you search high and low!'

Logan sat still. 'What do you mean, leave? Where's she going?'

'To the mainland. To work. And live. And...' Kyla faltered

and waved a hand. 'To do all the things that she used to do here. Did you accept her letter of resignation? Did you?'

'She's planning to resign?' Logan rose to his feet and Kyla folded her arms across her chest and narrowed her eyes.

'You're pretending that you don't know?'

'Of course I didn't know,' he snapped, and then drew in a deep breath and forced himself to think. This was all his fault. He'd compromised her. He'd destroyed their friendship. If she was leaving, it was because of him. 'It's my fault, Kyla.'

'Well, I know *that*. The whole thing is your fault.'

Logan frowned. She knew? Evanna had told her? It was true that Kyla and Evanna were close friends, but still… 'I'm not in the habit of discussing my sex life with my sister.'

'Your sex life? Why would I want to discuss your sex life?' Kyla threw him an impatient glance. 'I mean, it isn't as if you—' She broke off and stared at him. 'What did you just say?'

'I said that I'm not prepared to discuss my sex life with you.'

'We were talking about Evanna.'

'Yes.'

Kyla stared and then swallowed. 'You had sex with Evanna? You—'

Logan's gaze was icy. 'I've already told you, I won't discuss my sex life. If Evanna chose to confide in you, that's up to her, but—'

'She didn't.' Kyla sat down in the nearest chair and stared at the wall. 'She didn't, but now I see. You had sex? When?'

'Kyla!'

'Just tell me!' Kyla's voice was a threatening growl. 'For goodness' sake, this is important. When?'

He let out a long breath. 'The night of the barbecue.'

'Saturday.' Kyla gave a slow nod. 'That explains everything.'

'Does it?'

SARAH MORGAN   359

'Of course it does. Sex changes everything. Up until the sex part she was perfectly able to live with the fact that she loved you and you didn't love her back. But sex—sex for Evanna is extremely serious. Evanna doesn't do casual relationships.'

'I know that. I...' He frowned at her, trying to decipher the strange conversation they were having. 'Did you just say that she was able to live with the fact that she loved me, but I didn't love her back?'

'Yes. After both plan A and plan B failed, she decided to just give up and live with things as they are.' Kyla's tone was conversational and then she glanced up and saw the darkening expression on her brother's face. 'What?'

His tone was dangerously soft. 'I'd like to hear the details of plan A and plan B.'

Kyla squirmed. 'I probably shouldn't—'

'I'll give you five seconds to start talking.'

Kyla sighed. 'Oh, well, given that the whole thing is such a mess, I don't see any harm in it.'

She was going to miss Glenmore Island so much.

Evanna sat on the cliffs and stared across the sea towards the mainland. It was a view she'd grown up with. A view she'd believed she'd grow old with.

She couldn't imagine not seeing it on a daily basis as she drove to work. She couldn't imagine not popping into Meg's café for a coffee and a gossip. She couldn't imagine not running along the cliffs, swimming in the sea and sharing barbecues in Logan's garden with all their friends and family.

But she needed to build a new life and that was what she was going to do.

Somehow she'd struggled through her morning clinic, seeing patients on automatic, responding to their questions without even hearing her own answers. She'd intended to go straight into Logan's room and tell him her plans but instead she'd found herself walking up here to the cliffs for one last look.

Her letter of resignation sat in her pocket like a lump of lead.

After Kyla had left the previous evening, she'd read it over and over again and cried so hard that she'd thought her head might burst.

Then she'd made a supreme effort to pull herself together.

Enough.

Enough crying.

'Evanna?'

She turned and saw him standing there, his hair lifting in the breeze, his face so handsome that it made her catch her breath. 'Logan? What are you doing up here?'

His gaze was fixed on her face, his blue eyes sharply questioning. 'I should be asking you the same question.'

'Oh.' She scrambled to her feet and struggled to produce a smile. 'I just needed some fresh air.'

'Why would you need fresh air?' His eyes didn't shift from hers and she felt her stomach roll over.

Now. She should tell him now. It was the perfect opportunity. 'I—I'm glad you came up here. I was hoping to catch up with you later. I needed to give you something.' Her hand shaking, she delved into her pocket and pulled out the crumpled letter. 'Sorry. It's been in my pocket.' She thrust it towards him and he took it and tore it in half in a slow, purposeful movement and then handed it back to her.

She stared at him in confusion and then looked at the torn letter in her hand. 'You didn't even read it.'

'I didn't need to.' His voice was steady. 'I know what was in that letter, Evanna, and the answer is no. You're not resigning. You're not leaving Glenmore Island, you're not leaving the practice and most of all you're not leaving me.'

She stared at him and felt the emotion surge up inside her

again. He was being so unfair. This was hard enough for her without him making it even harder. 'I suppose Kyla told you. You can't stop me, Logan.' She almost choked on the words. 'I know it's inconvenient for you, but I'm not the only nurse in the world. You'll find someone else who can do the job just as well.'

'That isn't true. I wouldn't find a nurse as good as you if I searched Scotland, but that isn't why I'm not going to let you go.'

She gave a helpless shrug. 'Are you thinking of Kirsty? Because you needn't worry about that. I'll stay in touch.'

'It isn't about Kirsty.'

'I can't stay, Logan.' Her voice was a whisper. 'I have to go. I— It's complicated.'

'I've never minded complicated. Why do you have to go, Evanna?'

Their eyes held for a long moment and then she turned away and looked at the sea. 'That doesn't really matter.'

'It matters to me.'

'Why?' She swallowed hard and concentrated on the antics of a seagull swooping down to snatch a tidbit from the water.

'Because we have a relationship.' He gave soft curse and she felt his hands on her arms, his grip firm and purposeful as he turned her towards him. 'For goodness' sake, look at me, Evanna! This conversation is hard enough without trying to talk to your back. I want to know why you feel you have to leave the island. You owe me an explanation. And I want the truth.'

Given no alternative, she lifted her eyes to his face. He looked rough and rugged, strands of dark hair flopping over his forehead, his blue eyes sharp and observant. She'd grown up looking at his face. *Seen him grow from boy to man.* 'There's nothing more I can tell you, Logan.'

'No?' His eyes were very blue. 'You're not going to tell me exactly how long you've been in love with me? How long, Evanna?'

Her heart tripped over and she stood still, aware of his gaze on her face. Above them a seagull shrieked, but neither of them noticed. 'For ever.' The word was barely audible so she cleared her throat and tried again. 'For ever, Logan. I've been in love with you for ever. Girl, teenager and woman. There. You wanted the truth and now you have it.' She waited to feel humiliation or embarrassment but instead all she felt was relief. Finally there was no longer any need to pretend.

His gaze didn't flicker. 'And you're leaving because…?'

'I've just told you why I'm leaving.'

'No, you haven't. You told me that you love me. Girl, teenager and woman. You haven't told me why you're leaving.'

'How can you be so insensitive? I can't be this close to you any more. It hurts too much. I want to find a family, a home, a man who loves me, and I'm never going to find those things while you're in my line of vision because no one else exists for me.'

There was a long silence broken only by the distant rush of waves over rock. Then he let go of her arms and took her face in his hands. 'Look at me. I want you to look at me.'

'No.' She closed her eyes. 'This is so hard for me, Logan.'

'Then let me make it easier. I want you looking at me when I tell you that I love you, too. I love you, Evanna.' He stroked her face with his fingers and she opened her eyes.

'What did you say?'

'I love you. I should have told you the night we made love but you fell asleep and I had to get back to Kirsty. And then the next morning I was ready to tell you and you started talking about how much you wanted us to still be friends.'

She looked into his eyes, those lazy blue eyes that always made her weak at the knees. 'We had sex, Logan. It wasn't about love.'

'Yes, it was. It was all about love.' He gave a crooked smile and she felt suddenly peculiar. Her heart was hammering and her pulse was dancing. But she pushed down the little spurt of excitement.

'You've known me all your life, Logan. I'm sure you do love me. Like a sister.'

'*Not* like a sister.' His gaze dropped to her mouth and lingered there. 'Nothing like a sister.'

It was becoming hard to breathe. 'I've been under your nose for ever.'

'So maybe I'm just a bit slow.' He stroked her hair away from her face with a gentle hand. 'Or maybe, subconsciously, I always thought that you were out of bounds. You were my baby sister's best friend. Then you were a colleague.'

'You've kissed just about every girl on this island, Logan MacNeil. But you never kissed me until last Saturday.'

'If I'd known how good it was going to be, I would have been kissing you in the playground, right under Ann Carne's nose.' He hesitated. 'Perhaps I didn't kiss you because you were the only one that mattered to me. Our relationship was too important to risk messing it all up.'

She couldn't listen. *She couldn't allow herself to believe it.* 'Logan, you've had a terrible year, and—'

'Stop.' He covered her lips with his fingers. 'If you're going to suggest that this is rebound or therapy or anything like that, don't waste your breath. What I feel for you is real, Evanna. And it's for ever.'

'But—'

'It doesn't make sense, does it? You're going to ask me why I suddenly know I love you when you've always been in my life. Why haven't I felt it before? And I don't know the answer to that. I don't know why I haven't realised it before.'

'You loved Catherine.'

'Yes, I did.' His voice was soft. 'I won't lie to you about that. I did love Catherine. But she's gone. And now I'm in love with you. I'm crazy about you and I can't let you leave the island. You told me that I should grab happiness and I agree with you. But you're my happiness, Evanna.'

She struggled to speak. 'Logan…' Her voice shook and she tried again. 'I've dreamed about you for so long—wanted you for so long…'

'I never knew. I never knew that you felt like that.' He gave a groan and lowered his mouth to hers, his kiss warm and insistent. Then he lifted his head just enough to speak. 'I must be blind and stupid. Will you marry me?'

How could it happen? How could a person go from misery to happiness in one bound? 'It's too soon—you need time to think about things.'

He shook his head. 'Evanna, I've known you for twenty-six years. How much more time do you think I need? Will you be my wife? Will you be a mother to my daughter?'

Kirsty.

Tears filled her eyes. 'I've wanted this for so long I can't believe that it's true.'

'Believe it.' He muttered the words against her mouth. 'And then say yes. You said that you wanted a home and a family, a man who loves you, here on Glenmore Island. You have it, Evanna. If you want it, it's all yours.'

She slid her arms round his neck and buried her face in his neck. 'I want it. I want everything.' She lifted her head and melted into the heat of his kiss, excitement burning away the exhaustion and misery of the past few days. 'I love you, Logan. I can't believe you want me to be your wife and a mother to Kirsty. And your practice nurse.'

He gave a slow smile. 'For now.'

'What do you mean, for now?'

He kissed her once again. 'You can be my practice nurse until I find you something better to do. I'm planning on keeping you fairly busy in the bedroom, Evanna MacNeil. We're going to have a large family.'

'Really?'

'Really.' He brushed his lips over hers. 'How many children is a good number, do you think? Nine? Ten?'

She giggled. 'Ann Carne would have a fit if we gave her ten little MacNeil children to teach.'

His eyes gleamed. 'We have a duty to maintain the population of rural communities.'

Evanna felt a warm glow of happiness. It felt as though someone had touched her dreams with a magic wand and turned them into reality. 'You called me Evanna MacNeil. Have you any idea how many times I scribbled that name in my textbooks?'

'Did you? Well, I'm glad to hear it.' His mouth was still close to hers. 'It means that you won't need any practice writing it down once we're married.'

Her heart jumped. 'Married…'

'Yes, married. I love you, Evanna Duncan MacNeil. Are you going to say yes to me?'

'Yes.' She smiled and smiled. 'Yes. Yes. Yes-s-s.'

Read on for an exclusive extract from
Sarah Morgan's new novel,
Wish Upon A Star
coming this Christmas.

'MUM, where are we spending Christmas?'

Christy glanced up from the letter she was reading. 'I don't know. Here, I suppose, with Uncle Pete and your cousins. Why do you ask? Christmas is ages away.' And she was trying not to think about it. Christmas was a time for families and hers appeared to be disintegrating.

And it was all her fault. She'd done a *really* stupid thing and now they were all paying the price.

'Christmas is a month away. Not ages.' Katy leaned across the table and snatched the cereal packet from her little brother. 'And I don't want to stay here. I love Uncle Pete, but I hate London. I want to spend Christmas with Dad in the Lake District. I want to go home.'

Christy felt her insides knot with anguish. They wanted to spend Christmas with their father? She just couldn't begin to imagine spending Christmas without the children. 'All right.' Her voice was husky and she cleared her throat. 'Of course, that's fine, if you're sure that's what you want.' *Oh, dear God, how would she survive?* What would Christmas morning be without the children? 'I'll write to your father and tell him that you're both coming up to stay. You might need to spend some time at Grandma's because Daddy will be working at the hospital, of course, and it's always a busy time for the mountain rescue team and—'

'Not just us.' Katy reached for the sugar. 'I didn't mean that we go without you. That would be hideous. I meant that we all go.'

'What do you mean, all? And that's enough sugar, Katy. You'll rot your teeth.'

'They go into *holes*,' Ben breathed, with the gruesome delight of a seven-year-old. He picked up the milk jug and tried to pour milk into his cup but succeeded in slopping most of it over the table. 'I learned about it in school last week. You eat sugar, you get *holes*. Then the dentist has to drill a bigger hole and fill it with cement.'

'You are so lame! What do you know about anything, anyway?' Katy threw her brother a disdainful look and doubled the amount of sugar she was putting on her cereal. 'Stupid, idiot baby.'

'I'm not a baby! I'm seven!' Ben shot out of his chair and made a grab at his sister, who immediately put her hands round his throat.

'*Why* did I have to be lumbered with a brother?'

'Stop it, you two! Not his throat, Katy,' Christy admonished, her head starting to thump as she reached for a cloth and mopped up the milk on the table. 'You know that you don't put anything round each other's throats. You might strangle him.'

'That was the general idea,' Katy muttered, glaring at Ben before picking up her spoon and digging into her cereal. 'Anyway, as I was saying. I don't want Ben and I to go home for Christmas, I want all three of us to go.'

The throb in Christy's head grew worse and she rose to her feet in search of paracetamol. 'This is home now, sweetheart.' Thanks to her stupidity. 'London is home now.'

As if to remind herself of that depressing fact, she stared out of the window of their tiny flat, through the sheeting rain and down into the road below. There was a steady hiss as the traffic crawled along the wet, cheerless street. Brick buildings, old, tired and in need of repainting, rose up high, blocking out what there was of the restrained winter light. People shouted abuse and leaned on their horns and all the time the rain fell steadily, dampening streets and spirits with equal effectiveness. On the pavement people jostled and dodged, ears glued to mobile phones, walking and talking, eyes straight ahead, no contact with each other.

And then, just for a moment, the reality disappeared and Christy had a vision of the Lake District. Her real home. The sharp edges of the fells rising up against a perfectly blue sky on a crisp winter morning. The clank of metal and the sound of laughter as the mountain rescue team prepared for another callout. Friendship.

Oh, dear God, she didn't want to be here. *This wasn't how it was supposed to have turned out.*

As if picking up her mood, Ben's face crumpled as he flopped back into his chair. 'It isn't home. It'll never be home, it's horrid and I hate it. I hate London, I hate school and most of all I hate you.' And with that he scraped his chair away from the table and belted out of the door, sobbing noisily, leaving his cereal untouched.

Feeling sick with misery, Christy watched him go, suppressing a desperate urge to follow and give him a cuddle but knowing from experience that it was best to let him calm down in his own time. She sat back down at the table and tried to revive her flagging spirits. It was seven-thirty in the morning, she had to get two children to a school that they hated and she had to go on to a job that she hated, too. What on earth was she doing?

She topped up her coffee-cup and tried to retrieve the situation. 'London at Christmas will be pretty cool.'

Katy shot her a pitying look. 'Mum, *don't* try and communicate on my level. It's tragic when grown-ups do that. *I* can say cool, but it sounds ridiculous coming from anyone over the age of sixteen. Use grown-up words like "interesting" or "exciting". Leave "cool" and "wicked" to those of us who appreciate the true meaning.' With all the vast superiority of her eleven years, she pushed her bowl to one side and reached for a piece of toast. 'And, anyway, it won't be cool. The shopping's good, but you can only do so much of that.'

Christy wondered whether she ought to point out that so far her daughter hadn't shown any signs of tiring of that particular occupation but decided that the atmosphere around the breakfast table was already taut enough. 'I can't go back to the Lake District this Christmas,' she said finally, and Katy lifted the toast to her lips.

'Why not? Because you and Dad have had a row?' She shrugged. 'What's new?'

Christy bit her lip and reflected on the challenges of having a daughter who was growing up and saw too much. She picked up her coffee-cup, determined to be mature about the whole thing. 'Katy, we didn't—'

'Yes, you did, but it's hardly surprising, is it? He's Spanish and you're half-Irish with red hair. Uncle Pete says that makes for about as explosive combination as it's possible to get. I suppose things might have been different if you'd been born a blonde.' Katy chewed thoughtfully. 'Amazing, really, that the two of you managed to get it together for long enough to produce us.'

Christy choked on her coffee and made a mental note to have a sharp talk with her brother. 'Katy, that's enough.'

'I'm just pointing out that the fact that you two can't be in a room without trying to kill each other is no reason to keep us down here in London. We hate it, Mum. It's great seeing Uncle Pete but a short visit is plenty. You hate it, too, I know you do.'

Was it that obvious? 'I have a job here.' In the practice where her brother worked as a GP. And it was fine, she told herself firmly. Fine. Perfectly adequate. She was lucky to have it.

'You're a nurse, Mum. You can get a job anywhere.'

Oh, to be a child again, when everything seemed so simple and straightforward. 'Katy—'

'Just for Christmas. Please? Don't you miss Dad?'

The knot was back in her stomach. Christy closed her eyes and saw dark, handsome features. An arrogant, possessive smile and a mouth that could bring her close to madness. *Oh, yes.* Oh, yes, she missed him dreadfully. And, at this distance, some of her anger had faded. But the hurt was still there. All right, so she'd been stupid but she wouldn't have done it if he hadn't been so—so *aggravating*. 'I can't discuss my relationship with your father with you.'

'I'm eleven,' Katy reminded her. 'I know about relationships. And I know that the two of you are stubborn.'

He hadn't contacted her. Pride mingled with pain and Christy pressed her lips together to stop a sob escaping. He was *supposed* to have followed her. Dragged her back. He was supposed to have fought for what they had. But he hadn't even been in touch except when they made arrangements about the children. *He didn't care that she'd gone.* The knowledge sat like a heavy weight in her heart and stomach. Suddenly she felt a ridiculous urge to confide in her child but she knew that she couldn't do that, no matter how grown-up Katy seemed. 'I can't spend Christmas with your father.'

She'd started this but she didn't know how to finish it. He was supposed to have finished it. He was supposed to have come after her. That was why she'd left. To try and make him listen. 'A wake-up call', a marriage counsellor would probably call it.

'If I have a row with one of my friends you always say, "Sit down, Katy, and discuss it like a grown-up."' Katy rolled her eyes, her imitation next to perfect. 'And what do you do? You move to opposite ends of the country. Hardly a good example to set, is it?'

Christy stiffened and decided that some discipline was called for. 'I'm not sure I like your tone.'

'And I'm not sure I like being the product of a broken home.' Katy finished her toast and took a sip from her glass of milk. 'Goodness knows what it will do to me. You read about it every day in the papers. There's a strong chance I'm going to go off the rails. Theft. Pregnancy—'

Christy banged her cup down onto the table. 'What do you know about pregnancy?'

Katy shot her a pitying look. 'Oh, get a life, Mum. I know plenty.'

'You do?' She just wasn't ready to handle this stage of child development on her own, Christy thought weakly. She needed Alessandro. She needed—

Oh, help…

'And don't write to him. Ring him up.' Katy glanced at the clock and stood up, ponytail swinging. 'We'd better go or we'll be late. The traffic never moves in this awful place. I've never spent so many hours standing still in my whole life and I don't think I can stand it any more. I'll ring him if you're too cowardly.'

'I'm not cowardly.' Or maybe she was. He hadn't rung her. Gorgeous, sexy Alessandro, who was always wrapped up in his job or his role on the mountain rescue team, always the object of a million women's fantasies. Once she'd been wrapped up in the same things but then the children had come and somehow she'd been left behind…

And he didn't notice her any more. He didn't have time for their relationship. *For her.*

'Ben's upstairs, crying. I'm here eating far too much sugar and you're ingesting a lethal dose of caffeine,' Katy said dramatically as she walked to the door, her performance worthy of the London stage. 'We're a family in crisis. We need our father or *goodness knows* what might happen to us.'

Christy didn't know whether to laugh or cry. 'You haven't finished your milk,' she said wearily. 'All right, I'll talk to him. See what he says.'

It would be just for the festive season, she told herself. The children shouldn't suffer because of her stupidity and Alessandro's arrogant, stubborn nature.

'Really?'

'Really.'

'Yay!' Katy punched the air, her ponytail swinging. 'We're going back to the Lake District for Christmas. Snow. Rain.

Howling winds. I'll see my old friends. My phone bill will plummet. Thanks Mum, you're the best.'

As she danced out of the room, no doubt *en route* to pass the joyful news on to her brother, Christy felt her stomach sink down to her ankles. Now all she had to do was summon the courage to phone Alessandro and tell him that they were planning to return home for Christmas.

How on earth was she going to do that?

If you enjoyed **Summer Fling**,
why not share your thoughts with
hundreds of other Sarah Morgan
fans and post a review at:

amazon.co.uk   goodreads

Don't miss Sarah Morgan's first, irresistible O'Neil brothers story

Enjoy more sizzling summer stories from Sarah Morgan

Discover more at
www.millsandboon.co.uk/sarah-morgan